CRIMEWAVE 7
THE LAST SUNSET

Editor
Andy Cox

Publisher & UK Office
TTA Press, 5 Martins Lane, Witcham,
Ely, Cambs CB6 2LB
t: 01353 777931
e: ttapress@aol.com

US Office
Wayne Edwards, TTA Press, 360 W. 76th
Ave, #H, Anchorage, AK 99518
e: we21011@earthlink.net

w: www.ttapress.com

Four-Issue Subscriptions
UK £22 • Europe €40 • RoW £30 • USA $40

Submissions
Unsolicited submissions of short stories welcome. Please study several issues of Crimewave before submitting and always enclose a brief covering letter and a self-addressed stamped envelope. Overseas submissions should be disposable and accompanied by two IRCs or simply an email address (this option is for overseas submissions only). Writers from North America can send their stories to the USA office (SASE essential). Send no more than one story at a time, preferably mailed flat or folded no more than once. Do not send submissions by recorded delivery. There is no length restriction placed on the stories published in Crimewave, but we don't accept reprints or simultaneous submissions. Letters and queries are very welcome via email but unsolicited story submissions are not – they will simply be deleted. No responsibility can be accepted for loss or damage to unsolicited material, howsoever caused

ISSN
1463 1350

ISBN
0 9526947 8 6

GARY COUZENS

Gary Couzens was born in 1964 and lives and
works in Aldershot. He has had short stories
published in various magazines and is working
on novels in various genres. His previous story for
Crimewave, 'Miss Perfect', is included in his
collection *Second Contact & Other Stories*,
published by Elastic Press in May 2003.

Gary would like to dedicate this story to Tony
Lewing, who set the original challenge, and to
Roy King, who always did like the result. Thanks
also to Tiffany Bradford.

The air is thick as jelly. Greg finds each breath an effort, and the Atlantic breezes up the mouth of the Amazon give little relief. *You're a Northern European*, Roger Marks had said once, shortly after Greg's first visit to Brazil. *You don't function well in the heat. You're made for colder climates.* And with that, Roger had patted him on the back, one large paw of a hand between Greg's shoulder blades. *Me, I love hot weather*, he said. Greg replied, *Yeah, but you come from Texas, Roger. You didn't have a choice in the matter*.

Roger.

Soon it will rain again, the sky splitting from end to end, disgorging its latest load of water. It's as if a great wet mass tumbles from the heavens and shatters into millions of pieces about them. The weather is a fact of life here in Belém: locals often arrange meetings for *tomorrow, after it rains*. At least the wet will be a relief from the heat. Greg had asthma as a child; in this climate, twenty-five years on, he fears its recurrence.

Roger's last message.

The Amazon is seventy miles wide at this point. Small motorboats pass constantly, chugging upriver and returning laden with fruit. Greg and Laura, Roger's wife, walk slowly through the Mercado Ver-o-Peso, the big bustling market on the waterfront. The smell of mangos, sitting overripe in traders' stalls, is pervasive, a sweet thread in a weighty tapestry of rot. There are stands selling medicinal herbs, dead snakes, jacaré teeth and other things of which Greg can't begin to guess the function. "Look," says Laura in her throaty New York accent, "incense to ward off the evil eye." As Greg watches Laura, two steps ahead of him, chat with the stallholder in Portuguese far more fluent than Greg's own few tourist words, he wonders if Roger ever bought any of these trinkets. And if he needed them.

Roger's last message was recorded on the answer machine in the Marks' São Paulo apartment. Laura works in the city, teaching English as a foreign language, while Roger is away in the jungle, as he is often. He heads a construction company, building a dam; Greg is his accountant. Greg has listened to the tape countless times, Roger's basso-profundo voice rattling the tiny speaker. He's played it back again and again, in an effort to discern anything of significance, any implication he may have missed beneath the surface of trivialities. The day after recording this message, Roger Marks vanished.

Laura buys some incense and also a guias, a necklace especially blessed to connect the wearer with the spirit world. "Greg," she says, taking him out of his reverie. Greg curses himself: he ought not to wander around here in a daze, as pickpockets and muggers will find him too easy a target. He follows Laura. She's wearing a blue top and a long floral-printed cotton skirt, her face inscrutable under a straw sunhat. Greg can't tell what she's thinking. As she walks, she takes out a cigarette and lights it.

They walk to the end of the quay, where she finishes her cigarette and drops the stub into the heavy brown water. She says nothing. The first raindrops pinprick the river surface. Soon the rain will come crashing down, frothing up the river water, giving them nothing to breathe but vapour. Nature is far vaster than all of them, even Roger. It has swallowed him whole and they may spend a lifetime searching for any trace.

By the time they reach their hotel, Greg and Laura are drenched. Laura has the first shower. She sits on the bed, dressed only in a towel wrapped tightly about herself. She's using a dryer on her hair, now a mass of wet copper plastered to her scalp.

"Belém's one of the wettest places on Earth," Greg says as he reaches for a towel of his own. "It doesn't come home to you until you see it for yourself."

Laura says nothing.

Later, changed into fresh clothes and with dinner inside them, they sit in the hotel bar. The hotel is away from the waterfront, with less risk of robberies or disturbance by prostitutes. Laura calls Luis, Roger's foreman at the dam and talks to him in Portuguese for about half an hour. She sits in the armchair, knees drawn up to her chest, cradling the mobile phone to her ear. Even though Greg can't understand more than the very occasional word, he can sense the concern, the no doubt mutual supportiveness, that underlies the conversation.

As they'll be flying out to the dam tomorrow, Greg and Laura have an early night. Although they share a bed, they don't have sex. Their affair ended with Roger's disappearance. Greg wonders if it's guilt on her part; she was with him in his hotel room when she should have been back in her apartment. She should have been there for that final telephone call that the answer machine took. She should have been there to hear her husband's final words – if indeed that is what they will prove to be.

She should have been there for him.

She kisses him goodnight. "See you in the morning."

They lie naked side by side. Greg wants her to sob, to curse whatever fate has befallen Roger; he wants her to be tearful and vulnerable so that he can comfort her. There's something erotic to him about a woman crying, but so far she has denied him that pleasure. He listens to her even breathing, turns his head to watch her back. He's oddly absorbed by the fading pink marks left by her bra in her pale freckled skin, the incurve of her waist and the swell of her hip. The swell of her buttocks and the thin dark line between them: a backside firm enough to belong to a woman fifteen years younger. Laura is asleep now, dreaming whatever dreams she might, which he knows he will never share.

At University Greg slept around, took a few mild drugs and played in a couple of terrible student rock bands. Now and again, he took his old electric guitar out to see if he could still play along with some of his old CDs. But when the time came, he studied and achieved the grades he needed; he cut his hair, bought a suit and found himself a job.

When Greg first met Roger, Greg had climbed as far up in the accountancy profession as he thought he ought to have done. He had just passed thirty, had a house of his own and he could afford expensive holidays. It would be good, as well as useful, to have a wife he could show off at big company functions, as some of the senior partners did, and somewhere down the line he would like children of his own, but he still had time. In fact, he thought, he was at an advantage: with all those unmarried thirtysomething women out there with biological clocks ticking ever more loudly, as a presentable single straight man holding down a good job he might well be in demand over the next few years. He went to a private gym three times a week to keep himself in shape. He lived on his own and he could cook and clean for himself, so at the moment he didn't need any woman intruding on his space, unless it was for sex. He'd had several girlfriends over the years. The most recent was Kelly, a trainee accountant just graduated from University, barely five feet tall without her four-inch heels, with a mass of brunette curls and a wide lipsticked mouth. He was sure her habit of wearing blouses at least a size too small couldn't be accidental. The sex was good, but she was beginning to cling so this third trip to Brazil had been the perfect opportunity to call an end to it. Kelly hadn't seen it that way and there'd been tears, the kind he didn't find erotic.

All things considered, despite some jitters at entering his fourth decade, Greg thought he had done pretty well for himself.

Contacts were always vital, and Roger Marks came into his life through one. Greg knew nothing about dam construction, nor much about Brazil, but before their meeting he did his homework. He invited Roger to a good Chinese restaurant he knew in Soho, where Roger told him about his project. Greg was impressed by the detail Roger went into, both verbally and in the paperwork he handed to him. He was clearly no timewaster. Greg had done some discreet checks, so knew that Roger's business was legitimate, as far as he could tell.

Greg was five feet ten and he'd never thought of himself as short. But next to Roger he certainly did: Roger was not only tall, six five at a guess, but broad as well. He wore his hair in a crewcut, with a tightly curled black beard that had a few flecks of grey in it. *They grow 'em big in Texas*, Roger said once. But in England, Greg sensed, Roger was diminished. There was an icy January breeze in the air, and Roger sniffed into a handkerchief with the last of a cold.

"I can't get used to this weather you have here," he said.

"Not like Texas, is it?" Greg replied.

"No – in Texas you go from airconditioned house to airconditioned garage to air-conditioned car to airconditioned office. Never mind that it's 100 degrees plus outside. Have you ever been?"

"I backpacked to the States with a girlfriend at University, and I've been to New York and LA and San Francisco since. I never got as far as Texas."

After the meal, Greg took Roger to a pub he knew. It was futile trying to match Roger drink for drink, and Greg was hammered when they said goodbye at Piccadilly Circus Tube station. Greg nursed a hangover all the next day at work, for which Kelly teased him mercilessly.

Greg had nothing against Brazil as such, but it would never have occurred to him to travel there. It wasn't somewhere he knew much about, except for vague images of football, the Amazon jungle, the Sugar Loaf Mountain and women in skimpy bikinis on Rio's beaches. No one he knew had ever been there. Then Roger invited him: "You really have to see this, Greg." Throughout the flight, Greg dozed, read a Tom Clancy novel he'd bought at the airport, half-watched a forgettable inflight movie. He looked out of the window as the plane banked to land, to see São Paulo sprawl from one side of his vision to the other. When he left the plane it was surprisingly cold, considering the location: the Tropic of Capricorn ran just south of the city. It was winter in the Southern Hemisphere, and the city lay on a high plateau. Greg had followed Roger's advice and had packed warm clothing.

Greg's visit coincided with Roger's fortieth birthday, and he was invited to the party. Twenty of them went in taxis to an Italian restaurant in the city centre. It was there that Greg was introduced to Laura, Roger's wife. Tall and slim, late thirties, she was wearing a white backless evening dress, her red hair gathered up, gold, possibly native, earrings dangling from her earlobes. He smiled, shook her hand, said, "Pleased to meet you, Laura." She smiled back – "And you, Greg"— returned his handshake with one equally firm, her eyes maintaining contact with his. Greg could see how some men might find her attractive, though at first sight with her straight-backed, almost military bearing, she had a slightly mannish air to her that he had never warmed to in other women.

Roger introduced Greg to everyone else, mostly business colleagues and their partners. Most of them were Brazilians, though there were another American couple and a Japanese. Greg was still adjusting to the three-hour time difference, so he didn't say a lot, but he'd had years of practise in making small talk to cope. Roger and Laura were at the other end of the table, and he couldn't hear what they were saying over the mixture of English and Portuguese conversation. He found himself talking to the Japanese couple. Next to Laura was sitting a plump, balding Brazilian man who was on his own and had greeted Laura by kissing her hand. This was Luis, and he spent much of the meal talking to her. The food was excellent.

Afterwards, as they were retrieving their coats to leave, Greg heard Luis say, "We could go to a club!"

Laura laughed. "Not the type of club you go to, I dare say."

Greg asked, "Sorry, what sort of club?" He was tired, and the wine he'd had with the meal was beginning to affect him.

Laura rested her hand on his forearm. "Gay. Why, are you?" He sensed flirtation in her eyes.

"No I'm not."

They all took taxis back to Roger and Laura's apartment, where they drank some more and danced. Greg found himself with Fernanda, Roger's PA and the only other person apart from Luis on their own. She was dark-skinned, her Indian ancestry quite apparent, and was wearing a red dress and had thick black hair long enough for her to sit on. She was only five feet tall, so it was impossible for Greg to hold a conversation with her without gazing into her cleavage. Later in the evening, they danced together.

Towards midnight, Greg found himself on his own, gazing out of the window at the nighttime lights of São Paulo. Fernanda had gone somewhere, but in his drink-fuzzed way Greg wasn't sure. Then Laura said, "Is this is your first time in Brazil, Greg?"

She had a wineglass in her hand. "Let's go out on the balcony," she said. "It's warm in here."

The cool night air helped to at least partially clear Greg's head. "I'm sorry," he said. "I'm still a bit jetlagged."

"Don't worry about it." Laura leaned forward, resting her arms on the railings. In the distance Greg could hear faint music, and the lights twinkled, drowning out most of the unfamiliar stars of the Southern sky. Greg felt a long way from home.

Greg leaned back against the closed glass door, which blocked out most of the noise of the party. He gazed at her bare back, the points of her hips in the dress.

"The first time I came here, Roger and I went round Rio, the markets in the Central Station. While we were there, I heard someone on one of the stalls shout out *ladrão, thief!* I saw someone, only twenty years old if that, running away. The police caught him, they tackled him and brought him down. I was expecting them to make an arrest, but then they shot him. I just didn't expect that."

"A violent country."

"And I thought, *Jesus*, I'm from *New York*. I used to be a fucking cop before I met Roger. A lot of people in my country carry guns. Looks like you ought to here too. It's a whole different country, Greg."

They went back inside. Greg danced some more with Fernanda, who at the end of the evening kissed him on the cheek and said, "I will see you in the office tomorrow." Her strong perfume lingered in his nostrils. Greg barely remembered the taxi ride back to his hotel, or getting undressed for bed. But he certainly knew about the headache he had the next morning. Fernanda greeted him with a smile as he came into Roger's small office.

The following day, he flew out with Roger to the construction site and back again, which made for a very long day. On Greg's last night in São Paulo, he ate with Roger, Laura and Fernanda at a very good Japanese Restaurant, then they went off to a café where a live band wearing sequins and Stetsons played country music. Fernanda shared Greg's taxi as she lived close to his hotel. Greg invited her up to his room. Her blouse lost a button in their haste to remove their clothes. When they were both naked, she took his penis into her mouth. Then he entered her anally, as he masturbated her with one hand, stroking the soft underside of one breast and nipple with the other. Her body was warm; he breathed in the fresh smell of her long, loose hair.

He flew back to England the next day.

This is the second time that Greg has made the flight from Belém to the site of the dam, and the experience has not grown on him. He and Laura sit pressed side by side behind the pilot, his legs held so tightly behind the chair that they've become numb. He's glad he's not taller, and he wonders how the hell Roger ever managed. Laura chats to the pilot in Portuguese, but Greg gazes out of the window and concentrates on keeping his breakfast down.

The plane lands with a bump on the dam's airstrip, if a stretch of cleared jungle could be called that. The construction site is surrounded by a fence, but in the village grown up outside chaos reigns. Pigs amble freely. Children – boys in football shirts, girls in one-piece bathing costumes with short skirts – play at the side of the road. Gaudily-dressed Indian prostitutes eye every newcomer.

Think you could score, huh? Greg remembers Roger saying to him, the first time he came here, as he escorted him around. Greg's eyes had wandered at the sight of a particularly good-looking prostitute. *It's up to you, but you can catch things that'll rot your dick clean off. Or if you prefer, you'll find some willing Indian boy who'll sell you his cu for a few reais. Just ask Luis about that.*

I'm not gay, Greg said.

Roger clapped his hand on Greg's shoulder. *Greg, I don't care if you fuck women, men or one of those pigs over there. All I care is that you do the job I pay you for. What you do in you own time is up to you.*

Remembering that conversation, Greg glances at a prostitute standing up against the wire fence. It's a safe bet most of the locals have worms. *I'm with Laura now, so look but don't touch.*

Laura walks a pace ahead, saying nothing. She's wearing a loose-fitting top and trousers, sensible wear in this hot, mosquito-ridden place. She once told him about the infections women could catch in conditions like this, and that was more information than he had ever wanted to know.

Luis meets them at the gate, and kisses and embraces Laura. They hold each other for so long, talking in Portuguese (all Greg can make out are the words *Senhor Marks*, repeated several times) that it's almost as an afterthought that Luis shakes Greg's hand. He leads them along the inside of the barbed-wire fence to a row of Portakabins, hidden from the dam by trees. There's one large Portakabin, for meeting and administration, and four smaller ones for sleeping in. Footprints scar the ground outside, and paper and bits of plastic wrapping twist slowly across the clearing.

The smaller Portakabins are partitioned into three separate sleeping quarters each, all very basic with a bed, a table and chair and a basin. At one end are a shower and a chemical toilet. In the main building are Roger's office, a small kitchen and a rest area. The rest area has an assortment of CDs and a radio. On a low scratched-varnish coffee table are strewn newspapers and several magazines, most of them Brazilian porn. The hut is empty: with Roger's disappearance, Luis has suspended the construction of the dam and sent the workers home temporarily.

Greg's room is in the last Portakabin in the row. It's been a strenuous flight and he can see that Laura is as tired as he is. "Let's rest up for a while," she says.

"I would be honoured if you would both join me for lunch," Luis says.

"I'll call Fernanda and tell her we've arrived," Laura adds.

She and Luis walk away, back to the rest area. Greg can't think straight: it's too hot and airless and his shirt is soaked with sweat. They've gone back an hour, into another time zone, and that has confused him. He shuts the door and pulls the curtain to shut out the sunlight. There's no air conditioning, so he opens the window slightly, making sure to keep the mosquito net in place. The jungle sounds, bird cries, low roars and other darker sounds he can't identify, are very loud.

Greg takes all his clothes off and lies on the bed, soon drifting off to sleep regardless. From far away, he hears a woman singing. He can't make out the words. When he first visited this place, he'd wandered off on his own by the river and had found a young native woman swimming naked. She smiled as she saw him, waved. Her hair was plastered to her scalp and, as she stood up, Greg could see that it hung down past her waist. She wiggled her bottom and called out, *You are sexy boy – you like me?*

He didn't take up her invitation then but now, as he slips into that state where dreams and reality intertwine, he wonders what would have happened if he had. He takes her back to a tent, or a quiet jungle clearing; he runs his hands down her sides, kisses her breasts. As she takes his penis into her mouth, he realises that she's not some Indian girl he doesn't even know the name of, but Fernanda: he's back in his hotel room that last night in São Paulo. And as he enters her, it's Laura he has in his arms. She sighs, whispers in his ear, *Fuck me, Greg. Fuck me.*

I'd like you to look after my wife, says Roger, in the bed beside him.

Greg gasps out loud, sits up bolt upright. His heart is beating so fast he can hardly breathe. Is he having a panic attack? He doesn't have panic attacks. Or is it something worse?

He can't sleep again. He takes sips from a bottle of water beside his bed until he's calm again. As calm as he can be.

*

I'd like you to look after my wife. That was what Roger had said to him, as an aside, shortly after Greg had arrived in São Paulo a second time and just before Roger flew off to the construction site. He planned to be away a few days, and Laura would be alone. Greg had taken a fortnight's leave in addition to the work he was doing here. He emailed his photographs back to the office in London. Kelly's response, also by email, was terse: *See if I care, you lucky bastard!!!!* It was followed by another, from her home email address to his: *Just fuck off, OK!?*

Roger and Fernanda had always been efficient, and Greg's audit didn't take long. Greg sat with Fernanda in the office. Considering that the last time they'd met they'd slept together, there was a distance to Fernanda's manner that at first he found a little disconcerting. *Now we are professional colleagues, not in bed*, it was saying to him. In the office, Fernanda wore a white blouse and a short black skirt, which somehow made her brown skin seem darker; her hair was gathered up in a clasp and she wore glasses, a little touch he found appealingly cute. He sneaked a look at her backside every time she went to find a file.

Laura arrived in the office for lunch, two shopping bags in her hands. As Greg looked at the two women, momentarily side by side, there was an immediate and obvious imbalance: the American was some nine inches taller than the Brazilian. Laura, tall, slim and fit from her many gym sessions, fair-skinned and freckled, reflected back the noon daylight that came in through the window, while Fernanda, smaller, softer, more curved and rounded, darker, absorbed it. Sufficient light to make Fernanda visible would make Laura blaze like a beacon.

"How are things going?" asked Laura.

"We're ahead of ourselves," Greg said. "Fernanda's obviously highly efficient."

Fernanda beamed.

"Sure she is," said Laura. "Roger wouldn't have employed her otherwise. Talking of Roger, I had a phone call this morning. He's in Belém and he'll fly out to the dam tomorrow."

"Shall we finish tomorrow?" said Fernanda. "I have to be efficient to our clients for the rest of today."

"Yeah, sure." The thought of an afternoon off was certainly appealing to Greg. "*Mañana.*"

Fernanda giggled. "That is Spanish."

"The word you're looking for is *amanhã*," said Laura.

Greg and Laura spent the afternoon looking round a snake farm, then went to an Italian restaurant in the evening. Greg expected Fernanda to be with them, but she was at her evening class. Roger had developments in Africa in mind, and was paying for her to learn French.

"That's forward-thinking of him," Greg said.

"He likes her. And I can't dislike her either. She certainly likes *you.*"

Greg wondered if Laura knew about his one-night stand with Fernanda. He wasn't inclined to deny it, but had tried to be discreet.

"A good-looking gringo like you, of course she likes you. If I were her age I'm sure I would too."

"What do you mean?"

"I'm sorry, I shouldn't have said that. Please excuse me."

"What do you mean, Laura?"

"Well, you're a good-looking guy. I'm sure you don't need me to tell me that. You must get a lot of female attention."

"What's your point?" Greg wondered how much she had drunk.

"I'm not under any illusions that Roger's always been the faithful husband. I sort of wonder if I should've been the model wife all that time. No children, you see. Can't have them. I follow this brilliant man – that's why I fell for him, he was so fucking *brilliant* – I follow him all the way round the goddamned globe, all his business ventures. And we serve the great god Roger Marks. All of us. I play the wife role. And I'm sick of it, I need a break."

My God, she's making a pass at me, Greg thought. *A very clumsy one, but that's what it is.*

"Excuse me." Laura stood up.

Greg watched her as she went in the direction of the Ladies. She was gone fifteen minutes. Just as Greg was beginning to worry and was about to ask a waitress to look for her she walked slowly back to the table. Her expression was blank. Greg could see from the redness of her eyes that she had been crying.

"Are you okay?" he said.

"Yes, thank you."

"I was getting worried."

She didn't answer.

For the rest of the meal she kept the conversation on the level of small talk. Afterwards, they shared a taxi, sitting awkwardly side by side.

In her apartment, she made him a coffee. "I apologise about earlier. I've had a few things on my mind which I shouldn't have said."

"Don't worry about it."

"I'm sorry if I embarrassed you."

"You didn't." This wasn't entirely true. He paused, then said, "If there's anything you want to say – you know, get off your chest . . ."

"Thank you, that's sweet of you."

Laura was perched on an armchair, her knees pulling the material of her skirt tight. She was leaning forward, and Greg had to concentrate to keep his gaze fixed on her face and not to wander downwards.

"I really shouldn't drink," she said. "I do embarrass myself sometimes. But I get lonely sometimes, and that includes when Roger is around."

"He told me to look after you."

"Did he . . . ?" She made a weak smile, which suddenly became firmer. "While he's fucking some girl he's picked up in Belém tonight."

"You don't know that."

"Believe me, I do. I ask no questions and he tells me no lies. I don't want to know."

I wonder how much Luis has confided in her? Greg thinks.

"So, I think – I don't see what harm it would do me. If he can have a break from this marriage, why can't I?"

"Why not? It might do you some good."

"Don't be cute, Greg. You know what I'm talking about."

Greg said nothing as Laura sat next to him. Her hand rested on his thigh. Her mouth found his.

*

Lunch comes as something of a relief from himself for Greg. Luis and Laura have cooked feijoada, a stew of pork, sausage and smoked meat, black beans and garlic, garnished with orange slices. Afterwards, they eat some beiju, cooked tapioca pancakes filled with coconut; they drink coffee liberally sprinkled with manioc and açai juice, mashed dark purple fruit served in wooden bowls. Greg knows how to make small-talk, so he tries it with Luis. Football is usually a good subject, especially with men, increasingly so – he's noticed over the years – with women. Greg keeps up with the game, and has been to a few matches on corporate hospitality tickets, so knows enough to make conversation. He's gambling that Luis is a fan of what seems to be the national sport. And, as it happens, Greg is right: the two of them sustain a conversation, with Laura joining in here and there, especially at moments when Luis's broken English isn't up to the task.

Now, while Laura and Luis are elsewhere in the site, Greg is alone in Roger's office. As he looks up from the desk, he sees a black-haired spider monkey looking in through the window, dark-pink face pinched with curiosity. Greg starts. Most of the monkeys and birdlife live in the forest canopy, twenty metres or more above ground level. Normally, when he looks out of that window he sees hanging moss and not much else.

"Fuck off," Greg mutters, but the monkey does not react.

Roger's laptop was locked in a safe, otherwise Greg has no doubt it would have been stolen. It's connected to a satellite phone. Roger deliberately kept the laptop empty of all but basic software; each evening he would upload everything else to the server at work. Roger's office in São Paulo has a leased-line connection to the Internet; when he was outside Brazil, he would access it via CompuServe or AOL. Greg connects to the office server, entering the password Roger told him.

New email drops into Roger's mailbox but Greg does not read it. He feels he shouldn't be doing this, going through a missing man's post. Business correspondence, greetings from friends, and a large amount of spam that's escaped the filters. One of the new messages – dated the day before Roger's disappearance – catches his eye, one with an attachment. *You look at this*, it says. The attachment is a JPEG file: Roger's email software automatically displays the picture.

"Oh Christ," Greg mutters. He closes the email quickly, feeling sick. There are two men in the picture. One is Luis. The other one, being explicitly buggered by Luis, can be no more than a teenager. Also in the email was a phone number with a 092 dialling code: Manaus, about four hundred kilometres from here. Greg has never been to Manaus, a town deep in the jungle, but he knows its reputation for crime.

What is this, a blackmail attempt? Then surely it's Luis who is being blackmailed. Or has the blackmail progressed so far that it's escalated to Roger?

Greg closes Roger's email folder and lets himself wonder round the drives of Roger's office server, opening every word-processed document he can. Nothing of any use. He's still searching when Laura and Luis come back.

"Luis says there's something we should see," says Laura.

Greg lay back on the hotel double bed. He watched as Laura sat up, slowly swung her legs off the side of the bed, tangled her toes in the deep-pile carpet. The touch of her thighs, cool as marble, against his: the sensation still lingered. Laura stood, pulling up her knickers. Then she sat down on the side of the bed again, reaching for her bra where it lay on the floor.

Greg sat up, rested his palms on her shoulders. She didn't react.

"I'll have to go now," she said after a pause.

"Stay the night here."

"I can't."

"I'm sure the hotel won't mind."

"It isn't that. I won't be able to sleep in a strange bed."

Both dressed, they took the lift down to reception. Greg stood to one side, hands in pockets, as Laura ordered a taxi in Portuguese. He felt helpless and useless, completely disoriented. This had been the second time he and Laura had made love. Once you could, just about, forgive, blame on the moment, but twice had to be premeditated. Even *made love* seemed wrong. With Fernanda it had been different: sex had been the motivation then, pleasure the goal, for both of them. No complications wished for. With Laura that was surely the same, but it didn't seem that way to him.

Laura sat on one of the big armchairs to the left of the reception. She looked up significantly at him, and he took the hint and sat next to her.

"You look uncomfortable," she said.

"I am."

"Don't be."

I'm the one who gets called cold, Greg thinks. *Only in it for sex, and I lose interest in a woman once I've had that. Kelly was just the latest. But it's not like that now. Is it because Roger is a friend? And my employer?*

"I – I'd like to spend the night with you," Greg said.

Laura smiled. "That's sweet."

"Senhora Marks!" the man at reception shouted. The taxi had arrived.

"Good night, Greg." Laura kissed him quickly on the lips. "See you tomorrow."

That was the night that Roger left his final message on the answerphone.

Walking in single file, Greg and Laura follow Luis along a path hacked through the jungle. Ferns are trampled underfoot, while dark green bushes taller than any of them entwine thickly on either side. Even Roger would be dwarfed by them, Greg thinks. Luis warned them not to wander from the path, and Greg is quite willing to follow that advice. He has no idea what he might find in the shrubbery: a jaguar maybe, or an armadillo, or an anaconda. From high above in the forest canopy, he hears the trill of birdsong and the shrieks of monkeys. His nostrils are filled with the ripe scent of rotting fruit and vegetation. It's very humid and Greg is already tired and irritable. He's wearing cotton trousers and stout shoes, a baseball cap and the most powerful sunblock and insect repellent he can find.

Once they had to stop to make way for a wide, seething, chattering column of army ants to pass. If you wanted to dispose of someone or something, Greg thought, this is the perfect place. The army ants will eat everything in their path, and there are other scavengers prepared to pick your skeleton clean. Anything left will be consumed by the fungi and bacteria that live in the ground.

If someone wants to incriminate Luis, Greg thinks, then why has Roger disappeared? Or maybe Roger was the target and Luis simply the way of reaching him, of applying pressure on him? If Roger has been killed, then if his body was disposed of in the jungle they'd never find it. If that's the case, Greg thinks, I hope he didn't suffer.

"Here," says Luis.

They are in a clearing ten metres wide. Greg would think it natural if it wasn't so perfectly circular. The trees have extended across the gap, blotting out the sunlight and hiding the clearing from above. In the centre – the exact centre, he guesses, but he'd have to ask a surveyor to verify that – is a round grey object, metallic rock, about three metres across. It is buried in the ground, the visible part about a metre high.

Greg steps forward.

Luis says something in Portuguese. Laura says, "Be careful, Greg."

Close up, the object isn't a uniform grey: there are what look like burn marks and the surface is pitted where it isn't covered with lichen. Greg wonders how much of it is below the ground and how long it has been lying here. Judging by the growth around and above it, a long time.

"I showed this to Senhor Marks," Luis says. "He said it should belong in the Smith . . . Smiths . . . " He gazes at his feet; he's on the verge of breaking down.

Laura puts her arm about his shoulders. "The Smithsonian?" she says. Luis nods.

"How did you find it, Luis?" Greg asks.

"My friend showed me. My Indian friend."

"You mean your lover, Luis."

"Greg . . . " Laura muttered, resting her hand on Luis's forearm.

Luis looks down, nods again. "I was not supposed to see it. It fell out of the sky."

Greg first heard the news when Laura rang him, while he was eating a hotel breakfast. "I'll be right there," he said. Taxis were difficult to find at that time in the morning, so it was an hour later that he arrived at the Marks' apartment.

Roger was missing. Luis had called on him in the morning to find his door open, his bedlinen disturbed, but otherwise no sign of any struggle.

Laura let him in to the apartment, which to Greg now seemed vast, empty and unfriendly, its atmosphere changing overnight. Greg had an impulse to take Laura in her arms, comfort her, but she stood apart from him, her body language telling him that a closer approach would not be welcome.

He felt guilt, first of all – guilt that Roger had rung this apartment late. Late enough for Laura to be home, not so late that she would be asleep. And she hadn't been there. What would have gone through Roger's mind at that point? Did he suspect something had happened between his wife and Greg?

Laura, with Fernanda's assistance, organised a flight, which would involve a stop-over at Belém. Greg sat on a chair in the corner, suddenly feeling helpless and not a little scared.

"You can't go on your own, Laura," he said.

Greg suspected that, if he hadn't said those words, she would have done that very thing.

The rain begins to fall on the journey back, and they are drenched by the time they get back to the hut. There is no chance of flying back to Belém until it stops; the rattle of the drops on the roof is deafening. The rain persists until dusk, so they will need to stay the night here.

They eat a subdued dinner from the fridge. Greg wants to tell Laura that someone has attempted to influence Roger by blackmailing Luis – criminals in Manaus. Are they doing this simply because he was a rich American businessman, or have they got wind that he's found something, something potentially very valuable indeed, in the jungle? But he can't talk to her with Luis present. Laura seems to want Luis's company rather than his this evening. They sit together, listening to one CD after another; after a while, Laura puts her arm about Luis's shoulders. At eight o'clock Greg excuses himself and goes to his room.

A thick black loneliness is inside him, leaking into him like oil, filling him up. He feels alone, small and helpless. Normally, at times like this, he could distract himself: play his guitar, idly surf the Internet, or go out to a club with the intention of getting laid. But now he can't do any of these. Left to his own resources, he's frightened.

Did they come for Roger in the middle of night? Was it a quick death, a bullet to the brain, or slow and painful? A bullet to the head would do it, or repeated blows with a machete. Roger would take a lot of killing.

There's a knock on the door, and Greg's heart jolts.

"Greg, it's me," says Laura.

Greg climbs out of bed and opens the door. "Christ, don't do that. You made me jump."

Laura, dressed in a T-shirt and a pair of shorts, makes a faint smile. "I'm sorry. Do you want to talk?"

Greg nods.

"Come to my room."

He sees no need to tiptoe to Laura's hut, but he does so nonetheless. He sits on the edge of the bed. She pours whisky from a hip flask into two glasses and offers him one. He drinks more hurriedly than he should, the liquid a hot trail down his throat.

Laura sits heavily on a chair. "Poor Roger." She says it again, quieter: "Poor Roger."

Greg says nothing.

"I hope he didn't suffer."

Somehow this prompts Greg out of his silence. He tells her what he found in Roger's email inbox earlier.

Laura laughs harshly, incredulously. "We're not in São Paulo any more, Greg. This isn't New York or London. Did whoever sent that email think Roger gives a shit if Luis is gay or not? I know for a fact that he doesn't. And Carlos isn't a kid either: he just looks young."

"How old is he?"

"Old enough. Why, what's it to you?" Greg does not answer. "I know you have a problem with it, Greg. Roger didn't, and I don't."

"You're right. I don't like it. The thought of two guys shagging each other turns my stomach. But each to their own."

"Right. That's something we do agree on. Let's leave it at that, shall we?"

Slowly, Greg feels himself detach from the situation. The room drifts slowly out of focus, so soon all he can see is the window, the mosquitoes grey smears as they slap against the glass, attracted by the light within. He suddenly feels very very tired, as if the earth's gravity is sucking his substance out through his feet.

He opens his eyes. He is lying, still fully clothed, on the bed. Beside him, under the sheets, her back turned away from him, is Laura, asleep, still in her T-shirt and shorts, her chest rising and falling as she breathes. A headache pulses, a hot needle-point behind his forehead.

Click.

A noise from outside. Then a scraping sound.

Greg gets to his feet and tiptoes to the door, opens it a crack.

The clearing is dark, the only light from the stars, and it takes a few seconds for Greg's eyes to accustom themselves. The door of Greg's Portakabin is open. Just twenty feet away is a dark shape lying on the ground. Greg ducks down and hurries as quietly as he can up to it.

It's a man, lying on his back. Greg recognises him as Carlos from the photograph he saw earlier. Carlos's eyes are wide open, and the back of his head is matted with blood. A few feet further on is another body, at the entrance to Greg's room. This one is Luis, a bullet hole drilled neatly in the middle of his forehead.

Pressure. Pressure on Luis, hence the blackmail attempt. Pressure on Roger as well. Only Roger didn't respond to it. So they came for him. And killed him.

And now they're back.

Luis has let someone in, the men who took Roger. Luis led them straight to Greg's room, of course expecting Greg to be there.

Maybe he hoped to alert Laura. By sacrificing Greg.

But he didn't know that Greg wouldn't be in his room.

A fatal mistake.

Greg stands up, his gut trembling. He's about to run back to warn Laura, when a flashlight shines in his face, blinding him.

Greg yells out and runs straight at the light. The man holding it is much smaller and lighter than him, and falls back as Greg hits him. The man curses in some language Greg doesn't know. Greg stumbles and lands on top of him.

The man squirms under him. He has a machete in his other hand, but Greg kneels on his forearm preventing him from using it. Greg takes it out of the man's hands. The machete is heavy. He lifts the weapon up and brings the blade down hard on the man's forehead.

The man shrieks. He twitches in his death agonies, the machete embedded in his skull. His blood pours out over his face, the spray staining Greg's hands and shirt.

Greg stands up again. Something very hard hits him on the head and he gasps out loud. His legs buckle under him.

For a brief moment he must have been unconscious, for he is lying on his side looking up, pain clustering thickly at the back of his skull. Another man is staring down at him.

Is this how Roger died? Will it be over quickly, a shot to the head? Or will they take their time?

In his ear is a noise so loud that Greg can't hear anything any more. The Brazilian opens his mouth in surprise, as blood and bone erupts from the side of his head. His mouth remains open as his eyes dim, and he falls sideways, tripping over Greg's legs.

Laura steps over them both.

Greg is unable to move now, except to turn his eyes. There are other men in the clearing and the entrance to the Portakabin, backing away from Laura as she points a gun at them, holding the weapon in both hands. One man's head jolts back as his brains splash against a wall. He slides down to the ground. A third man turns and runs, and Laura shoots him in the back of the neck.

Laura looks down at Greg. She says something that he lip-reads: "Are you okay?"

Greg mumbles something, as blackness creeps over him. He closes his eyes. ✿

MAT COWARD

Mat Coward lives in Somerset. His crime, sf/f/h and children's short stories have appeared in numerous anthologies and magazines in the UK, US, Europe and Japan, and on radio. His first collection is out now from Five Star in the US, under the title *Do the World a Favour and Other Stories*. The same publisher puts out his series of crime novels featuring DI Don Packham and DC Frank Mitchell, which are also available in paperback from Worldwide. Mat's latest book is *Classic Radio Comedy* in the Pocket Essentials series. His hilarious and informative antidote to useless 'howtorite' books, *Success . . . and How to Avoid It*, is published soon by TTA Press.

So many people die. That's the main thing I've learned from life: so many people seem to die. And when they're not busy dying, they generally pass the time being unhappy, or else making other people unhappy, or else getting drunk and dancing and throwing up. Which puts getting drunk and dancing and throwing up in a whole new light, when you think about it.

I was never much of a dancer, to be honest, except for very briefly, when I was 17. I lacked the ability to just let go and let it happen. But my mate Andy danced. I'm not saying he was a *good* dancer, necessarily; not saying he had any particular talent for it. That wasn't the point: he enjoyed dancing, so he did it. Andy had a true punk rock soul, by which I mean that he didn't give a toss what other people thought of him. As long as what he was doing was right by his lights, then that was all he needed to know. And if you didn't like it, then that was your problem, not his.

For a while, in the late summer or early autumn of 1977, there was a sign in the window of one of the West End venues – the Vortex, possibly – which showed a picture of a punk rocker in all his glory (bondage trousers, ripped leather jacket, safety pins, spiky hair) and written underneath was the message: IF YOU DON'T LOOK LIKE THIS, FUCK OFF. The police made the club take it down eventually. I think there might even have been a threat of prosecution. I thought it was brilliant, hilarious. It was tribal, and aggressive, and punky and it said *Go to hell* to the entire Establishment – to anyone who wasn't us. Andy thought it was stupid.

"If they want to wear a uniform," he said, "why don't they join the army?" Next time we went to a punk gig, Andy wore a sports jacket and tie.

The dance that everyone associates with punk wasn't really a dance at all. Pogoing didn't involve learning any steps; it didn't require an ability to keep time, or to co-ordinate with a partner. That was the point of it, really. If you could jump up and down, you could pogo. If you could jump up and down even though your trouser legs were linked at the ankles by a short length of khaki fabric, or black mock leather, then you could *really* pogo. Not that it would have mattered; those were not competitive days, punk was not a competitive scene. To be better at pogoing than someone else – or rather, to have tried to be better – would have been to miss the idea entirely. Can you jump up and down? So, you can pogo. I even remember seeing two kids in wheelchairs, at one gig, bumping their wheels up against the side of the stage, pogoing away with the rest of us. Even if you *can't* jump up and down, you can pogo.

Slamming and choking are not as well remembered today, but were just as important at the time, and both were a little more involved than pogoing, a little more demanding. Slamming required timing. As you hurled your body at your mate – or he hurled his at you – at distances ranging from a few feet to a few inches, depending on whether the floor was illegally overcrowded or catastrophically overcrowded, if you didn't time it right you could end up with all sorts of trouble. Not that anyone ever did get injured, as far as I know. Those were wild times, and in wild times the wild children are protected. Today, people live more safely, and children are killed everywhere.

The choke (I'm not sure if we actually called it that, or even if we called it anything; 1977 was more a time of doing than of branding) was a frenzied dance, even more so than the pogo or the slam. There was a strange sense of thrill to choking a total stranger; how would he react?

To an uninitiated onlooker, seeing two teenagers gripping each other about the throat and shaking each other back and forth, while simultaneously leaping into the air, bouncing on the rubber soles of their French kickers, it must have looked like a fight to the death. It is this one image of the punk era – of my friend Andy strangling Jamie Holmes, holding on and tightening his wrists even after Jamie's hands had dropped to his sides – that stayed in my mind over the years more than any other.

I hired a room for the reunion above a suitably dingy pub near Waterloo. That wasn't as easy as it sounds; dingy pubs were not so plentiful in 1997 as they had been twenty years earlier.

I got there first, to set up. I had a few homemade tapes of the classics: Elvis Costello, The Clash, The Pistols, Wreckless Eric, Eddie and the Hot Rods. There was a small bar in the functions room, staffed by a friendly teenage girl. She asked me what it was, a stag night? A works do? I told her. She was delighted. "Oh, wow! I love all that old punk stuff, it's so naff isn't it? So camp? Like, you know, so *Seventies*."

I wondered when irony had become the only acceptable response to anything; when, precisely, people had decided that it just wasn't safe to actually *feel* anything any more.

The girl passed me the clingfilmed plates of sandwiches I'd ordered, and I distributed them around the room. I stuck a few treasured old posters to the walls: creased fold-outs of the Pistols in their pomp; red-and-white handbills advertising gigs at the Marquee or The Other Cinema.

I drank a quick half, and smoked half a cigarette. I was nervous. The fact was, I hadn't kept in close touch with any of the old crowd. I'd seen Andy maybe once or twice a year for a quick drink in town; most of the others I'd seen even less than that. The last time we were all together in the same room was . . . well, shit, *forever* ago.

"Can you keep an eye on things for a moment? I just need to change."

"Sure," said the barmaid. "No problem."

I took my holdall into the Gents, locked myself in a cubicle, and took off my jeans and jacket and shirt. I put on my Army surplus straights held together with an old bike padlock and chain, and a black T-shirt, faded to grey. I took off my slip-ons and replaced them with French kickers. I hadn't needed to visit a barber – my hair, these days, being short enough by nature – but I did spike up what remained of it with a comb and a blob of gel; I'd have used Brylcreem, or perhaps sugar water, back then.

"Oh, wow!" said the barmaid when I emerged. "Where did you get all that fantastic stuff?"

"I don't know. Just stuff I never threw away."

"Wow, you mean it's *authentic*! Hey, you know, that stuff might be worth something."

"I don't know. I wouldn't think so."

She looked at me more closely. "But shouldn't the T-shirt be, like, ripped?"

I just shook my head, smiled; I couldn't be bothered to explain. A ripped T-shirt was one that *got* ripped; a T-shirt ripped on purpose was for posers.

Well, I was dressed. The posters were up. The tapes were standing by. The sandwiches were sweating. Everything was ready. I'd invited seven blokes, those I still had fairly recent addresses for, and asked them to invite anyone else they thought of. How many would turn up? Just me? Or, just me and Andy . . . I didn't fancy that.

That would be even worse.

The first bloke to arrive wasn't a bloke. It was Anne. I must have looked as astonished as I felt (perhaps even – though I hoped not – as *horrified* as I felt), because she laughed and said, "Hi, Steve. Hope you don't mind? I know I wasn't really invited, but . . ."

She obviously had been invited, I thought, because otherwise how would she have known about it? But who had invited her, I couldn't imagine.

"Of course not, Anne, I'm delighted to see you. It's – you look wonderful." She did. She was dressed up like Gaye Advert, black leather jacket and tight PVC trousers. Long black hair, and black eye make up. She looked stunning.

We kissed awkwardly. You didn't kiss when you met people in the old days; that's something of the modern age, of who we've become.

To my relief – and Anne's, no doubt – the door banged again, and three men walked in. I recognised one of them (Chaz, he'd been in the Hammersmith squat with me and Andy), but I didn't know his companions. All three had dyed hair: green, with yellow highlights. It looked as if someone had been sick on their heads – someone with a streaming cold, at that – which I suppose was the idea.

Chaz introduced his nephews. Now I came to look at them, they were a good bit younger than him – nearer the barmaid's age. I was annoyed: this wasn't supposed to be a fancy dress party, for heaven's sake. But I tried not to show my annoyance, not even to myself. After all, it was only a reunion, not a sacred rite.

More people drifted in over the next half-hour or so. Old friends, old acquaintances, wives and girlfriends, friends of friends. Almost everyone had made some effort with their clothes, though the results were astonishingly varied. It seemed to me (though I don't pretend my memory's any better than anyone else's), that most of them were dressed according to 1990s ideas of what 1977 looked like.

I reckoned I was the only one wearing his own original clothes from back then – and I wasn't sure what that said about me. The worst word a modern kid can use about anyone is 'sad', which seems to mean something like 'enthusiastic'. But the barmaid had said I looked fantastic, hadn't she? Well, no . . . she'd said my *clothes* were fantastic.

In the end, there were more people present than I'd feared might be the case: must have been getting on for twenty-five, which was about right for the occasion. A few I didn't know. A few, to be honest, I didn't remember, or barely. Rob was there; I was glad to see him, we'd been good mates. He hadn't lived in the squat, but he had got me a job in a pub near Whitehall, which had become our HQ. He was wearing straight black jeans and a long, thin tie and he was completely bald, smooth as a shaved egg. I'd pretty much lost contact with Rob some time in the late 80s, but when you've been close to someone when you were seventeen, the years don't matter that much.

"How you doing?" I asked him, and he just shrugged and said, "Oh, you know, mustn't grumble," and then we talked about old times instead. Which – fair enough – was the reason we were there. I noticed he could hardly take his eyes off Anne. I wasn't sure if that was because he shared my shock at her presence, or just because she looked so sexy.

I was pretty busy acting like a host, so I didn't notice Andy had arrived until he tapped me on the back while I was turning over a cassette and said: "Wotcher, Stevey-boy. Good turnout."

His hair was slightly longer than was fashionable; he was wearing blue jeans, a sports jacket, and a smart denim shirt. We went up to the bar to get him a drink. While I ordered, Andy looked around him, smiling. "I see Anne made it," he said.

For the second time that night Anne caused my jaw to drop open.

"You knew she was coming?" I handed him his pint.

"Cheers. Yeah, I invited her."

"*You* invited her?"

"Sure. Who wants to spend the evening at a stag do?"

"No, right. No, I'm glad she's here. I just – I didn't even know you were still in touch."

"Why wouldn't we be, Stevey? We were married, you know, albeit briefly."

A hand fell on his shoulder from behind, and Chaz said, "Andy, mate – is that you? Oh man, great to see you. Great!"

"Chaz." Andy put down his beer, and they shook hands. I got the impression Chaz was trying to do some black-kid thing with fingers and thumbs, but if he was it crumbled inside Andy's firm, conventional grip.

Chaz fingered one of Andy's lapels. "But mate, shame on you – you're not dressed up."

"Never mind, Chaz. You're punk enough for both of us. Nice hair."

Chaz ran his fingers through his Day-Glo spikes. "Oh, yeah. Well, no harm in a little nostalgia, right?"

Andy shrugged. "Sure."

"You don't agree?" Chaz smiled in the fixed way people do when they're not going to have a fight, but they're not going to let it go, either.

"I just think being nostalgic for punk is maybe a contradiction in terms."

"Sort of un-punk?" I said. I felt I knew what he meant.

"If you like. Besides, life is better now than it was then. We had a revolution and it worked – so why look back?"

"Surprised you turned up, then," said Chaz. "Still – great to see you." He moved further down the bar, and began waving a tenner to attract the barmaid's attention.

"Always was a bit of a poser," I said.

"Bloke's entitled to his point of view. They're *his* memories. Tell you what, I should have come in my work gear." Andy worked as a nurse in a busy casualty department. "Head to toe in blood and vomit – he'd have liked that."

"So. Why did you come, if you're not into All Our Yesterdays?"

He clinked his glass against mine. "See some old mates. It's good to keep in touch. No, all I'm saying is, punk wasn't a fashion, something that can be reproduced by wearing the right clothes or dyeing your hair. It was about how you walked, stood, the expression on your face, your tone of voice. Your outlook."

"Fair point," I said. But I couldn't help wondering if there was another reason why Andy didn't feel nostalgic about 1977: because that was the year he killed a kid with his bare hands.

When I first arrived at the squat, all I knew about punks was what I'd seen on the news, or read in the *Daily Mirror*. They couldn't play their instruments, they looked like freaks, they had no respect for anything and they were violent. When Andy persuaded me to go to my first punk rock gig I was nervous, frankly. Excited but nervous.

I never knew Andy's full story; his accent was from somewhere up in the Midlands, maybe Wolverhampton, but it soon faded, and he ended up speaking the kind of universal sub-Cockney that was youth's Esperanto. He never admitted to a surname, not in those days, and he never offered much in the way of biography, except to say that he'd come down to London for the music, and because back home everything and everyone was 'dead'. I took this to mean that, like the rest of us, he wanted a few laughs before he got old and died. Obviously, there was something he wasn't talking about: a violent dad, maybe, or a juvenile criminal conviction. It wasn't a mystery that I found interesting enough to pursue. I was simply glad that he wanted to be mates with me, this quiet, rather serious-minded, grown-up man (he was 19, I was 17), who always knew where things were happening, and shared his knowledge without con-descension. As a new boy in the big city, I felt safe in his company. In part this was because there was, behind his wry eyes and hidden in his understanding smile, an unmistakeable glint of danger. The first time I met him, I remember thinking *You wouldn't want to be his enemy.*

My own story was a simple one. Born in Kent, didn't much take to school, moved to London as soon as I could. I got on OK with my parents; even phoned them, every now and then. I wasn't a runaway – I was just a teenager who'd moved to London. Where else was there to be, if you were young in the summer of '77?

Andy, Jamie and Rob were already regular attendees at various of London's mush-rooming punk venues. They'd seen all the bands I'd heard of, and many that I hadn't. Chaz used to tag along as well, although I don't think he really had any close friends at the squat. He was in some ways the opposite of Andy: he tried to be a mystery man, and failed. Jamie's summing-up of him was blunt, typically Glaswegian, and generally accepted: "He's a middle-class tosser, thinks wearing anarchy symbols makes him cool, but he's harmless enough."

If I'd been on my own at that first gig, I would never have got into the dancing. In fact, if I'd been on my own, I'd quite likely have turned tail the moment I passed through the weapons search in the corridor, and walked through the doors into a living definition of claustrophobia.

There were a few hundred kids there, mostly boys, and their collective *thrum* of newness and rebellion was something the press reports could never have prepared me for. It was alien and frightening and my stomach walls were squirting cold-hot liquid at each other . . . and as my heartbeat and my breathing gradually attuned themselves to this new world, I began to think that maybe I'd come home.

Between us and the small stage there were rows of tip-back chairs, and there was hardly room to get into the place, let alone to move around. Drinking from the plastic beer glasses was difficult enough, hemmed in by elbows and hips; rolling a cigarette would have required a dexterity far beyond my skills.

The lights went down, and Jimmy Pursey yelled *One two three four!* and Sham 69 leapt into – I don't know, I don't remember exactly. It could have been 'What Have We Got', though I seem to remember they used that as a closer, so maybe it was 'They Don't Understand'. Whatever it was, it was big and strong and hard and relentless, and I'd never in my life heard music so driving, so physical. The guitar chords raced each other up the hall and tore holes in my body.

"Come on," Andy shouted in my ear. "Let's go down the front."

I'd have preferred to stay put, not too far from the illuminated exit sign. Apart from anything, getting to the front would involve fighting through an almost solid mass of leaping, screaming flesh. But the others set off towards the stage, and I had either to follow them or lose them.

You couldn't actually stand in the space immediately in front of the stage. It was too crowded for that; the only way that many people could all occupy such a small floor simultaneously was by jumping up and down, taking turns to annex the vertical so that your neighbours could occupy the horizontal. In 1977, choreography wasn't an art or a science, it was a force of nature.

That's how the pogo was born, I would guess; from teenagers full of uncontrollable energy, responding to music that could never be listened to static, played in venues designed for audiences half the size. That – and the sheer speed of the beat. The conduits of information between brain and limbs weren't up to a job like this. By the time the message had travelled from head to knees, the beat had gone – and you were already too late to catch the next one. Just jump up and down: that's all there was time for.

I'd never done it before, or even seen it done, but it seemed as if my legs were veterans of the pogo while my brain was still back at the box office queuing for a ticket.

I jumped, jerking my body upwards from the hips, twisting and writhing at the point where my ascent peaked, forcing out an extra inch of flight, then using my landing to shoot me back up. It sounds effortful, but really I seemed to be hovering more than jumping. A teenager is a kind of furnace, who burns his childhood inside his belly for fuel.

My glasses flew off my nose. I caught them and shoved them in my pocket. Andy grabbed me round the throat and began to shake me. *Oh Christ*, I thought. *Here's the violence.*

His eyes were pure danger now, all rage and no wry. I didn't want to do it, but I had no choice – to save myself, I put my own hands around his throat, trying to hold him at arm's length. It was only as his mouth split into a wild smile, and then as he goggled his eyes and lolled his tongue, making believe he was choking, that I realised: my neck didn't hurt. I could breathe normally. I relaxed my own fingers, suddenly embarrassed and afraid at the force with which they'd been digging into him.

Locked together, we took it in turns to jump and kick our legs out, leaving our weight momentarily on the other guy's shoulders. We caromed around the floor, bouncing off other people, knocking them sprawling, sweat flying from our hair, and at the song's peremptory end, we spun away from each other, ending up on our arses amid a million legs.

I wondered how that was possible: how did we have enough space to fall over? I looked at Andy's laughing face and saw the answer: we'd made our own space.

The singer was swearing at the people who were still standing at the bar, clutching pints. "Tossers! Why ain't you dancing? This lot down here, they're the ones that count. They're the only ones we're playing for!"

And he pointed at me and my mates. We were the ones they were playing for. If you've ever been 17, you'll know how good that felt.

About half an hour after the last tape had finished, no one at the reunion had bothered to turn it over – including me. It wasn't that sort of evening. There wasn't going to be any pogoing tonight, let alone throttling.

By ten o'clock there were only half a dozen of us left, sitting round a couple of the tables, chatting, drinking moderately. Andy and Anne seemed relaxed, courteous with each other, though they didn't have much to say to each other. Chaz had left early, with his cousins – to go on to a Seventies disco that one of them ran. Chaz at least had the decency to look a little embarrassed when his cousin let that slip. They offered us free tickets, but no one took them up. I might have been arrested for assault if anybody had.

Nobody had mentioned Jamie all night. I hadn't expected anyone would. For all I knew, I was the only one who remembered him.

I looked around at my old punk rock comrades: a nurse, a computer guy, a plumber. Anne was a housewife, with two children at school. Having spent twenty years doing crap jobs, I was halfway through a non-graduate-entry teacher training course. I was proud of that; didn't like to say so, didn't seem very punk to say it, but I was a not very academic bloke who'd left school a few days before my sixteenth birthday. I wanted to be a teacher because almost all the teachers I ever had were sadists or morons or defeatists.

The conversation at first was of the catching-up type you'd expect, and then, as the alcohol did its gentle work, we moved on to soul-searching. Rob and Andy held the floor mostly, while the rest of listened and nodded and contributed the occasional affectionate insult. I gathered from what they said that the two of them had seen quite a bit of each other over the years, though I'd never had them down as big pals, particularly, in the old days.

Rob was the punkiest of us, so it seemed, despite his bald dome and the fact that he was on orange juice. He'd never had a steady job, never been married, still went to gigs, still lived the punk life. "Unlike you load of BOFs," he said, and we all laughed at Anne, who had to have the phrase *Boring Old Fart* explained to her.

Andy was as I remembered him; calm and quiet, serious but always amused. Never a shouter, but never one to say something just to make people comfortable. "For the record, Andy," I told him, "I reckon you're the only authentic-looking ex-punk here."

He gave me a puzzled frown, though I'm sure he knew what I meant.

I gestured at his sports jacket and clean jeans. "Well, that's what real ex-punks look like when they're knocking 40, isn't it?"

Amid the jeers and cries of "Never trust anyone over 30," Andy said: "I'm not an ex-punk. I'm a punk. I always was punk, and I always will be."

Someone said: "In *those* shoes?"

"DIY," said Andy, and we all fell quiet, ready to hear something worthwhile. "Do-it-yourself, use the materials at hand to make the world a place you want to inhabit, that was punk. And you can do that all your life. I don't just mean music – any aspect of life. Give you an example. I'm a good cook, you know? Dab-hand with the old wok, maestro of the flung-together stir-fry. But I've never read a recipe in my life."

Anne and Andy met in an all-night snack bar not far from Big Ben. She was working there, he was eating there. He asked her out and she said, "Yeah, why not?" It was two a.m. Their first date, later that morning, consisted of having sex in an empty car park. For the second date, she took him to the pictures.

She was never into punk, which would have made her all but invisible to the rest of us except that she was too pretty to be invisible. The announcement of their wedding came as a shock; getting married wasn't a very punk thing to do. As wedding announcements go, it wasn't very formal. One evening, Anne came into the pub where I was working and asked me if Andy had been in yet.

"Not yet. You supposed to be meeting him here?"

She shrugged. "Yeah, you know. Talk about the wedding and that."

"What, you're going to a wedding?" I gave my lips a little twist as I released the words, like a bowler putting on spin. We didn't go to weddings, our sort. Funerals, maybe, they might be quite cool. But not *weddings*!

"Yeah," said Anne. "So are you – you've got to be a witness."

"What witness?"

"At the registry. Yeah? You and one of the others. Jamie, maybe. Me and Andy, we need two witnesses, when we get married. You've got to have two, it's the law. I don't know why. In case one of them's lying or something, I don't know."

It was mostly Andy's friends at the registry office. A cousin of Anne's did attend, wearing a hat, but she cleared off as soon as she decently could, and that was it for family on either side. After the ceremony, about half a dozen of us went off to somewhere in the country, on a train. A cottage in Kent, or somewhere, owned by some old hippies that Anne knew. They'd lent her the place for a sort of combination wedding party and honey-moon.

Speed was the true punk drug – a fast, urban buzz, harmonising with the fast, loud guitars of the music – but for that occasion it didn't seem appropriate, so we compromised our principles and stuck with dope and cider. My only big memory of our rural sojourn is of staying up all night – the weather was very hot, must have been high summer – and at one point, sitting outside the house on the front step of the cottage watching the sun come up. Feeling tired, but completely awake. Shivering slightly from the brief period of chill that comes at the dawn of even the hottest day. Pulling my jacket across my chest, and putting my hands deep in the pockets: we'd all worn hired suits to the wedding, as a laugh. (Oh, God – is *punk* responsible for irony?)

Then, about six in the morning, going into the little house, seeing a pile of people snoring and farting on the living-room floor, going up to use the bog, looking out of the landing window and seeing Anne and Jamie, kissing in the back garden. She was wearing his jacket, and she had one hand behind his head, a cigarette between the fingers.

It was a very short marriage. I never said anything to Andy, so I can only assume that Anne did, or Jamie maybe, or perhaps Andy himself looked out of a window and saw what I saw. At any rate, by the time we headed back to London that evening, they were no longer a married couple in any but the legal sense.

These days, the 1970s is packaged as a fashionable, cherishable decade, the greatest flowering of a sweetly naive kind of cool. That's not how those of us who were there remember it. Before punk rock, with its snarling singers and its rude graphics, the mid-70s were cold and grey, unfriendly and above all *boring*.

Let me tell you about punk music, about what it meant to us. Or to me, at least. It wasn't about anarchy – we weren't anarchists, you have to study to be an anarchist. It was simpler than that: for the first time, or at least the first time for white kids since skiffle, pop music became something you could *do* instead of just something you consumed. Just before punk detonated, you could buy a Yes concept album, and listen to it – and that was it, that was your part of the process finished. Punk was as different as it could have been. If you liked the noise, you just *became* punk. Thousands of kids formed bands, about ten minutes after hearing their first punk single. People used to say "But they can't play their instruments," not realising that was the whole point! Music isn't as hard as people make out – that's something all the young punks discovered, as bluesmen thirty or forty years earlier had discovered.

All you needed was two chords on the guitar, a bassist who could count up to four by tapping his feet, and someone who could shout loud enough to be heard over the drums – the technical, musicological term for this latter Herbert being 'lead vocalist'.

The lyrics; that was the easiest bit of all. You just said what was going on in your life, in your head: "I'm bored. Working is crap. School is crap. I want excitement. I'm scared." Same with the dancing. You can jump up and down, can't you? Fine, then you're dancing – so get down the front and dance.

You didn't even need to be in a band to be part of punk. If you wanted to be part of it, believed you were part of it, acted like you were part of it, you were part of it. If you felt punk, you were punk, whether you were the editor of a Roneo'd fanzine in the heart of punkland, or a school kid in rural Wales. There was no distance between the band and the crowd; they were just the same as us, except they'd managed to get hold of an amp from somewhere, and we hadn't, or hadn't yet, or didn't want to. In 1977, all the bands were garage bands.

If you wanted to be a punk, the only thing that could stop you was death.

The night Jamie died, about a fortnight after the wedding, we'd been to see an all-girl group in the cellar of a pub near Kings Cross. By then, just about every space in London was putting on gigs, live music was alive again for the first time in ages.

This particular place was even less suitable as a venue for a music club than most: the sound was dreadful, the heat was unbearable, and the beer was warmer than the fug. We were having a great time; me, Andy, Rob and Jamie. Anne had been there – not with anyone as far as I could tell, just hanging around, almost as if the wedding, and the break-up with Andy had never happened. But it wasn't really her sort of place, and she left well before the end, saying she'd meet us later at a pub down the road.

"I'm going outside," Rob told me, though I understood him mainly by sign language. "Get some air."

"Right," I said, thinking I might follow him, but just then the band went into a number that was even faster than the stuff they'd been playing so far, and I decided to have one last jump around the floor.

Andy and Jamie were already on the floor, slamming into each other, ricocheting off strangers. One of Jamie's slams pretty near knocked Andy off his feet, and I felt a flash of unease; neither of them was smiling. I pogoed over to them, with the vague idea of doing some kind of peace-keeping, but I was too late. They had their hands around each other's throats, and even if no one else in the place noticed it, I could tell they weren't dancing.

I couldn't get to them through the crowd, so I just had to watch as Jamie's mouth worked – to take in air, or to expel curses, or both – and as his fingers lost their hold on Andy's neck, and dropped to his sides. Andy was smiling. Jamie's teeth danced and his bones rattled, and Andy smiled.

Two guys I didn't know very well were at the bar getting a round in, and Rob was lost in conversation with Anne, when Andy put his arm along the back of my chair and leaned forward and spoke directly into my ear. "I didn't kill Jamie, you know."

I couldn't quite manage to say *What?*, so I just looked at him.

"All these years it's been bothering you, Stevey-boy, and you've never said anything, and I thought tonight might be the time to get it sorted."

"All right."

"Not now, obviously. Later – when everyone else has pissed off. I'll stay behind, help you to pack up. All right?"

"All right," I said, and was surprised I managed to say that much.

One long, distorting chord ended the set, and a bunch of punks rushed the stage. The girls in the band beat them off with kung fu kicks and spittle.

The lights came up, and Andy dropped Jamie – dropped him, I mean, like you'd drop a bag of rubbish into a swing-bin. I caught Andy's eye. He just shook his head, and marched off towards the exit.

"You all right, mate?" Jamie was slumped against a big speaker, holding his throat with one hand and rubbing at his ribs with the other. I reached out a hand to help him up.

"Just sod off, Steve," he said. So I did. I deliberately didn't catch up with Andy.

The next morning, Jamie was found dead in an alley, in amongst the dustbins of a Chinese restaurant, a few yards from the club we'd been in. It said in the *Evening Standard* that he'd been throttled.

Most people remember pogoing as the punk dance, but to me, the choke has far greater symbolic resonance. It epitomises so much of that era: the desire to break with the past, the need to shock, the way everything was a laugh, even though every-thing was deadly serious; the pretend violence. Except, of course, that violence never is pretend.

Rob was the last to leave the reunion, apart from the two of us. He drained his final orange juice, smacked his lips as if it had been best ale, and got up to go. We'd already told the barmaid to get off home, not to worry about the clearing up.

"Well, lads," he said. "That was a quick twenty years. Not bad, but a bit quick."

Twenty years, I thought. *Bloody hell.* "Let's make the next twenty count more, yeah? I mean, I really wish we'd kept in touch better. You know? This time, let's do it, not just say it." I held out my hand for a handshake. I really meant what I was saying. How had I virtually lost touch with someone who used to be such a mate?

Rob blinked, and his cheeks crinkled. He put his arms out and around me, and I could feel his bald scalp against my ear and his dry lips pressed for a short second against my neck.

I was amazed. I'd never have expected to see him act so emotional, especially when he hadn't been drinking. It took me a moment to recover, but when I did, I patted his back, squeezed his shoulder. "Look after yourself, Rob. Keep the faith, eh?"

Andy didn't wait to be asked. He enfolded Rob in a solid embrace, and said, "I'll phone you."

We sipped at our drinks when he'd gone, and smoked a couple of cigarettes, and then I said: "So?"

Andy nodded. "I want to thank you for organising tonight, Steve. It's been good for me."

"Despite the nostalgia?"

"Reminded me what it's all about."

"Which was?"

"Is," he said. "What it is all about. Breaking up the established order. Bringing music back to the kids."

"Yeah, but did it work?" By 1978, people were saying punk was just another fashion. You'd see trendies wearing expensive bondage gear. Genuinely individual, rebel New Wave bands were being turned down by major labels for being 'not punk enough', despite the fact that the real punk rockers had always admired, and worked with musicians from all sorts of different styles. "I mean, look at the kids nowadays – "

"Look at the kids nowadays," said Andy, and we both laughed.

"Yeah, I know, it's what every generation says. But don't you reckon? We set out to murder boredom, but boredom's become a lifestyle option. It's all satellite TV and computer games and music that would have sounded tame half a century ago! Even the drugs are boring. You've got kids of 19 talking about careers, for Christ's sake. They either put up with boredom, or they actively *treasure* it – because life's so dangerous and horrible that a bit of boredom is a relief."

"Sure," he said. "But their children won't. I'll bet you. You can't keep the kids quiet forever. One tame generation, maybe, then it'll turn again. 70-year-old punks and their grandchildren'll be out to all hours smashing up clubs and getting arrested. Don't you worry, Stevey: boy bands and tribute bands contain within themselves the seeds of their own destruction."

I hoped he was right, and listening to him tell it, I was far from sure he wasn't. I drained my glass, and said: "If it wasn't you, who was it?"

For me – for all of us, I would guess – the punk summer disintegrated the day we heard about Jamie's death and everybody split up. The way we lived, the way we thought, it was only natural that we'd run rather than talk to cops, innocent or guilty.

The punk explosion was more or less dead by that autumn, in any case. Which was no bad thing. Previous youth movements had made the mistake of thinking they were going to go on forever; we believed the exact opposite right from the start. We didn't despise people for selling out, we despised them for pretending not to sell out.

I found another squat for a while, then a bedsit, and eventually I got a council flat near my parents. I took a job in a local factory, and helped my mum look after my dad while he was dying.

I never went to the police with what I knew, the half-strangling I'd seen in that club. I never mentioned it to anyone, and never confronted Andy with it, after we'd met up again by chance three or four years later. At the time, my silence was instinctive, but as Rat Scabies once said, "You can't help growing up." So, after twenty years of growing up, I held a punk reunion above a pub near Waterloo, and they all came.

"It was Rob," said Andy, and I knew at once that it was true.

"Why?"

"Rob's never gone into details, and I've never demanded any, but my belief is that when Rob left the club, he went to meet Anne at that pub. He made a pass at her, she turned him down. He headed back towards the club, met Jamie coming out, and – well, you know old Jamie could have quite a sharp tongue on him."

"You think they had a row?"

"More likely Jamie figured out where Rob had been, what he'd been up to, and taunted him about it. Rob went for him, and of course Jamie was in a weakened state, because of . . ." He spread his fingers, like a manual shrug.

"You and him, choking each other on the dance floor."

"You thought I'd killed him because of him and Anne. Well, Stevey-boy, I almost did."

"I know. I thought you had, for a moment."

"But I didn't." Andy stubbed out his cigarette, and his face looked as serious – and yet as happy – as I had ever seen it. "It just came to me, from nowhere. Lack of oxygen to the brain, maybe, I don't know. But I had a sudden realisation – that I didn't have to be like that any more. I was a *punk*: I could be what I wanted. I was a self-made man, made of safety pins and glue."

"Who else knows?"

"Not Anne," he said. "She probably still thinks it was me. Or maybe she doesn't. She's never talked about it. For her, it's something that happened in the past, and therefore something that doesn't exist."

"How do you mean?"

"You never saw her wearing punk gear before tonight, did you? She was more into disco back then. As far as she's concerned, you're a kid, then you grow up, and whatever happened when you were a kid doesn't count when you're grown up. If she didn't think that, she'd never have agreed to come tonight."

"Just you and Rob?"

Andy smiled. "And Chaz."

"You're joking!"

"Chaz knew. He was there when Rob told me. He knew, and he's never said a word."

"Just like Anne."

"Except that with him, what happened when we were young is nostalgia. Same result; the past isn't real."

"And you?" I asked the inevitable question. "Why didn't you ever say anything?"

"What good would have it done? Rob was just unlucky."

"*Unlucky* to have killed a mate?"

"Sure. Millions of lads fight over birds and booze, all over the planet, every day of every year. A boy doesn't deserve to have his life destroyed for a bit of bad luck – not if he's fundamentally a good man."

"And Rob is?"

"I've kept an eye on him, over the years. If he'd disappointed me, I might have acted differently."

"But what's he done that's so great? What's he done with his life?"

"He's stuck to being who he thinks he ought to be. You can't ask more than that of a man."

"So why tell me now?"

Andy paused, as if waiting for me to catch up, and then said: "He asked me to."

"Rob did? Why?" But even as I put the question, I saw the answer. "Oh, God . . ."

"Yeah. He won't be around for the next reunion, I'm afraid."

"Oh my God." Bald Rob with his orange juice and his dry kiss.

"He wanted you to know, because he wishes he'd told you years ago. Because he's never stopped thinking of you as a friend."

The weight of twenty years wasted on occasional acquaintanceship, where there might have been constant friendship, almost crushed the air from my lungs. Rob, Andy – even Chaz and Anne, maybe, who could say? It wasn't going to happen again. "Andy. You said that when you were strangling Jamie in the club, and you stopped, it was because you realised you didn't have to be like that any more."

"Yeah. That's something else I came here to tell you. Before I moved to London, all those years ago, I killed a man."

"Why? I mean – who?"

He shook his head. "Doesn't matter. It was a – a *friend* of my mother's. Point is, I'm giving you my secret for the same reason Rob gave you his." He leant forward, locked onto my eyes. "You understand?"

"Sure. Yes, I do."

"Good. I was thinking, maybe you could come round and meet my family some time?"

"Yes. I'd like to."

"You've never met my wife. My little daughter." He laughed. "The flat that eats my wages up, paying off the mortgage. You've never met my life. And I'd like you to, because it's a good life."

"Redemption through punk rock," I said.

He shook his head, lit another cigarette. "If you like. I don't know about redemption, but . . . I don't know if I told you, I'm a union rep. I led a strike last Christmas. They wanted to reduce the number of emergency beds at our hospital, and we weren't having it."

"What happened?"

"We won." His face glowed. "We were fierce and full of rage and acting unafraid, and they backed down and we won. You see what we were doing, Steve? You know what we were doing?"

I nodded. I did know. "You were jumping up and down."

"*Right*, Stevey-boy! We were pogoing in their faces and gobbing on their shiny shoes and shouting in their ears and shocking them with our war paint. The fact that half of us couldn't have *actually* pogoed if our lives depended on it, because our old knees are too knackered, and the other half were too young to have ever *heard* of pogoing, didn't matter. We were punk, and that's why we won."

Let me tell you about punk rock. For an exhilarating few months, the kids controlled the music. The business, the media, they had no influence over what was happening. They recovered quickly, of course, and re-established the status quo, and they learned from it – they determined never to let things get out of hand again.

They learned from it; but so did we.

'No Future' was the big slogan back then, and it's only taken me half a lifetime to figure out what it means. The future never arrives, and the past never departs, and what matters in between isn't *how* you dance – it's *why* you dance. And the day you realise that, is the day you go punk.

We're still out there, us old punk rockers. We don't bother with the safety pins any more, or the bondage trousers, or the gobbing. But you'll know us when you see us. We're the ones jumping up and down.   ✿

DEBBIE MOON

Though primarily a screenwriter, Debbie Moon has been publishing short fiction under various names for many years, and won the 2001 Shamus Award for PI short stories. She has tried her hand at novels, but every publisher that accepted her first novel immediately went bankrupt, and in the end she gave up in order to save the British publishing industry. Her life's ambition is to win an Oscar and a Golden Raspberry award – preferably for the same script.

E ven here in the elevator, gliding serenely upward in a miasma of vomit and piss, Ellen could already hear their cries. The building seemed to vibrate with them, calling her in. Welcoming her back.

She still had one hand in her jeans pocket, between the torn lining and the fake, empty wallet she kept to give to muggers, fingering a coin greasy with body warmth. The coin she'd intended to give the girl on the doorstep. Who, from the look of her, would have been happier with fifty pence than with this eerie, unprecedented invitation.

With the army-surplus blanket hunched round her shoulders, she looked thin and frail and defiantly scared. Her lashes were clogged with old mascara, and her left ear-lobe torn and bloody. Lost earring. Tried to take a pitch from a beggar or a working girl, and paid for it.

Girls floated into Butetown every day, as hollow and fragile as the driftwood that clogged the docks after a storm. They flocked first to the bright lights a little further north, but the park and Queen's Street cleared like lightning at five, when the gleaming, self-conscious malls closed, and then the police appeared out of nowhere and moved them on, to please the non-existent tourists.

"So," the girl said. East London accent, hoarse with the cold. "Are you, like, from China, or Japan?"

"Try Pontypool."

"Oh. I thought you . . . I've never been abroad."

"It's overrated. The drivers are lunatics, and the hotels are always freezing." The elevator doors slid open, onto forty watt gloom and a familiar, acrid smell. "This way."

"What's that noise?"

"My pets."

Her dark eyes widened. "You've got monkeys?"

Despite herself, Ellen smiled. "Come on."

Relaxing her grip on the safety rail uncertainly, as if it was the only thing holding her up, the girl followed.

They were beating at the door now, a tremulous, arrhythmic pattern of excitement. They heard her footsteps; they knew it was her, recognised her step, whatever the experts might think.

The girl beside her shivered, tightened her grip on the blanket, but kept walking.

They expected bad things to happen, girls like her. That was what killed them. Not the cold, or the drugs, or the pimps. The fact that they saw the signs and just kept on walking.

There were new scratches on the lock, the scars of another unsuccessful burglary attempt. The guitarist downstairs, Ellen suspected, though she was careful to say nothing. She was breaking the terms of her lease: 'no pets', here and everywhere, because tenants didn't deserve to have friends. So was he – those weren't exactly marigolds in his carefully tended windowbox – but tit for tat had never been a game she enjoyed.

She turned the key and pushed the damp, stubborn door, and even before she touched the light switch, the room was alive with colour. Feathers brushed her cheeks, tangled her hair, stirred breezes thick with air freshener and guano. She forgot the girl, standing breathless at her back, easing the blanket up over her short, dirty hair like a shroud. She forgot everything except the playful pecks stinging her hands as she raised them, and the fluttering bundles of brilliant colour settling on her arms, squealing and squawking their delight that mummy had come home.

"That's birdshit," the girl said, as if explaining quantum physics to a child. "Your room's covered in birdshit."

Ellen shrugged. "You should have seen it before I moved in."

"You can't live like this. It's filthy."

"Does that mean you don't want anything to eat?"

The girl pouted, turned her attention to the birds. Clustered on top of their cages now, jostling idly for space, they returned her stare.

She probably didn't know what half of them were, even. Most people hardly knew a parrot from a budgie, let along the cockatoos and linnet and the glowing, shimmering hummingbird, black market contraband in feathered form.

Never mind. She'd learn.

Ellen pulled a couple of plastic trays from the freezer, tossed them on the table. "Korma or rogan josh."

"Korma. Thought you'd have chinese."

"Three minute ready-meal chinese? That really is shit." She shut the door on the korma, and the feather rustle of the restless birds vanished under the hum of the microwave. "What's your name, then?"

"Beth. Bethan, really. Me mum was from Newport. I went there to find her dad, when I first ran away, but he didn't want me. So I came here."

Batting away the cockatoo picking through the korma's discarded outer cellophane, Ellen leaned back on the kitchen counter and considered. "That's not a bad spiel, kiddo, but you want to learn to adapt it to your audience. For a start – "

"It's not a – "

"For a start, you're talking to a woman, so play up the sex war. Your mum was practically a saint, but she's dead. It was your nan you went to; and she would have had you, but she was sick and the council put her in a home. Your dad's the villain of the piece. He used to hit you – "

Beth pulled a face. "And do things to me, yeah, I get the idea."

"No, no. Never play the abuse card. You want to seem as much like their kids as possible – and that would never happen to nice kids like theirs. So they think. He hit you, then he took up with a younger woman, and she wanted you out. Plausible and quick. Don't give them chance to walk away."

"How'd you know so much about this?"

"There are several good reasons why I'm not up in Pontypool right now, serving sweet-and-sour to drunks at the Red Pagoda takeaway. Some of them are in my spiel. But the most important is: there are better ways to make money."

And the best of them take two people.

The cockatoo hopped up onto the microwave, shifted uneasily from foot to foot, and leapt into flight just as the bell pinged.

Beth slept in her bed. The birds didn't go in there, and she looked like she hadn't slept since she was born, she deserved a soft mattress for once. Ten minutes after

Ellen closed the door on her, she heard the chest of drawers being hauled across to block the doorway.

Daft kid. The door opened outwards, what good did she think that would do?

Paranoid, daft – and obviously not local. She'd do. She'd have to. The rent was due next week, and that would be the last of the cash. The clothing refund scam was getting harder; she was running out of shops, and everywhere wanted receipts. You could pick them up in the shopping mall toilets sometimes, scattered like confetti, but then you had to shoplift exactly the right item to go with them, and if the receipt only had a code number, it was useless.

Ellen thought about selling the birds – just for a moment, the way she always did, just to remind herself that it was impossible. Then she reached into the bag beside her, scooped a handful of seed, and let the budgerigars settle on her fingertips to feed.

At least the old dear in the pet shop hadn't installed security cameras yet – only place in town that hadn't – so her babies were still eating half price. Pity, preying on a small trader like that. Just think of it as a special offer. Buy one, pop one unnoticed in your shopping bag.

Little Boy Blue, losing the squabble for the last grain to the yellow one she still hadn't named, pecked her palm instead. Ellen ran a finger down his plumage, tracing the distinctive pattern of turquoise and grey. He shivered, fluffing his plumage as if expecting an attack.

They didn't appreciate her concern, any of them. She enjoyed that. If you wanted something to need you, get a dog. Birds had pride. They needed her, needed the water and the seed and the safety of their always-open cages, but they'd die rather than admit it.

Beth needed her, too, but it would be her turn to be unconcerned there.

Setting her coffee aside, Ellen shook the squawking budgerigars from her wrist and sat back in the chair. No, that flight to the South of France was no closer today than it had been yesterday – and it wasn't just the ticket, of course, it was finding a way to get the birds past customs and around quarantine, entirely possible but breath-takingly expensive . . .

Behind her, the bedroom door opened. She looked round. Beth was standing there – behind the useless fortifications, round-shouldered and overwhelmed by Ellen's spare nightdress. "I just wanted to say," she mumbled. "You know. Thanks. And this, urm, scam thing. It sounds really good. I'll do my best. Really I will."

Ellen smiled.

The door closed. The girl would do, and the bills would get paid this month after all, and if she closed her eyes, she could almost smell the grapes ripening in the sun. One day soon, my little ones. One day.

The Royal Cathays Tearoom thought it was the Hilton, with damask tablecloths and cut glass to match. The staff knew it for what it was, a pretender attached to an over-priced department store, and lounged behind the gateaux display case picking lint from their black aprons, muttering about whose turn it was for a fag break. They resented their customers, probably fantasised about dropping Ex-Lax in their over-priced green tea – and better than that, it was pay day.

She'd sent Beth in almost an hour earlier, pathologically careful not to enter the building until she'd been and gone. It was the easy part of the job, the set-up. Designer shirt and stonewash jeans, rich kid playing casual; a slightly desperate enquiry about a lost necklace, she'd had tea here with grandma yesterday and she'd borrowed mummy's pearls . . .

A reward? Of course, she'd happily give, oh, a thousand to get them back before Mummy gets back from Paris. Here's a description, and her card, ring the mobile if there's any news at all . . .

Then it was Ellen's turn. The perfume department, for a free sample to add to the illusion of the twin set she'd picked up last week. A little loitering in accessories, checking security, blending in. That silk scarf would have topped off the outfit perfectly, but the wizened woman at the hat counter had too much time on her hands and was using it to spy on the customers, she couldn't risk it.

And then, afternoon tea.

She took her time. At that price, she wanted her money's worth. Fat old women and silent, brow-beaten men came and went, fortifying their tables with mounds of high-quality carrier bags before eating.

Then, when she was sure the staff were impatient to clear her table, and beginning to give her the hard stare, she reached down to pick up her handbag. The pearls slid smoothly from her sleeve, and from that distance, it must have looked exactly like she'd drawn them from under the radiator.

Just a glimpse as she lifted them to the table; just a frown, and a raised eyebrow, *this must be my lucky day* . . . Then tuck them quickly into a pocket, and stand up to leave.

The waitress was at her table so fast that she turned heads. "Those are lost property," she said, straightening her apron. "You'd best hand them over."

"Those what?" Ellen asked benignly, dropping a tip beside her empty plate.

"Those pearls. Come on, we all saw you. I could call the police, you know."

"And tell them what? You saw me pick up some pearls – which I could have dropped?"

She frowned. "All right. Maybe we could give you a reward. For being honest enough to hand them in. Ten quid?"

Ellen rolled her eyes heavenward. "For pearls that must be worth, oh, five hundred pounds? And would tone quite divinely with my gold evening dress?"

They knew now – knew she was playing a part, dressed above her station and treating herself to a slice of the high life she couldn't afford. Knew she was screwing them. But they didn't have the imagination to see how – and they thought they were going to have the last laugh. The waitress cast a glance at her fellow workers, bit her lip. "All right. Let's see what we can do."

They scraped a hundred and fifty out of their pay packets, and Ellen left them grinning like coyotes, proud of their ability to con a rich housewife out of the full reward. They wouldn't be smiling when they found out the phone number was a fake, and the pearls were free with the first order from a clothing catalogue, but that was life. Someone always got hurt. Just make sure it's never you.

The bus was crowded; long raincoat huddled round her to hide the designer suit, out of place down in the backstreets, Ellen hugged the Pets Paradise carrier bag to her chest and imagined the parrots squabbling over their new toys.

She'd promised half the proceeds to Beth, but she'd been careful to say this scam rarely pulled more than fifty quid. Give her thirty-five, maybe, say they'd had a good day. After all, she was sleeping and eating for free right now, it was only fair she should take a smaller cut. They'd formalise the household expenses soon, and then they'd split their income evenly then. If she deserved it.

Ellen found herself smiling faintly. It was good to be working with someone again. Someone who wouldn't argue with her, tell her how to improve on her routines, get greedy or violent. Someone who wouldn't dispute the amount of their take that went to support the birds – if only because she was never going to find out.

The bus shelter glistened in the aftermath of a shower, and the wind was picking up. She hated winter. She'd lost two canaries last year when the heating failed, and the electricity bill was a nightmare. Winter was a blur of black skies and rain and a longing for escape that gnawed at her like hunger. Winter was a time for dreaming, and dreams frightened her.

On the pavement outside her block, a thin man was pulling at the arm of a toddler strangely interested in something in the gutter. The wind brought her a snatch of his petulant order: " – alone, Josh, it's dirty – "

The toddler finally admitted defeat and turned to face the same direction as his father, out into the grey and the wind and the blank unlit windows of Butetown. Leaving the luminous flash of primrose and gold abandoned in the gutter, framed by muddy tyre marks where someone had bumped a van up on the pavement.

Ellen stood there for a moment, oblivious to the wind and the traffic, staring down at the mauled corpse of the nameless yellow budgerigar.

She'd told Beth never to open the windows, always to be careful with the doors; she'd made that absolutely, perfectly clear, how could the silly little cow have been so stupid?

Then she looked up at the fourth floor windows, reflecting the lamplight exactly as they always did, and she realised they were closed, and all her petty scams faded into insignificance.

The silence was unbearable. The long walk along the corridor, suddenly soundtracked by neighbours' voices that she'd never heard before. A child squealed, a television blared about prizes and winners, hammering shook the flimsy walls.

She nudged the door with her knuckles, and it swung open. It was on the latch; the hole plugged with blu-tac to hold it in place when Beth closed it on the way out, preserving the illusion of security.

The living room was strangely still, and all the cages were gone.

Beth hadn't needed any lessons from her. She'd had her own grift, and played it to perfection. The parrots alone were worth hundreds, the illegal imports thousands. If her accomplice had picked her up outside the store, she could have been back here, loaded up, and gone, before Ellen had even ordered her Earl Grey and strawberry shortbread.

The silence was crushing her. She wrestled with the security locks for a moment, threw the windows open to the monoxide-choked night. Suddenly the smell in here seemed unbearable, and she wanted to run, head for the sea and the south and the sun. Anywhere away from the memory of the flutter of wings.

She stood there for a while, just breathing, and listening to the cries of the children in the next room, shrill and strangely familiar. Then, in the last of the blood-red light, a flock of lost gulls wheeled and turned seaward, and Ellen pulled her battered suitcase from under the table and went into the bedroom to pack.   ✿

ANTONY MANN

Antony Mann's short stories have been published in four previous issues of *Crimewave*. 'Taking Care of Frank' from *Crimewave 2: Deepest Red* won the 1999 CWA/Macallan Short Story Dagger. A film of 'Shopping' from *Crimewave 4: Mood Indigo* is currently in production, and he has recently been commissioned to write a feature screenplay based on his own (as yet unpublished) novel *The Suicide Club*.

"How about a late seventeenth century Russian peasant?" I asked. Across the room, my agent Myra raised an eyebrow. "North or south?"

"South."

"Been done."

"Ah, I meant north," I said quickly.

Myra shook her head. "Sorry, been done," she said. "Sheila Trescothick's Ivan the Irascible series. Ivan's an irascible Russian peasant, disliked by all and sundry in his small northern Russian village, tolerated only because of his extraordinary ability to solve the most perplexing of crimes."

"Yeah, yeah, I get the idea. Okay. Try this on for size." I read from the bottom of my list. "A nineteenth century Peruvian goatherd, male, between thirteen and sixteen years old, an amateur sleuth who solves crimes across the local mountain community?"

"Nu-uh. Stan Archer. The Miguel Goatchild books."

I didn't think it was necessary that Myra smile so hugely, but you can't say she didn't have a sense of humour. She all but clapped her hands in merriment. A slim and businesslike thirty-five with wavy auburn hair and sharp, intelligent eyes, she'd been taking fifteen percent of my very little for three years now.

"Oh yeah." I nodded. "I've heard of them. Vaguely."

"They've won awards," said Myra.

"Of course they have. Works of genius."

The room was as light as the small windows and the overtaxed bulb in the frilly shade would allow. The main office was out the door left. Out there, clacking and ringing noises sank meekly into the thick carpet. This was reception, where Myra sat her writers down for chats. It smelled of my grandfather's aftershave. He was dead. One wall – floor to ceiling – was devoted entirely to books on shelves, both fiction and non-fiction, hardback and soft. These were the books that over the years Myra had sold on behalf of her clients. It was impressive. It said, *I'm a successful agent, I place lots of manuscripts*, and as always, I was impressed. But not one of them was mine.

I sighed and turned my attention back to my list. I'd started with thirty-six brilliant ideas for crime fiction sleuths that didn't yet exist. Or so I'd thought. Now, there remained only one not crossed off. "Myra, don't piss me around now, because this is my last shot. Are you sitting comfortably? A dominant Neanderthal male at the time of the Cro-Magnon . . ."

Myra was already shaking her head.

"No?" I whispered.

"Merlene Trent's Ug Oglog novels. You mean to say you don't know them?"

"They've won awards?"

"They're big in New Zealand."

"Lucky New Zealand. May it sink without a ripple, both islands. Well that's that. By my reckoning, there's now a fictional detective for every profession across every social class from each and every region in the entire history of mankind, including the future, parallel universes and q-space."

"What can I say? Crime fiction's going through a purple patch."

I took my cup from the glass table between us and poured the dark tepid coffee down my throat. Like it was going to quench my thirst. "So unless a writer dies – or gets murdered – there isn't a single opening left for a series gumshoe. And I'm stuck trying to write one-offs."

"No, no, that's no good," said Myra.

"I've got a great idea for one. There's this zeppelin pilot, see, and he gets drunk one night and accidentally kills the son of a wealthy local politician in a bar fight. He panics and runs off, but then this other guy who was at the bar finds him and blackmails him into flying the zeppelin into the Arctic Circle where the rich politician is secretly mining – "

"Nobody reads one-offs," said Myra firmly, stopping me in mid-plot. "If there isn't a recurring central character from book to book, readers simply get muddled and don't know what's happening. Sure, a resilient few can cope, but others tend to lose all sense of direction, even when they're sitting down. They get confused and worried. Some throw up. Do you really want to be responsible for making people ill?"

"Yes."

"I'm sorry, Paul," said Myra as though she'd just told me no, she didn't want to change her gas supplier, not today, not any day. "Maybe if you'd been lead singer of a trendy Britpop band, if you were a stand-up comic or celebrity gardener, you could get away with it."

"So what are you saying? That I'm all washed up before I get started? That it doesn't matter what I write, it won't find a publisher? This sucks. I'm going back to law school."

"I like your writing, Paul. I think you've got potential. That's why I'm going to tell you this. Esther Gordon Framlingham is dead."

"Who?"

"Esther Gordon Framlingham. She wrote the Father Rufus Mysteries."

"Really? The little old lady with curly white hair and spectacles? I thought that was Mary Margaret Whitmore."

"It was Esther Gordon Framlingham too. They both have white hair."

"Oh. Dead, huh? That's a shame. Father Rufus, you say?" Now that I thought about it, I knew those books! Between Father Quentin and Father Septus in the alphabet, sixteenth century abbot, sixteenth century Exeter. "Yeah, yeah, I read some when I was growing up. They're kind of fruity, aren't they?"

"Fruity? No. Maybe you're thinking of Father Rastus. This is Father Rufus. There's no fruit. Anyhow, if you'll just let me finish my fucking thought for a change, what I was going to say was, Cantor aren't certain any more that they want Esther Gordon Framlingham dead."

"Publishers can do that now, bring people back to life?"

"No, no, well not the mid-size ones like Cantor anyway. She's dead, but they haven't released the news yet."

"Crikey, does her family know?"

"Not yet. She's been a recluse for decades anyway."

"How did she die?"

"Boredom. Shut up and let me finish. Cantor would ideally like to keep the Father Rufus series going indefinitely, maybe even until the world is destroyed by a giant asteroid or consumed in the final implosion of the universe. Rufus is a brand name, and of course there's the TV series."

I filled Myra's pause, because she just left it out there for me. "And they want someone to step into Esther Gordon Framlingham's shoes, ghostwrite the Rufus books?"

I filled another. "And you want me to do it? Wouldn't that mean writing under her name?"

"To begin with. Esther Gordon Framlingham was frankly churning out shite towards the end there, and sales were drooping like my husband's dick. Cantor want a team player, someone energetic and enthusiastic to become part of the brand."

"Someone who'll write for peanuts and do what they're told."

"You got it."

"I always thought you were a lesbian."

"Married twelve years this March. And so what if I'm gay? You threatened by that? But enough about me. The point is, Cantor might eventually be willing to let a new writer come up with their own books. If said writer can demonstrate increased sales with the ghostwritten stuff. And, of course, when society moves on and new gumshoe professions develop."

"How about lifestyle coach?" I said. "I've always wanted to write about a mystery-solving lifestyle coach, at any rate for the last four seconds. You can't say it's not contemporary, and no one else has – "

"Anne Portman. The Ralph de Silvian mysteries. De Silvian is a lifestyle coach who solves murders while coaching . . ."

"Yeah, yeah, put a sock in it yourself for a change. I get the picture."

"Good. If you've got it, then don't go losing it. Anyhow, there is just the one other catch that I've omitted as yet to tell you about. Cantor have asked me to audition *two* writers for the Esther Gordon Framlingham job. You and one other."

And, she could do basic arithmetic.

"Who's the other lucky fool?"

"Jack Pantango."

"Doesn't ring a bell."

"That's the idea. The one who comes up with the best synopsis-and-three-chapters in the next fortnight gets the nod."

"Didn't Esther Gordon Framlingham leave any storylines behind?"

"At least four hundred, but you don't get to see them unless you win."

"What if I don't like the idea of writing Father Rufus books?"

"Have a ball at law school."

Sleuth. Gumshoe. Detective. Private eye. They're all just another name for soft-spoken tonsured fifteenth century cleric. I didn't do any research. I didn't need to. The more I thought about it, the more I vividly remembered the Father Rufus books from my childhood. It was my Dad bought the whole set by mail order, except for the ones that hadn't yet been written. I liked them so much I would always get to them first and devour them in a sitting. *The White Raven. Candlestyx. The False Witch. The Third Chamber.*

I recalled Dad reading them by the fire on chilly winter evenings. Whenever he finished one, he'd toss it into the flames, and reflectively watch it burn. What was he thinking about? Fire? Books? Books on fire? They were big thick volumes, but quick to read, and it wasn't exactly a huge fireplace. We were never cold, though.

It took me no more than a couple of days to thrash out the synopsis. I came up with a clever plot: this ship's captain gets drunk one night in an inn, see? And accidentally kills the son of a wealthy local nobleman during a fight. He panics and runs off, but then this other guy who was at the inn finds him and blackmails him into sailing the ship to the Arctic Circle where the rich nobleman is running a secret mining operation. Then Father Rufus is called in to solve all the assorted murders and associated mysteries that would no doubt crop up from time to time.

I was half way through Chapter One when Jack Pantango got in touch.

He was ten years younger than me, and that was only the start of what irked me about him. For some reason he'd wanted to meet in The Juniper Tree, a crummy pub a half mile from Liverpool Street Station, which for me meant an inconvenient trek up from Tooting Broadway by tube. The Juniper Tree was undecorated in olive green wall carpet and those stupid bar mirrors covered in swirly bits that reflect life in swirls. The place was replete with fruit machines going ding, and tired-looking blue-collar types at the bar who'd never figured out how to get some expression into their faces.

Pantango himself was lean and boy-faced, good-looking, with his dark hair slicked back behind his ears. "For some reason, I thought you'd be older," I was saying. "What are you? Twenty-two? Twenty-three?"

Across the table, Pantango was using the tips of his fingers to edge his half pint of lime-and-lemonade in a circle, watching the ice try to keep up as the glass moved round it. He was from the East End, and spoke deliberately, as though it was me who was the idiot. "Mr Gadd, it's like this."

"Call me Paul," I said.

"I won't, if you don't mind. It'll make it easier what I have to say, if we keep it on a business footing."

"Ha, that sounds a bit serious." My attempt at a laugh betrayed me somewhat by sticking fast to the insides of my throat. "Congratulations, by the way, on getting in on this Esther Gordon Framlingham audition. Have you been on Myra's books for long?"

"Who?"

"She's not your agent? Well, congrats anyway. It's very young to be expecting to land this sort of job, so don't be too disappointed if it's me who ends up with the banana. But don't feel you don't have a chance, because I honestly think you do."

"End up with the banana? What the fuck are you talking about?" He stopped spinning the glass and raised his voice, and the heads of blokes at the bar moved the inch required for their eyes to note what was going on. I got annoyed again as I realised I was up against an authentic cheeky chappy Cockney geezer who no doubt didn't baulk at having to punch people in the face. Plus he was probably a super-gifted natural writer who'd be great on TV and radio and look smooth on the back of a jacket sleeve, who'd most likely soon write the definitive London working-class novel on the proceeds of the Esther Gordon Framlingham job. Which should have been mine.

"Is that a South American name?" I said. "Pantango? You do look a bit Spanish."

Though I only meant to a little, I was making him angry a lot, and now, in my general direction, he poked at the air with his finger.

"Mr Gadd," he said, keeping something nasty corked up that I was glad not to see. "Believe me, I want to say this twice, but if it does end up being only once, then you've saved yourself a smashed kneecap. The Esther Gordon Framlingham job is Jack Pantango's, right? It's a payday for me that I not going to miss, plus apparently there's other perks that go with. Like there's chicks and drugs, yeah? So get it fucking straight. There's no discussion on this that won't lead to some breakage."

The further annoyance of this upstart punk who wanted to steal my big chance referring to himself in the third person as though he could present himself objectively to the world at large – a habit I've always despised, even in myself – was the last straw. Though by his expression he was almost begging me to, I had no choice but to protest.

"Sorry," I said, standing and draining my glass in one. "I've been working towards this Esther Gordon Framlingham thing for the last five years. Actually, I haven't been working towards it at all, but it'll have to do until something better comes along. Do what you have to, but don't forget, a writer writes with his brain, not his kneecaps. I cite as an example that French guy who was paralysed but still wrote a book using his eyelid to press down the keys on his typewriter? Or what was it? Come to think of it, it couldn't have been that." I turned to the assembled heads at the bar, all now facing in my direction, assaulting me with their mild amusement and indifference. "Does anyone remember the name of that book, or the guy's name even? I never read it myself. Anyway, don't forget him!"

With that, I walked out, turning no more than four or five times to see if Pantango was following. But he just sat there, staring at me, a small, hard smile on his face, and I could tell, he would soon be beating my fucking head in.

As it turned out, he didn't want to beat me up. He wanted to kill me. I found out soon enough when, half way along the darkest stretch of the lane which ran from The Juniper Tree towards Liverpool Street Station, where the only real illumination in fifty yards came from the filthed-up windows of a heat-trap chippie selling last month's grease in tonight's batter, he came at me from the shadows near a roll-up corrugated doorway with a blade that somehow found light enough to glint back into my eyes.

It turned out also that, even supposing he was a young upstart writer of some talent, he was lousy at killing people. Lunging forward to puncture my squawk of surprise, he tripped on the cobbles of the footpath and his feet skittered out from under him. In retrospect, it was comical, the way he twisted as he fell, the way the air and city smog was forced from his lungs with a grunt as he hit the ground. Even funnier, if you're amused by that kind of thing, was the way the knife in his hand went straight through his eye into his brain. Ha ha. Ha.

I would have called the police, or at least simply walked away, but I was still finding Jack Pantango pretty annoying, not least because he'd just tried to stab me. So, avoiding the spreading pool of blood, I searched his pockets for wallet and keys. I had a vague notion of finding out where he lived and breaking in. On the slim chance his Esther Gordon Framlingham idea was superior to my own, I could steal it with impunity.

It was his wallet that told me he wasn't Jack Pantango at all. According to his driver's license, Gardner Beam had been twenty-five years old, and had lived in Bow, and had looked less like a thug in real life than in passport-sized photos. I also found a sheet of ruled notebook paper, fold in four. On it someone had written, in inverted commas, 'Jack Pantango', and an address in Highgate.

It was dark, but early still, so I bought an A–Z from the kiosk at Liverpool Street and caught the tube across town. Pantango lived in a modern block of flats half way up North Hill, a corner place set back behind a laurel hedge – three stories of pocket-sized balconies painted white, faintly luminous in the moonlight amidst the beige brickwork.

I got through the security entrance on the coat tails of an old man in a black business suit who didn't see me. He was half way up the first flight of stairs before the front door had gently squeezed against my foot.

It was a woman who opened the door to Flat 9. Maybe because I hadn't buzzed she was expecting to see a neighbour – she opened her mouth to speak, then shut it again, and I saw a shadow of trepidation cross her eyes. "Yes?" She was fiftyish, a short frump in a kitchen-curtain floral dress that was keeping her ample bosom in check. Her hair was stiff and dark and looked like a wooden salad bowl, something you'd maybe pay a tenner for at a craft fair, inverted and plonked on her head.

"Hi," I said. "I'm looking for Jack Pantango." That made her start, and she would have shut the door in my face if I hadn't stuck out a hand and stopped her. "I don't mean to be rude, but it's important. Is he home?"

She didn't turn around and look back into the flat like I thought she might have done if he'd been there. She just stared straight at me, then sighed deeply, and her shoulders sagged along with her face. "You'd better come in."

"It's okay for *you*," she said, not bothering to hide the bitterness. "You're not all that fat and you're not that old."

"Thanks very much."

We sat in her kitchen, at the table, drinking weak tea by the light of the fluorescent tube. The wall tiles were gaudy with cutesy kitten pictures, and there was a plastic water filter near the sink. She was a Jackie, not a Jack, but she was a Pantango.

"Me?" she went on. "I'm fifty-four and plain ugly. I'm a part-time surveyor with an arthritic left knee. Do you really think I could ever make it as writer? What publisher is going to want to promote *me*?"

"What about your writing?"

"What's it got to do with that? Sure, if I had some claim to fame. Christ, why didn't I become a politician? Or a bus driver?"

"Do something quirky, like wheel a microwave round the Outer Hebrides. Write about that," I said. "Are you a virgin? That'd help."

"Maybe, but only if I was proud of it. That's why I hired Beam, you see? He was going to be my public face, do the interviews and appearances when I got famous, and I was going to pay him a retainer from my royalties. Plus he was a cheap Cockney thug, so I thought he could scare you off into the bargain."

"You didn't tell him that being a writer meant that he'd gets lots of women and drugs, did you?"

"I thought that might make the deal more attractive."

"He believed you on that?"

She refilled my cup. "I'm sorry about the knife thing. Did he really try to kill you?"

"I think that was just for his own enjoyment," I said. "Jesus, Jackie, what was the point? The Esther Gordon Framlingham job, it's faceless anyway! It's anonymous hackwork for a few bucks!"

"Oh, but it could lead to other things, don't you think?" she said, almost plaintively.

"Oh, it could do," I said. "But for me, not for you."

It was simple enough. Pantango didn't have a choice. In return for me not going to the police about Gardner Beam, she left the way clear for me to secure the Esther Gordon

Framlingham gig.

I finished my Father Rufus chapters, then sent them off to Myra, and a week or so later she called me into her office.

"This is good stuff," she told me as she slapped the typescript down onto the reception room table. "The writing is tight. The characters are real. The story is strong."

I was grinning in anticipation.

"And it's funny," said Myra, "because Jack Pantango rang me during the week and told me she was no longer interested. Wouldn't say why. But that leaves just you."

"You knew Jack Pantango was a woman?"

"Of course I knew he was a woman. He's one of my people."

"Christ, why didn't you tell me?"

"Why the fuck should I? What's it to you? Anyhow, you didn't get the job."

There was nothing I could say to that which wouldn't come out all sulky and disappointed and wrong, so I said, "Why not? You just told me yourself you liked what I wrote! What's the problem? This isn't fair!"

"What's the problem?" She slid the chapters over. "I wanted synopsis-and-three-chapters on Father Rufus. You've given me *Brother* Rufus."

"I've . . . what?"

"I don't want sixteenth century Exeter! I want fifteenth century Bath! I want Esther Gordon Framlingham, not Edna Williams Dickinson!"

Bloody hell, I'd written about the wrong detective. Sure, a mistake anyone could have made, but could I really have *remembered* it all so wrong, those vivid unimpeachable memories, my father by the fire with a book, my father, the book, the fire? How clear it still seemed. "Whoops," I said. "But no harm done. Let's just switch the dates and places, and make it a Father Rufus story anyway."

"What, and destroy the authenticity? No thanks buster. In any case, I was going to tell you this if you *had* got the job, so I'll tell you now too. Cantor have decided to keep Esther Gordon Framlingham breathing a while longer. So there's no big break."

"What do you mean, keep her breathing and there's no big break? I thought that was the precise reason there *was* a big break!"

"There's another teensy thing I neglected to tell you. The real Esther Gordon Framlingham has actually been dead sixteen years. When I told you that Cantor were looking for someone to ghostwrite the Esther Gordon Framlinghams, maybe I should have said they were really looking for someone to replace the Esther Gordon Framlingham ghostwriter who's been churning the books out for the last decade and a half. But now they've changed their minds and keep it to the status quo. Sorry about that."

"Esther Gordon Framlingham has been dead sixteen years?"

"Her flesh has."

"Does her family know?" In a way, I was relieved. I was a big fan of Brother Rufus, but Father Rufus I could take or leave. But I had an idea. "Hey, what about this? Contemporary fifty-something virginal female part-time surveyor from Highgate with an arthritic left knee."

"*Part-time* surveyor, you say? Because of course you know the Donna Cable Mysteries by Rod Binks, but I think she's full-time . . ."

"Definitely part-time," I said.

"Hmm. Interesting. You might have hit on something. Why don't you write me synopsis-and-three-chapters?" ✿

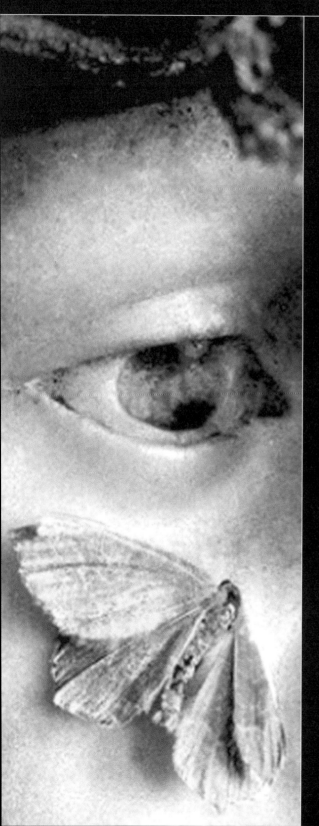

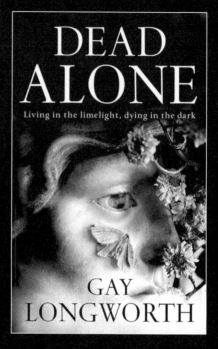

DEAD ALONE

Living in the limelight, dying in the dark

GAY LONGWORTH

Born in 1970, Gay Longworth trained as an oil trader after graduating from university. It was during this time that the idea for her first novel, *Bimba*, came to her. Eventually she took courage, left the job, and moved to Cornwall to write. *Bimba* was published in 1998, and her second novel, *Wicked Peace*, came out two years later.

During that time Gay had too many jobs to mention, though donning fishnets for Club Med was probably a low point. Thankfully she is now a full-time writer.

Dead Alone is the first in a series of Jessie Driver novels, and she is currently working on the second. Gay lives in London with her husband, theatre producer Adam Spiegel, and their daughter.

Dead Alone is published in paperback in May 2003. ISBN 0 00 713956 X

HarperCollins*Publishers*
77–85 Fulham Palace Road, London W6 8JB
www.fireandwater.com

J essie Driver had her thighs clamped round the leg of a man she hadn't been in-troduced to. Hanging upside down, she could feel the sweat running through her short spiky hair. From the corner of her eye she watched two men shake hands. The small envelope of folded lottery paper passed from one palm to another. Jessie was pulled back up and spun around. It was time to leave this club. Local boys from the nearby estate were eclipsing the dance aficionados and the atmosphere was becoming increasingly hostile. Jessie couldn't relax any more. She ran her hand down the perfectly smooth biceps of the man she'd been dancing with, squeezed his hand reluctantly and left. Her flatmate, Maggie Hall, was signing a flurry of autographs by the bar. All men, Jessie mused as she approached.

"Jesus, you're soaking," said Maggie, looking at Jessie in disgust.

"Properly purged." Jessie leant closer. "Can we go?"

Maggie nodded, flashed an 'if only' smile to the admirer she would instantly forget and walked with Jessie to the coat check. Maggie was a presenter; with ruthless ambition she had come up through the highly competitive ranks to become a household name. It was strange watching an old friend gain in fame. Of course, at thirty, it hadn't come soon enough for Maggie. People asked Jessie whether Maggie had changed. The answer was no. She'd always been ambitious.

They had reached the motorbike bay when Jessie heard the sound of a van back-firing. Twice. In quick succession. She turned abruptly towards the noise. Like a solitary clap in a crowded room, the sound silenced the world around them. For a second. And then people started to scream. A man ran across the road and climbed into a waiting car. From the narrow doorway and two fire-exits people spilled out into the street. Jessie threw her helmet at Maggie.

49

"No, Jessie!" shouted Maggie. But Jessie didn't hear her. She ran straight into the sea of oncoming frightened faces. Ducking, side-stepping, shouldering against the out-pour. She battled against the tide down the narrow staircase. At the bottom, a young man lay on the ground. He'd been shot. Twice. Two girls stood next to him screaming and jumping up and down intermittently. She threw her phone at one of them.

"Call the police and ambulance service," barked Jessie. Her commanding voice silenced them as swiftly as the gunshot had set them off. "And someone turn that music off!"

Only the man made a noise now. He wasn't dead. But he was bleeding profusely.

"What's your name?" asked Jessie.

"Carl," he whimpered.

"Carl," she said, "the ambulance is on the way. Meantime, I've got to try and stop this bleeding. You stay focused, concentrate on me." Jessie ripped his trousers and T-shirt and examined the singed, bloody holes. "Perhaps you should think about a change of career," said Jessie. "Small-time dealing on someone else's patch is a sure-fire way to get yourself killed." She smiled at him. "And I think that would be a waste. Good-looking boy like you." One bullet had embedded itself in his right thigh. The other had passed through his left flank. Jessie guessed he must have spun round from the impact of the first bullet and been hit by the second in the leg. Better aim and the boy would have died instantly. "Well, Carl, seems it was your lucky day," said Jessie.

The boy continued to blink at her, mesmerised. The girls stepped forward to get a better look. Jessie pulled a couple of super-sized tampons from her bag, ripped the plastic off with her teeth, and inserted one gently into the bullet wound in the boy's leg. It was soon plump with blood. Carl clenched his jaw and shuddered. Jessie inserted the second into the boy's fleshy side. "Carl," said Jessie, "you still with me?"

"Man," said one of the girls, "she just stuck a Lil-let in your leg."

Carl groaned and passed out.

The sight of two uniformed officers careering down the stairs made the girls jump.

"Step away from the body," shouted one of the officers.

"Show your hands, slowly," shouted the other.

Jessie turned around. "Everyone calm down. Where is the ambulance?"

"Move aside," ordered the police officer.

Jessie did.

They stared down at the gunshot wounds. "What the hell is this?"

"Don't worry, they're sterile. Thought it best, given the length of time ambulances take to get to shootings in this part of town."

The coppers didn't appreciate the snide comment. "And who are you – Florence Nightingale?"

Jessie reached into the back pocket of her tight blue jeans and held up a leather wallet. "I'm Detective Inspector Driver from West End Central CID, and if you want to know who shot this man, he is five foot eight, medium build, mixed race, wearing a red Polo running top. He left in a dark blue Audi 80, number plate T33 X9R." Jessie looked over to the girls. "Sound familiar?" she asked.

Neither of them spoke.

"Thought so," said Jessie, standing up.

Two paramedics arrived. Jessie stepped away. The uniformed officers stared at her as she began to mount the stairs.

"You know where to find me," she said to their fixed expressions.

The paramedic looked up at her. "Thanks for bridging the gap," he said, folding out a stretcher.

"My pleasure," said Jessie, and left.

Out on the street, Maggie stood holding both helmets. She smiled at Jessie. "All right, Mad Max. You done with your life-saving antics?"

"Yes thank you, Anne Robinson, I am."

"Sure? No burning buildings to run into? No pile-ups to attend?"

Jessie swung her leg across the leather seat of the chrome-and-black Virago and started the engine. "Finished?" Jessie asked, backing out of the parking bay.

"Yes."

"Then get on."

Maggie smiled. "I love it when you get all masterful."

"Kebab?" asked Jessie.

"No," said Maggie. "I'm off to Istanbul, that means bikini and camera crew in close quarters, that means no kebab."

"I'm hungry," complained Jessie, revving the bike.

"You're weird. Now, take me home, Arnie. And don't blast that music in your ears, it makes me nervous. You have precious cargo on board."

Dutifully placing her minidisk player back in her pocket, Jessie pressed the bike into gear. It heaved forward. Jessie turned out of the cul-de-sac and raced down Goldhawk Road just as police reinforcements arrived.

West End Central was an old-fashioned, York stone building in the heart of Mayfair. Jessie had recently been assigned to the Detective Chief Inspector there, a man called Jones, a legendary police officer who had her hanging off his every softly spoken word. His Area Major Investigating Team were responsible for a large portion of Central London, and with around two hundred murders in London a year, they were kept reasonably busy.

She loved this new posting. She loved being back in London after four years in the regionals doing exam after exam to gain the necessary qualifications to make her the youngest DI on the team. Though her brothers, parents and friends were proud, there were others who did not appreciate her achievement. Jessie draped her leather jacket over the back of her chair and sat at her desk. A large box of Tampax had been placed in the middle of her blotting pad. The subtlety was not lost on her. She rested her chin in her cupped hand and stared at it. She could see the humour, really – if it had been left by anyone other than Mark Ward. Her professional equal. Her personal opposite.

A small, curvaceous girl was pacing the corridor outside her open doorway. Jessie watched the vaguely familiar creature wiggle, swivel and sigh dramatically. Puppy fat on heels. "Can I help you?" Jessie enquired politely.

The girl stopped in the doorway, weighed up Jessie's role and decided on secretary. "I'm waiting for Mr Ward. He's a friend of my father's. Can you check his diary, he should be here."

"What are you seeing him about?"

"Someone is out to kill me."

"Oh." Jessie nodded in a manner she hoped looked sympathetic. "Your name is . . . ?"

"Jami," she shrieked. "With an 'i'. I'm a singer. Some man has been sending me these letters."

"How do you know it's a man?"

"It always is."

Jessie took the 'death threats' from her just as Mark Ward appeared. The forty-eight-year-old glanced downwards, unable to resist the gravitational pull of the well-mounted chest on display. Jessie could hear the saliva in his throat when he spoke. "Sorry to keep you waiting. You must be feeling terrible." He snatched the letters back from Jessie and gave her a warning look before leading the girl away. Jessie gave it a few minutes before following them across the corridor. The great divide.

"Thought you might want to take a DNA swab," said Jessie, leaning into the room. "The person sending these threatening letters may already have acquired personal items belonging to Jami."

"We don't need your help, thank you," said Mark bitterly.

"No, that sounds good. People will want to know what you're doing to protect me," said Jami.

"We can also compare it to the saliva on the envelope," said Jessie. The young performer held the smile until she fully comprehended Jessie's words. "Then we'll know when we've found the person responsible," she continued.

"Excuse me, Driver," said Mark furiously. "I'm in charge of this."

"I'm sorry. I was only trying to help. I've brought a couple of swabs – " She showed Jami the white spatula in its grey plastic case. "We'll just scrape the inside of your cheek, and that's it."

"I . . ." Jami looked around the room for an exit. "I can't have any foreign objects in my mouth. It could damage my vocal cords. I'm a singer!"

"They are completely sterile," assured Jessie as she took a big step towards the shrinking girl.

Jami started backing out of the room, reached the door and picked up speed. "I need to talk to my manager about this. I'll come back." Her six-inch heels clicked like castanets as she made her getaway.

Jessie turned back to Mark, smiling.

"What the hell do you think you are doing?!"

"Come on, you didn't – "

"Go away, Driver. Why don't you do us all a favour and fast-track your tight arse back to the classroom, eh? Leave the real jobs to the real policemen. And stop sticking your oar and any other pussy paraphernalia where it's not wanted, needed or desired."

Ah, thought Jessie, that was the line he'd been working on. Quite inventive, *pussy paraphernalia*; quite a poetic ring about it. She flashed him a smile. "Tell me, Mark, do you play with yourself as much as you amuse yourself?"

Mark picked up the phone. "I need to call the press office, tell them they won't be getting their photo op."

"*Their* photo op. Right."

He raised his eyebrows. "Yes, actually, their photo op." He paused dramatically. "Imagine that, Driver, you don't know everything, after all."

Coming out of Mark's office, Jessie bumped into their boss, DCI Jones. He was an un-assuming man with grey eyes that matched his suits. As far as Jessie could tell, his only mistake was thinking that she and Mark Ward could learn from each other. Ward had been in the Force nearly thirty years, starting on the beat and working his way up until he was made a detective twelve years ago. He'd dragged bodies from burning cars, rivers and ditches, picked bomb victims' remains off buildings, and dismembered bodies off railway lines – a hard-drinking, notebook-carrying copper who was being phased out. She was thirty-three, same rank, and all her experience was two-dimension-al. They were vastly different species occupying the same ecosystem; it couldn't last.

"Jessie! Perfect. I'd like you to come with me," said Jones.

"I've got to go to the press office."

"Not that bunch of interfering old bags."

"I've made a – "

"This is important. You can read the file on the way." Jones suddenly tensed.

"You all right, sir?"

"Old age. I'll meet you downstairs."

When she went to retrieve her jacket from her chair, Mark appeared in her doorway. "Managed to wiggle your way out of trouble again?"

She didn't bother looking at him. "Fuck off, Mark."

"Thought you lot were supposed to use long words."

Jessie zipped her leather jacket and stood back. "I'm sorry I got in the way of your voyeurism. Had I known it was the closest you'd get to the female form, I'd have left you to it."

Mark watched from his office window as Jones and Jessie crossed the car park. When they'd pulled out of the gate, he called the duty officer. "Who's doing the next few shifts?"

"I'm on double," said the man. "Getting married, need the overtime."

"Next duff DOA you get in, give it to DI Driver. The duffer the better. I want to teach that little upstart a lesson in good policing."

"Yes, sir."

"When you go off duty, pass the message on to whoever comes on."

"Yes, sir."

"I'll get a pot going, for your wedding."

"Thanks, sir. Much appreciated."

"This is between us."

"Of course."

Mark put down the phone and prayed for a fly-infested OAP.

Jessie stood alongside Jones as he knocked sharply on the door twice. The flat was on the third floor of a council block that overlooked a poorly maintained central courtyard deep in the heart of Bethnal Green. The square mile's adjunct; as poor as its closest relation was rich. Robed women pushed prams, men stood in groups on street corners and bored kids kicked a deflated football against a wall. Jessie felt the resolute atmosphere of foiled expectation all around her. They heard the unmistakable scrape of a chain and a large brown eye peered out at them. Jones held up his badge. Clare Mills, the woman they had come to see, drew the door back. She was a thin woman, tall, and very lined. She had a thick crease etched between her eyebrows. A permanent worry line. Her light brown hair was short, thinning, and Jessie could see strands of wiry grey in amongst it. This woman looked as though she'd been worrying all her life and, according to Jones' story, she obviously had.

Twenty-four years ago an innocent passer-by was shot during a robbery. That man was Clare's father, Trevor Mills. He'd been on his way home from a job interview. Carrying an innocuous brown paper bag. Sweets for his kids – he'd got the job. The stray bullet had been fired by a man called Raymond Giles, a notorious gangster of his time. At first the police thought Giles had fled to Spain, but after an anonymous tip-off he was found hiding out at a hotel in Southend. Eventually Raymond Giles was sentenced to sixteen years for manslaughter. The tariff was high because, although the prosecution could not prove intent, the judge knew men like Raymond Giles. Intent to harm was not specific. It was innate. His arrest was a coup for all concerned.

But for Clare Mills it was only the beginning of the nightmare. Her large brown eyes were suspicious, she blinked nervously, continuously. The torn skin around her nails was bitten back to the knuckle on her long, thin fingers. Jessie followed Clare through to the surprisingly light, bright yellow kitchen and tried to break the ice as she made tea. "I don't sleep much," was the answer she gave to most questions. Hardly surprising, thought Jessie as they returned to the small sitting room. The day Clare saw her father lowered into the grave was the day her mother committed suicide. She was eight when she found her mother hanging from the back of the wardrobe, the mascara-stained tear tracks barely dry on her cheeks. Even that was not the worst thing that was to happen to Clare Mills.

Jessie tried again. How did she manage to do so many shifts at work and look after the elderly lady next door? How did she find time to draw and paint? The answer always came back the same. "I don't sleep much."

It was different when they started talking about Frank.

"My little brother. Five years younger than me. Their miracle child, Mum and Dad used to say. They were so happy. We were. He was a gorgeous kid, simply gorgeous. I played with him every day, every day until . . ." Clare turned away from them and stared out of the rectangular window. The day after their mother died a car came to take the children into care. Except that two cars came. One took Clare and one took Frank. It was the last time she saw him.

Clare's pleas had gone unheard for years. Until she had begun chaining herself to the gates of Woolwich Cemetery, where her mother was buried. It had become a PR nightmare. The search for Frank had at last become a matter for the AMIT team, and Jones had been given the case. Now he was talking, apologising, trying to find the right words. ". . . and whatever happens, we'll find out what happened to Frank and we'll make those responsible for what has happened pay – "

"There is only one, and you've let him out." Clare spat out the words. "The man who shot Dad. That thieving bastard, swanning about – "

Jones leant forward. "He spent a long time in prison, Clare. He did his time. Let's concentrate on Frank and the people who were supposed to be looking after him. And you."

"Mum and Dad were supposed to be looking after us."

"Clare . . ." pleaded Jones.

Clare turned to Jessie. "My mother sat by my dad's hospital bed for three weeks. She didn't sleep, she didn't eat, she just sat there and waited for him to wake up. He fought, I've seen the records, I've spoken to one of the nurses who was there, she re-membered my mum, sitting there, praying for him. Mum refused to leave, she wouldn't let anyone in neither, except her friend Irene, of course. They remember Dad fighting to stay alive. He fought so hard he came round a few times, just to tell Mum he loved her, and us, but it was a losing battle. Stray bullet? Stray? Tell me, how does a stray bullet hit a man point-blank in the heart?"

"We can't change the law," said Jones. "He served nine years behind bars. That's a long time."

So, thought Jessie, the man who ruined Clare's life was out. A free man again. Jessie believed in repaying one's debt to society. She believed time served meant a slate wiped clean. She actively dissuaded her team from reaching for the con-list every time a body appeared. But she could see in Clare Mills's saucer-sized eyes that she would never be free of this crime. Her sentence meant life.

"Not long enough for three murders." She was shaking now. "No, make that four."

Clare had no other family. Her father's parents had died before she was born. Clare's mother, Veronica, hadn't spoken to her family in years. Clare had never met them, her mother had never talked about them. All the information Clare had came from Veronica's best friend, Irene. A hairdresser who had never left the area.

"They changed my name. Those people in care. Care! Don't make me laugh. I knew I wasn't Samantha Griffin, I was Clare. I kept telling them, "I'm Clare."" She paused. "I was punished for lying." Clare closed her eyes for a brief moment. The nervous energy was eating her alive.

Jessie and Jones exchanged knowing glances. The seventies were not childcare's proudest era. "We'll start with his birth date and the day he was taken into care. I don't know who has tried to help you with this, but the truth is that you've been misdirected at every turn, and for that I am truly sorry. You have my word," said Jones, "we'll find him."

Clare seemed to retract into herself. "Dead or alive?"

Jones nodded. "Dead or alive."

The timer on the video switched itself on to record. Clare stared wide-eyed at the empty television screen. "I'm not normally here in the daytime," she said, sounding far away again. "There are certain programmes I can't miss."

Jessie wondered which daytime host held Clare's attention. Kilroy. Oprah. Trisha. Vanessa. Ricki. Springer. Pick a card. Any card. "I'm surprised you ever get time to watch television," she said.

Clare bit at her forefinger. "I don't sleep much."

"Pull. Pull. Pull. Three, straighten up." The tip of the boat cut through the deep cold water, parting the mist. "Three, are you listening?" Oars collided. A whistle blew long and loud. The boat started to drift out of line, carried along by the rush of the tide. The muddy brown water slapped heavily against the fibreglass hull. Cold spray covered the girls' bare pink thighs, mottled with exertion. "What on earth is going on?"

"I thought I saw something on the shoreline. I'm sorry, it looked like . . ." the girl paused, her fellow rowers peered to where she was pointing, ". . . bones."

"Oh God," said the cox. "Any excuse for a break! It's pathetic – get rowing."

"No, I swear. I think we should turn around."

They rowed the boat round and backed towards the muddy stretch of bank. The tide was rushing out, they had to fight it to stay still. The five girls stared over the water. Patches of mist clung to the river, reluctant to leave.

"There!" shouted the girl.

There was something lying on the thick, black, slimy surface. Strange outstretched fingers, poking out of the mud like the relic of a wooden hull.

"It's just wood," said the cox.

"White wood?"

"Yes. Let's go."

The girl at the back of the boat was closest. "I think I can make out a pelvis and legs."

The girls began to row away from the bank. They didn't want to get closer. They didn't want to get a better look.

"What do we do?" asked a shaky voice from the back of the boat.

"Row. We'll call the police from the boathouse. Get a marking so that we can tell them where it is."

"It's right below the nature reserve. We'd better hurry, it'll be open soon."

"Oh shit. Okay, okay . . . um, pull, pull – fuck it, you know what to do . . ."

A fully decomposed skeleton had been found in the mud on the bank of the Thames. No skull. No extremities. Probably a forgotten suicide. A local PC was on site. It warranted nothing more from CID than a detective constable. It was perfect. Jessie was early to work, as usual, and when she asked what was in, as usual, all he had to do was obey. "Headless body on a towpath," said the duty officer, crossing his fingers. Her leather coated arse didn't even touch the seat. ✿

STEPHEN VOLK

Stephen Volk is best known as a screenwriter. He wrote the Ken Russell film *Gothic*, starring Gabriel Byrne, and the BBC's notorious 'live' Halloween night 1992 drama *Ghostwatch* featuring Michael Parkinson. He has also written for the BBC TV anthology series *Ghosts* and Channel Four's *Shockers*, and won a BAFTA award for Best Short Film for *The Deadness of Dad*. He is currently writing a new big screen adaptation of John Masefield's *The Box of Delights* for director Mike Newell, and a novel for RazorBlade Press. A new psycho-thriller he has written, *Octane*, starring Madeleine Stowe, will be released in the UK later this year.

In all my memories of my father, I cannot remember him once telling me a story. There were few books in the house: sports magazines collected in binders, the odd political memoir, a few non-fiction books about aviation, an unopened, unwanted gift or two, and newspapers, always newspapers, but hardly any books. I think he was probably rather like the accountant overheard by John Mortimer on a holiday beach who couldn't see the point in reading anything that wasn't true.

There are many possible stories. Even now, I am not sure which this is to be. There is the story of my father's life. Of course, that has been told, and will be told, ad infinitum, in some cheaply printed paperback by some tabloid gnome, or in tiresomely creative television documentaries. Close up, the exhaust with the pipe running from it. Close up, the fumes filling the car. Close up, a bulky, indistinguishable actor slumped over the wheel.

Then there is my story, meagre though it is for any kind of drama, which I am presently negotiating with a publisher friend of Dad's. My brother has got a damn good advance from HarperCollins, and I confidently expect a few k more than that. After all, he is a bachelor, and I have a wife and kids. Added interest. We've been in *Hello* magazine, for Christ's sake.

Then there is the story of the abominable trial. Everyone seems to tell that one differently. According to the judge I'm innocent. According to the man in the street, "He got away with it, didn't he?" The poor old man in the street who can just about understand his bank balance or his betting slip.

Today we heard the verdict. Perhaps that's why I'm in this kind of mood. We came out to face the phalanx of lenses, the massed ranks of BBC and ITN, chattering like baboons in a cage. I took my wife's hand in mine, tightly, giving them time to frame up and focus on it. Then I delivered my statement. Handwritten.

"The last five years have been a protracted hell not only for myself and my brother, but for those around us, completely uninvolved parties nevertheless affected by the relentless and malicious pressure of media accusation. Also those accusations were perniciously directed at my father in his role as Treasurer of the Inner London Development Council and the man directly and personally responsible for those funds." I faintly emphasised the word *personally*. "He, sadly, tragically, is no longer with us to answer to those charges in a court of law." A quaver came to my voice. The requisite flashes strobed. "I am glad and feel vindicated at last that the judge has said categorically that my brother and I at no time acted unlawfully. Were we naive not to ask where the funds came from which our father invested in our construction companies? Yes. Was there nepotism? Arguably. Were there back-handers? No. Was there any sort of criminal collusion? No. Did I believe my father? Yes. Did I trust my father? Yes. Was my father a difficult man to say no to? Absolutely.

"I do not believe however that he had any selfish interest at heart. I do believe, on the contrary, he was doing what he thought best to rescue an impossibly difficult financial situation. Sadly he is not here to defend his reputation. I however have defended mine. I am not a crook. I am not a liar. I am innocent."

*

Simon is waiting for the car with Dougal McRae in the back seat. We get in and he says, so much for the press release. I say, it's much better from the horse's mouth. The Daimler snails along Fleet Street and turns at Ludgate Circus, its indicator ticking like a metronome.

"Are you all right?" says Dougal. His starched collar cuts into his red shaving-raw neck.

"Fine," I say.

"You look wrecked."

"I'm meant to be," I say. I flip the drinks cabinet open and take out one of the two Monte Cristos. "I didn't shave or wash my hair this morning. Does it look all right?"

"They'd never let you in the bloody Garrick."

As we drive across Blackfriar's Bridge, there is a white van in front with CLEAN ME finger-written in the dirt. I look out at the happy throng and their simple lives. The cigar smoke slowly fills the car, like burned earth, like ashes, like Christmas. The interior of the car is muggy again after the sobering chill of the pavement. I run my words through my head, editing them this way and that for *News at Ten*. I am reasonably satisfied that they can't do too much of a hatchet job, but I am inured to that now.

When the car stops again, I look behind to see that my brother is still there in his BMW, alone. I ask Dougal what Kenneth is doing tonight. Dougal says he is booked on a flight to Goa. Booked? That took more optimism than I gave him credit for. On his own, I ask? He says he doesn't know.

Arabella, whose short, tight dress is riding up her stockings, says, "Are you coming to the country?"

I say, "No, I don't think so. There are a few things to see to. I promised Ronnie Philp a celebratory binge at Wheeler's. I'll stay in the flat tonight. I'll be down first thing tomorrow."

She looks out of the car window. She tucks a strand of ash blonde hair behind each ear. "Do you want Simon?"

"You take Simon. I'll come down in the XJ. Helps me unwind, the XJ."

"Call me," she says. "Won't you?"

The cigar smoke prickles my eyes. I remember how I used to sneak one from Dad's cigar box and suck it, unlit, trying it for size. Somehow the smell was always the smell of his breath, his goodnight kiss.

You know you're famous when people make up jokes about you. There's a joke going round about Dad.

— Did you know that Geoffrey Cush has invented a new car?

— Oh really? How many gears has it got?

— Four. First, second, third, and (teller of joke lapses into a coughing fit).

Boom boom. There are plenty of others. Then there are plenty who don't find the jokes funny. I don't suppose the rate payers down in the docklands who feel that my family took the Christmas stuffing out of their mouths think they're very funny either.

I arrive at Butler's Wharf alone and the flat seems more than usually empty. I rattle round my privacy, the air around me suddenly empty of manic, slanging or sycophantic voices. I have only the sound of my own voice. I almost expect accusations from the furniture, a haranguing from the wall coverings. The silence is like someone who knows, but won't say.

I turn on the telly and pour myself a small Calvados. I recognise the figures of Bogart and Bacall in *To Have and Have Not*, an ironically appropriate title. As Donald Trump said when he owed 600 million, that bum on the street is better off than me – he's just skint. But the truth is, whether Donald Trump has 600 million or owes 600 million, the same number of bankers follow him round by his shirt tails and laugh at his jokes. And I daresay he eats at the same restaurants.

I phone the direct line to Nina Hopkins's office.

"Did you watch the news?"

"How are you?"

"Great."

"Congratulations."

"I'll catch it on the six o'clock," I say. "How did I come across?"

"Tired. Relieved. On the edge of tears," then after a pause, the word I most want to hear: "Honest." She must hear the tinkle of ice cubes against my teeth, because she says: "Are you on your own?"

"I am."

"I'll come round."

I hang up. I immediately ring the office. I've received a bundle of faxes, mostly well wishers. I tell Siobhan to bin the rest, and fire off some three line thank-yous, apart from two which would need to be personal.

I roll up my tie in a ball. It is unbelievable to think that it is all over. On the first day, when I came into the light, I raised my hand, palm outwards, to shield the sun, and that was the image that greeted me, cropped, blown up, doctored, from every broadsheet and tabloid front page the following morning. I was panned, zoomed, freeze framed, exploded into pixels and whizzed into a box, parrot-like, over the shoulder of Trevor McDonald.

Of course, they said in the beginning, "He must have known." As I'm sure they said as the Daimler sped away, "The bugger must've known. How could the sons not know?"

I telephone Philp and wriggle out of dinner. I say the emotion of the day has taken it out of me, just feel completely drained. He understands. Get an early night, old boy. I shall, I say. Well done, he signs off, uncertainly stumbling over each word, great relief to us all.

"Bless you," I say in a hushed tone, immediately aware it is my father speaking. His smile stays on my lips till I wipe it away. I'd seen him hang up the phone so many times with a blown kiss like that. But what did I expect? I learned at the knee of the master.

Now, I realise, the master is me.

I almost always, in my hour of need, over the past five years, have heard my father's voice in my ear. That trout-tickling basso profundo that so often accompanied his monolithic rise over the boardroom table, usually before his hand-kissing charm turned like a knife into a weltering verbal demolition. "Power was the only thing in the world that stopped him feeling useless." This I found myself saying to ITN the day after my father's suicide. Kenneth, my brother, as became habitual, kept a low profile. (As a result, the research poll we commissioned privately found that whilst the public 'despised' me, it merely 'felt sorry' for him.) The newspapers said that the Cush brothers seemed 'remarkably composed' that day. I don't know. I once read that when a person falls from a great height they look to all intents and purposes unharmed, but when they do the autopsy, every organ is ruptured, every bone shattered, inside they're a complete write-off. That's what it felt like to me.

Dad was alive when my mother found him in the car. When my brother and I were informed, he was already being hurtled in an ambulance to a place in West London where they train deep sea divers. The policeman explained to me that, apparently, the only way to treat carbon monoxide poisoning is to de-pressurise the body, and this was the closest place they could do it. So we arrived at this grotty industrial estate protected by Rottweilers, at this ramshackle Nissen hut in Southall, with a colourful mural of a deep sea diver surrounded by fish over the walls. The place was padlocked and the lights were out. We became suddenly optimistic: obviously he had recovered and they'd taken him to the nearest hospital to recuperate. We were wrong. Dad had never recovered. He'd died in that concrete shed surrounded by badly painted fishes. By the time we'd reached the hospital, he was in the morgue. The nurse we collared used a wonderful euphemism, 'Rose Cottage'. "He's been taken to Rose Cottage," she said to the policeman. Not to me.

Dad was a Quaker, and if you've ever been to a Quaker funeral, it's a peculiar business. It begins in absolute silence, and there are spoken contributions from anyone and everyone who wishes to speak. In this day and age, to sit in 'silent reflection' for any period of time is shamefully agonising. As the seconds tick by, one finds oneself thinking not of the deceased, but of whether one has set the car alarm, or whether one's mobile phone has any messages. I loved my father, but I found myself examining with immense scrutiny the polished toe-cap of my shoe rather than thinking of him. The Meeting House was foetid with macs and morning coats and stillness. Most disconcerting of all, I found my eyes wandering to an object on a desk to one side of the room, marked with a Sellotaped label reading boldly OUT TRAY.

Several people spoke ministries. Outside a *Sun* reporter's mobile rang, and crates of bottles were being delivered to the Bunch of Grapes. Someone afterwards told me that that was the origin of the term Quaker: that people would quake with fear before standing up and speaking at a meeting. Ever since, I've thought it curious that a whole faith should be based on stage fright.

At the graveside – the family only now – one of Dad's jokes came back to me. "Dead centre of town," he'd say, expecting us to look puzzled. "Graveyard," came the punchline as he tapped the car window, followed by his over-loud, ghost train laugh. My brother and I came to anticipate this joke every time we drove down the Holt Road. He used to tell it anyway, and it would invariably be capped by his own laughter. Eventually, it had a kind of comfort attached to it: the joke that is no longer funny.

I could see him, driving, smiling.

Mum always said that if Dad saw one of his cronies and waved when he passed them in Market Street, he'd still be grinning like a fool ten minutes later when we got to Trowbridge Road. That was the public Geoffrey Cush that everyone knew and loved, not his private face. To the outside world he was always "A hell of a nice feller, Geoff." I often saw his arm around the shoulders of a councillor or a mate, but never around his wife's. He kissed her only at times when it could clearly be seen by others. I suppose my mother came to make the most of these sparse shows of affection when she could. It was never a particular priority to him.

One priority he did have, always, was winning. Six years old, he never allowed us to score goals. When we played Monopoly he was always the Banker and he always cheated, sneaking money from the box whilst our eyes were misdirected elsewhere. It was "All part of the fun." Once when I got fed up with him and upset the board and made Kenny cry, my father said, "You have to grow up and learn to be a good loser."

Nina Hopkins arrives at four thirty. She lets herself in with her own key. The straggling residue of the hack pack outside think she's another resident of the block, they ignore her. I am already undressed. She seems harassed to begin with, or she is uptight on my behalf. I have a Scotch ready for her and I ask how her day was. She says, "Shitty." She works as a feature writer for *The Guardian*, small and Welsh, well-muscled and squat like a female scrum half, dressed like a social worker in Camden Town baggies and rattling Bombay jewellery. She takes off her clothes and jumps into bed. Her skin is cold and her lips taste of whisky. Her Peter Pan hair is bleached blond, and her pubic hair black as seaweed in a Chinese restaurant.

"You've started without me," she says, finding my erection under the sheets.

"Almost," I say.

She pulls back my foreskin and I'm like a rock. It pleasantly surprises me.

"You're excited," she says. "I thought I might have my work cut out this afternoon."

"Fuck 'em," I say, rolling on top of her. "Fuck the lot of them." Her vagina is loose and wet. I wonder if she masturbated in the ladies at *The Guardian* before she got in a cab. It's a mad fiction, I know. I run it through my mind like a film clip, behind my closed eyes, and I'm there in the cubicle with her when I come – it's ridiculous.

As we lie in the bath, later, I hear the music of the six o'clock news to the smell of Angels on Bare Skin, from Lush. Hopkins drops her cigarette in the toilet bowl and reaches out to pull the flush. The long hairs in her armpit fan and then close. Her attention is focused on a blackhead on my knee, which she anoints with soapy water.

"Daniel and Kenneth Cush have today been acquitted of all charges of fraud. They had been living with the threat of criminal proceedings since the suicide of their father Sir Geoffrey Cush and the scandal surrounding the alleged misappropriation of Inner London Development Council funds . . . " I climb out of the water and drip into the bedroom, turning up the volume on the remote control. ". . . Daniel said he regretted the huge investment of time and money by the SFO in their bid to convict him . . ." A pink nosed reporter outside the Law Courts. "It felt close to madness, he said, when everything you do and say is construed only as deception, and it particularly offended him that his father had been branded a liar, a cheat, and some kind of despotic monster . . ."

I see Dad's face up on the screen. No, it isn't Dad in the blue shirt and white collar behind the desk: it is me, the docklands outside the office window. My lips are moving.

"The whole idea that the public, if we are to believe the media, had in their head, that there was this grand conspiracy to divert funds to the sons' companies, that my father was somehow skimming off the cream to line our collective pockets . . ." Mixed bloody metaphor. A touch of humanity. Not bad. ". . . it's simply repugnant. It's simply, terrifyingly untrue. This notion that rate payers money which was supposed to be helping amenities, housing in the inner city, getting the homeless off the street, keeping pensioners warm, et cetera, was finding its way into my father's cheque book, is errant nonsense."

Hopkins lays down a bath towel and sits naked on the bed beside me. She lights a Marlboro Light. I can smell the bath-water on her. With one hand she manipulates my penis, and she puts her open mouth to my shoulder and blows. I think it is meant to arouse me. Almost immediately after coming, I realise, I wanted to be alone. Even while I was still inside her, I wanted her not to be there.

My close up says: "Dad made a foolish . . . a series of foolish, bad decisions, but he was doing his job, as he saw it, to manage the funds at his disposal, so that a potential disaster could be overcome. He was guilty of bad judgement, bad practice, hubris – and if I was guilty of anything at all, I was guilty of not standing up to him and saying, what is going on, Dad? But nobody, including myself, was able to say to Sir Geoffrey Cush, are you sure this is not a mistake? That was simply a foreign language to him."

Interviewer: "Do you wish that you could turn the clock back?"

Me: "Of course."

Interviewer: "Would you have done things differently?"

Me: "Of course. Of course I would. My father is dead. Of course I would. Hundreds of millions of pounds were lost, and many, many people suffered considerable loss and hardship as a result. Of course I would."

I reach to the bedside table and put on my watch.

Hopkins stands on the other side of the room, catching herself unwillingly in a full-length mirror. She picks up her own watch and looks at it, then dries herself and pulls on her knickers and leggings. Her knickers have seen better days. Without asking, it's a ritual now, she calls the usual number from my phone's memory and within a few minutes I hear a black cab purring up outside.

"Give me a call," she says.

She understands the situation and she is happy with it. We have discussed it many times.

Unexpectedly, she moves to the bed where I lie naked. She pulls at my flaccid penis as a person tweaks the rubber of a balloon. Then she kisses my cheek, pulls on her various layers of outer covering, Eskimo like, and leaves.

Dad's picture comes up. The beetle brow, the broken veins in his cheeks, the big pancake roll fingers. If Dad had been in that court, he'd have had the SFO for breakfast. Crook, liar, double-crosser – to his face? I don't think so. Never in a million years. That's the great, deep, shifty cowardice of it all.

He was worth ten times any of them, and they knew it. He'd been through more than they could even contemplate. He'd been one of the first soldiers to step through the gates of Belsen. I don't remember him ever talking about it. I first knew when I was fifteen, from my mother. All the times we'd been watching *633 Squadron* or *Colditz* and he'd say "Rubbish" or "Shut up" and switch channels suddenly made sense. My mother told me he'd had a nervous breakdown shortly afterwards and got invalided out of the army. Once, I asked him why he didn't like watching war films, and his answer was typically evasive, but precise. "The actors," he said, "It's the *acting*."

Within thirty-six hours of him dying, surprise surprise, the SFO suddenly thought they had a case. My brother and I sat through seventy days of prosecution evidence. I was shaking by the end of it. I was white. It was like a witch hunt. The pressure was on them for someone to pay. I stuck to the facts: that every action taken by us was a legitimate and legal action. But I never lost sight of the possibility I could be in jail by Christmas, and neither did my wife or my children that they could have their husband and Dad taken away from them.

The BBC Nine O'Clock News: "Daniel and Kenneth Cush have been cleared of conspiracy to defraud over 100 million pounds of ratepayers' money from regional council funds . . ."

I remember the way Arabella threw her arms around me earlier today, so tight I thought that she might literally break my neck.

"I love you," she said.

" . . . The Cush brothers will not face further prosecutions. The Judge said that subsequent charges would be unjustified and a flagrant abuse of power . . ."

I decide to go to Hamley's tomorrow and get Kit and Zoe a pre-Christmas treat, and something for Arabella. A perfume a little less exotic perhaps. Arabella says the children are spoiled. She's hard on them, being with them all day, every day, she's always the one to blow her top. And Daddy comes in as the big softie to wipe the tears. It makes her so mad sometimes, that their Dad can do no wrong.

In my dressing gown now, I look out of the picture window across the black of the Thames at Alderman's Stairs, at the lights of the Tower Hotel and St Katherine's Wharf, and Wapping. Beyond my grey reflection, I think of the black-and-white PR photos of Dad, shirt sleeves rolled up, hairy arms, gorilla like, meaty knuckles pressing down the conference table. A Neanderthal baby, more built for a donkey jacket than a Saville Row suit.

As I raise the telephone receiver to my face and listen to the ringing tone I can smell the spermicide from Nina Hopkins's cap on my fingers.

"Hi. Did I wake the kids?"

"No, they're watching a video." Down to earth Arabella, cleverly avoiding them watching TV. Kit had already been in punch-ups in the playground with yobs who called his Dad a swindler and a crook who murdered old age pensioners who couldn't pay their heating bills.

"What are they watching?"

"*Childsplay 3*," she jokes.

A breath goes through my nose, a kind of laugh.

"You didn't ask if you woke me."

"Did I?"

"No."

"Listen," I say. "I'll be down tonight."

"Are you sure?"

"It'll be an easier drive. The roads'll be deserted."

"How was dinner?"

"Oh, Philp chickened out. I was quite relieved. Ended up sleeping for about six hours, spark out."

"Poor sweet, you must be shattered. Will you be OK to drive?"

"I'll be perfect. I'm wide awake now."

"Shall I wait up? When will you be here?"

I looked at my watch. It was getting on for ten. "About midnight. Don't worry if you're asleep. I'll try not to wake you." I have an image of slipping out of my clothes, leaving them in a pile in the dark, and squeezing into the creaky cottage bed with its clean sheets.

I am driving down the M4 with the needle fidgeting under 70, aware that the Calvados is still in my system, though I don't feel it. I feel a kind of out-of-body remoteness now. The car doesn't seem to exist, the dark of it melding into the surrounding night, the only thing hinging it to reality being the lights of the dashboard, like the points in a dot-to-dot puzzle not yet completed.

The road is empty. I do not have the radio on, the tarmac under me providing a rumbling, abstract melody. I watch cars loom up in my rear view mirror, indicating, and overtaking, tail lights disappearing into the dark.

It's remarkable. When we used to go for a run in my grandfather's Hillman Hunter, we used to think we were speeding at 35.

I used to have one of those toy steering wheels when my father had his first car. It was yellow. You'd stick it to the dashboard with spit and pretend it was you who was driving. "Sterling Moss," he called me. With my free hand I'd make up arbitrary gear changes. And I remember, when *Goldfinger* came out we'd all want stick on bullet holes for the car windows, except Dad wouldn't let us have those. Or a nodding Boxer dog in the back window, like my cousin had.

A Volvo overtakes me. Its indicator seems bright and insistent, a warning, an asterisk, an accusation.

It's funny how things come back when you least expect them. The memory comes up like a fish out of water, a flash at first, then so clear I can touch it.

I was eight. I must have been eight, because we were on our way to Bradford hospital and the only reason I can think for going to Bradford hospital was when my brother was born, and he's eight years younger than me. My mother was in the car, so she must've been pregnant with Kenny at the time. I presume she was going for a check-up.

I remember Dad asking me if I'd like to give the baby its middle name. I'm pleased as punch. I ask for him to be called Gregory, because Gregory Follows was my best friend in school. (I fell out with Gregory that summer, and I never saw him again once I left primary school. So Kenny was landed with a stupid middle name nobody liked, including me. It was the name of a friend I didn't have any more.)

On this day, we are driving to Bradford hospital in Dad's first car, the green Morris Minor. It is sunny. Dad is smiling. Perhaps he's seen one of his cronies ten minutes ago, I don't remember, but he has one of those grins which was nothing to do with my mother in the passenger seat or me in the back.

I say I feel really happy and I can't remember why. Dad laughs and says it's because I'm going to have a baby brother. I say, oh yes. But I think to myself the real reason is that I've got an afternoon off school.

We are going down the Winsley Road and come up to the T-junction with the Bath Road, and stop at the broken white lines. I am asking Mum if Gregory can come round for tea and play Scalextric and my Dad looks right and left and pulls out to turn left and suddenly *smash*. A van has gone right into the side of us, or for a second it seems as though it has. In fact it has clipped the driver's side wing and bumper, crunching and sprinkling the glass from the headlight all over the road. It makes a sharp bang and my mother, of a nervous disposition at the best of times, shrieks and holds her arms stiffly against the dashboard. "Oh, hell!" she says, her voice drawing it out musically like an opera singer. I am sure she is going to faint.

I, on the other hand, feel calm. I quickly realise that the worst is already over. My mother's fear and panic is retroactive, almost as if reliving the anticipatory graph of horror she has missed by the suddenness of the crash.

"Are you all right, Mum?"

"Of course she's bloody all right," says Dad.

"Daniel?" says my Mum, her voice rising shrilly. She turns and reaches out her hands to me. I am not sure whether she is going to comfort me, or me her.

"Sit down," says Dad. I am standing up in the gap between the driver's and the passenger seat. I see his face from a three-quarters angle from behind. A redness begins to seep from his collar upwards, his lips are pulled tight, and I can tell from the crow's feet vanished from his cheeks that he isn't smiling any more. He asserts a kind of terrifying calm over himself and methodically moves the gear stick into neutral and switches off the engine, completely oblivious to my mother's stifled sobbing. My mother's emotionality was never a serious consideration. Beyond him, I can see the van framed in the Cinemascope of the dusty windscreen, sunlit, a hefty vehicle pock-holed with rust, the automotive equivalent of the kind of boys in school who my Mum tells me not to play with.

"Quiet," my Dad says.

"Oh Geoff. What happened, love . . . ?" My mother's voice flirts with tears. There's a suggestion of blame in her sympathetic tone. My father doesn't ask if she was hurt, or comfort her in any way. He doesn't even look at her. His unblinking eyes are on the van door as it opens and creakily slams shut.

"Leave this to me."

He opens the car door and my mother says, "Now don't start anything, Geoff, for goodness sake. Please, promise me you won't." She reaches out towards him, her fingers not quite touching the sleeve of his royal blue blazer in the second before there is emptiness behind the steering wheel and the door is slammed in our faces.

"Who's the bloody idiot, then, eh?" I can hear my father booming dully outside our car. Mum cringes.

He stands with his hands on his hips, his trilby on head, shirt tight across his pot belly and his cricket club tie, a maroon squiggle, dancing in the wind. The man from the van, a good six inches shorter and thin as a whippet, is a builder of some sort. He has overalls caked in white limey residue, cement or plaster, which salt his face and sticky-up Stan Laurel hair. The lines in his face seem to all point to his powder blue eyes. Some plastic twine ties his overalls together at the hip, where a button is missing.

"Is anybody hurt?" says the man, quietly spoken, and obviously shaken and trying to peer into our car. He hunches down, catches sight of Mum and me and looks concerned.

"No thanks to you there isn't," says my Dad. Dad has his back to us.

The man looks at him now. "What? What are you talking about?" He sounds genuinely baffled. He sounds like somebody picked on for something they didn't do. "What are you on about?"

"On about!"

"You're in the wrong, pal, not me," the small man says, a slight tremor in his voice.

Not somebody used to or relishing confrontation, this chap. He shifts from foot to foot as if trying to avoid it. "You want to read your Highway Code."

"You what?"

"Well. Coming out into a main road without looking. Christ. Who the hell's fault do you think it is?"

"You must be bloody joking!"

"Me? I'm not joking, no. You're the joker."

"I've got a pregnant woman in that car!" says my Dad with an expressive gesture in our direction.

"What, I suppose that's my fault too, is it?" says the man. "I wouldn't be surprised."

"Oi. You watch it!" My Dad shuffles closer to him, making the most of his height advantage to intimidate. "You watch what you're saying, you. That's my wife in there, that is."

"God, God alive . . ." breathes my mother against the car window. She has turned her head away from the confrontation, only to be faced by two passersby, a woman a shopping trolley and another with a pram, transfixed as the altercation gets more and more heated. My Mum closes her eyes. "Geoff. No. Please. Don't . . ." she prays under her breath, in vain. But she knows her husband of old and since she can't prevent it, what she really wants is for this to be over as soon as possible. Please. Please.

Outside the car, his stubby index finger is stabbing at the small man's chest.

"Hey. Don't point that finger at me, pal."

"What?"

"I said don't point that bloody finger at me, *all right?*"

"I'll do what I want with my finger. It's my bloody finger. If I want to point it at you I'll bloody *point* it at you. Who are you to tell me what to do with my finger!"

The small man does the only thing he can do. He laughs, and turns away, shaking his head. My father goes after him as if to grab him by the arm or the throat. The man turns, unexpectedly. Disarmed, my father backs up a step, a coward, his neck as maroon as his cricket club tie. His chin is in the air, Mussolini-like now, hands on hips, a big strutting cock.

My eight year old mind races with the question: *Is this what Dads do?*

This was not a hero and baddie, like in the pictures. This was not John Wayne and Sitting Bull, this wasn't even Ernest Borgnine and Richard Widmark – this was something I recognise all too well, just a big blow-up version of a scrap in the playground. I think: this is how it is. This is how it will be, then. The playground just gets bigger.

Mum dabs her nose with a hankie and puts it back up the sleeve of her cardigan. She sniffs.

I say, "I'm all right," quietly – not to her, but as a statement of fact, to myself, to convince me.

Outside the mute chorus of onlookers is growing, none of them with the slight intention to either arbitrate or interfere. They are like cows in a field.

It seems like we have been there for hours but it is probably less than five minutes. My Dad is putting on a laboured tone of voice now, as if talking to a congenital idiot: "You were coming down that road, let's face it. And you indicated to turn left. *I saw you.* A hundred yards away. Your left indicator was merrily flashing away, I saw it! *That's why I pulled out.* Because *you* were indicating to turn left. *Except you didn't, did you?* Oh no. You changed your mind and you just . . . you just came along straight and went straight into the blinking side of me!" He is becalmed now, more considered, so *blinking* replaces the involuntary *bloody*. "Didn't you? Pal. Pally . . ." A touch of mockery now. Victory in sight, he can smell it. "Go on. Admit it! Didn't you?"

Silence.

The small man whispers something beginning with F under his breath, a bad word I haven't heard a grown-up say before. He looks up and, seeing the wild triumphant gleam in my father's eyes, he says, "You're half cracked, you are."

"Am I? Oh, yes," says my father, showing his teeth. "You would say that, wouldn't you?"

"So I indicated I was turning left?"

My Dad laughs incredulously. "You *know* you did!"

"Bollocks did I."

"Are you telling me I don't know what I can see with my own two eyes?" says my father.

"Your bloody eyes need seeing to, mate, if that's what you saw. I'm on my way to the A4. Why the hell would I by taking a turning to go through Winsley?"

"Well, we only have *your* word for that, don't we? We don't know *where* you're travelling. You could be travelling to *Timbuctoo* for all we know!" The man doesn't move. There is a flicker in my father's face that he might have overstepped the mark. "I – I don't know, do I? For – For all I know you might have flicked the indicator on by accident. All I know is, *that indicator was bloody on!*"

"I didn't do anything by *accident*. Look. Look at my van, look at the front." He moves to his vehicle but my father doesn't follow. "Look. Is the indicator on? No."

"Not *now*, no! Obviously!"

The skinny man looks at the big man. Not yet the elephant seal who will go to Buckingham Palace to collect his knighthood for services to charity. Not yet the chairman of one of the top five banks. Now, back then, a Co-op man, selling insurance and picking up small change from old ladies in terraced houses once a week, invited in for tea and digestives and to listen to their troubles by the heat of a two-bar electric fire, while his two little sons do their homework.

"You don't believe me. Fair enough. No, fair enough!" says my father, straightening his tie. "We'll ask the boy.

I feel a coldness like tapwater run down my back and suddenly I want to go to the toilet. I'm sure I haven't heard correctly. I couldn't have heard correctly.

"The boy was watching," my father is saying in some distant world. "He saw what happened. Exactly what happened. Didn't you son?" The voice grows louder as it grows closer.

My father's face is up to the window beside me, his enormous palms flattened against the glass. His bushy eyebrows cast caterpillar shadows over his eyes. I see the small black dots of bristle on his top lip, cartoon clear. Behind him, more indistinct, I see the builder looking at the sky, folding his arms, moving his weight from one foot to the other, saying, "Listen, pal . . ."

"No no. No no," insists my father, holding up a hand. The builder puts his hands deep in his pockets and looks at the clouds, squinting.

My Dad's face fills the window. All of a sudden, I can't see anything else. He's filling my eyes and my head. "Now, Dan. You know I want you to tell the truth, don't you?"

I can smell the warm leather of the seats.

I nod.

My father says, "You know that, whatever happened just now, you must say the truth. Never mind what you think your Dad wants you to say. Your Dad – listen to me, son – " I look into his big chocolate coloured eyes " – Your Dad wants you to tell the truth, that's all." I can see every pore in the tip of his nose. I am closer to him now than when he tucks me into bed and turns out the light. I watch his lips form the words. "That's all that matters, all right?"

"Wait a minute," says the builder, behind.

Dad straightens up. All I see now is the maroon tie and an expanse of shirt filling the window.

"What's the matter?"

"Come off it . . ."

"What?" my father sounds pained. Affronted. Hurt. "Are you saying – what? That my boy, that – come on, out with it. If you've got something to say, say it!"

"This is bloody ridiculous and you know it is."

"Is it?" Now my father addresses the pram lady and the four people standing at the bus stop, who have listened to everything. He is playing to the stalls. "*Is* it ridiculous?" He walks over to the bus stop and returns, arms outstretched.

Then the builder silently looks my father from head to toe, inwardly summing him up. I don't know what he thinks he sees, apart from not thinking much of him, but he also looks over to me, and he looks in my eyes for quite a long time. Like he feels sorry for me. Then he looks at my Dad, like he thinks even less of him, and folds his arms and says quietly, "All right then. You're the boss. Ask the lad, go on. Ask the lad if he saw the indicator on." He sees my father hesitate slightly and he picks a flake of plaster dust from his sleeve and flicks it away.

"Right then," says my father. He rolls on his heels, nodding at him. "Right then. We'll settle this. Right. We'll settle this once and for all."

He comes closer and wipes the window next to me with his hand, then taps the glass with his hairy knuckles.

"All right, Daniel. You've heard what we're talking about. Have you?"

I nod.

"The truth. Dad won't be angry at you. You won't be in trouble, whatever you say – all right? All I want you to say is what you *know* to be absolutely true, all right?"

I nod.

It is warm and the seat smell is horrible and I want to go for a wee. I don't look at my Mum. My Mum is no part of this now. I forget she is even there.

"The truth, lad, remember," says the builder. "Nobody will blame you for telling the truth, I promise." He looks in a packet of Woodbines for a cigarette but the packet is empty. He drops it into a nearby the gutter, poking it down the drain with his toe. He looks like a nice, kind man. I wonder if he is somebody's Dad, if he is one of those Dads who take their children to the park, to the swings on a Sunday afternoon.

Dad backs away from the car, away from me, hands raised, as if saying, look, no hands, the boy is on his own. He has no expression on his face now but complete, abject innocence, removing himself from the action, from the equation, from the accusation. He steps the same distance from our car as the builder. I feel abandoned. Alone. Empty. Both are bathed in the same dusty sunlight beyond the smeary glass of the Morris.

The smell of the sun on the leather seats is almost making me sick. I try not to breathe too deeply, because I know it will.

"Just the truth, laddo," says the small man softly. "That's all I want. That's all your Dad wants, isn't it?" He looks across at my father, sideways.

I look into my Dad's eyes, but I can't find them. I know they are there, somewhere, but the sun is too bright. "That's all I want, son. All you have to do is answer the question. Was it off or was it on?"

"That's all you have to answer," says the builder. "Was the indicator off or on?"

I open my mouth. I hear my breath come out. Except it isn't my breath, it's a word. And I'm curious as to what word it is that has come out of my mouth, and I say it again so that I can listen to it this time. And I say, "On."

My father cups a hand behind his ear. "What? What did you say, Danny? Speak up!"

"On," I hear myself say again, then louder: "*On.*" And in my mind I see the word on a blackboard and I am trying to rub it out.

"On! Did you hear that?" says my Dad outside, standing in the road, advancing on the man. "Did you hear that, eh? *On!*" The small man's shoulders fall against the side of his van.

My Dad asks for the man's insurance company and it turns out the man doesn't have insurance. He looks ashamed, humiliated. He doesn't have a tax disk on his van either. My Dad says, "Ho." It doesn't take a genius to work out his vehicle isn't fit to be on the road, and he knows it. And that means just one thing we all know now, Dad, my mother, me: that the man is *poor*. And that somehow seals it.

They have more words, but I don't really hear any of it, it is like being underwater, maybe for minutes, I don't know how long – then Dad backs off, flattening his tie against his paunch and buttoning his blazer across it.

The man stands propped against his van, his arms hanging. He looks at me. He looks at me as if everything makes complete sense, as if he knows everything, more even than I know or would ever know.

I duck down a fraction, hiding my sight line under the frame of the window. And I hear him laughing. I look up again, and he is shaking his head and laughing. Dad says nothing to him after that.

I look the other way, keep my eyes inside the car, on a copy of *Look and Learn* beside me on the back seat, until I hear the van rev and reverse and clatter away with a miner's lung of an engine. And I hear my father get a dust-pan and brush from the boot and sweep up the broken glass from the front of the car, and as he is doing it he is whistling.

Afterwards, he gets in behind the steering wheel and he shows my mother a fan of twenty pound notes. My mother doesn't say anything and neither does he.

As we drive to Bradford hospital, I can see my Dad's big brown eyes in the rear view mirror. It might be the sun, but there are big crow's feet round his eyes and it looks like he is smiling. Without taking his eyes off the road ahead, he says, "Well done, son." I have that feeling again, that I am really happy and I don't know why.

And he has the smile on his face all the way to Bradford hospital, and all the way home. Twenty minutes, because I am counting. One thousand two hundred seconds. That is more than when he sees one of his cronies, even. Much, much more. ✿

John Grant, born in Scotland but now resident in the US, is the author of over fifty books, both fiction and non-fiction, and a few under other names – including his real name, Paul Barnett. His non-fiction includes three standard reference works: the phenomenally successful *Encyclopedia of Walt Disney's Animated Characters*, now in its third edition; *The Encyclopedia of Fantasy* (done with John Clute); and *Masters of Animation*. His most recent books are *Perceptualistics: The Art of Jael*, *Dragonhenge* (done with Bob Eggleton), the novella *Qinmeartha and the Girl Child LoChi* (half of a 'double' book, the other half being by Colin Wilson), and the novel *The Far-Enough Window*. Among his genre novels are the twelve books in the *Legends of Lone Wolf* series and, as Paul Barnett, the on-going series begun with *Strider's Galaxy*. His two major novels to date, aside from *The Far-Enough Window*, are *Albion* and *The World*.

A recipient of the Hugo, the World Fantasy Award, the J. Lloyd Eaton Award, the Mythopoeic Society Scholarship Award, the Locus Award, the Chesley Award, and a rare British Science Fiction Association Special Award, he is, when not writing, the Commissioning Editor of Paper Tiger, the world's leading publisher of fantasy/sf art books, and the US Reviews Editor of the webzine *InfinityPlus*. He is married to Pamela D. Scoville, Director of the Animation Art Guild.

Heddie had been missing for several days before someone called the police. Hours later a search party was raised – a dozen or so of the police, and half a hundred or so local residents like myself – and only a few hours after *that* we found her. She was lying naked alongside one of the many baffling stone-age artefacts that litter Dartmoor. Her skull had been battered in, so that her brains were scattered across the grass (pink, not grey as I'd always imagined). She had been sexually assaulted with a sharp instrument. I was third on the scene, after a pair of hardened police sergeants. I was not the first to throw up. The body which had once been so warm and filled with motion was now cold and clammy and still. The blonde hair was no longer something with which to stroke an appreciative body: it was a mat of sodden keratin. I felt very selfish and particularly necrophiliac thinking of her corpse in sexual terms – remembering the few friendly nights we had spent together – but at the same time I couldn't help it. *Yes*, one part of my mind remembered her laugh and the way the wind bullied her hair and made her eyes shine; but at the same time, *yes*, I remembered her soft breasts against my chest.

Somewhere in another universe they'll tell you about Alan. I don't know the story that he belongs to.

After throwing up again, I cried for several minutes until there were too many people gathered around. I wiped my nose on the back of my sleeve and tried to look like an adult.

A little while later the cops sent most of us away. A forensic scientist was arriving. The police set up a tent over the body, so that eager sightseers would have nothing to sightsee. A plain-clothes detective held me back for some moments after the others had gone.

"I believe you knew the murdered woman," he said.

"Yes. She was a family friend."

"A little more than that, I think."

"How do you mean?"

"She was your mistress, wasn't she?" He lit a cigarette. Like his grubby fawn raincoat, the cigarette seemed to be a part of the uniform.

"Only slightly."

"Like being 'only slightly' pregnant – that sort of 'only slightly'?"

"No. We slept together a few times. Only when we both wanted to. It wasn't a regular arrangement. Just when my wife was away and Heddie didn't happen to have a boyfriend. Really, we were just friends. Honestly. Sex was only a sort of pleasant extra. God – you're not going to repeat this, are you?"

"We may have to. At the inquest." However, he looked as if he would be reluctant to destroy my life.

"But Jan! My wife, Inspector – "

"Detective-Sergeant."

" – it would kill her if ever this got out."

"Perhaps you ought to have thought of that before, sir."

"Would *you*?"

"No." He smiled. It made him look thirty-five rather than fifty. "I'm not *judging* you, you understand. I'm just trying to tell you what might happen. The coroner might think it a piece of material evidence. But God alone knows what coroners are going to think. If you're lucky the subject'll never come up."

"Hope you're right," I said.

"By the way," he said, as if on afterthought, "I don't suppose *you* killed her, did you?"

"No. Bloody hell! She and I weren't passionate enough for a *crime passionel*. Like I said, she was a friend who I sometimes slept with. It was a different sort of relationship. She wasn't the great passion of a middle-aged life. I don't think she was involved with *anyone* that deeply – and certainly not me."

"She might have been threatening to tell your wife?"

"She wasn't. And . . . she wouldn't. Even if she had, I'd have lived with it."

"I thought you said it would kill Mrs Wethering if she heard about it?" He threw the half-smoked cigarette into a puddle. It hissed and died.

"That was a figure of speech." I looked over his shoulder at one of the tors. "It would just make life very unpleasant for a while, that's all. But Jan and I would get over it. I know it sounds odd coming from someone who's just confessed adultery, but . . ." I was embarrassed " . . . I love my wife very dearly." Why in hell is it that we British always feel so bloody ashamed to admit things like this? It was a lot easier to say I'd committed adultery than to say I loved my wife. Surely it should be the other way around?

"Don't worry, sir," he said. "I really don't think it was you. You just don't seem to me to have the guts."

As I left I didn't know whether to be relieved or insulted. I ended up being a mixture of both.

Later I wondered at the man's insensitivity. Someone quicker on the uptake than me might have objected to the term 'guts'. In the context, you understand.

Alan would have understood my qualms.

I didn't really feel like going in to work, but I didn't really feel like doing anything else, either, so in to work I went. Besides, there was the evening show to do, and it would look curious if Mick Wethering was off the air simply because an assumed distant friend had died, however revoltingly. The big electric clock on the wall stared at me as Jim Paxton handed the studio over. He gave me a can of lager as he left – "Just to keep you happy through the long night hours." He obviously hadn't heard about Heddie. So far as I knew, he was the only one who knew about the depth of our friendship – except, it seemed, for the police. Hm. How the hell had *they* known?

The question tormented me as I slotted in the cassettes for the ads and my own signature tune, and stuck the first couple of CDs on the decks. Jim would never tell anyone – I was sure of that.

Seven o'clock came and with it the news summary, which Andy read from the adjacent studio. I could see his adam's apple bouncing as he read from his scruffy heap of badly typed script. It was, as ever, odd that I couldn't hear anything he said directly, but could hear his voice blasting in from the speakers in my studio as well as pipsqueaking through my cans. I'd had the sensation a thousand times before, but it was still strange. So at first I hardly registered Heddie's name when the speakers mentioned it. Then I realized that this wasn't Andy reading: IRN had picked the item up. Heddie had made the national news by dying. Ironic. She'd tried so hard to make it while alive.

Sorry, some explanations are needed. Heddie was, in life, a painter. In commercial terms, she wasn't a successful one. She might have been if she'd stuck to fussy little watercolours of Dartmoor scenes – twenty-five quid apiece in the Ashburton Arts Centre – but that hadn't been her style. If she'd produced a canvas less than six feet across I'd never seen it. Her pictures took two strong men to lift and could be attached to only the strongest walls. But it wasn't just because of their size that they dominated any room they were in. They featured exuberant clashes of colour and heavy forms. Somehow they seemed to give out more light than they received. The net result was that her exhibitions got good write-ups from John Dalton in *The Guardian* but hardly ever sold. If Jackson Pollock had painted them they'd have been worth millions, but no one was prepared to pay even £500 for a Heddie Metcalf original.

Except, that is, for me and Jan. We'd been married for about a month when we first saw an exhibition of Heddie's work on a rainy Saturday afternoon in Barnstaple. It was surprising we were out of doors, really. We were still in that stage of early marriage when, aside from the demands of work and shopping for food, we usually left the house only to make love in a field for a change. However it happened, there we were in front of a canvas called, in uncompromising defiance of the Barnstaple magistrates, 'Fucking'. It was an abstract, like all of Heddie's work, and I've *still* never been able to work out why it's so erotic. Maybe it's just that Jan and I were in the right frame of mind, but the two of us were shot instantly into a sort of tingling sexuality the moment we saw it. We were short of money at the time, and convention demanded that we buy ourselves a three-piece suite, but nevertheless we found ourselves asking the attendant the cost of Picture 7 (we couldn't bring ourselves to call it by its real name to the elderly gentleman, who looked like a stalwart of the British Legion). The price was much more than we'd expected, but Jan pulled out the joint-account chequebook anyway. Why? Well, first because we wanted the picture – aphrodisiacs have always commanded a high price. Second, because of the price itself: £499.99. Any artist with a sense of humour's got to be good.

Jan was scribbling the cheque when a pretty girl I'd vaguely noticed hanging around spoke to us. She looked about sixteen, and was dressed accordingly. She had longish fair hair held together in a pony-tail. There wasn't a trace of make-up on her face. Her skirt was grey, made of some soft material I couldn't identify. She wore a white blouse, through which you could see she had on a pale blue bra. She was wearing also a navy-blue blazer-type jacket, which confirmed the general impression that she was a schoolgirl.

"Sorry to intrude," she said confidently, "but I was wondering why you'd decided to buy that picture."

Jan looked annoyed. I certainly felt it. This wasn't so much intrusion as voyeurism.

"Well," I said, "we don't know much about art but we're . . . er . . . impressed by the use of colour, and the juxtaposition of hard lines and soft, and . . ."

"Oh, shut up, Michael," said Jan, squeezing my hand. (She always called me 'Michael'. Most of my close friends did. Actually, I loathe being called 'Mick', but there are professional considerations.) Jan continued: "We like it because we like it. Isn't that enough?"

"Yes," said the girl. "I'm sorry – again. I must seem very rude to you. You see, I have a sort of special interest. I painted it . . . and I wanted to know *why* you liked it."

"Then you must be . . . ," I said, squinting at the greyly gestetnered catalogue, "ah, Heddie Metcalf?"

"Too true," she said. She looked nervous, her eyes suddenly tracing the pattern of the cigarette-burnt carpet.

"That's fantastic!" said Jan. The attendant handed her a receipt and told her that we could pick up the painting in a fortnight's time when the exhibition closed. Long enough for the cheque to be cleared, a part of my mind reflected. Most of my mind was wondering how quickly we could get home to bed, however, so I was infuriated when Jan impulsively said: "Would you have coffee with us? We'd like to talk to you."

Heddie immediately said yes, with gratitude so obvious that I wished I were some-where else. So we had coffee, drove to Exeter, ate a meal in the Curry House, and drove back out to Kingsparson-on-the-Moor. During all of this time Heddie explained that this was only the second painting she had sold, despite the fact that it was her eighth one-person show; that she was 26, despite her appearance, and therefore the same age as me and one year younger than Jan; that this was the first time she had had a chance to talk to someone who liked her work enough to pull out a chequebook (I gathered the other purchaser had been an unusually adventurous pension fund); and that she'd painted 'Fucking' because she wanted to try and capture on canvas how much she enjoyed doing just that. We were all a bit drunk by this time, so the final comment was less of a shocker than it might have been had it emerged over the birianis.

Jan and Heddie had been talking together now since five o'clock. I checked my watch and discovered that it was a quarter past ten. During five and a quarter hours I had contributed at most three paragraphs to the conversation.

I swivelled my slightly hazy gaze to Jan's face. She looked readier for bed than I'd ever seen her, which at that stage in our marriage was a spectacular sight.

"It's been a long day," I said to Heddie. "Would you like me to drive you home?"

"Nonsense," said Jan. "Michael, you're in no condition to drive anyone home. Come to that" – she giggled – "neither am I. Heddie, would you like to kip here? I'm afraid all we can offer is a camp-bed and a sleeping-bag, but . . ."

I can still remember Heddie's clear, thin voice as she said: "If you don't mind, I'd rather sleep with you two."

Try as I might, I cannot remember all that happened then. At a guess, I turned in shock towards Jan. At another guess, she did the same towards me. Guesses aside, the next thing I knew was that the three of us were more or less naked. I was on my back on the sheepskin rug Jan's mother had given us as a wedding present. The only clear image I have is of opening my eyes to find Heddie eagerly kissing the musty triangle between my wife's thighs.

My wife. Had it been a man doing the same I would have been incensed. As it was a woman, it seemed somehow all right.

Further gaps of memory. I do know that we all reached bed together, but I cannot recall climbing the stairs. I have just one more visual flicker from that night. Jan went to switch out the light, and as she turned to look at Heddie and I sprawled across the bed my eyes focused on the black triangle of her pubic hair. For some reason I found I wanted to check the colour of Heddie's. Was she like so many blondes: fair on the head but dark beneath? As I turned to look, Jan switched out the light.

In the chilly hungover morning, over a dismal breakfast, we all agreed that the night before had been a product of the booze, and that it should never, *never* be repeated. It was six weeks later that I found out that Heddie's pubic hair was almost as blonde as that on her head.

I *had* to phone Jan. Even though, to her, Heddie was nothing more than a good friend with whom, six years earlier, she had engaged in an episode that was best left un-remembered, I knew that she would be upset by Heddie's death. I did not want her to hear about it on the radio news. I had to tell her myself. As the ads finished – with the inevitable carpet sale – I pulled the new Backstreet Boys single off the deck and put Al Stewart's *Past, Present and Future* album on instead. I'd just changed the speed control when it was time for me to speak.

"The cock of the evening to all of you listening to Dart Radio," I said. "This is Mick Wethering speaking, and I'm going to be with you right through till closedown at midnight. At ten we'll have the sports round-up from Jenny Judson, at eleven we'll have the Independent Radio News from Andy Mulveen, but aside from that it'll be music all the way. And we're going to start with a golden oldie that's as popular now as it was when it first came out in the 1970s, Al Stewart's 'Nostradamus'. I'll be right here, listening with you. Hope it brings back happy memories . . ."

I switched the mike off. Nine minutes of 'Nostradamus' would give me enough time to call Jan. Without really thinking I stuck Meat Loaf's *Bat Out of Hell II* into the other deck; 'I'd Do Anything For Love' would give me an extra twelve minutes, if I needed it – it was going to be a good show for golden-oldie lovers. Thank God there wasn't a fucking *guest* on tonight: most nights I was stuck with spending half an hour pretending to be interested in some touring author and his lacklustre book. Dart Radio doesn't pay its visiting 'celebrities', and so has to make do with whatever the publicists send it.

I felt Alan almost.

I put the earphones around my neck, so that I would know how Al Stewart was getting on without actually having to listen to him, and picked up the phone. I'd expected a direct line out, but Denise had obviously decided to linger around the switchboard for a few extra minutes. (Denise is another story, but one that happened so long ago that I can't remember any of the details. It was long before I met Jan, and it was only a one-nighter. Denise was now unhappily married with two kids, and occasionally told me firmly to keep my hands to myself when they weren't even remotely near her. This was her way of trying to be tantalizing. If I'd been the one behaving like that towards *her* she'd probably have called the vice squad.)

"Hi, Mick," she said sweetly.

"Oh, uh, hi, Denise," I said. "I thought you'd have gone by now."

"A woman's work is never done." She was fond of clichés, and this was one of her all-time faves.

"I wanted an outside line," I said.

"Outside line coming up," she said, and my ear was filled with the purr of the tone. The trouble was, I wouldn't have put it past Denise to listen in. I dithered. Al Stewart was into the central section of 'Nostradamus'. The minutes were ticking away. I pulled the Meat Loaf CD off the deck, hunted for the remastered *Tubular Bells* only to find that someone had liberated it, and instead dragged out an ancient copy of the Incredible String Band's *Changing Horses*. 'Creation' lasts eighteen – count 'em, eighteen – minutes. Another golden oldie. No one would like it much, not even me, and I'd have to put on seven ads in a row at the end of the track, but I didn't care any longer: I had to speak to Jan.

I listened with one ear to the mind-numbing purr of the phone and with the other to the squeaky version of Al Stewart I could hear directly from the stylus. He finally finished, and I switched my own mike on. "Takes you back, doesn't it?" I said, filling my voice with synthetic friendliness. "This is Dart Radio and I'm Mick Wethering, and I'm glad to know that you – yes, *you* – are listening to the show tonight. And I'm sure you'll be just as glad to know that I'm going to follow that track with another from the same period. Yes, it's one for all of you out there who love the Incredible String Band. Here it is: 'Creation.'" Listen to the first few bars. Switch the mike off. Denise *must* have gone home by now. Dial. Listen to the dialling tone. Was Jan in the bath?

Finally:

"Kingsparson 364. Jan Wethering speaking."

"Jan. It's Michael here. Something terrible has happened."

"Let me sit down." She wasn't joking. I could hear her pulling up a chair. "OK, tell me."

"It's Heddie. She's dead."

"*What?*"

"Dead. She's been murdered."

"Oh God. Who by?"

"Darling, I don't know. I don't think the police do, either. I was one of the first to find her. It was . . . not good." Robin Williamson was speaking intently into my neck and I couldn't make out a word of what he was saying.

"Do they think it was one of us two?"

"I don't believe so," I said. "Why should they? There must have been thousands of other people who knew her."

"Yes, but . . ." She was thinking about that night, six years back. Her thoughts were very loud down the line, drowning even the crackles and hisses that we always referred to as the MI5 tappers lighting up their roll-your-own cigarettes.

"That was a long time ago, darling," I said. "It doesn't make any difference now. She's been involved with a dozen people since then. Remember, there was that biker she brought to dinner, and Hector the Lie-Detector Tax Inspector, and . . ."

"I know, Michael, but we were the only *couple* she . . ."

"We don't know that," I said, trying not to snap. Jan was on the verge of tears, I could hear. "The whole thing is nothing to do with us."

"I'm sorry, lovie," she said, her voice thickening. "The news hurts, that's all. I'm being selfish. Who killed her isn't really important. I'm just so upset for Heddie, that's all. She's . . . she was so young."

"'Too young to die,'" I muttered. Denise would have been proud of that one. But it was true: Heddie at 32 had still looked like a schoolgirl. Even dead on the cold, wet moor, with a great gash from her genitals to her breasts, she had looked like a school-girl. I gagged.

"Can we stop talking?" whispered Jan.

"What? Oh. Yes. If you like."

"I want to go and . . . I don't know . . . say a prayer, or something. I want to have a quiet time to weep for Heddie. Very primitive. I . . ."

"I know what you mean. I'll be home as early as I can. Don't get too sad."

"I love you," she said.

"I love you too," I said. "*Je t'aime, moi non plus.* I'll be with you soon."

"Yes," she said. "I think that would be best."

She hung up. I started to concentrate on trying to retrieve a few listeners.

Jan. (Alan has nothing to do with this.)

The only woman I have ever deeply loved in a man-loves-woman sense. My wife. My lover. My mistress. My whore and my ever-new shy virgin bride. The exact centre of my Universe. The person with whom I was utterly infatuated. But, unfortunately, only my second-best friend.

Equally unfortunately, my first-best friend was female.

Which was why I'd ended up leading a curious form of double life – not the usual sort of double life, in which there is an element of falseness in at least one relationship, if not both. No, both of my relationships were genuine and profound. On the one hand, there was Jan, who was everything to my soul. On the other, there was Heddie, who was everything to my intellect, so that the intellectual satisfaction of her company somehow spilled over into the emotional part of my mind, too. When she and I were in bed together, which was surprisingly less often than you might think, we weren't just fucking, we were genuinely making love . . . except that it was a different type of love from the one which Jan and I shared. I never once felt that there was any betrayal involved in my adultery (a silly, cold word). With both women, the interaction of my body with theirs was merely a physical rendition of the love I had for them. With Jan, love-making was a complete and utter surrender of the self. Yet, oddly, with Heddie there were fewer inhibitions: I doubt whether there was a square centimetre of her body that I had not at one time kissed. And yet . . . and yet, in a way, with Heddie there was less *involvement*. I'm not sure that I quite understand why this was the case, but it was. Perhaps there were fewer inhibitions because whatever we did physically was less important than it would have been between Jan and me. As I say, I don't really understand it.

I often wondered what I'd have done had some King Solomon figure come along and told me that I must give up one or other of the relationships. I never did – and still cannot – work out which of the two was more important to me. They were just . . . *different*. Ideally, I guess I should have tried to talk Jan into allowing Heddie to live with us: that would probably have been the best thing, now that I use hindsight. But now is now and then was then. At the time, I was caught up in both relationships. It was as if both of the women were two different aspects of the same person. Heddie was the one with whom I walked the shoreline of the Exe estuary talking about post-Impressionism – a subject of which I knew nothing, but about which I liked to think I sounded knowledgeable. Jan was the one with whom, in the cold hours of the early morning, I muttered about how particle physics seemed incapable of explaining the phenomenon of love. Particle physics was another subject of which I knew nothing.

So who *was* Jan? I realize, guiltily, that I've told you a lot about Heddie and next to nothing about Jan.

Oddly, I find it hard to describe Jan's physical appearance. Oh, yes, the particulars are easy enough: long dark hair, oval face, 5 foot 6, trim figure, looked best in tight blue jeans. But aside from that I'm stalled. I could give a better description of a woman I'd seen and idly fancied on the train than I could of Jan. She just *was*, as far as I was concerned. She was there. She was everything.

In bed together it was less as if we were making love with each other, more as if we were a single organism confirming its identity: there was a great deal of physical ecstasy, but it was almost incidental.

Jan was a virgin when we met – a 'late developer', she used to say. She was no longer a virgin by the time, eighteen months later, we went to bed together; but she might as well have been. She had gone through a very rapid phase of promiscuity, during which she'd lost count, she always said, of the men she'd been screwed by. I use the expression carefully. She had made love with no man; she had screwed no man; she had been screwed by many. None of her 'lovers' had paused to make love with her. When she and I first made love it was a first time for her.

As far as she was concerned, beforehand, I was simply a prestige one-night stand – local-radio DJ, and all that – while, for me, it was rather different. We'd met because she was an astronomer at Exeter University and Dart Radio, ever desperate to find people who would come and be interviewed for free, had asked her to speak about the new supernova the Hubble had spotted in M31. For half an hour, interrupted by the ads and two puerile records, we discussed supernovae on air. I pretended that I was being the 'voice of the people', whereas the truth was that I didn't know what the hell she was talking about. The interview was really killed in the first few moments when she pointed out that astronomers are constantly spotting supernovae in other galaxies – this one was no big deal.

After the show I asked her out for a drink, but she declined the offer. She had things to do at home, she said, and I felt that the excuse was a real one, not just a polite put-off. Dart Radio not worrying too much about repeat performances, she was invited onto the show several times and invited out for that drink the same number of times before, one night, she agreed. The intensity of my interest in her can be gathered from the fact that, during those eighteen months, I went to bed with a woman only one time. That was the sad time with Denise, and for me (and for her too, I think) it was merely a case of releasing tension. It was mindless fucking. Jan was the person with whom I wished to be the whole night long.

The first night Jan and I had a drink together – in the Horse and Groom – was also the first night we made love together. The transition from pub to her flat in Polsloe Road was a swift one: we never finished the first drink. The transformation in her personality was spectacular. As soon as we were inside the peeling-paint blue door she flung her spectacles at the worn couch and the studious astronomer disappeared. She almost strangled me as she ripped the T-shirt from me. We had the usual tussle with her brassiere as we worked our way like a pair of professional wrestlers into her somewhat seedy bedroom, where the sheets and blankets lay on the bed like a scale model of the Andes. She threw herself down.

"Go on," she said. "Do it. Now."

"Not yet," I said, easing myself down beside her and gently kissing her left breast.

"Let's wait a little."

Although it was a long while later that we had intercourse, it was at this early moment that she started to make love for the first time.

To hell with it, I thought for the umpteenth time that night as I looked around the studio. Time had passed. The usual crap singles had been played. Jenny had done her stuff and gone, as had Andy: people who wanted to know about sports and/or news would either have to switch over to the Beeb or wait until the morning. Forty-five minutes to go before I and Dart Radio could knock off for the night, too. The listeners in their hundreds would just have to accept that the Mick Wethering Show was concentrating almost to exclusion on golden oldies – *long* golden oldies – this time. Made a change from the usual top-twenty drek, anyway.

"Bob Dylan," I said. "A lot of people feel he's lost his way over the last few years. Well, maybe he has and maybe he hasn't." (That's the art of the DJ – to use a lot of words to say nothing.) "Perhaps you think he has. I don't know. Perhaps you think he hasn't. But, whatever you think, I'm sure you'll agree that he hadn't lost his way all those years ago when he recorded that magnificent double album, *Blonde on Blonde*. And here's what's probably the best track from it." I finished speaking as the opening bars of the satisfyingly thirteen-minute-long 'Sad-Eyed Lady of the Low-lands' sounded tinnily from the pick-up. I switched my mike off, and then began to think about me, and Jan, and Heddie . . . all over again.

The phone rang. I jumped. Jesus – that could have happened while I was on air! I stared at the instrument. Normally I was punctilious about turning the volume-control down to zero while working, but tonight I'd forgotten. Still, I had an excuse . . .

I picked up the receiver.

"Mick," said a voice. It was vaguely familiar.

"Michael Wethering," I said. "How did you get this number? Who are you?"

"I've known the number for years," said the voice. "A Dart Radio DJ gave it to me. He's a cunt. My name's Alan. That's all of my name you need to know. Alan."

"Who *are* you?" I asked again.

"I've told you my name."

Curiosity turned into uneasiness. This telephone call should never have come through.

"I don't want to know your name. I want to know who you are and why you're calling me. This number's for emergencies only."

The man at the other end of the line giggled, shrilly, like a young girl. "I'm surprised you have to ask," he said eventually. "You know me very well."

I thought hard. I couldn't think of any Alan that I knew outside Rider Haggard. Oh, yes, there was Alan behind the counter in the post office, but three months ago he'd gone off to live in Finland or somewhere. I was suddenly very conscious of the emptiness of the building. I was alone. I was supposed to lock up after closing down the studio. It was foolish, but I began to think about ghosties and ghoulies and things going bump in the night. We often had phone calls from crackpots, but this 'Alan' didn't sound like the average pub loonie to me. He sounded sinister. There was a timbre in his voice that suggested he knew exactly what he was doing, and the in-flection of his words reinforced the impression.

Besides . . . besides, there *was* that something in his voice I recognized . . .

"I don't know you at all," I said.

"Do you know the second-rate, stuck-in-a-shit-filled-rut DJ who gave me the number of the direct line into the studio?"

"I probably do, if he's at Dart," I said. In my more honest moments I'd have admitted the description could be applied to any of us on your soaraway local radio station.

"But do you know *exactly* who this fucking shit was?"

"No."

"I'll give you some clues. He's about six feet tall and he has a silly-looking little moustache that for some reason he's very proud of. Perhaps he thinks it suits his image of being virile and manly, cock-swingingly bollock-laden like all the other guys."

I winced. I was the only person at Dart Radio who fitted the physical description. The taunt about sexual neuroses was all too accurate – Jan and I had often joked about it. So had Heddie and I. Both of them had said it was OK, not to worry, and that anyway, it didn't matter, what was important was that I was good in bed. I'd have been more convinced if both of them had not, independently, thought to mention the fact.

"You're talking about me, I think," I said. It was difficult getting the words out. Bob Dylan was having no trouble getting the words out, I thought absent-mindedly, as I heard him buzzing away into my neck.

Alan responded immediately. "Right on the button, *and* you get the ceegar. But shall I tell you a little more about this DJ?"

"What?"

"This turd has been screwing my lover, on and off, for six years now."

"You mean you're Heddie's boyfriend? But I thought she . . . She always told me there was no one special."

"Well, there was, buster. Me. For six years now I've been with her, loving her, caring for her, sleeping with her whenever I could. And then last week . . . " Alan began to cry. I looked despairingly across at the timer. Thank God. Two-thirds of 'Sad-Eyed Lady of the Lowlands' still to go. Hardly thinking, I stretched for a CD and got Pat Benatar in concert. Six minutes of 'Hell is for Children' would be better than nothing.

"Pull yourself together, man," I said. "Heddie's dead, so it would make a lot more sense if you and I got together as friends and drank to her memory. She'd like that. She wouldn't want us to go for each other's throats . . . especially since I never even knew you existed."

"You *shit*!" came the scream. "You bastard shit! You fucker! God, how can you speak like that? You killed her, you cunt! I told the fucking fuzz. You. Killed. Her. You. Cunt."

There was only the one phone-set in the studio – the same one served for calls routed through the switchboard and those coming in on the direct number. I might make a dash for the switchboard, but the blackness of the corridor I could see through the heavy glass door was almost as terrifying as Alan had become. I felt as if someone had stapled me to my swivel-chair. "I didn't kill her," I said limply.

Alan's voice was a whisper this time. "Yes . . . you . . . did," he hissed. "I held the knife but it was you who killed her, cocksucker. You and the filth you spread all over her. What do you think it was like for me to hold her in my arms and know that some man had been with her, imagining her still sticky from being with you. But I didn't know who the man was until last week, when she said the wrong name in bed. And then I knew it was you."

"How did . . . "

"It was easy, arsehole. Have you ever thought how rare your name is? There are thousands of 'Micks' and 'Mikes' for every 'Michael'. When she said 'Michael' to me I was sure, but I made her tell me, anyway. You'd better put on another record. 'Sad-Eyed Lady' is nearly over."

I thought I was going to be sick as I voiced the link. I had to keep this . . . psychopath . . . on the line, but I also had to contact the police. I couldn't do both. If I went on air to summon the police Alan would surely hear me – clearly he had Dart Radio playing somewhere near. I didn't want him to hang up. My reasons were not just the logical ones. Some masochistic part of me *needed* to go on listening to him.

Once 'Hell is for Children' was well under way I noticed that I'd forgotten to switch my mike on. Dart devotees had just been treated to a three-minute silence. I grabbed the phone. Had Alan interpreted the silence as me taking time out to call the police?

"Don't worry, wanker," said his almost reassuring voice. "I know what happened. It's not the first time. I listen to your show a lot. Only this time I would guess that you're not going to break into the song and apologize with a laugh. No, not this time. And not ever again."

Sod that, I thought. I broke into the record and laughingly apologized for my little mistake. "Must be getting later than you think," I said to the listeners, who probably totalled two necking teenagers and a taxi driver.

And Alan.

"OK," he said, and I was startled by the increased bitterness in his voice, "so you've had your tiny triumph. Enjoy it. You don't have long. You killed Heddie, with me as your instrument. Now you're going to kill yourself the same way." Abruptly he burst into tears again.

This time I was – definitely was – going to slam down the phone and dial 999, but then a new voice came on the line.

"Darling – Michael, darling."

"Jan," I said. "What for Jesus's love are you – "

"Michael, please Michael – please. I can't stop him. I know all about you and Heddie, and it's all right, I don't mind, we can live with it. But Alan – he's . . . he's *insane*. He means it when he says he's going to kill you."

"Jan," I said, trying to sound calm. "If you're with that fucking homicidal maniac, then get away from him. Right now. At once."

"Oh God, Michael," she shrieked. "I *can't*. Don't you understand? I *can't*!"

Pat Benatar was off the airwaves. So was Dart Radio. I didn't care.

"What do you mean, you can't?" I said. "Darling, he's nuts. You *must* get away from him. Are you tied to him, or something? Has he got a knife on you?" A picture of Heddie's gutted body flashed into my mind. Jesus! The way I loved Heddie I could live with her death. The way I loved Jan . . .

"No, it's not that. Michael," and her voice was momentarily icy-cool, "I can never never never never get away from Alan. Don't you understand?"

And then, of course, I did understand. I understood why Alan's voice had seemed so familiar. It was Jan's, but in a lower register.

"Dearest," I said, "I'm going to put the phone down and I'm going to call some doctors, and I'm going to drive out to the house with them. There's no need to be frightened. The police may come with us, but I'll be there and I'll make sure they're gentle with you. You mustn't panic."

"But – but," she said, and then, with one of those maddening inconsequentialities with which we litter our lives: "You can't come away now. What about the show?"

"Oh, dear heart, to hell with the show." There were tears in my eyes. They stung, too: I'd always thought they only stung in books. "Anyway, Dart has been off the air for nearly four minutes now" – instinctive glance at the electric clock – "and so it can just stay that way till tomorrow. Nobody minds. Probably nobody's even listening. *I* don't mind. Just let me call the doctors, and we'll come for you."

Privately, I was worried about how quickly the psychiatrists would come. A friend of ours had waited two days while her husband, talking about being the reincarnation of Benito Mussolini, had systematically smashed every object in the house.

"There's no need to come for me," said a voice which was Alan's on a couple of the words and Jan's for the others. "No need to call the doctors. I'll come to you."

"But you can't drive when you're like this, darling."

"No need to drive," said the voice. "I'm just downstairs."

I put the phone down. I switched on my mike, and then realized it was now after midnight: studio transmission had automatically been cut off and we were carrying Radio 2 for the night owls. No more access to the airwaves for Dart Radio this night. I picked the phone back up again. The person who was Jan/Alan had cut it off at the switchboard. I looked around me for a weapon, but there was nothing I could see. Fend off a murderer with an empty lager can? – no way. I looked at the glass door, and it was as staunchly boltless as ever. I saw Heddie's brains on the moss of the moor, her intestines glistening on the same moss. I decided my only chance was to move. I made for the door but, before I got there, it opened. Framed in it was the woman I loved.

Except that she was a man.

I don't mean that she was dressed any differently from normal – in fact, she was in a skirt, the short skirt I'd bought her a couple of birthdays ago because I'd always fantasized about making love up against a wall with a woman who still had her skirt on. (We'd done it, too. On a holiday we couldn't really afford we'd made love leaning against the Great Wall of China. At the time it had seemed funny, and hence intensely erotic; now the memory brought acid to my mouth.) Costume aside, however, Jan/Alan was male. There was no five o'clock shadow on her/his face, but I could almost see one there.

I could see, also, the carving knife that Aunt Edith had given us for Christmas. It reflected a sparkle from the studio's fluorescent lighting at me. The reflection was not from the steel but from the bright redness that covered the blade, as well as the whole of Jan/Alan's front. There was even a spatter of blood on her nose. It looked incongruously fetching.

"Jan," I said.

"I'm Alan."

"Alan. Alan – look, you're invading Jan's body. I mean, fuck off out of there and let me speak to Jan."

To my surprise, he did exactly that. All at once the figure in front of me was female.

I took a step towards her. The knife stayed pointing at me, so I stopped. "Darling," I said, loving her.

"Stay there," she said. "This is very difficult for me."

For a moment it seemed like a domestic quarrel. "It's pretty bloody difficult for – "

"Shut up," she said. "I can't keep Alan down for long. Not now. He wants to kill you. He's already killed Heddie. And Denise, downstairs. She was waiting for you. Her marriage was all fucked up and she thought she might seduce you to Prove Something to her husband. Well, she'll prove something to him, all right, when he has to identify her." Jan began to cry.

Instinct: I moved towards her. The knife gestured me back.

"I want to tell you the truth," said Jan, "before I let Alan come back. You see . . . while it was Alan who killed Heddie, it was *me* who was her lover. Making love with her was like nothing you can imagine. The very first time, when the two of us were in bed with you, you were nothing but a sort of . . . impediment. You were the second-best. We kept you happy, and it was something of a vague turn-on, but most of the time we just wanted to be *together*. You were . . . you were . . . you were an *excuse*. Yes, I enjoyed making love with you when we were on our own. Yes, I loved you. I loved you, but I was not *in love* with you. I was in love with Heddie. And she was in love with you . . . and with me. I'm . . . I'm sorry."

"So you killed Heddie," I said. A knife couldn't kill me now.

"No," Jan corrected, "*Alan* killed Heddie. When he discovered she'd been betraying us, all these years, he took her out on the moor and he smeared his saliva all over her and he stuck his knife into her and he ripped her. And then he beat her brains out with a rock, to make sure she had died."

The way Jan was telling it, the whole episode seemed somehow logical. The memory was clearly hurting her. Tears came to her eyes. Her face crumpled. One moment it was Alan's, the next it was hers. Both faces expressed the horror of the killings she/he/they had done.

The knife dropped to the floor.

I picked it up.

And here I am. The judge said I was evil. He said any confessed adulterer who slaughtered his mistress, his wife, and a casual girlfriend from long ago, all because he was worried about his sexual adequacy, deserved to be put away for life.

Really life – none of your out-in-a-few-years jobs.

He didn't believe me, and I can see that neither do you, which is why you're all going to have some recreational fun kicking the shit out of me. Again. Just like him, you think that people are either good or evil, that Jan was Jan and I killed her because she'd found out about me and Heddie. That I killed Heddie because she was going to tell or had told Jan. That I killed Denise – poor, godforsaken Denise – because she'd eavesdropped on some of my phone conversations with Heddie.

Jan: I touched the upper part of your arm, just above the elbow, and I loved my fingertips against your hairless skin.

I explain myself sometimes.

It was only Alan I killed.

And I killed him to defend myself.

My *self*.

MURIEL GRAY

Muriel Gray's broadcasting career began in 1982 as a co-presenter of Channel 4's music show *The Tube* with Paula Yates and Jools Holland, which led to a twenty year career in television and radio, encompassing everything from the arts and entertainment to long running factual series and current affairs. She was the first woman rector of Edinburgh University, a post she served for three years. She began her own production company in 1987, initially named Gallus Besom, now called Ideal World Productions, which was awarded Independent Company of the Year 2003 by *Broadcast* magazine. It is one of the UK's leading companyies, producing a wide range of television and drama projects.

Her writing career began first with a non-fiction best selling mountaineering book in the late eighties entitled *The First Fifty*, and in 1993 with the publication of her first horror novel *The Trickster*. This was followed by two more horror novels: *Furnace* and *The Ancient*. Stephen King called *The Ancient* the 'one thriller you have to read in 2001. Scary and un-putdownable'.

Muriel has won many awards for both writing and presenting, and is currently working on an original horror screenplay commissioned by Little Bird films. She lives in Glasgow with her husband and three children. After her family, her other passions are mountaineering, snowboarding and growing trees.

"Ah, interesting," said Lesley Henderson, her mouth contorting to articulate the words around the impediment of a half masticated Bourbon biscuit. "That must be Roger Rabbit's mum."

The three women crunching biscuits and nursing plastic cups of tea craned their necks. A small, unremarkable, dark-haired woman waited in line at the trestle table for her own refreshment, her head turning occasionally to gaze at a wall barnacled with grotesque paintings of oversized heads entitled 'my mummy' that glared down on the hall's occupants like a surveillance device. Holding her hand was a small boy with curly hair and prominent front teeth.

Lesley leant forward conspiratorially. "Well, we're honoured indeed. Mrs Rabbit has clearly found time in her busy diary to come and see what young Roger does in her lengthy absence."

The two other women smiled and moved their shoulders as though shrugging off invisible perching birds. Dorothy Stevens gesticulated at Rosemary McKendrick beside her. "Move Lesley's coat off that seat Rose. Get her over here."

A grey wool coat and an orange silk scarf adorned with a childlike pattern of bumble bees was hastily shifted from the one remaining vacant plastic seat to the floor beneath an occupied one. The dark-haired woman accepted a cup of tea from a plump parent helper behind the trestle, then bent down and kissed her son on the forehead. He ran off towards a group of boys at the back of the school assembly hall, his slapping feet joining the muted thunder that the boys' cavorting drummed on the scoured oak floorboards. She watched him go, then her shy gaze roamed the room in search of refuge before coming to rest on the three women staring at her. With a pause that betrayed it as a considered effort, she smiled with an accompanying upward nod of the head. Lesley raised a hand. The gesture was returned.

"Sorted," said Dorothy under her breath.

Cautiously, the dark-haired woman threaded her way through the labyrinthine obstacle course of formally and sensibly arranged plastic stacking chairs, that had been informally and ludicrously rearranged by the groups of women who now occupied them, gabbling together like startled geese and booby trapping the way between them with handbags and jackets. In this sea of shrill femininity, only one or two ugly, gangly men, whose beards, wire rimmed spectacles, cagoules and bicycle-clipped trousers advertised a very particular kind of personal failure, indicated that this was a parent's open day rather than a mother's one. The dark-haired woman arrived at her destination and stood awkwardly, like a child called to a stern father's study waiting to be asked to sit. All three seated women noted her discomfort with pleasure and said nothing.

"Hello," said the standing woman quietly to Lesley. "Are you Sandy's mum?"

Lesley grinned. "Guilty!"

The dark-haired woman laughed politely, trying to look amused despite the weakness of the joke. Regardless of its disingenuous provenance, it was a nice laugh. "I'm Thomas's mum, Irene. I think Thomas plays with Sandy quite a lot."

The seated women exchanged furtive and amused glances.

"Why don't you sit down?" suggested Lesley, neither confirming nor denying Irene's statement.

"Thank you."

"We don't see much of you at the school gates," said Rosemary as Irene sat down on the prepared chair.

"No. I work. My mum drops off and collects Thomas most days. A child minder on the days she can't manage."

"Ah," said Lesley.

"Do you work?" asked Irene pressing a finger to the top lip she'd just burnt by sipping the unpleasant tea.

"At the hardest job they've come up with yet," said Dorothy.

Irene raised her eyebrows in polite enquiry, her head inclined to invite fuller explanation.

"It's called being a full time mum."

Irene nodded sagely, ignoring the heavy theatrical emphasis on the last three words. "Yes, no one realises how tough it is, all this, do they? Not until they do it themselves."

Lesley snorted.

Irene looked at her quizzically.

"So what it is that you do then?" demanded Lesley in a voice that was rather too rough for a pleasantry.

"I work in computers," said Irene, her eyes drifting to the group of boys at the back of the hall, pushing and jostling by the tables where the projects they'd been working on were laid out for their parents to admire. The boys were growing rowdy, the high-pitched yelling giving way to a subtle but audible drop in key and tempo.

"Keep you busy?" enquired Rosemary with a barely concealed sneer.

Irene sipped her tea again, eyes still on the boys. "Yes. I have to travel a lot. It's hard sometimes."

Dorothy crossed her arms over the large breasts that were fighting to get out of a zippy up fleece that advertised her husband's polytechnic by way of a badly designed embroidered logo. "Well of course there's hard and there's hard isn't there?"

"Yes," said Irene. "There certainly is."

A shout rang out from the back of the hall and then a scuffle. Irene was on her feet and over to the boys with a speed and agility that surprised the seated women. Thomas was already on the floor, Sandy Henderson standing triumphantly amongst a small group of hooting admirers. Irene picked up her son and straightened out his crumpled uniform with quiet motherly efficiency. Neither mother nor son spoke, but instead looked intently at each other as the group of boys watched with shining eyes to see what Sandy would do next. But Sandy was looking at Thomas's mother's face. She moved her gaze slowly to meet his and his cheeks coloured.

"Buck-toothed freak," he muttered to his nearest companion as he turned and walked away.

Irene waited until she and Thomas were alone in the small space they had defined with crouched bodies, then put an arm around his shoulders and said something quietly into his ear. Thomas looked into her dark eyes, moved off, head bent, and began looking at the scrapbooks, poking at them to turn the pages with a limp disinterested finger.

The three women were quiet as Irene rejoined them and sat down, smoothing her grey suit skirt over short muscular legs. Lesley looked at her friends. All three exchanged mirthful glances, trying hard not to laugh.

"The projects are rather good, aren't they?" said Irene in a steady voice.

Alasdair Henderson didn't kiss his wife goodbye in the morning any more. Nor did he kiss or hug his two boys. For the last two years he had worked hard at making his exits from number fifteen Churchill Avenue as swift as he could manage, and now after a breakfast that had been punctuated with the usual sly contemptuous insults from his sullen brutish sons, fuelled by tiny encouragements from his wife, he was free and happy behind the wheel of his car. Sonya's flat had been broken into last night and he was going straight there to act her saviour. His whispered comforts to her over the mobile in the garden last night at midnight had been well received, and his crotch ached at the prospect of the many ways he would relieve her anxiety when he got inside the small and trendy Hyndland apartment that he paid for.

He was not disappointed. She had calmed down, mostly because nothing had been taken, and it looked like kids had just kicked in the door. They took an hour to make each feel better about the whole thing and the Alasdair that kissed her goodbye, and left for work for the second time that day, was a man who felt the world was on his side. As he accelerated through an amber traffic light and glanced in his mirror at some pathetic little white Japanese car behind him that hadn't his kind of horse-power to make it through, he felt like a real man, and one to be reckoned with.

Lesley walked a few steps out of her prime territory by the main gate and sidled up to the elderly woman. "Am I right in thinking you're Thomas's granny?"

The older woman turned and regarded her over the top of her spectacles without warmth. "Yes?"

"I'm the mum of one of his friends."

"Which friend exactly?" said the woman curtly and with an accent of upper class origin that took Lesley by surprise. This wouldn't do. Surely everyone realised that in school gate hierarchy grandparents were only one step up the food chain from nannies, who were undisputed pond scum and not to be acknowledged under any circumstances. This granny was clearly getting above herself. Who did she think she was? After all, Lesley had made the effort to come and speak to her in full view of the troops. Gratitude would be appropriate. A snippy response was quite wrong, and the surprise of the woman's class had thrown her.

Lesley's pulse quickened. "One of the few he has, I believe," she said, working hard to elevate her middle class status to a slightly higher plane with a mannered and clipped diction, her gaze deliberately leaving the woman's face as though already bored. "Well, considering his rather noticeable orthodontic problems," she added. "You know how cruel children can be."

"Indeed," replied the older woman noncommittally while consulting an elegant and expensive wristwatch, thereby trumping the semblance of boredom to a considerable degree.

Lesley fumed. How dare the old cow treat her like this? She glanced over at the girls, still waiting, whispering to each other and smiling, anxious to see what titbit she would return with. Lesley composed herself. "Is Irene working today?"

"What do you think?"

A rage boiled in Lesley's belly that threatened to affect her voice. That couldn't happen. The placid delivery of slights and covert insults was essential to their efficacy. She must remain calm. She breathed deeply. "I imagine it must be rather hard, that's all. You know, for mothers who don't get to do much mothering."

The elegant and expensively dressed old woman looked once more at Lesley over the top of her spectacles, her eyes and nose screwed up as though examining an offensive piece of graffiti on a wall. "What are you anyway? A dentist or something?"

Lesley could feel colour rising in her cheeks. "No."

"Then what is it you do exactly?"

"I'm a mother."

"As are we all. But what do you do?"

"Isn't that enough?" There was a nervous laugh in Lesley's voice.

The old woman wrinkled her nose again and turned her gaze back to the playground with an air of finality. "Self-evidently not."

Thomas Barker's *Monsters Incorporated* lunch box travelled at least fifteen feet before coming to rest against the wall. It split open and spilled its contents onto the wet concrete. The small comforts of home, the ham sandwich and round wax coated cheeses, the chocolate bar and hardboiled egg his mother had packed that morning as they'd laughed at something on breakfast telly, all lay like crash casualties in a muddy puddle as Thomas viewed them side on from his own prone position in a similar body of water.

"Get up, you fucking rabbit faced twat!"

Thomas pushed himself up on his palms and knees. His trousers were wet through and black with mud. His anorak had at least saved his torso from a soaking.

Sandy Henderson kicked at the puddle and splashed Thomas in the face. Thomas stood up, wiping his eyes.

"Say it. Go on."

Thomas shook his head.

Sandy's eyes narrowed. He gripped the smaller boy by the hair. "Say 'my mum has to work because she can't keep a man and she's a fucking moron.'"

Thomas shook his head, eyes fixed on the ground. "My dad's dead."

Sandy snorted, just like his mother. "Yeah? My mum says yours just works because she's a stupid lazy tart who can't be bothered doing the proper job of being a mother."

Thomas didn't react. This was what Sandy hated the most. As he contemplated another kick to Thomas's stomach just to get a response, Mr Strang appeared around the corner of the canteen block. The crowd of boys dispersed like mayflies on the wind.

Thomas Barker watched them go, then wiped his mouth with the back of his arm and went to fetch his lunch box.

Lesley and Alasdair Henderson shook hands with the Reverend Paterson and exchanged a few pleasantries, mostly about the Scotland verses England rugby match the day before, while Sandy and his younger brother Andrew kicked at the gravel.

"Well, I tell you this my old son, we'll give them what for next time," said the reverend as he gripped the big man's elbow.

"Here now! Could you not have put in a word with the boss upstairs?" grinned Alasdair.

Lesley hit her husband playfully. She was about to add her own little *bon mot*, but the reverend was already pumping the hands of the next exiting congregation member, making a joke about sailing. She composed herself and walked down the gravel drive of the church a few paces behind her children, concentrating on not ruining the heels on her new kitten heeled shoes from Princes' Square. As they stepped out onto the street Sandy booted Andrew's ankle and he screamed.

"Stop that! Right now!" hissed Lesley through bared teeth, her eyes scanning the crowd of church goers to check no one was witnessing this insubordination, only adding "You little bastards!" when she was sure it was safe to do so. The children ran off down the street and started to swing on the low branches of a flowering cherry, pulling off the blossom in handfuls and throwing it on the ground to wither and die. Following their progress made her miss Irene Barker's appearance from the door of a small white Nissan Micra, and so it took her by surprise when Irene stepped in front of her, her face calm, hard to read.

"Hello Lesley."

"Irene," cooed Lesley. "Were you in church? We didn't see you."

"No."

Alasdair slipped in beside his wife and took her arm, the grin of the village idiot painted across his face.

"This is my husband Alasdair."

Irene shook his hand.

"Irene's in computers Alasdair. Thomas's mum."

"Ah!" grinned Alasdair. "Computers. Bloody brilliant. Keep telling Lesley that's the kind of thing she should be studying. Get her up off her bloody backside instead of drinking coffee in Fraser's all day with her pals while she spends my money."

Lesley pulled her arm free of her husband's and ground her back teeth together. If he noted the movement then Alasdair didn't register it, on his way as he was to slap the back of another church member standing on the kerb shaking some keys to a new BMW estate.

"Is Thomas with you?" said Lesley coolly.

"No," said Irene. "But I'd like to talk to you about him if I may."

This was good. Lesley liked this very much. She was coming to her to beg. That was the way it should be. It was the way it had to be. Lesley smiled, beatific, understanding. "Do you want a coffee? We're just here." She indicated one of the neat identical terraced Edwardian houses stretching away from the church that made up this dependably middle class Glasgow district.

"Thank you," said Irene. She locked the car with a key, as Lesley noted with pleasure the absence of central locking on the tiny vehicle, and together they walked quietly down the street.

"So what brought you to Jarrowhill then?" said Lesley as she placed the mug of coffee on the glass top of the low table.

"Well, I'm sure you know yourself the school has a very good academic reputation. And luckily my mother lives in the catchment area."

Lesley sat down heavily and pushed a biscuit into her mouth. "So you live with your mother then?"

"Just since John died. We're looking for something more permanent."

"That must be hard," said Lesley without feeling, as she washed down the biscuit with a gulp of coffee.

"Yes."

"And where were you before?"

"We moved around. John's job, and now mine I suppose, takes us wherever the work is."

"Ah," mused Lesley. "Difficult for Thomas."

"Not really. He settles quickly."

"Does he?" said Lesley sitting back, enjoying herself.

Irene looked at Lesley, unblinking, and Lesley looked back, trying hard to do the same. She really was a very plain woman, thought Lesley. The kind of face you would never remember in a crowd. Pretty enough, but so very ordinary. It made her feel good that she was considerably more attractive and certainly more notable in appearance. But then she worked at it. You had to.

"May I ask you a great favour?" said Irene quietly.

"Of course. Anything I can do to help." Lesley hugged herself. Power was a wonderfully intoxicating thing. She knew what was coming, and she was going to savour it.

"I have to go away for ten days. To the States, on business."

You show-off cow, thought Lesley. "How exciting," said Lesley.

"I wonder if while I'm gone, Sandy could perhaps be a little kinder to Thomas."

She had planned for this moment. It was a beautiful and delightful thing when an anticipated pleasure came to fruition so perfectly. Lesley savoured it before raising her eyebrows in surprise and leaning back as if in horror. "I don't know what you mean Irene."

"I think there's a little tension between them."

Lesley adopted a posture of placation, hand held shoulder high, patting the air. "I'm sure you've got that wrong. It must be just schoolboy scrapping. Sandy thinks of Thomas as one of the gang."

Irene nodded. "Perhaps you're right. But if you could just ask him to be kind for this very short trip, it would mean a great deal to me."

"Well, I mean, I'll have a word, but I really don't . . ."

Irene leant forward. "When I'm working away from Thomas," she said in a voice so low that Lesley had to strain to hear it, "I have to concentrate one hundred percent on the job. One hundred percent. It's important to me that I don't worry about what's going at home. I don't like to make mistakes at work."

Lesley was slightly discomforted by the peculiar and measured emphasis on her last sentence, but she sat back and half smiled. "Then perhaps you shouldn't work away from home."

"Perhaps not."

"We all have choices Irene," said Lesley and drained her cup. Irene Barker sat very still, waiting. It unnerved her. "Yes. Well, of course I'll have a word with Sandy. But don't be surprised if he hasn't a clue what I'm talking about. He's a very friendly and popular boy, you know."

Irene continued to stare for a moment, then got up. "Thank you Lesley."

She left the room and Lesley followed.

As Irene's small figure walked back down the tree-lined road to her tiny cheap car, Lesley Henderson reflected on how good life was. It was good to be the strong one, the one in control. The one who'd done well for herself, with the wealthy popular husband, the two expensive cars, and two strapping boys. The one who people had to ask for help, who had the power to grant respite or the power to turn up the heat. It was good, in fact, just to be alive.

Sonya Fergusson fumbled through her drawers looking for the red lace bra and pants set that Alasdair had bought her, until she remembered with a smile what they had been through and knew they'd be in the wash. But curiously she didn't remember putting them in the washing machine. She thought for a moment with a mind befuddled with sleep and then dismissed it. They'd turn up. She opted instead for a black silk teddy, slipping it over her shoulders before looking at herself in the mirror to admire the way her small upturned breasts protruded through the smooth black material.

Sonya yawned and went to start the coffee machine. Behind her in the quiet bedroom, the rummaged drawer remained open, and to an owner who might have been more interested, it revealed that not only was it short of a bra and pants set, but also of some six letters that Alasdair Henderson had clumsily composed, written and sent in the heat of his passion for the recipient. But more than that. Beneath the chest of drawers on the floor, in the dark shadows against the skirting board, lay a crumpled orange scarf with bumblebees.

Irene Barker looked in on her sleeping mother and then kissed her restlessly sleeping son goodbye before she left the house for Glasgow airport.

She carried only a small holdall as hand luggage as she caught the six fifteen shuttle to Heathrow. On arrival at Heathrow she went directly to Costa Coffee and sat on a high stool at the only beech wood table that was out of range of the video camera covering the catered area, on account of it being behind a pillar. The man sat beside her within five minutes. He read his paper from cover to cover, finished his coffee and left the envelope on the table. She picked it up and walked to the ladies' room. In the cubicle Irene Barker sat on the closed toilet seat, removed her new passport, the coded instructions and three credit cards in the name of Mrs Lindsey Scott.

On the flight to Denver she talked to a woman beside her who was going to visit her sister. She had the chicken, watched a movie about some rich people in a big country house and then slept for four hours. In Denver Irene hired a small car and drove to the address she had been given. The bag with her equipment and the mark's file was concealed in a log pile at the back of the house. In the car she read the file before destroying it. Cats, she thought.

Seven and a half hours later at a Holiday Inn in Colorado Springs, Irene phoned home.

"How are you darling?" she said to Thomas.

"I'm fine. How are you?"

"Fine." There was a silence.

"Is everything okay at school?"

"Yes," said Thomas.

"We'll be moving on again soon darling."

"When?"

"Very soon. Mummy's big contract is nearly finished and then we'll live a little. I promise."

"With Granny?"

"Yes. Granny's coming too this time."

"He ripped up my spelling book today."

Irene stared at herself in the smoked hotel mirror. "That will stop."

"I miss you."

"I miss you too."

The safe house was in a quiet street with neat square lawns but few trees for cover. It was clever and she admired it. He would see a car coming for miles. Irene stopped at the hydrant outside his house to let the mongrel she'd just picked out from the town dog pound pee against it. She committed the layout of the house to memory, calculated the distance between the front door and the sidewalk, and paid special attention to the garage door. Then she walked on with the happy animal, an unremarkable housewife walking a dog that couldn't believe its luck.

When he heard the cat screaming, he looked out of the side window of the study. The animal lay half on the sidewalk, half on the road, its back legs twitching. He felt his heart atrophy. The stupid fucking Americans and their fucking cars. Couldn't they see an animal when it crossed the road? He'd seen those bumper stickers, the ones that proudly declared I DON'T BRAKE FOR CRITTERS and they made him sick. They had no respect for life. For a second he hesitated. But he was a professional. He could smell danger. No one knew he was here, and this was simply a cat that needed help. He thought of Gammshead, his wife's white Persian at home, and how he would feel if someone failed to come to their beautiful pet's aid in such circumstances.

Carefully, he opened the front door, looked up and down the street, then walked forward quickly to the stricken cat. The neighbour across the road was watching him as usual from the window. He always watched. Of course he had routinely searched the man's house when he was out and found it safe. An old nosey interfering redneck, just irritated that the new neighbour who lived across the street had a better lawn mower and pick up. Nothing to cause concern. He waved at the man and the figure stepped away from the window, embarrassed to be caught. The animal was in a bad way. By the time he bent down and gently picked it up Irene was in the house, her latex gloves already on.

She let him close the front door and then stuck the needle into the back of his neck. His hand and arm flew up in the beginning of a killer defensive move but she was already three steps back and the drug was instantaneous. He fell, his legs folding beneath him like a shot deer. Irene quickly snapped the neck of the cat she'd maimed. It had done its job. No need to let it suffer. She took out two tiny castors from a deep pocket, placed them under his heels, then wheeled the man's body through the house to the garage and opened the car door. They could tell from the shoes these days when a body had been dragged. He was overweight and she was small, but she had been trained how to lift. She re-pocketed the wheels, propped him at the wheel, inserted the hosepipe to the exhaust and brought it round to the driver's side. Taking off her small rucksack, she opened it and found the bottle of vodka, the nasal gastric tube and syringe. Inserting the greased tube up his nose and feeding it carefully down his throat she syringed in half the bottle of vodka, taking her time, spilling nothing. She glanced at her watch. It was important he stayed alive long enough for the alcohol to enter his bloodstream. Removing the tube, she put the hose between his legs, wrapped his hands around them, turned on the ignition and shut the door.

Back in the house Irene checked her watch, quickly found the computer, inserted the disc and watched for a moment with mild curiosity to see what had been chosen to incriminate their target. As the files of hard core paedophile porn downloaded onto the hard drive she raised an eyebrow, glancing over his desk and around the room at the tiny clues that told her instantly that this was unlikely to be the man's vice but would mean nothing to the lumpen FBI dolts who would be crawling over the house in the next twelve hours. It was the detail that mattered to Irene. The enigmatic decisions she acted upon without question, and the variety of the challenges kept her interest, but the detail was what kept her alive. As the computer continued to consume pictures of inhuman depravity, she moved to the kitchen, fetched a glass he'd just used and filled it with a generous measure of vodka. She returned to his study, sat it by the computer as the disc finished its business, and then carefully knocked it over. She watched the vodka spill over the desk and dribble onto the floor as she removed the disc and pocketed it. Irene folded the dead cat into her bag, checked that all the doors and windows were locked and secure from the inside, and returned to the garage. She looked out through the dusty strip of glass that revealed the street and the house opposite and checked it was clear. Reassured she opened the car door, pressed the remote garage door-opening device on the car keys and then closed the car door again. It took her seconds to slip out as it opened, and minutes while she hid, to watch it close again automatically, the engine of his modest Lincoln ticking over innocently on the other side. She walked away.

On the plane home Irene had the beef. She sat beside a man who had been on a fly-drive holiday and had very much enjoyed it. She watched a movie about wizards and elves, and before she went to sleep she took out her calculator. After this job, that would make her total savings in the bank accounts in Switzerland and the Caymans come to nearly nineteen and a half million pounds. It was enough. It was nearly time to stop.

"So, Thomas tells us you're moving on then?" said Lesley adjusting her sitting position to the posture they taught at her Palates class.

"Yes," replied Irene, smiling. "Next month."

The stage in front of them started to fill with small boys and girls, clattering and shoving in their excitement about their impending performance. Thomas looked smart and proud, his curly head just visible in the back row of the choir. Rosemary and Dorothy came breathless along the row and sat down in the seats that Lesley had kept.

"Sorry," said Rosemary.

"God," said Dorothy. "Nearly didn't make it. Who'd be a bloody mum, eh?" She glanced sourly at Irene. "I don't know how we manage, I really don't," she said pointedly.

Irene smiled sympathetically. Lesley watched the choir assemble for a moment, studying Irene's face from the corner of her eye and registering the pride that shone there. Sandy hadn't made the choir. Sandy was handing out programmes. Sandy was only good at rugby, allowing him as it did to use his skills at knocking people over and hurting them. But even then he was only average. No one made Lesley proud. She relied on herself to do that. Lesley leant into Irene's ear. "I don't want this to sound the wrong way Irene," she whispered, "but have you ever considered getting Thomas some cosmetic dentistry?"

"Yes," said Irene, still watching her son. "I have."

"And?"

"There's plenty of time."

Lesley raised her chin. "Well, I don't know. You don't want him being made fun of again wherever it is you're going next, do you?"

"That won't happen," said Irene.

Lesley sat back with a cruel smile playing on her lips. Maybe it would or wouldn't happen where they were going. She didn't care. But it was up to her if it was going to happen or not in the next month before snivelling Roger Rabbit and his smug working mum left for pastures new. But then the most intoxicating thing about power was the ability to withhold it. Would she withhold it? Would she call Sandy off or encourage him? It was up to her. Power. She pulled in her pelvic floor muscles and relished the choice, although she already knew which it would be.

Alasdair Henderson turned off the television and took his whisky glass through to the dishwasher in the kitchen. He could hear Lesley thumping around upstairs getting ready for bed. He wondered if they should try and have sex tonight in case she started to suspect him, then decided against it. The memory of Sonya's twenty eight year old tongue licking the inside of his thigh quickly turned the idea of wrestling with Lesley's spongey bulk into a horror he couldn't face. He needn't have worried. Lesley had other things on her mind than the dull predictable sex offered occasionally by her dull and predictable husband. She was thinking about strategy, about the placing and timing of small hurts and how good it felt to get them right. It was these thoughts that so absorbed her that she fell asleep without noticing that the kitchen knife she'd used to make a repulsive chicken casserole was not in the dishwasher where it belonged, but lying in the dark beneath her bed. Nor did she know that a dusty hat box on her wardrobe contained more than simply the garish green velvet affair she had bought for Amanda Findlay's ghastly cheap little wedding, but in fact a semen-soiled set of red lace underwear and some badly written love letters.

But then her husband's attention was no more acute than hers.

As Alasdair Henderson ripped open a dishwasher tablet, leaving the packet on the worktop in a habit that he knew annoyed Lesley, stacked his glass, turned on the dishwasher and put out the lights, his thoughts were very far away. So far indeed, that as he closed the dishwasher and went to lock and chain the front door, he failed to register the tiny breeze from the kitchen window that had been propped open with a pebble, the breeze that as he left the room nudged the discarded wrapper off the worktop and made it flutter gently to the floor. ✿

BEST OF TOUGH GANGSTER AUTHORS

HANK JANSON

Announcing a range of brand new re-issues of classic Hank Janson titles of the 1940s and 1950s, complete with their original covers, and with new introductions by Steve Holland.

Each title costs £9.99 (+£2.50p&p) from Telos Publishing Ltd, c/o Beech House, Chapel Lane, Moulton, Cheshire, England, CW9 8PQ

Worldwide credit card ordering is available from our website at www.telos.co.uk

June 2003:
Torment
Women Hate Till Death

December 2003:
Some Look Better Dead
Skirts Bring Me Sorrow

Telos Publishing Ltd,
61 Elgar Avenue, Tolworth, Surrey, KT5 9JP.
Visit us online at www.telos.co.uk

COMMITTED TO QUALITY

trademarks of Telos Publishing Ltd.

STEVE MOHN

Steve Mohn's comic sf monologue, 'The Producer', recently ran in *The 3rd Alternative*. Other monologues, stories and film essays have appeared in *On Spec*. He lives in Montreal with a medievalist.

Jonathan Kerner was nine years old. He rarely minded his mother. "Do you mind?" Hope warned him, muffling the phone. Jon said he did. He knew that he should. She sent him to his room without supper to wait till his father got home but Gordon Kerner telephoned: "No, one of these teachers-college specials has to have his hand held and Julie's out a town so I'll have to do it. I'll be home pretty late." Holding the bedroom receiver, Jon heard his mother dial out. "It's me, I have a few hours." A man said, "Fine." Jonathan crept to his own room, the floor creaking under him. His sister Barb was out with a boy and his brother Brian out with boys who wished they were out with girls. His mother left the house and took the Falcon.

Jon stood with his shoulders hunched almost to his ears. The open garage door made a drive-in movie of the barn, black trees, cobalt sky, a crescent moon like a boat. He crossed corn stubble then meadow. Burdocks clawed his jeans. Jon took a path through woods then pasture smooth as felt, clumpy with manure, thistle. He smelled cows, saw safety lights on a big barn. He'd hiked this way with Barb and Brian once. Skirting NO TRESPASSING signs, they had followed a stream that bored beneath the road and found a waterfall roaring off a limestone ledge:

You're my parents! he told them. You have to tell me what to do! He ran ahead like a monkey, looking back when Barb called: Jon, wait up – I'm telling you what to do, you listening?

No! But waited for his dour brother, his wise sister, to catch up, striding in laced boots, hands in pockets, like paired animals out of the Ark. I mean when I think that she's balling this guy, Barb said. Jon's eyes cut to her. The green water flexed in its narrow bed. Barb picked her way, frowning at her feet. Brian grabbed a sapling for balance – both so worried over getting wet that Jonathan beat them to where the stream ended in the air, turning down like a flywheel belt. Jon cut across on big stones. Jon, come on back this side! The shallow water skimmed flat limestone but Jon had rubber boots on. He waded in.

Jon, not that way! Brian yelled. Go back use them stones you crossed on.

He rolled his eyes. You're not my parents! And started across. His legs split like a cheerleader's. Strong water dragged him to the edge. He churned on hands and knees. Barb dug her heels into the bank, held Brian's arm – Brian, gritting his teeth, extended his free hand.

Though soaked to the waist, Jonathan would not go home: he would see the falls from below. They worked down a deer path and stood by a pool scoured into the stone. The water fell fifty feet, exploding on haunches of rock.

I would of lived, Jon said. But it was crap . . .

Now, by thin moonlight, he crossed a lawn to a farmhouse in which two windows glowed. Inside an old man and his wife watched TV – Red Skelton, telling a joke; Red laugh as if weeping at the punchline. He waved goodnight as a child would.

The old man and woman sat watching as if they had died. Jonathan stood, head tipped, seeing himself knock at their front door to say he'd been left by his parents. The farmer and his wife would take him in, raise him to manhood. He would cry at their funerals.

Back home he found his father in the den. Gordon sat at his easel, ruining a sable brush, crushing the bristles out to make weedy streaks on canvas.

Jon felt behind himself, clutched his elbow. "Okay if I watch TV?"

Gordon examined his brush. "Watch upstairs. Where you been?"

They might not have been related: Jon puny with hair as fine and pale as the angel floss they spread around the creche in the advent wreathe, and Gordon dark, face weathered by tobacco and scotch. His square hands had slammed them all against walls.

"I went for a walk. There's a crescent moon."

Gordon swiped clean canvas with the weed brush, flicked the bristles with his finger. "Full moon's a woman, you know that?"

Jon said, "I didn't have supper."

"How's come?" His father squeezed paint like toothpaste onto a palette.

"Mom sent me to bed without."

The splayed brush got shot into a jar of turpentine. "So I'm s'posed to kick the slats out of you?" He squeezed raw umber from a tube. "Your Mom's funny that way. She can't belt you but I can. That makes me the ogre. What'd you do?"

"She said do you mind, I said yes." He shrugged. "I thought I should."

Gordon messed the paints together with a palette knife. His teeth crackled on his pipestem. "There's ham in the fridge. Make us both a sandwich. Mustard. Pour yourself a glass a milk, get me a beer. Your mother say when she be home?"

"She told this man she had a couple hours."

His father drew the splayed brush from the jar and wiped it on a rag, blew on it then hung his pipe back on his teeth – the pipe crouched like a saxophone, ready to lunge. "Listen. Next time someone says do you mind, say I'm sorry. Say yes or no if someone asks mind if I smoke. If it's just do you mind, say I'm sorry. You won't get in trouble that way."

Hope returned late. "I'm not waiting till Jon's out of school." Gordon sat flicking weed streaks onto the canvas. Jonathan stood in the hall, motionless in shadow, hidden. "I'll wait till he's twelve, not longer."

"You're not waiting till he's twelve, you're waiting for me to make dean." Scant paint left bright cuts on other cuts: you could see through weeds and other weeds to the wash. "I won't dig my grave to pay alimony, Hope. I told you that." He examined his field, unfinished barn, sky like the fog in a light bulb.

Her head went down. "Look."

He poked his brush in turpentine. "Want me to take Jon?"

In the night-black windows Jon saw his mother blink.

She said, "I don't think he wants to live with you."

"I think he's scared to death he might have to. But I don't think he wants to live with you. You'll get him 'cause you're the mother. And I drink and knock them around." He faced her. "I know how I'd look – I can look at myself."

"Meaning I can't. Not even look, 'cause you're the artist." Her lip trembled on the old useless fight. What she had loved was still there but withdrawn. The offer had depended on being loved. But his paintings were shallow, derivative. Unloved, he would not love.

She said: "I look at what I've got and what time I've got left."

Except she keeps waiting, Jon thought in the shadows. She's his moon – goes around him in this orbit?

The farmer's wife died. She'd been dying when Jonathan looked through the window. Linus Webb sold his pasture, his herd and had his barn torn down. He bought an old trailer painted machinery-green, had it set up on the lawn and rented the house.

That first year he had trusty tenants: because he was too old to drive they picked things up for him down the store: eggs, tobacco, coffee, bread. His face was wrinkled like a net. He had eyes like blue drops of water. He did nothing all day but chew Red Man and watch TV in his trailer. Key Bank in Tacitus took in his social security checks for automatic deposit; he wrote checks to pay electric and phone bills and reimburse his tenants for things they'd bought him at Menotti's Big M. When these tenants left, Linus posted a FOR RENT sign out front. That was where he shook hands one spring day with Fred and Wilma Spillit.

Wilma was tall with a small bust, pear-shape hips, light brown hair at jaw length: she tucked the forward strands behind her ears. Her gray eyes were dry as two buttons. To look at you she turned her whole head. Her smiles came and went like the slow sweeps of an airport beacon. Fred's shovel-face made him look crafty and stupid when he grinned. His eyelids drooped. When he talked he droned. They could sit the same way for hours, Wilma upright, Fred resting on his elbows. They often went on unemployment, dealt grass, took odd jobs. They had never been arrested. Her father was dead, her mother was in the Clara Mah Home. She never visited. His folks had moved out of state.

That spring they both had jobs. Linus wanted low rent. The Spillits moved in. Each week Wilma got Linus's groceries and Fred mowed lawn. He did some painting to keep up the outside, using what he found down cellar or in the attic. But inside the house grew filthy. Dust clouded the corners. Trash built up. Every couple weeks they swept everything into black garbage bags to toss off Hogsback Ledge. Wilma would dust her hands and say: "Clean house." Fred would put his feet up and brush cookie dust from his chest to the floor, chewing.

A porn movie, *Behind the Green Door*, was big that year – the star's face had decorated Ivory Soap boxes. It played at the Franklin Art Cinema in Syracuse and Fred and Wilma went. During the credits a cameraman on the film mugged for the camera, hefting his own movie camera. Fred said, "Let's get one a those." They bought a used super-8 Kodak and film. A needle in the viewfinder swung to show they didn't have enough light. They brought all the lamps in the house into the bedroom, screwed in the highest-watt bulbs they had and left them bare then took turns with the camera when it wasn't watching from the nightstand. Fred knew a guy at Syracuse Movie Lab and added an ounce of grass to the usual development charge. They bought a used projector.

The film was all orange but Wilma thought that made it look homey.

Fred said, "Old man have a heart attack he saw this."

Wilma lolled on him, gazing at her image on the wall. Even orange, she looked better on the wall than in the mirror. The camera liked Wilma. Watching herself astride Fred, she asked, "What if he did have? A heart attack."

Fred guessed they'd have to move.

"But if he died and no one knew."

Fred bucked upwards. "*We'd* know."

"But if we didn't say anything."

A splice jerked the second reel through the gate. Orange fog sharpened to pictures: she lay on her side, a leg cocked. Fred strove in her. The frame left them headless.

The divorce gave Hope her three children and the farm. Gordon escaped Central New York for a job in Oregon. The alimony staggered in then ceased. By then Brian was out of school, working at a local plant called the bean mill – a dried-bean packing plant. Barb worked for a realtor in Tacitus. Jonathan wanted to work. He was sixteen and could take a job with parental consent so Brian got him into the bean mill.

Four screeners and elevators fed the production lines in the packing room. Green splits or baby limas or red kidney beans rattled down metal tubes a pound at a time into polythene bags shaped by the tubes. Pneumatic jaws rose and fell, biting off the bags – kk-sss *chunk* kk-sss *chunk* – to fall onto a conveyor, which plopped them onto a small turntable. On Jonathan's line, Wilma Spillit packed the bean bags into cardboard cases and shoved the full cases down a roller ramp for Jonathan to glue shut and stack on a pallet. He did it all day. Fifteen minute break at ten, another at two, half hour for lunch.

Jon wondered why Wilma kept watching him with her gray button eyes, almost as if she didn't see him. Her job was so automatic she didn't have to keep her eyes on her hands and Jonathan was good to look at. Not yet as tall as Brian and Barb, he was lean as lath. His jeans fit like tights. His pale hair was long as a high school girl's; at work he wore it tied back under his white plastic bump cap. Feeling Wilma's eyes on him, or meeting her eyes and getting that slow smile, like an airport beacon sweeping by, his long fingers dithered at his sides.

He had no one to talk to. It was too noisy. And Brian drove lift truck in the warehouse; nor did Brian eat in the men's lunchroom: his girlfriend, Jill, worked in the office and they ate together in there. So Jonathan ate with Dan, one of the foremen, Ben, Scotty and Mink and with Fred Spillit. Fred worked in Receiving. He dragged hundred-weight sacks of dried beans out of box cars and slit the bags with his knife to slam the beans down an iron chute. In the lunchroom the men played hands of pitch for high, low, jack and game during breaks and over lunch.

Wilma started eating in the men's lunchroom to be with Fred. Finished eating, she'd hand Fred a fresh pack of cigarettes: "Sweetie, pack my cigarettes." He'd smack them on his palm, filters down, and hand them back. Looking past Jonathan's shoulder, she would tear the red ribbon around the top edge to open the pack then park a cigarette on her lip for Fred to light.

She often sat across from Jon. One day she slid her foot under the table and pressed the toe of his work boot. Her gaze passing through him, her foot rubbed. Jon cut his eyes to Fred, cut to Wilma. She sat vacantly, smoke seeping from her.

Jon looked down, pulled his foot away and dealt the cards. He didn't like Wilma but her interest made him feel the way nude foldouts did: women who looked right at you, legs open, showing you where to put it like you were dumb? Showing too what you couldn't get? He'd have let Wilma do what she wanted but he was scared of Fred, who was big like his dad. Still, Jon knew from guys at the bean mill that Fred bought grass in pounds and sold ounces. If Fred got mad about Jon and Wilma doing stuff, Jon could call the TIP line – Turn In a Pusher.

⋆

After work Jon asked Wilma if he could score an ounce: "I've bought from Mink before. Scotty too." As Fred came out of the time-clock room Wilma fell-in beside him. "Sweetie?" Wilma talked all the way to the warehouse exit. But Fred said, "I hear he's a narc."

That evening, when Wilma brought in Linus's groceries, she asked Linus if he still had family.

"No family no more. No brudders, no sister." Linus leaned to one side and expectorated into a three-gallon pail by his chair. "Dere all dead now, all a dem."

The TV was loud. She yelled, "Don't you have friends?"

Linus shook his bald head. His blue eyes glittered with the video light that slicked the brown-green surface of the sludge in that nearly full three-gallon pail, a tobacco sputum deposit Wilma couldn't help but stare at.

"You got a doctor?" she yelled at the sludge.

With a spotted hand Linus clawed the air. She was in his way. She stepped aside. Wilma watched *Hawaii Five-0* for a minute then put away his groceries.

Monday morning the car wouldn't start. Fred called the bean mill; a boy in Receiving drove out. "You gotta get that mother fixed," the boy said. "Dan's kind a pissed off, it's like once a week? I don't mind drivin' out, I'm just sayin', is all."

At morning break Wilma found Fred. "Sell Jon an ounce – all we need is spark-plugs. Mink swears Jonathan's cool."

A different guy drove them home and Jon, whom Brian usually drove to work, rode with them. Wilma sat in back with Jon, smoking, asking how old he was, what shows he liked, did he have a girlfriend?

Jon lied that he had a girl. Wilma asked who. Jon said she lived in North Syracuse. When he saw the old two-story house, woods all around and out back, he felt he knew it. But not the green trailer. "Who lives there?"

Wilma said, "Just a old man."

"I have a uncle who's ninety."

Wilma thumbed hair behind an ear. "Sweetie, how old's Linus. Seventy?"

"Seventy-three." Fred got out. The mailbox had LINUS WEBB painted on it. A yellow sedan rested on the gravel driveway.

"My dad," said Jon, "had that same exact car once?"

"All it needs is sparkplugs." Fred looked very big walking, head up, pelvis angled forward. Wilma too walked as if presenting herself. Jon thought of how her foot had rubbed his beneath the table. It was why he was here, buying grass. His chest felt carbonated worse than how it usually felt when he bought grass or like how it felt when he looked at foldouts? He minded their frayed curtains, the grit underfoot, cracked bowls by the TV chairs holding chips and crumbs of other foods. A rock slide of dirty dishes filled the kitchen sink. Jon wanted to buy the dope and leave, cut across lots and get high but if he bought without trying it first they'd think he was a narc. He sat on their sofa where Wilma sweetly asked him to sit. She and Fred sat to either side. Fred stuck his feet out, rolled a fat joint.

"Look, he's shivering." Wilma leaned across Jon, passing the joint to Fred. Her breast mooshed on Jon's shoulder. He said he was cold.

"Think the house is cold?" Fred asked, taking the smoke in sips.

"Sweetie, turn the heat up."

Jon said he wasn't cold.

"So you want it?" Fred asked.

Upping his hips, Jon dug out his wallet. In his hand the twenty shook like a leaf. Fred plucked it. Wilma stared at Jon's ear. "Why so nervous?"

"Not nervous." Jon exhaled smoke. "Just paranoid. Like when I smoke?"

"You don't need to get paranoid with us." She opened her denim legs on the sofa: one flat, the knee against Jon, one with the knee up to lean on. Fred left to get an ounce from his stash. Wilma blew in Jon's ear. He nerved himself to face her vacant eyes, parted lips. Hot sand poured through Jonathan's belly to his crotch and filled his muscle. Tap water ran in the kitchen. He looked that way as Fred clumped back in, drinking from a filmy tumbler. Wilma said, "You want a shotgun?" Jon shook his head. "Sweetie, gimme a shotgun." Fred set the tumbler down, scraped the coal end of the joint clean and put that end carefully into his mouth then leaned across Jon, who sank into the sofa. Fred blew smoke through the joint. Wilma held her face in the erupting cloud and sucked in. She gripped Jon's shoulder, convulsing to keep the smoke in her chest. Her eyes leaked.

Fred drew the coal end from his mouth. "Wanna play pass-out?"

Jon shook his head but Wilma pinched his nose shut, muscled her tongue through his lips and made him breathe her smoke.

"Take that deep," Fred said.

Jonathan pushed Wilma off, stood coughing into one fist.

"I gotta get goin' but thanks, it's good pot."

"You gotta go?" Wilma asked. Fred snorted, clumped back to the kitchen. The tap ran hard. Wilma asked, "What's a matter, don't you like us?"

Jon resisted wiping his mouth. He did not like them but wanted what they offered. All he had to do was nothing. He could blame being stoned. He sat again. He'd never seen such life in Wilma's eyes. So vacant, like decorative eyes on a doll, now they gave light. He saw himself in a fleshy moil with Fred and Wilma and touched her denim thigh.

Fred clumped in, drinking water. Jon's hand leaped.

"I gotta go."

"Come back some time you can't stay so long," Fred said.

Wilma said, "Yeah, Jon, come back see us now."

He walked staring at the grass growing up through the gravel and started home, along the road, then ducked into the woods on a tractor path to cut across lots and get high. He had some foldouts, old ones, hidden in a place?

For a long time Wilma sat as if dazed. She slept and when she woke it was dark. Fred sat in the kitchen eating. Wilma went to work on the dishes – a week of plates, mugs, glasses, bent flatware. Fred said, "Think I'll walk around to Rick's Auto-body, get them sparkplugs." Wilma said she'd watch TV but stared at the trailer through the window above the sink. Slats of bluish video light, slanted by glass louvers on Linus's windows, gleamed through thin fog.

She went out to do a bowl alone then went to the trailer. Linus didn't pay me for the groceries other day. Video light edged the glass louvers on the door. She heard forced laughter, a sitcom, and tried the door. It clicked softly off the latch. Linus slept in his chair, his head forward, his baldness like a blank face or the yellow pad of a giant thumb. Wilma gentled the door shut. He didn't wake. She crept to the bedroom end of the trailer and stood in the dark. I'm gonna do something. Stood waiting for something to take her there. Her hand touched her thigh where Jonathan's had. I'm going to, Sweetie. I'm gonna do something, just watch. She took Linus's pillow. Scene-change music on TV giggled. Wilma held the pillow to her chest. She had seen it a thousand times. Just watch. She was tall and easily straddled the chair and Linus, then sat on his lap, hugged him into the pillow. All her weight on his lap, Linus kicked, threw his bony arms, clawed her. Wilma sank her face in the pillow, heard him squeal through it. Felt his erection and rocked on it, scooted down to get it right, jolted on it. His chair jumped, hit the wall. A framed picture fell. Wilma couldn't breathe through the pillow. But she was going. Linus's jabbing arms descended in jerks. She turned a side of her face to the pillow, eyes crossed in blue lunacy, and drew air, inhaling a stench of tobacco sludge. I've really done something. Wilma's body shook. The television laughed. I've ever really done something now!

She told Fred nothing and Linus remained in the trailer. She turned off his TV, lights and electric heater and, one evening when Fred was out, went in to open all the rear windows. She wanted Linus Webb to get cold.

Every June the Tacitus Volunteer Fire Department held a carnival called, locally, the field days. Itinerant carnival people drove in to set up game stalls and truck-mounted rides. The firemen put up their enormous tent (old yellow light filled it and clouds of cooking smoke) where they sold beer and burgers and steak sandwiches. Jonathan's eyes reflected peaked waves of colored lights. Iron rides roared around him like war machines. Leaving the beer tent, he stood with a can of Coke, fingers thrust into one front pocket, bellbottoms frayed at the heels. His white hair hung to his shoulders. Girls with moist mouths, big eyes and nervous behinds passed as if hunting, themselves hunted by lean, grinning boys.

Then Fred and Wilma Spillit walked by slowly like a pair of large dolls. He backed into a shadow. He realized that he was always ready to do that – step back into darkness like a spy. He'd learned it at home. He hadn't seen Fred and Wilma since that day at their house – Wilma's button eyes coming alive, Fred's weight across his lap as he gave her the shotgun toke, her wet mouth eating and kissing the smoke into his chest. He had quit the bean mill next day. Brian had yelled at him: "I got you that job, you little knucklehead. You don't just quit!" But Jon had quit then spent the next three weeks densely stoned: picturing Wilma, strangling his goose. When his pot ran out he bought more. Then his money ran out. He'd found another job a boy his age could do, forking ensilage at Brinkerhoff's Dairy. He'd saved enough to buy a used bike, a 250 cc Suzuki.

He wasn't licenced to ride at night so he'd walked down from Hart Lot. He lived there with Brian but Brian's Jill might move in soon, then Jon would have to live with his mother – she lived with the man she'd been seeing before the divorce, the same realtor Barb worked for in the village. His mother was in realty too. Houses, occasionally farm lots.

Jon hung around the field days a while, aware of being tall and of looking good but afraid to talk. If he talked to a girl she would cut him with a look or one poisonous word. If he talked to a guy wrong the guy might think Jon was queer – he imagined, as boys that age do, that he probably was. Rejected in advance on every front, Jonathan wandered from the field days on foot as if the whole thing bored him. Cars behind him stretched his long shadow ahead on the gravel and barnyard grass. He crossed the highway and started up the steep S-curve: but now if a car came he stepped off into the shadows of trees, as if practising, and waited till they'd passed. A pointless game but he won every time. No one saw him. Jon felt stronger each time, as if he'd eaten meat.

On the high level road there were fewer cars. It was still early enough that most people who had gone to the field days would be there for some time. There was no moon. The trees wove together above but he knew the road lay straight. Car headlights bloomed ahead. Jon stepped into the weeds to stand behind a tree. The car passed.

A little further up stood a house.

Dark, completely. Chenoweth's house. They were on vacation. Their boy, Eddy, half Jonathan's age, had a dirt bike and they met on their bikes sometimes on the road between their houses, just gooning around, talking bikes? And Eddy had said they were going on vacation, Poconos maybe. Eddy's dad had *Playboys* down cellar. Years of them, foldouts intact, Eddy had said. Jonathan thought how great that would be, to sort through all those foldouts and take what you wanted, instead of pot luck? He could picture every one he'd ever seen.

He went up the driveway and the sky opened out. Stars watched him cross the lawn to check cellar windows flush to the grass on one side, then around the back. Locked, locked. His heart thumped. He could kick one in but he'd rather get in and have people not know. Locked, locked. He wanted in.

On the north end of the house, near one corner, Chenoweth's had hung a wooden door like one side of a crate. He crouched to examine it. He could see the door was meant to swing out so big stuff like a canoe or old bed frame could pass through instead of struggling them down the cellar stairs. It didn't have a lock on the outside. It was locked but he knew it was just a latch inside that lifts a piece of metal from a notch when you squeeze a kind of trigger? Then you push the door out and feed stuff through. The door didn't fit its frame well. Jon could hear that metal piece clink when he jiggled the handle.

He used his penknife, slipping it through the crack at an angle to try to lift that metal piece. He had it a few times but it slipped before he could pull exactly right on the handle. Each little sound was like hammering dishes. The lawn felt enormous, every star in the clear sky a searchlight. Once he was sure he heard hooves thud across the lawn, like the ghost of a horse, and his heart slammed adrenalin through him in a sheet of white electric discharge that blinded him – he ran halfway up a maple out front before he realized he had imagined it. And the scare was so good! He felt full of buzzing helium. Really great scare.

Jonathan went back and used the penknife and finally swung the door out. Blackness solid as a wall absorbed him.

Wilma had always taken in Linus Webb's mail. After murdering him she began to read it. The phone and electric bills frightened her. They were small but had to be paid. Wilma and Fred had a checking account but she wanted Linus's checkbook. He sat in the trailer like a chair with a sheet over it. He stank but she searched and found his checkbook, a box of blank checks, all his cancelled checks in packets clenched in rubber bands. All from Key Bank in Tacitus – her same bank. She found his old phone and electric receipts, his bank statements. He had a savings account passbook, nine hundred dollars in it, the last update three years ago. She found a land deed, receipts for sales of pasture and livestock. He'd had his own well so had not been buying water from the county.

She left all this in the trailer and was careful to stay out of there when Fred was home. Wilma liked being out there after Linus stopped smelling, would sit with him for hours. But the phone and electric had to be paid. She worked out a way to do it. She'd tried copying his signature from cancelled checks but it never looked right so she laid an old check on a blank and traced his name, pressing hard, going through old checks to find appropriate dates and numbers and filling in these impressions. She wrote checks to herself this way as if to cover Linus's needs. When these checks first returned with the statements they were obviously unlike the last few Linus had written but soon they all looked alike. Confidently, Wilma went through all his records and put them in calendar order. She found the name of a doctor and made a note of that. But aside from themselves, his last tenants, the local tax collector, power and phone companies, he'd had no regular contact with anyone in years.

One evening she showed it all to Fred, who grinned but not as if he got the joke. "Where'd you get this stuff?"

"He saved it," Wilma said. "He's like a clock, he just ticks: phone, lectric, phone. Four times a year he files tax. All we got to do is figure how to disconnect his lectric and phone."

Fred watched her. "Why?"

"'Cause he's dead, Sweetie."

Fred's mouth opened like a pocket.

She said, "He's been dead two months."

He stared till his eyes fluttered shut. "How do you know that – that it's two months, exact?"

"'Cause I made him that way."

She held her tight face up, her dim gray eyes wide, waiting for Fred to say anything. He finally sat back and gaped.

"We gotta get the fuck out a here."

Wilma wagged her head. "We could stay thirty years. He's just seventy."

"Seventy-three." Fred went deep with it. Stayed down. Came up. "That's a hunnerd an three."

"All right, so twenty. But twenty years living on him? Know how much we'd save?"

"Yeah, if we don't get caught. You must be crazy as shit. What if someone stops in to see him?"

"Who?" she asked with sweetening all over.

"Fuck should I know!" He threw his arms out. "A person! Some person – oh, Wilma – fucking shit!" He slapped both hands on the table. Stood. "I need a bowl." Pressed his eyeballs into his head. "I need a whole fucking pound!"

But later he went with her to the trailer, took a flashlight. It was January. Fred lifted the sheet. Linus looked leathery and black.

"Just see callin' the cops now," Fred said, "like we forgot check up on him – why didn't you *ask* me about this? We could of done it together. 'Sides, what you kill him with, your breath?"

She told him what she'd done. How it had been. How she spazzed.

They put their movie on later. The projector clattered on the nightstand, near the wall, the picture like a window into another house, the room on fire, the orange people in it burning.

Wilma didn't tell Fred about the savings passbook. She didn't understand interest, only that savings accounts earned it. She felt Fred would try to empty the account and get caught. And she'd heard of money machines: slide in a card and money came out? She wanted one for Linus.

She stopped at Key Bank to cash a Linus check. The teller, who'd been with the branch for years and knew their arrangement, asked, "How old's he now?"

Wilma stared like a doll with painted eyes. "Seventy-three."

The teller's mouth tucked in at one corner. She stamped the check.

On the way out Wilma took a card application from a rack by the door and stood on the bank steps. Main Street lay scuffed with ice. Trees cut black veins on the sky. Black cinders encrusted snow peeled back by the plows. Wilma buttoned up her new warm red coat.

After months of feeling spooky about even mentioning Linus, Fred began making jokes: "What's Uncle Linus bought us this week?" Wilma's slow smile came and went. But Fred stayed out of the trailer: he considered it her place. She went out for an hour each week to do her bookkeeping, pulling the curtains wide for light. Fred did appreciate the extra money. It was not a lot but it doubled what they made on their own and when they weren't making any they were not broke. He could put his feet up.

He and Wilma both minded how scratchy their movie had become. Their camera still worked but the boy at the movie lab had left and Fred didn't trust the commercial processors. They bought color porn magazines and super-8 movies. Talked about hookers downtown. But as they discussed what they might do with one they heard the ice groan with the weight of what they left unsaid. Shrugged and figured it was too much money. So Linus haunted and restrained them, like a stern father, upright in his trailer, who knew the worst they could do.

Otisco Lake lay sparkling blue as a swimming pool full of club soda. Skiers pulled by motorboats cut up the water. There were many people all around the lake but not many thumbing rides from one end to the other. By that hour, most had reached where they had wanted to be.

South of Orion, the east shore road passed few houses. Two girls, walking under baking sun, were trying to get to the causeway swimming spot on the west shore, which you couldn't reach by crossing the causeway itself. They had wasted most of an hour trying that. So they were hitching. One was dynamically pretty, a blue-eyed blond in full make-up that made her skin look burnished. She wore a romper of tight denim shorts with a farmer bib over a red check shirt. The other was plain, sullen, with long brown hair, a lemon top, brown shorts. She wanted to go home. Whenever she went anywhere with her friend, she was the one boys looked at second and both girls understood this.

A car slowed, driven by a couple.

"Wanna smoke a joint?" asked Wilma from the front seat. The blond girl said, "Sure." When Fred turned onto a dirt road she asked, "Is this the right way to go?"

Fred said, "Sure. Comes out the other side then you go north again? Only other way to get over is go around the north end." Which was true. The dirt road bumped down into dense woods; yellow light slashed green leaves. A glade, long grass under locust trees. Old campfires, blackened stones. Fred wheeled suddenly into the glade, tossing the girls in the back. He parked and he and Wilma got out. They hadn't discussed it or signalled each other. Fred pulled the blond girl out of the car. Wilma pulled the other girl. "Let's play a game!" They pulled the yelling girls through bushes.

Another couple drove by, saw the parked car and kept going.

In Linus's trailer, Wilma washed the blond girl's head over the sink and blotted it dry. She held it in both hands. It was light and pale and wore a faint smile. The eyes had turned up as if to see out the window above the sink. Water swishing outside meant Fred was washing the car. Wilma could just hear the car radio nattering. "We're gonna do something," Wilma told the indifferent face. She traced the blue lips with her tongue.

A car motor revved. Wilma blinked. A car ripped across the lawn past the trailer. She dropped the head in the sink. She had cranked the translucent green louvers shut. Someone ran to the trailer and pounded on the door, stiffening her electrically. "Wilma!" Fred yanked the door wide. She stepped back from the sink like a doll whose knees and elbows can't bend. "Somebody saw the fucking car!" Fred yelled. "It's on the radio!"

A white station wagon with a chrome roof rack and coat-hanger aerial – Fred had rushed it behind the house so it couldn't be seen from the road. They painted it with brushes and a can of exterior oil base the same brown color as the house, a disguise that would last long enough for them to ditch the car after dark. It could not be traced to them easily. Fred had swapped his yellow sedan for it at Rick's Auto-body but hadn't yet registered the car, had just put his old plate on it and the registration sticker from his yellow sedan. Rick sold him an inspection sticker for an ounce. Fred and Wilma hadn't been working, hadn't been parking it in anybody's lot. Still, Fred tore off the chrome rack, stickers and plate.

He told Wilma this was the perfect time to get rid of Linus – in the car. Wilma said, "How will they explain a old man in a car when they find it? They'll look for old men around here. The people at the bank know Linus is old." Linus stayed in the trailer. Wilma put the blond girl's head in a fridge down cellar.

That evening they drove to Hogsback Ledge, where a dump of rusted cans, bald tires, cracked porcelain sinks and bottles laid a broad fan across the face of a hill. They pushed the car over to one side: it rolled almost silently over grass and weeds to plunge through a dark wall of trees at the bottom. A stream down there. The car hit rock. They walked home, stepping off the road to avoid headlights.

Jonathan Kerner's Honda 750 four-stroke was black with gold trim. So was his helmet and so was the riding outfit that coated him like skin, more costume than clothing, threatening and effeminate, right to the mid-calf boots and gloves like gauntlets. Nineteen years of age now and out of high school, Jon rolled into the annual field days like a flashy outlaw: past Tacitus Lanes and a car wash; past the DPW quonset hut and its conical heaps of gravel and sand; past young men and women in shit-stain camo and denim and billed caps worn backward, with CARRIER and ARCTIC CAT stitched above the bills? Growling in first gear, Jonathan entered the congestion of booths, food stalls and iron rides crowned by the struts and lights of a ferris wheel that lifted hanging seats up high then let them down and away like water. Below black goggles, the pout of his lower lip needed only a gold ring piercing the flesh to make him terrific against his background of soda can pull tabs, paper tickets, stamped-flat popcorn dotting the ground. He was silly and perfect. Seeing him made you want to have sex but maybe not with him.

"The King!" cried a boy like a drunken hippopotamus. "The King *lives!*" He threw his arms wide. Kids laughed.

Jon rode past, minding but seeing through them. Bet I've done things you haven't – done things you wouldn't *know* how to do.

Sawhorses blocked his way. Jon squeezed the brakes and put out a thin leg boled at the knee like a colt's to take the weight of the bike. On a wire stretched between two poles firemen had hung a fat ball droopy as an udder: a loop let the ball slide along the wire. Below, in two teams of six, laughing drunken firemen held hoses. "Stan clear everbuddy!" the PA barked. "This is Loki versus Signal Falls." Each hose gushed violent water. The hissing streams fought the ball back and forth along the wire. Jon looked through the crowd into the smoky tent in which men fried steak and sausages and peppers, stuffed ragged buns, ladled on tomato sauce. Above the tent and fire hall and the plateau of Hart Lot hung a few early stars occluded by thunderheads building up like brains.

The yelling firemen leaned back, clutching hoses. People on the sidelines cheered. The cheering peaked as the ball slid to one end of the wire and the white water pushing it cascaded onto the losers. "Winners are Loki!" barked the PA. "Loki Volunteer Fire Department, ladies an gentlemen!" Final water spattered the pavement. The soaked losers shook fists, laughing at the winners. Jonathan rolled through a gap in the sawhorses, hissed through the waterball puddle. A fireman yelled: "Hey!" then yelled at one of the town cops: "See what he's doin' – he can't do that!" Jon stopped, balanced on the square toe box of a boot. He and the town cop looked at each other like an android observing an overdressed man (necktie, stetson) but the cop waved him through and Jonathan flatulently roared out of town.

He boomed up Hart Lot Road. His headlight hurried shadows through the trees. At the Y-intersection he veered east. The trees fell away. South would take him to Brian's farm. Jill was there alone, Brian having gone to Marietta to look at brood sows. Jon knew he shouldn't stop to see Jill. She was pretty and she had big tits. Also, she would let him talk – Jon might talk too much.

Corn stood guard along the road then the ground sloped to the village. In his handlebar mirrors the carnival lights and ferris wheel shivered. He wanted to go see Jill. He wanted to break into a house. He wondered if he had an actual chance with Jill. It was like breaking in, that tight lightness in his chest, when he thought about Jill. When he broke into Chenoweth's and found those *Playboys* down cellar, Jon had taken five foldouts, in his opinion the best. One had looked like Jill. (Her name was Rita and she was supposed to be Spanish but still.) Jon had kept it. Perfect condition. The older ones were better. Now there was *Hustler* and harder-core stuff in Syracuse that showed everything? But they didn't have the charm. Those women couldn't smile right, their eyes didn't smoke.

But Jill. The motorcycle roar whipped behind him and the wind got into his mouth. If he could just bang Jill once! He leaned over the ovoid gas tank and pushed the bike to eighty before easing off, the pipes barking at his heels. He took the curve onto Baylor Road at forty-five degrees, heeled over like a sailboat, then righted and shifted down, erect in the saddle, coasting between two wood lots. In a clearing on his right stood a black square two-story house, beside it the black rectangle of a trailer. Both might have been abandoned but an old van sat in the driveway, red reflectors catching his light. He saw the place with a sense of loss. Out one night when he was nine or ten, Jonathan had snuck up, had seen an old farmer and his wife watching Red Skelton. There had been a crescent moon. Jon glanced up for any sign of moonlight. It should have been full, had been just off the full other night but lay behind the brainy thunderheads piling up, lightning flickering within.

The mailbox read: LINUS WEBB. He wondered if that had been the old man's name. It sounded like a minister or like a sea captain with a long white beard or a farmer who had plowed with a horse.

He could keep going on Baylor (he passed between the concrete guardrails denoting a stream, one of dozens that poured rain and snow melt off the plateau) and cut west on Hogsback to hook up with Hart Lot Road again, then cut north to the farm. But he shouldn't go there. Goddamn Jill! He swung a tight U-turn and revved passed the dark house and trailer – recalling now those people, that Fred and Wilma and the stupid thing he'd nearly done there. They must have moved out long time ago. The place looked dead-empty, not even worth breaking into. It might storm soon anyway: he should be in the village when it did. He worked at The Lafayette House, mornings doing laundry from the guest rooms and helping in the kitchen afternoons. He might be a cook maybe. Jon had a room there, kept his bike out back. He should go there, do a bowl and go through his foldouts? He had one like that Wilma, kind of stupid-looking? He could whack on it.

Below the high road the village lay simplified by distance, the field days foremost, a thick constellation of colored lights, the ferris wheel churning it like a propeller. In the east Syracuse was a pillow of soft light. Thunder through the motorcycle roar made Jon glance behind. Quick filaments lit the thunderheads inside. He might not make the village. Might get soaked. He headed for Brian's.

Somewhere in a cellar a refrigerator whammed and shuddered on. A boy tied to a chair in one room of that cellar woke but saw nothing. It was black down there. He had been sunk in sleep so empty of thought that his sudden awareness of life going on, and that it was his own life, ached like the death of a loved one. He had been a week in that cellar. He was so used up he didn't know his name, had no more thought in his mind now than he had had while asleep, only the sense of his physical self and what his deprived senses conveyed in meaningless automatic sequence to his brain. He had gone under language and merely knew what he knew. He was alone. He no longer wept. He had broken his prayers to little pieces of useless print. He'd stopped beating the back of his head on the wall – they had moved his chair away from the wall so he wouldn't hurt himself and that had made him laugh till he was sick in his lap. Just yellow like mucus. They had given him nothing to eat and only water to drink. Then the man had washed him down with a garden hose then had thought of another way to wash him down then had made him drink it. He had thought: At least let me drown! As indifferent to death as he would have been, out in the world, to the fall of a leaf. He indifferently remembered that now. He was indifferent to the belt that squeezed his waist and had to be tightened each day to adjust for the weight he had lost; to the shredded black stockings tied onto the belt; to a wig so moldy it smelled like feet; to the ache in his rectum and the slow blood seepage that more than once had glued him to the chair – indifferent even to the sounds the man and woman made upstairs as they watched TV or ate food or streamed into the toilet. The boy had renounced the world. Nothing hurt him anymore. Nothing could. He could have done again what they had made him do the first night – it wouldn't matter at all. He had offered to, they wouldn't have to tie his hands or anything. My, you *are* a little pervert, that nude woman told him. And with that he had given up language, had begun to disconnect from the world.

The refrigerator in one corner of the cellar shuddered off. That refrigerator was his clock. The woman needed him every nine or ten refrigerators. The man could wait about twelve. The lights would blare; in mirrors he would see himself in his chair like one of those big plastic girl dolls. The woman would come down naked, eyes glazed, smoking or maybe chewing something she had been eating, and would start saying lines from some play she had written for herself. Well, it looks like you'll just *have* to sit there, don't it! As if she had given up language too but had yet to learn to do without the actual words. The boy was way ahead of her. It struck him how far ahead of her he'd already gone.

Shadows spidered through trees on the lane into Brian's farm. Jill had the house lights off though the safety lights glowed in the barn. He smelled sour pigs and let the bike roll to a stop, took the weight of the bike on one leg and switched it off. He pried up his helmet as if pulling off his head. It popped out wearing the pale flossy hair but cut back for a more punk look. Not many guys in central New York were doing that but Jon was right on it. He clawed the goggles down around his neck, set his black and gold helmet on the black and gold gas tank and pulled his fingers one at a time from his black and gold gloves. His hands were white as school paste.

He popped his ears with his fingers, heard thunder, heard corn crackle as it grew, scratchy in the husks. Backed the bike onto its stand and went through the open garage to the screen door. Pulling it wide made the spring groan like piano wire. He felt in, flipped on the light. Above the kitchen table a fluorescent ring in the ceiling jumped, jumped on. Black smiles leaned behind hanging cups, angles struck black from behind the cupboards.

Jill, coming from the den where his father used to paint, said, "You caught me asleep."

She wore khaki cutoffs, a white buttondown shirt that had lost its sleeves. Her shiny hair was straight and black with bangs. Her eyes were cornflower blue. Her breasts and bottom were heavy but she was narrow in the waist and looked strong enough to dropkick Jonathan over the barn. Her feet were bare. "Time is it?" But looked for herself: near ten. Pulling a hair clip loose, she held it in her teeth as she shook out her straight black hair to gather and clip it again. "I was so knocked out after supper." She ran tap water, one finger in the flow, filled a glass when it ran cold. "There's beer in the fridge."

"Where's Brian?"

Jill held a finger up, drinking, throat bobbing. Dashed out the last gulp.

"Went to Marietta, look at a brood sow – he said he told you, other day. Invited you along. Should be back soon. Want a beer?" Jill smiled handsomely. "I'll get you a glass."

"I don't want one. How you been?" He leaned on the table, looking in his riding outfit like a circus performer, perhaps out of work.

"I'm *fine*." As if he had asked three times. She stood in refrigerator steam, twisted off the cap, drank. "You just riding around?"

Jon shrugged. "Yeah, mostly – hey, thought that was mine."

"Thought you didn't want one."

"I didn't want a glass."

With her shirt tail Jill wiped the bottle, gave it to him.

"Checked out the field days." Jon's face lit up. "Wanna ride down with me on my bike?"

She grabbed her own beer from the fridge and shut the door. She laughed without a sound, just the shape of her mouth. "Got a helmet I can wear?"

"No – you can wear mine."

"Thanks. I'll pass. Brian and me prob'ly go down Saturday – tomorrow." She angled a hip against the table, staring at the floor but not as if she saw it. "He should be back soon."

He set his weight more on one leg, waiting.

Jill glanced at him, cut her eyes away.

"You look nice," he told her, his ears full of surf, his tight chest fizzing.

Jill turned away.

"Jill, I'm breaking into houses again."

As he said this he knew she'd been waiting to hear it. He'd told her about Cheno-weth's, had even shown her Spanish Rita with the sad brown eyes, pale skin, stiff black lace framing her luscious body, a tiara in her ebony hair. She the kind a girl you wanna sleep with? Jon had squirmed. I don't know, I don't think I could. Shouldn't be afraid a girls, Jon. They just want guys to like 'em. They don't mind if you're nervous, shows you care about being turned down. But he never believed it. He'd sworn Jill to secrecy that time and again last year, when he broke into two other houses. Because he had confessed to Jill, and believed he was in love with her or something, he considered her the only one who could help him past the risk and make him stop.

The fluorescent ring flung hard light into the dark living room. Jill stood staring into the room, legs together, tipping the beer into herself. Jonathan went past her, holding his beer by the neck, and stopped at the fieldstone fireplace. He set the bottle on the mantel.

"I don't even take things, Jill. Like I get inside and try to *think* of things to take." He smacked the bottle off the mantel but caught it before it could fly and sat with it on the couch, the bottle upright on his crotch. Jon gazed as if reading the label. "It's the dark, I guess. But other people's things too – I mean, all their furniture just sitting there? Refrigerator humming? Most a those people never knew I broke in. I'd been in their bedrooms? Seen their underwear? I never used a flashlight, you get like a cat, you can see in the dark. There's lots a light, silvery dark." One of his legs started jigging. "It's crazy but when I'm inside it's like I'm finally doing the one thing I really want to do – like Dad must of felt when he started a painting? Like you know everything, you know exactly what time it is and where you are and there's no God and if there is it's you." His leg jigged up and down faster. He saw Jill sitting on the arm of the couch, just her dark shape with the kitchen light behind it. "Two weeks ago, I was in the village, up in this big end room? Bedroom with a slant ceiling? Had my back to this hall and this light moved through. Like my shadow's on the wall in front a me? Car lights – someone's pulling into the driveway, just coming home. So I run for the stairs and this is pure rush, pure adrenalin rush. Like everything's carpeted wall to wall so it doesn't make a sound. It's like running in a dream. Stairs go down an turn an down an turn? Damn living room's full a light? I hear voices out there and then the light's out: they're on their way in. It's like I turned into some kind a gas, like I'm all through that house like gas in every corner. I couldn't . . ." Here Jon groped for the right word: "*Get* myself back into just one person and get out. I forgot how I got in." He set his head back, leg jigging fast, shut his eyes. "It was a car turning around. They pulled in to back out. You know, no lights in the house so they pick that one. Turn around in." He ground his head into the back of the couch and flexed both legs straight, breathing through his mouth.

Jill left the room. The fluorescent ring in the kitchen wheeled her shadow across the floor. She stood at the casements above the sink, watching for Brian's truck. Jonathan thought he heard calliope music.

She said: "You have to see someone."

"Jill, I can't help it."

"Then you have to see someone. You can't just keep doing this."

"I haven't told you about the other yet."

Jill unclipped her hair, angrily pulled it tighter, clipped it again.

Jon waited, sly. Settled into the couch. His leg started jigging but stopped when he looked at it. He started tapping his knee with the beer bottle held by the neck. "I went up – this is just the other night? – up from the football field and the pines? Into this back yard slopes up to one a those houses on Highland? One for sale. So I'm taping this cellar window with masking tape before I break it and suddenly there's this face in the window? This old guy with scotty-dog whiskers, like someone's uncle in a movie? Jumping at the window, yelling right at me. I jump back and start running down into those pines and I realize, just as I get off running, that it wasn't a man, it was a dog, jumping up, barking at the window."

"You really have to see someone," Jill said. "It's just gonna go on, it's like Peeping Toms."

He said, "I guess."

"You guess!" She clamped her arms across her chest.

Jonathan shrugged. His leg started jigging but he made it swing idly back and forth. "Anyways, I run down through the pines." (Glanced at her to see if it was okay.) "Like this dog is after me. It's locked in that cellar but like I *think* it's after me. I keep running and I'm running into trees and getting whipped, almost stabbed where them little lower branches all get broken off? So I'm finally out a that and I'm way the hell over behind the school. I come out around front and go along the tennis courts and there's this water all over in front a the school. Then I hear people running. I see two of 'em off in a field. They'd been opening up fire hydrants. Been doing it all week and the cops and fireman are after 'em? No way I'm following them so I cross into that big weed lot, they never mow it, it's like meadow. And just then this light sweeps in. I drop flat – I just lay flat, like Jesus, just this once, I'll never ever do it again!"

"You *want* to get caught!" Jill yelled from the kitchen. "That's what this is about. You keep pushing it. You want that rush 'cause getting caught's gonna be the best rush!" She glared through the casements. "Will you please see someone, please – if I set it up?"

"Jill, I won't do it again." (Like maybe if she banged him?)

"Yeah, right." She crossed to the phone.

He sat up. "Who you calling?"

"Your sister."

Jon stood. "You're calling *Barb*?"

"I'm not gonna be the only one who knows about this anymore."

"You can't fuckin' call Barb!"

"Want me tell your brother instead? – and watch your mouth."

Jonathan froze. He had confided in her: that was like a holy act. How could she betray him? How could she betray him to *Barb*, his prim sister in her bifocal glasses and her pony tail down to her tight-together ass? And Brian no better. Jon had run into both of them couple weeks ago in Barb's realty office and she, at her desk, glancing over the bifocal rims at his riding outfit: Jon, you can't go around in stuff like that, people will laugh and point. And Brian, in his Amish farmer clothes, toothpick jutting from his lip: You mean like wearing mom's underwear then he has an accident and at the hospital they say he got his mom's underwear on? Jon stopped worryin' about that long time ago. And Jon: Hey, fuck you, you know? His empty beer bottle hit the floor and rolled as he crossed toward Jill. She sat leafing through the little book on the desk where she did her telephoning. It felt wrong that Jill had to look it up. She knew Barb's numbers. Jonathan felt she didn't really mean to call but he was out the screen door anyway, heels hitting concrete, then on his bike, revving it, stuffing his head into his helmet. Working his hands into his gloves a finger at a time, adjusting his goggles. Jill didn't come out. Peeling away sprayed the garage with dirt and gravel. He nearly lost the bike then fishtailed down the lane with his light off.

Somebody called. Fred didn't like it. "Nobody ever calls here."

"It was just a wrong number," said Wilma, turning the page of a dog-eared paperback called *Bitch of Buchenwald*. The cover showed a startled blond tied to a stone bier, her face muffled by the cleft of an ugly Gestapo woman. Wilma liked reading it anyway but tonight they were going to use up the boy down cellar, take him past the point and this time no hurry.

"I don't like he called me *Fred*."

"There's lots a people named Fred." She hadn't even heard the phone ring or Fred talking downstairs. Just a wrong number. She didn't like being bothered. She turned a page, skimming plot. She was feeling like getting to it. "You should get undressed."

He stood in jeans, sneakers, T-shirt, smoking as if he might eat the whole pack. Wilma had a cigarette going but hers gave up a steady ribbon of smoke. She wore her red negligee, sat with legs crossed. She would make this her ritual: to sit reading, smoking in the nice red negligee Linus had bought her, then go take one past the point, use it up.

After that she would rock back and forth, go into herself, empty her mind. She didn't care for people. She knew no one but Fred and he was not a person, he was just *there*, agreeable and slow, a body that liked to do what Wilma's body like to do.

She saw herself as a body that did things to other bodies, saw the world as a place where bodies moved around. Bodies could give you this big deep pleasure in the gut but after that they were nothing. Just dead. They were dead – dead while she could soar.

Wilma turned a page and looked at Fred. It wasn't the same with Fred. He didn't understand putting things off. Fred rammed. Smoked pot, ate, watched TV – worried too much. Like that wrong number, someone calling Ned or Ed.

The room light dimmed. Her refrigerator rumbled down cellar, going on.

She said, "If it'll make you feel better load the gun tonight."

Smoking the filter made Fred Spillit cough into his fist. He coughs way too much anymore. His face purpled. She wondered what exactly she would do if he started to die. I don't really need him anymore. She had found and given the boy a ride, let him feel her up in the car. You wanna get high? I got some great reefer home. She marked her page.

"You should get undressed. I'll load the gun."

Fred nodded, coughing on his fist.

The boy heard the door rattle. Light struck down the stairs. She had gone almost twelve refrigerators. One of his eyes was permanently shut.

Jonathan thundered on the turnpike through a winking red light and up to the top of the highest hill in Onondaga County as if, on reaching the top, he might wing out into empty space and die laughing and they would all sit around the kitchen table not saying anything and Jill would be the first to get up and go outside to hang herself. But the hill steeped over and sank toward a swamp. Jon turned south. He knew where he was going and resented it. It's because there's other people in the world, he thought bitterly. Like those kids opening hydrants – because of them he could not break into a village house tonight.

He had been riding for an hour when he turned onto Baylor Road toward Linus Webb's house, that horny feeling hitting his chest and stomach. He could almost not sit his bike. He had to be on his feet, cutting through a lawn toward a house growing larger to his eyes, becoming the wall meant to frustrate him. But he would get in. He always did. In fact the breaking-in was merely an effect of the far greater pleasure of approach. Had someone told him: This time you're gonna get caught! he would have curled his lip. It was none of their business. Even the people whose homes he'd broken into had no legitimate gripe. It was just a pane of glass. But more important than any of that was the house he was heading for, his first house – first because he had *not* broken into it. Tonight he would close that circle, one so wide it felt like the orbit of a moon.

He straddle-walked the bike onto a tractor path, let his eyes adjust, took off his helmet and goggles. He pinched his nose to pop both ears then crunched into the woods, feeling ahead with gloved hands. The thunderheads had not rained, had moved along, and the full moon showed the scratchy lawn and the angular house. His heart thudded. He passed where the barn had stood, the concrete slab overgrown, cracked by weeds, freeze and thaw. Stubble crackled under his boots, all that was left of the lawn. Halting, he looked up. The full moon glowed within a misty ring.

Jon didn't have masking tape; he'd dropped it behind that house, other night. This far from the village he didn't care about noise. There were two cellar windows in back: he would kick out one pane, unlock the latch (if it even *was* locked) and climb through. Leave by the front door. The trailer bothered him. He walked to it, watching the grass for things he might kick or trip on. Moonlight hung a silver curl on the trailer door. Combination lock. The trailer was just for storage. And that van out front – by moonlight he saw one wheel on a red jack, a tire leaning on the front fender?

There might be people home. There was that chance. The best way to close his private circle, make it shine like the ring enclosing the moon, might be to up and leave. This house could remain unviolated. Holy. (Something.) Going back to his bike could be bittersweet. Complete the orbit, he thought. He stood behind the house, recalling that farmer and his wife watching TV, his square boot toes facing one cellar window. The moon burned directly overhead. Shadow hugged the house low. He should *not* break into this house, should summon the will to put an end to this! But the will to ruin what he knew to be right held Jon:

because I want in
but I can't get in
because I'm not good enough
I try to be good enough
and I get in
but I have to get out
because I'm not good enough
so I try to be good enough
because I want *in*
so Jonathan kicked in the window.

Hot light shot out. He backed off, bent to look. He did not understand what he saw.

Beyond the jagged teeth of black-painted glass, surrounding the scene like a cartoon explosion, two people became three, one being the meat in a standing sandwich. Cracked flaking mirrors multiplied a big man striving in some kid's rump. Pressed up to the kid was a woman pulling on a rope that looped a pulley and tightened to a noose around the kid's neck. One of his eyes was shut but the other looked crossed. His tongue was out: all this like a snapshot before the glass clattered. Then the grunting woman and man groped out of their mutual stupor to look for the cause of the noise.

Wilma saw the pale face and white hair as if projected on what she knew to be glass painted black. She knew Jon right off. The splintered glass snapped the truth into her. She let go the rope. Fred flopped out of the hanging boy. The boy dropped to hands and knees, gasping like a fish. Jon lunged to one side, slipped on damp grass, fell flat and scrambled away. Wilma's eyes cast around. Fred had the gun, a revolver. Naked, Wilma took the cellar steps three at a time. Reaching for the gun, she yelled: "Stay here – clean it up!" Fred slipped, holding the gun by the barrel. Wilma gripped the handle. A hammer slammed. Red slush backed out of Fred's head. He broke that step he should of fixed. It was what she believed as Fred fell. Wilma ran out through the house.

Jon heard the front door bang wide. He could hide in the woods across the road but Wilma (he knew it was her) ran fast, naked with a gun raised as if she meant to throw it. The roadside brush looked thorny. Jon might snag. The creek would let him into the woods.

Wilma fired into the next township then ran like a horse down the road. Concrete guardrails isolated the creek – vaulting one, Jon banged his knee. The jolt turned him, dropped him in the water. Another shot went high.

After rainstorms all week the water surged and flexed. Jon's riding outfit drugged him. He slid on scummy stones, thrashing, scattering moonlight flakes. Through the white noise he heard footfalls thud, looked back. A fringe of leaves framed Wilma. The flow added Jon to a dam of tires and branches. Blocking the muzzle flash with one hand, Wilma fired. The strobe caught Jon's bleached face. She fired again then leaped the guardrail.

Clawing over the dam, Jonathan was carried downstream so fast he caught at anything to stop himself. Here the creek bed was flat rock, slick, swept clear. He hung flat out by his fingers, nose just above the flow. Water plumped his cheeks, fought down his throat. He knew where he was, knew the flat rock preceded that fifty-foot drop. Barb and Brian had pulled him out. He hung in the swollen creek trying to get air past the water in his mouth. He wished hard for Wilma to think he had already slipped away, fallen, died. Or that police would arrive soon – she ought to give up, go back to the house, go away from *him*.

Jon hung on but couldn't breathe. If he dunked his head and coughed hard then flung his head up he might get air.

He did. But it made a noise like yelling.

Wilma stood in the water, head and shoulders dark against the moonlit concrete. She skidded on the slick stone, the gun waving up once. Holding on, Jon's chin met the water like the prow of a boat. Wilma stepped on his hand – she fired down. Lead cracked rock. And Jon let go, thought fuck it. Wilma fell on him, grabbed his hair. A perfectly round steel tunnel kissed his forehead. He was glad he would be shot. He would not have to go to the cellar. He told his mother he was sorry. That covered everything. But when Wilma finally fired she hit the first blank. She didn't know she had shot Fred back in the cellar and had thought she had one more left. She triggered again then hit with the gun. Jon clawed soft flesh. The gun hit harder. They slid and Wilma slid under Jon. The creek carried them like sticks into open air.

Dark sweet lightness. Wilma's soaked hair in his fists. Rock stopped them, stopped, stopped them on the steps of the waterfall – like smashing through the floors of a flooded house.

And floated in whirling black water, the roaring falls above, behind, still present but past, still strong. He let the hair go, felt down. Here the shallow water let him move on all fours through its wan spiral, the water as if itself dazed. The falls roared. Jon crawled onto gravel to lay in cool air and fine mist.

He woke before morning light found him. Falling water thundered within a purple darkness suggesting depth, sheer walls that held sound in a cup.

When he sat up a pain snapped on in his left leg. That leg lay in water. He turned the leg from the hip. The pain snapped. It was pain he could bear but still pain. He made himself sit up. Each move spoke a new pain, naming his muscles, bones, other limbs. He braced on his arms.

He sat letting the light come up from lavender to palest gray. The waterfall was not what he had pictured last night in the dark nor what he remembered. It had aged. Great blocks had come down to build a pile, with no more than twenty feet between the sheer curl coming off the top and the first of many steps down. Water exploded on the blocks.

It had been prettier before. Now it was old and violent.

The waterfall had scoured a pool from which a limestone shelf extended, littered with rubble and boulders. Among the rubble lay a pale shape, not solid. It might have been one of Brian's hogs that had nosed under a fence then found a bad end. Wilma lay on the stone shelf, in water just inches deep. A rip in the leg of Jon's outfit meant more to him: the rip showed a long pink gash from thigh to shin. Not deep. It had lain in cold water overnight, had stopped bleeding without forming a scab. Did not bleed now as he moved but burned. When he made to touch it he saw that two right-hand fingers were swollen and blue. They had no feeling while one knee, a shoulder, a rack of ribs were solid aches.

But on hands and one knee he crawled over to Wilma. He wanted to see. She lay naked and no one was watching.

She lay face down. Pulses of water current jostled the flesh of her buttocks. He raised her head from the water by its hair. The head fell open, nearly in half. Jon looked and looked but there was no brain inside. Just a scoured reddish-blue vessel. A plug of like cooked egg where the neck joined but the whole brain was gone. He let the head down into the water.

Jonathan gazed downstream, struggled briefly with an urge to go that way and look for Wilma's brain – he felt that he *should* look for it. But what he had to do was get out somehow. He felt he knew the way. He and Barb and Brian had found a deer path, steeply turned. He began: clutching thin trees, bracing himself on boulders, crawling on his belly.

His pain made him old, like the waterfall. But he raised himself out of the deepness the falls had carved and stood at the edge of the road.

The sky had that frail gray light of early-morning overcast. The old brown house stood open, the green trailer dark beside it, the lame van out front. By the mailbox stood a boy wearing shreds of a lady's black stockings – that kid. So the man (Fred, it must have been) had run off. A dirty wig sat on the boy's head. He wore a black evening glove and was holding another. Red speckles showed about his genitals where he'd been shaved. He was like a foldout girl but one who had passed through fire then acid then lime.

Jon limped across the road. The boy watched with one eye. His other eyelid drooped and he was splashed all down one side with blood as if someone beside him had exploded. Except where the evening glove had been: that arm was clean.

Jon didn't know what to say, his head as empty as Wilma's, on that ledge.

"I gotta find my mom," the boy said, earnestly reinventing language.

Jon pointed. "My bike's off that way."

The boy stood still.

Jon took him by the cleaner hand and walked him down the road to the tractor path. No cars happened by. Jon would have loaned the boy something to wear but all he had was his helmet so he loaned him that. Threw that filthy wig down. Let him sit forward on the saddle – Jon was tall enough to reach all right. He turned the key in the ignition, reversed the big bike slowly onto Baylor, put up his goggles and drove to the village then up Litton to a small police station – entering like an appari-tion to the person on duty, or like maybe two apparitions for the price of one? ✿

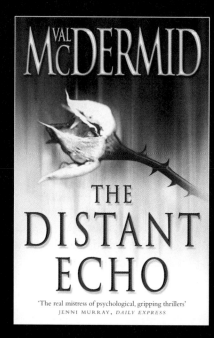

THE
DISTANT
ECHO

'The real mistress of psychological, gripping thrillers'
JENNI MURRAY, *DAILY EXPRESS*

Val McDermind is the author of *Killing the Shadows*; *A Place of Execution*; the Tony Hill novels *The Last Temptation*, *The Wire in the Blood*, *The Mermaids Singing*; the Kate Brannigan novels *Star Struck*, *Blue Genes*, *Clean Break*, *Crack Down*, *Kick Back*, *Dead Beat*; the Lindsay Gordon novels *Booked for Murder*, *Union Jack*, *Final Edition*, *Common Murder*, *Report for Murder*; and the nonfiction book *A Suitable Job for a Woman*.

The hardback edition of *The Distant Echo* is published in May 2003. ISBN 0 00 714282 X

HarperCollins*Publishers*
77–85 Fulham Palace Road, London W6 8JB
www.fireandwater.com

November 2003, St Andrews, Scotland

He always liked the cemetery at dawn. Not because daybreak offered any promise of a fresh beginning, but because it was too early for there to be anyone else around. Even in the dead of winter, when the pale light was so late in coming, he could guarantee solitude. No prying eyes to wonder who he was and why he was there, head bowed before that one particular grave. No nosy parkers to question his right to be there.

It had been a long and troublesome journey to reach this destination. But he was very good at uncovering information. Obsessive, some might say. He preferred persistent. He'd learned how to trawl official and unofficial sources, and eventually, after months of searching, he'd found the answers he'd been looking for. Unsatisfactory as they'd been, they had at least provided him with this marker. For some people, a grave represented an ending. Not for him. He saw it as a beginning. Of sorts.

He'd always known it wouldn't be sufficient in itself. So he'd waited, hoping for a sign to show him the way forward. And it had finally come. As the sky changed its colour from the outside to the inside of a mussel shell, he reached into his pocket and unfolded the clipping he'd taken from the local paper.

FIFE POLICE IN COLD CASES REVIEW

Unsolved murders in Fife going back as far as thirty years are to be re-examined in a full-scale cold case review, police announced this week.

Chief Constable Sam Haig said that new forensic breakthroughs meant that cases which had lain dormant for many years could now be reopened with some hope of success. Old evidence which has lain in police property stores for decades will be the subject of such methods as DNA analysis to see whether fresh progress can be made.

Assistant Chief Constable (Crime) James Lawson will head the review. He told the Courier, "Murder files are never closed. We owe it to the victims and their families to keep working the cases.

"In some instances, we had a strong suspect at the time, though we didn't have enough evidence to tie them to the crime. But with modern forensic techniques, a single hair, a bloodstain or a trace of semen could give us all we need to obtain a conviction. There have been several recent instances in England of cases being successfully prosecuted after twenty years or more.

"A team of senior detectives will now make these cases their number one priority."

ACC Lawson was unwilling to reveal which specific cases will be top of the list for his detectives.

But among them must surely be the tragic murder of local teenager Rosie Duff.

The 19-year-old from Strathkinness was raped, stabbed and left for dead on Hallow Hill almost 25 years ago. No one was ever arrested in connection with her brutal murder.

Her brother Brian, 46, who still lives in the family home, Caber-feidh Cottage, and works at the paper mill in Guardbridge, said last night, "We have never given up hope that Rosie's killer would one day face justice. There were suspects at the time, but the police were never able to find enough evidence to nail them.

"Sadly, my parents went to their grave not knowing who did this terrible thing to Rosie. But perhaps now we'll get the answer they deserved."

He could recite the article by heart, but he still liked to look at it. It was a talisman, reminding him that his life was no longer aimless. For so long, he'd wanted someone to blame. He'd hardly dared hope for revenge. But now, at long last, vengeance might possibly be his.

1978, St Andrews, Scotland

Four in the morning, the dead of December. Four bleary outlines wavered in the snow flurries that drifted at the beck and call of the snell north-easterly wind whipping across the North Sea from the Urals. The eight stumbling feet of the self-styled Laddies fi' Kirkcaldy traced the familiar path of their short cut over Hallow Hill to Fife Park, the most modern of the halls of residence attached to St Andrews University, where their perpetually unmade beds yawned a welcome, lolling tongues of sheets and blankets trailing to the floors.

The conversation staggered along lines as habitual as their route. "I'm telling you, Bowie is the king," Sigmund Malkiewicz slurred loudly, his normally impassive face loosened with drink. A few steps behind him, Alex Gilbey yanked the hood of his parka closer to his face and giggled inwardly as he silently mouthed the reply he knew would come.

"Bollocks," said Davey Kerr.

"Bowie's just a big jessie. Pink Floyd can run rings round Bowie any day of the week. *Dark Side of the Moon*, that's an epic. Bowie's done nothing to touch that." His long dark curls were loosening under the weight of melted snowflakes and he pushed them back impatiently from his waif-like face.

And they were off. Like wizards casting combative spells at each other, Sigmund and Davey threw song titles, lyrics and guitar riffs back and forth in the ritual dance of an argument they'd been having for the past six or seven years. It didn't matter that, these days, the music rattling the windows of their student rooms was more likely to come from the Clash, the Jam or the Skids. Even their nicknames spoke of their early passions. From the very first afternoon they'd congregated in Alex's bedroom after school to listen to his purchase of *Ziggy Stardust and the Spiders from Mars*, it had been inevitable that the charismatic Sigmund would be Ziggy, the leper messiah, for eternity. And the others would have to settle for being the Spiders. Alex had become Gilly, in spite of his protestations that it was a jessie nickname for someone who aspired to the burly build of a rugby player. But there was no arguing with the accident of his surname. And none of them had a moment's doubt about the appropriateness of christening the fourth member of their quartet Weird. Because Tom Mackie was weird, make no mistake about it. The tallest in their year, his long gangling limbs even looked like a mutation, matching a personality that delighted in being perverse.

That left Davey, loyal to the cause of the Floyd, steadfastly refusing to accept any nickname from the Bowie canon. For a while, he'd been known half-heartedly as Pink, but from the first time they'd all heard 'Shine On, You Crazy Diamond' there had been no further debate; Davey was a crazy diamond, right enough, flashing fire in unpredictable directions, edgy and uncomfortable out of the right setting. Diamond soon became Mondo, and Mondo Davey Kerr had remained through the remaining year of high school and on to university.

Alex shook his head in quiet amazement. Even through the blur of far too much beer, he wondered at the glue that had held the four of them fast all those years. The very thought provoked a warm glow that kept the vicious cold at bay as he tripped over a raised root smothered under the soft blanket of snow. "Bugger," he grumbled, cannoning into Weird, who gave him a friendly shove that sent Alex sprawling. Flailing to keep his balance, he let his momentum carry him forward and stumbled up the short slope, suddenly exhilarated with the feel of the snow against his flushed skin. As he reached the summit, he hit an unexpected dip that pulled the feet from under him. Alex found himself crashing head over heels to the ground.

His fall was broken by something soft. Alex struggled to sit up, pushing against whatever it was he had landed on. Spluttering snow, he wiped his eyes with his tingling fingers, breathing hard through his nose in a bid to clear it of the freezing melt. He glanced around to see what had cushioned his landing just as the heads of his three companions appeared on the hillside to gloat over his farcical calamity.

Even in the eerie dimness of snow light, he could see that the bulwark against his fall was no botanical feature. The outline of a human form was unmistakable. The heavy white flakes began to melt as soon as they landed, allowing Alex to see it was a woman, the wet tendrils of her dark hair spread against the snow in Medusa locks. Her skirt was pushed up to her waist, her knee-length black boots looking all the more incongruous against her pale legs. Strange dark patches stained her flesh and the pale blouse that clung to her chest. Alex stared uncomprehendingly for a long moment, then he looked at his hands and saw the same darkness contaminating his own skin.

Blood. The realization dawned at the same instant that the snow in his ears melted and allowed him to hear the faint but stertorous wheeze of her breath.

"Jesus Christ," Alex stuttered, trying to scramble away from the horror that he had stumbled into. But he kept banging into what felt like little stone walls as he squirmed backwards. "Jesus Christ." He looked up desperately, as if the sight of his companions would break this spell and make it all go away. He glanced back at the nightmare vision in the snow. It was no drunken hallucination. It was the real thing. He turned again to his friends.

"There's a lassie up here," he shouted.

Weird Mackie's voice floated back eerily. "Lucky bastard."

"No, stop messing, she's bleeding."

Weird's laughter split the night. "No' so lucky after all, Gilly."

Alex felt sudden rage well up in him. "I'm not fucking joking. Get up here. Ziggy, come on, man."

Now they could hear the urgency in Alex's voice. Ziggy in the lead as always, they wallowed through the snow to the crest of the hill. Ziggy took the slope at a jerky run, Weird plunged headlong towards Alex, and Mondo brought up the rear, cautiously planting one foot in front of the other.

Weird ended up diving head over heels, landing on top of Alex and driving them both on top of the woman's body. They thrashed around, trying to free themselves, Weird giggling inanely. "Hey, Gilly, this must be the closest you've ever got to a woman."

"You've had too much fucking dope," Ziggy said angrily, pulling him away and crouching down beside the woman, feeling for a pulse in her neck. It was there, but it was terrifyingly weak. Apprehension turned him instantly sober as he took in what he was seeing in the dim light. He was only a final-year medical student, but he knew life-threatening injury when he saw it.

Weird leaned back on his haunches and frowned. "Hey, man, you know where this is?" Nobody was paying him any attention, but he continued anyway. "It's the Pictish cemetery. These humps in the snow, like wee walls? That's the stones they used like coffins. Fuck, Alex found a body in the cemetery." And he began to giggle, an uncanny sound in the snow-muffled air.

"Shut the fuck up, Weird." Ziggy continued to run his hands over her torso, feeling the unnerving give of a deep wound under his searching fingers. He cocked his head to one side, trying to examine her more clearly. "Mondo, got your lighter?"

Mondo moved forward reluctantly and produced his Zippo. He flicked the wheel and moved the feeble light at arm's length over the woman's body and up towards her face. His free hand covered his mouth, ineffectually stifling a groan. His blue eyes widened in horror and the flame trembled in his grasp.

Ziggy inhaled sharply, the planes of his face eerie in the shivering light.

"Shit," he gasped. "It's Rosie from the Lammas Bar."

Alex didn't think it was possible to feel worse. But Ziggy's words were like a punch to his heart. With a soft moan, he turned away and vomited a mess of beer, crisps and garlic bread into the snow.

"We've got to get help," Ziggy said firmly. "She's still alive, but she won't be for long in this state. Weird, Mondo – get your coats off." As he spoke, he was stripping off his own sheepskin jacket and wrapping it gently round Rosie's shoulders. "Gilly, you're the fastest. Go and get help. Get a phone. Get somebody out of their bed if you have to. Just get them here, right? Alex?"

Dazed, Alex forced himself to his feet. He scrambled back down the slope, churning the snow beneath his boots as he fought for purchase. He emerged from the straggle of trees into the streetlights that marked the newest cul-de-sac in the new housing estate that had sprung up over the past half-dozen years. Back the way they'd come, that was the quickest route.

Alex tucked his head down and set off at a slithering run up the middle of the road, trying to lose the image of what he'd just witnessed. It was as impossible as maintaining a steady pace on the powdery snow. How could that grievous thing among the Pictish graves be Rosie from the Lammas Bar? They'd been in there drinking that very evening, cheery and boisterous in the warm yellow glow of the public bar, knocking back pints of Tennent's, making the most of the last of their university freedom before they had to return to the stifling constraints of family Christmases thirty miles down the road.

He'd been speaking to Rosie himself, flirting with her in the clumsy way of twenty-one-year-olds uncertain whether they're still daft boys or mature men of the world. Not for the first time, he'd asked her what time she was due to finish. He'd even told her whose party they were going on to. He'd scribbled the address down on the back of a beer mat and pushed it across the damp wooden bar towards her. She'd given him a pitying smile and picked it up. He suspected it had probably gone straight in the bucket. What would a woman like Rosie want with a callow lad like him, after all? With her looks and her figure, she could take her pick, go for somebody who could show her a good time, not some penniless student trying to eke his grant out till his holiday job stacking supermarket shelves.

So how could that be Rosie lying bleeding in the snow on Hallow Hill? Ziggy must have got it wrong, Alex insisted to himself as he veered left, heading for the main road. Anybody could get confused in the flickering glow of Mondo's Zippo. And it wasn't as if Ziggy had ever paid much attention to the dark-haired barmaid. He'd left that to Alex himself and Mondo. It must just be some poor lassie that looked like Rosie. That would be it, he reassured himself. A mistake, that's what it was.

Alex hesitated for a moment, catching his breath and wondering where to run. There were plenty of houses nearby, but none of them was showing a light. Even if he could rouse someone, Alex doubted whether anyone would be inclined to open their door to a sweaty youth smelling of drink in the middle of a blizzard.

Then he remembered. This time of night, there was regularly a police car parked up by the main entrance to the Botanic Gardens a mere quarter of a mile away. They'd seen it often enough when they'd been staggering home in the small hours of the morning, aware of the car's single occupant giving them the once-over as they attempted to act sober for his benefit. It was a sight that always set Weird off on one of his rants about how corrupt and idle the police were. "Should be out catching the real villains, nailing the grey men in suits that rip the rest of us off, not sitting there all night with a flask of tea and a bag of scones, hoping to score some drunk peeing in a hedge or some eejit driving home too fast. Idle bastards." Well, maybe tonight Weird would get part of his wish. Because it looked like tonight the idle bastard in the car would get more than he bargained for.

Alex turned towards the Canongate and began to run again, the fresh snow creaking beneath his boots. He wished he'd kept up his rugby training as a stitch seized his side, turning his rhythm into a lopsided hop and skip as he fought to pull enough air into his lungs. Only a few dozen more yards, he told himself. He couldn't stop now, when Rosie's life might depend on his speed. He peered ahead, but the snow was falling more heavily now and he could barely see further than a couple of yards.

He was almost upon the police car before he saw it. Even as relief flooded his perspiring body, apprehension clawed at his heart. Sobered by shock and exertion, Alex realized he bore no resemblance to the sort of respectable citizen who normally reported a crime. He was dishevelled and sweaty, bloodstained and staggering like a half-shut knife. Somehow, he had to convince the policeman who was already halfway out of his panda car that he was neither imagining things nor playing some kind of prank. He slowed to a halt a couple of feet from the car, trying not to look like a threat, waiting for the driver to emerge.

The policeman set his cap straight on his short dark hair. His head was cocked to one side as he eyed Alex warily. Even masked by the heavy uniform anorak, Alex could see the tension in his body. "What's going on, son?" he asked. In spite of the diminutive form of address, he didn't look much older than Alex himself, and he possessed an air of unease that sat ill with his uniform.

Alex tried to control his breathing, but failed. "There's a lassie on Hallow Hill," he blurted out. "She's been attacked. She's bleeding really badly. She needs help."

The policeman narrowed his eyes against the snow, frowning. "She's been attacked, you say. How do you know that?"

"She's got blood all over her. And . . . " Alex paused for thought. "She's not dressed for the weather. She's not got a coat on. Look, can you get an ambulance or a doctor or something? She's really hurt, man."

"And you just happened to find her in the middle of a blizzard, eh? Have you been drinking, son?" The words were patronizing, but the voice betrayed anxiety.

Alex didn't imagine this was the kind of thing that happened often in the middle of the night in douce, suburban St Andrews. Somehow he had to convince this plod that he was serious. "Of course I've been drinking," he said, his frustration spilling over. "Why else would I be out at this time in the morning? Look, me and my pals, we were taking a short cut back to halls and we were messing about and I ran up the top of the hill and tripped and landed right on top of her." His voice rose in a plea. "Please. You've got to help. She could die out there."

The policeman studied him for what felt like minutes, then leaned into his car and launched into an unintelligible conversation over the radio. He stuck his head out of the door. "Get in. We'll drive up to Trinity Place. You better not be playing the goat, son," he said grimly.

The car fishtailed up the street, tyres inadequate for the conditions. The few cars that had travelled the road earlier had left tracks that were now only faint depressions in the smooth white surface, testament to the heaviness of the snowfall. The policeman swore under his breath as he avoided skidding into a lamppost at the turning. At the end of Trinity Place, he turned to Alex. "Come on then, show me where she is."

Alex set off at a trot, following his own rapidly disappearing tracks in the snow. He kept glancing back to check the policeman was still in his wake. He nearly went headlong at one point, his eyes taking a few moments to adjust to the greater darkness where the streetlights were cut off by the tree trunks. The snow seemed to cast its own strange light over the landscape, exaggerating the bulk of bushes and turning the path into a narrower ribbon than it normally appeared. "It's this way," Alex said, swerving off to the left. A quick look over his shoulder reassured him that his companion was right behind him.

The policeman hung back. "Are you sure you're no' on drugs, son?" he said suspiciously.

"Come on," Alex shouted urgently as he caught sight of the dark shapes above him. Without waiting to see if the policeman was following, Alex hurried up the slope. He was almost there when the young officer overtook him, brushing past and stopping abruptly a few feet short of the small group.

Ziggy was still hunkered down beside the woman's body, his shirt plastered to his slim torso with a mixture of snow and sweat. Weird and Mondo stood behind him, arms folded across their chests, hands tucked in their armpits, heads thrust down between their raised shoulders. They were only trying to stay warm in the absence of coats, but they presented an unfortunate image of arrogance.

"What's going on here, then, lads?" the policeman asked, his voice an aggressive attempt to stamp authority in spite of the greater weight of numbers arrayed against him.

Ziggy pushed himself wearily to his feet and shoved his wet hair out of his eyes. "You're too late. She's dead."

Nothing in Alex's twenty-one years had prepared him for a police interrogation in the middle of the night. TV cop shows and movies always made it look so regimented. But the very disorganization of the process was somehow more nerve-wracking than military precision would have been. The four of them had arrived at the police station in a flurry of chaos. They'd been hustled off the hill, bathed in the strobing blue lights of panda cars and ambulances, and nobody seemed to have any clear idea of what to do with them.

They'd stood under a streetlamp for what felt like a very long time, shivering under the frowning gaze of the constable Alex had summoned to the scene and one of his colleagues, a grizzled man in uniform with a scowl and a stoop. Neither officer spoke to the four young men, though their eyes never strayed from them.

Eventually, a harassed-looking man huddled into an overcoat that looked two sizes too big for him slithered over to them, his thin-soled shoes no match for the terrain. "Lawson, Mackenzie, take these boys down to the station, keep them apart when you get there. We'll be down in a wee while to talk to them." Then he turned and stumbled back in the direction of their terrible discovery, now hidden behind canvas screens through which an eerie green light permeated, staining the snow.

The younger policeman gave his colleague a worried look. "How are we going to get them back?"

He shrugged. "You'll have to squeeze them in your panda. I came up in the Sherpa van."

"Can we not take them back down in that? Then you could keep an eye on them while I'm driving."

The older man shook his head, pursing his lips. "If you say so, Lawson." He gestured to the Laddies fi' Kirkcaldy. "Come on, youse. Into the van. And no messing about, right?" He herded them towards a police van, calling over his shoulder to Lawson, "You better get the keys off Tam Watt."

Lawson set off up the slope, leaving them with Mackenzie. "I wouldnae like to be in your shoes when the CID get off that hill," he said conversationally as he climbed in behind them. Alex shivered, though not from the cold. It was slowly dawning on him that the police were regarding him and his companions as potential suspects rather than witnesses. They'd been given no opportunity to confer, to get their ducks in a row. The four of them exchanged uneasy looks. Even Weird had straightened out enough to realize this wasn't some daft game.

When Mackenzie hustled them into the van, there had been a few seconds when they'd been left alone. Just sufficient time for Ziggy to mutter loud enough for their ears, "For fuck's sake, don't mention the Land Rover." Instant comprehension had filled their eyes.

"Christ, aye," Weird said, head jerking back in terrified realization. Mondo chewed the skin round his thumbnail, saying nothing. Alex merely nodded.

The police station hadn't felt any more composed than the crime scene. The desk sergeant complained bitterly when the two uniformed officers arrived with four bodies who were supposed to be prevented from communicating with each other. It turned out there were insufficient interview rooms to keep them separate. Weird and Mondo were taken to wait in unlocked cells, while Alex and Ziggy were left to their own devices in the station's two interview rooms.

The room Alex found himself in was claustrophobically small. It was barely three paces square, as he established within minutes of being shut in to kick his heels. There were no windows, and the low ceiling with its greying polystyrene tiles made it all the more oppressive. It contained a chipped wooden table and four unmatching wooden chairs that looked exactly as uncomfortable as they felt. Alex tried them all in turn, finally settling for one that didn't dig into his thighs as much as the others.

He wondered if he was allowed to smoke. Judging by the smell of the stale air, he wouldn't have been the first. But he was a well-brought-up lad, and the absence of an ashtray gave him pause. He searched his pockets and found the screwed-up silver paper from a packet of Polo mints. Carefully, he spread it out, folding the edges up to form a rough tray. Then he took out his packet of Bensons and flipped the top open. Nine left. That should see him through, he thought.

Alex lit his cigarette and allowed himself to think about his position for the first time since they'd arrived at the police station. It was obvious, now he thought about it. They'd found a body. They had to be suspects. Everybody knew that the prime candidates for arrest in a murder investigation were either the ones who last saw the victim alive or the ones who found the body. Well, that was them on both counts.

He shook his head. The body. He was starting to think like them. This wasn't just a body, it was Rosie. Somebody he knew, however slightly. He supposed that made it all the more suspicious. But he didn't want to consider that now. He wanted that horror far from his mind. Whenever he closed his eyes, flashbacks to the hill played like a movie. Beautiful, sexy Rosie broken and bleeding on the snow. "Think about something else," he said aloud.

He wondered how the others would react to questioning. Weird was off his head, that was for sure. He'd had more than drink tonight. Alex had seen him with a joint in his hand earlier, but with Weird, there was no telling what else he might have indulged in. There had been tabs of acid floating around. Alex had refused it himself a couple of times. He didn't mind dope but he preferred not to fry his brains. But Weird was definitely in the market for anything that would allegedly expand his consciousness. Alex fervently hoped that whatever he'd swallowed, inhaled or snorted, it would have worn off before it was his turn to be interviewed. Otherwise, Weird was likely to piss the cops off very badly indeed. And any fool knew that was a bad idea in the middle of a murder investigation.

Mondo would be another kettle of fish. This would freak him out in a totally different way. Mondo was, when you got right down to it, too sensitive for his own good. He'd always been the one picked on at school, called a jessie partly because of the way he looked and partly because he never fought back. His hair hung in tight ringlets round his pixie face, his big sapphire eyes always wide like a mouse keeking out from a divot. The lassies liked it, that was for sure. Alex had once overheard a pair of them giggling that Davey Kerr looked just like Marc Bolan. But in a school like Kirkcaldy High, what won you favour with the lassies could equally earn you a kicking in the cloakroom. If Mondo hadn't had the other three to back him up, he'd have had a pretty thin time of it. To his credit, he knew that, and he repaid their services with interest. Alex knew he'd never have got through Higher French without Mondo's help.

But Mondo would be on his own with the police. Nobody to hide behind. Alex could picture him now, head hung low, tossing the odd glance out from under his brows, picking at the skin round his thumbnail or flicking the lid of his Zippo open and shut. They'd get frustrated with him, think he had something to hide. The thing they'd never suss, not in a million years, was that the big secret with Mondo was that ninety-nine times out of a hundred, there was no secret. There was no mystery wrapped in an enigma. There was just a guy who liked Pink Floyd, fish suppers with lashings of vinegar, Tennent's lager and getting laid. And who, bizarrely, spoke French like he'd learned it at his mother's knee.

Except of course tonight there was a secret. And if anybody was going to blow it, it would be Mondo. *Please God, let him not give up the Land Rover*, Alex thought. At the very least, they'd all be landed with the charge of taking and driving away without the owner's consent. At the very worst, the cops would realize one or all of them had the perfect means to transport a dying girl's body to a quiet hillside.

Weird wouldn't tell; he had most to lose. He'd been the one who'd turned up at the Lammas grinning from ear to ear, dangling Henry Cavendish's key-ring from his finger like the winner at a wife-swapping party.

Alex wouldn't tell, he knew that. Keeping secrets was one of the things he did best. If the price of avoiding suspicion was to keep his mouth shut, he had no doubts he could manage it.

Ziggy wouldn't tell either. It was always safety first with Ziggy. After all, he was the one who had sneaked away from the party to move the Land Rover once he'd realized how off his head Weird was getting. He'd taken Alex to one side and said, "I've taken the keys out of Weird's coat pocket. I'm going to shift the Land Rover, put it out of temptation's way. He's already been taking people for a spin round the block, it's time to put a stop to it before he kills himself or somebody else." Alex had no idea how long he'd been gone, but when he'd returned, Ziggy had told him the Land Rover was safely stowed up behind one of the industrial units off the Largo Road. "We can go and pick it up in the morning," he'd said.

Alex had grinned.

"Or we could just leave it there. A nice wee puzzle for Hooray Henry when he comes back next term."

"I don't think so. As soon as he realized his precious wheels weren't parked where he left them, he'd go to the police and drop us right in it. And our fingerprints are all over it."

He'd been right, Alex thought. There was no love lost between the Laddies fi' Kirkcaldy and the two Englishmen who shared their six-room campus house. There was no way Henry would see the funny side of Weird helping himself to the Land Rover. Henry didn't see the funny side of much that his house-mates did. So, Ziggy wouldn't tell. That was for sure.

But Mondo just might. Alex hoped Ziggy's warning had penetrated Mondo's self-absorption enough for him to think through the consequences. Telling the cops about Weird helping himself to someone else's car wouldn't get Mondo off the hook. It would only put all four of them firmly on it. Besides, he'd been driving it himself, taking that lassie home to Guardbridge. *For once in your life, think it through, Mondo.*

Now, if it was a thinker you wanted, Ziggy was your man. Behind the apparent openness, the easy charm and the quick intellect, there was a lot more going on than anyone knew. Alex had been pals with Ziggy for nine and a half years, and he felt as though he'd only scratched the surface. Ziggy was the one who would surprise you with an insight, knock you off balance with a question, make you look at something through fresh eyes because he'd twisted the world like a Rubik's Cube and seen it differently. Alex knew one or two things about Ziggy that he felt pretty sure were still hidden from Mondo and Weird. That was because Ziggy had wanted him to know, and because Ziggy knew his secrets would always be safe with Alex.

He imagined how Ziggy would be with his interrogators. He'd seem relaxed, calm, at ease with himself. If anyone could persuade the cops that their involvement with the body on Hallow Hill was entirely innocent, it was Ziggy.

Detective Inspector Barney Maclennan threw his damp coat over the nearest chair in the CID office. It was about the size of a primary school classroom, bigger than they normally needed. St Andrews wasn't high on Fife Constabulary's list of crime hotspots, and that was reflected in their staffing levels. Maclennan was head of CID out at the edge of the empire not because he lacked ambition but because he was a fully paid-up member of the awkward squad, the sort of bolshie copper senior officers liked best at a distance. Normally, he chafed at the lack of anything interesting to keep him occupied, but that didn't mean he welcomed the murder of a young lassie on his patch.

They'd got an ID right away. The pub Rosie Duff worked in was an occasional drop-in for some of the uniformed boys, and PC Jimmy Lawson, the first man at the locus, had recognized her immediately. Like most of the men at the scene, he'd looked shell-shocked and nauseous. Maclennan couldn't remember the last time they'd had a murder on his patch that hadn't been a straightforward domestic; these lads hadn't seen enough to harden them to the sight they'd come upon on the snowy hilltop. Come to that, he'd only seen a couple of murder victims himself, and never anything quite as pathetic as the abused body of Rosie Duff.

According to the police surgeon, it looked like she'd been raped and stabbed in the lower abdomen. A single, vicious blow carving its lethal track upwards through her gut. And it had probably taken her quite a while to die. Just thinking about it made Maclennan want to lay hands on the man responsible and beat the crap out of him. At times like this, the law felt more like a hindrance than a help when it came to achieving justice.

Maclennan sighed and lit a cigarette. He sat down at his desk and made notes of what little information he'd learned so far. Rosemary Duff. Nineteen years old. Worked in the Lammas Bar. Lived in Strathkinness with her parents and two older brothers. The brothers worked in the paper mill out at Guardbridge, her father was a grounds-man up at Craigtoun Park. Maclennan didn't envy Detective Constable Iain Shaw and the WPC he'd sent up to the village to break the news. He'd have to talk to the family himself in due course, he knew that. But he was better employed trying to get this investigation moving. It wasn't as if they were swarming with detectives who had a clue about running a major inquiry. If they were going to avoid being pushed out to the sidelines by the big boys from headquarters, Maclennan had to get the show on the road and make it look good.

He looked impatiently at his watch. He needed another CID man before he could start interviewing the four students who claimed they'd found the body. He'd told DC Allan Burnside to get back down to the station as soon as he could, but there was still no sign of him. Maclennan sighed. Goons and balloons, that was what he was stuck with out here.

He slipped his feet out of his damp shoes and swivelled round so he could rest them on the radiator. God, but it was a hell of a night to be starting a murder inquiry. The snow had turned the crime scene into a nightmare, masking evidence, making everything a hundred times more difficult. Who could tell which traces had been left by the killer, and which by the witnesses? That was assuming, of course, that those were separate entities. Rubbing the sleep from his eyes, Maclennan thought about his interview strategy.

All the received wisdom indicated he should speak first to the lad who'd actually found the body. Well-built lad, broad-shouldered, hard to see much of his face inside the big snorkel hood of the parka. Maclennan leaned back for his notebook. Alex Gilbey, that was the one. But he had a funny feeling about that one. It wasn't that he'd been exactly shifty, more that he'd not met Maclennan's eyes with the kind of piteous candour that most young lads in his shoes would have shown. And he certainly looked strong enough to carry Rosie's dying body up the gentle slope of Hallow Hill. Maybe there was more going on here than met the eye. It wouldn't be the first time a murderer had engineered the discovery of his victim's body to include himself. No, he'd let young Mr Gilbey sweat a wee bit longer.

The desk sergeant had told him that the other interview room was occupied by the medical student with the Polish name. He was the one who had been adamant that Rosie had still been alive when they found her, claiming he'd done all he could to keep her that way. He'd seemed pretty cool in the circumstances, cooler than Maclennan would have managed. He thought he'd start there. Just as soon as Burnside showed his face.

The interview room that housed Ziggy was the double of Alex's. Somehow, Ziggy managed to look comfortable in it. He slouched in his chair, half-leaning against the wall, his eyes fixed on the middle distance. He was so exhausted he could easily have fallen asleep, except that every time he closed his eyes, the image of Rosie's body flared brilliant in his mind. No amount of theoretical medical study had prepared Ziggy for the brutal reality of a human being so wantonly destroyed. He just hadn't known enough to be any use to Rosie when it mattered, and that galled him. He knew he should feel pity for the dead woman, but his frustration left no room for any other emotion. Not even fear.

But Ziggy was also smart enough to know he should be afraid. He had Rosie Duff's blood all over his clothes, under his fingernails. Probably even in his hair; he remembered pushing his wet fringe out of his eyes as he'd desperately tried to see where the blood was coming from. That was innocent enough, if the police believed his story. But he was also the man without an alibi, thanks to Weird's contrary notions of what constituted a bit of fun. He really couldn't afford for the police to find the best possible vehicle for driving in a blizzard with his fingerprints all over it. Ziggy was usually so circumspect, but now his life could be blown apart by one careless word. It didn't bear thinking about.

It was almost a relief when the door opened and two policemen walked in. He recognized the one who had told the uniforms to bring them to the station. Stripped of his overwhelming overcoat, he was a lean whippet of a man, his mousy hair a little longer than was fashionable. The stubbled cheeks revealed he had been rousted from bed in the middle of the night, though the neat white shirt and the smart suit looked as if they'd come straight from the dry cleaner's hanger. He dropped into the chair opposite Ziggy and said, "I'm Detective Inspector Maclennan and this is Detective Constable Burnside. We need to have a wee chat about what happened tonight." He nodded towards Burnside. "My colleague will take notes and then we'll prepare a statement for you to sign."

Ziggy nodded. "That's fine. Ask away." He straightened up in his seat. "I don't suppose I could get a cup of tea?"

Maclennan turned to Burnside and nodded. Burnside rose and left the room. Maclennan leaned back in his chair and checked out his witness. Funny how the mod haircuts had come back into fashion. The dark-haired lad opposite him wouldn't have looked out of place a dozen years earlier in the Small Faces. He didn't look like a Pole to Maclennan's way of thinking. He had the pale skin and red cheeks of a Fifer, though the brown eyes were a bit unusual with that colouring. Wide cheekbones gave his face a chiselled, exotic air. A bit like that Russian dancer, Rudolph Nearenough, or whatever his name was.

Burnside returned almost immediately. "It's on its way," he said, sitting down and picking up his pen.

Maclennan placed his forearms on the table and locked his fingers together. "Personal details first." They ran through the preliminaries quickly, then the detective said, "A bad business. You must be feeling pretty shaken up."

Ziggy began to feel as if he was trapped in the land of clichés. "You could say that."

"I want you to tell me in your own words what happened tonight."

Ziggy cleared his throat. "We were walking back to Fife Park . . ."

Maclennan stopped him with a raised palm. "Back up a bit. Let's have the whole evening, eh?"

Ziggy's heart sank. He was hoping he might avoid mentioning their earlier visit to the Lammas Bar. "OK. The four of us, we live in the same unit in Fife Park so we usually eat together. Tonight, it was my turn to cook. We had egg and chips and beans and about nine o'clock we went down into the town. We were going to a party later on and we wanted to have a few pints first." He paused to make sure Burnside was getting it down.

"Where did you go for your drinks?"

"The Lammas Bar." The words hung in the air between them.

Maclennan showed no reaction, though he felt his pulse quicken. "Did you often drink there?"

"Pretty regularly. The beer's cheap and they don't mind students, not like some of the places in town."

"So you'll have seen Rosie Duff? The dead girl?"

Ziggy shrugged. "I didn't really pay attention."

"What? A bonnie lassie like that, you didn't notice her?"

"It wasn't her that served me when I went up for my round."

"But you must have spoken to her in the past?"

Ziggy took a deep breath. "Like I said, I never really paid attention. Chatting up barmaids isn't my scene."

"Not good enough for you, eh?" Maclennan said grimly.

"I'm not a snob, Inspector. I come from a council house myself. I just don't get my kicks playing macho man in the pub, OK? Yes, I knew who she was, but I'd never had a conversation with her that went beyond 'Four pints of Tennent's, please.'"

"Did any of your friends take more of an interest in her?"

"Not that I noticed." Ziggy's nonchalance hid a sudden wariness at the line of questioning.

"So, you had a few pints in the Lammas. What then?"

"Like I said, we went on to a party. A third-year mathematician called Pete that Tom Mackie knows. He lives in St Andrews, in Learmonth Gardens. I don't know what number. His parents were away and he threw a party. We got there about midnight and it was getting on for four o'clock when we left."

"Were you all together at the party?"

Ziggy snorted. "Have you ever been to a student party, Inspector? You know what it's like. You walk through the door together, you get a beer, you drift apart. Then when you've had enough, you see who's still standing and you gather them together and stagger off into the night. The good shepherd, that's me." He gave an ironic smile.

"So the four of you arrived together and the four of you left together, but you've no idea what the others were doing in between?"

"That's about the size of it, yeah."

"You couldn't even swear that none of them left and came back later?"

If Maclennan had expected alarm from Ziggy, he was disappointed. Instead, he cocked his head to one side, thoughtful. "Probably not, no," he admitted. "I spent most of the time in the conservatory at the back of the house. Me and a couple of English guys. Sorry, I can't remember their names. We were talking about music, politics, that sort of thing. It got quite heated when we got on to Scottish devolution, as you can imagine. I wandered through a few times for another beer, went through to the dining room to grab something to eat, but no, I wasn't being my brothers' keeper."

"Do you usually all end up going back together?" Maclennan wasn't quite sure where he was going with this, but it felt like the right question.

"Depends if anybody's got off with somebody."

He was definitely on the defensive now, the policeman thought. "Does that happen often?"

"Sometimes." Ziggy's smile was a little strained. "Hey, we're healthy, red-blooded young men, you know?"

"But the four of you usually end up going home together? Very cosy."

"You know, Inspector, not all students are obsessed with sex. Some of us know how lucky we are to be here and we don't want to screw it up."

"So you prefer each other's company? Where I come from, people might think you were queer."

Ziggy's composure slipped momentarily. "So what? It's not against the law."

"That depends on what you're doing and who you're doing it with," Maclennan said, any pretence of amiability gone.

"Look, what has any of this got to do with the fact that we stumbled over the dying body of a young woman?" Ziggy demanded, leaning forward. "What are you trying to suggest? We're gay, therefore we raped a lassie and murdered her?"

"Your words, not mine. It's a well-known fact that some homosexuals hate women."

Ziggy shook his head in disbelief. "Well known to whom? The prejudiced and ignorant? Look, just because Alex and Tom and Davey left the party with me doesn't make them gay, right? They could give you a list of girls who could show you just how wrong you are."

"And what about you, Sigmund? Could you do the same thing?"

Ziggy held himself rigid, willing his body not to betray him. There was a world of difference the size of Scotland between legal and comprehended. He'd arrived at a place where the truth was not going to be his friend. "Can we get back on track here, Inspector? I left the party about four o'clock with my three friends. We walked down Learmonth Place, turned left up the Canongate then went down Trinity Place. Hallow Hill is a short cut back to Fife Park . . ."

"Did you see anyone else as you walked down towards the hill?" Maclennan interrupted.

"No. But the visibility wasn't great because of the snow. Anyway, we were walking along the footpath at the bottom of the hill and Alex started running up the hill. I don't know why, I was ahead of him and I didn't see what set him off. When he got to the top, he tripped and fell into the hollow. The next thing I knew was he was shouting to us to come up, that there was a young woman bleeding." Ziggy closed his eyes, but opened them hastily as the dead girl rose before him again. "We climbed up and we found Rosie lying in the snow. I felt her carotid pulse. It was very faint, but it was still there. She seemed to be bleeding from a wound to the abdomen. Quite a large slit, it felt like. Maybe three or four inches long. I told Alex to go and get help. To call the police. We covered her with our coats and I tried to put pressure on the wound. But it was too late. Too much internal damage. Too much blood loss. She died within a couple of minutes." He gave a long exhalation. "There was nothing I could do."

Even Maclennan was momentarily silenced by the intensity of Ziggy's words. He glanced at Burnside, who was scribbling furiously. "Why did you ask Alex Gilbey to go for help?"

"Because Alex was more sober than Tom. And Davey tends to go to pieces in a crisis."

It made perfect sense. Almost too perfect. Maclennan pushed his chair back. "One of my officers will take you home now, Mr Malkiewicz. We'll want the clothes you're wearing, for forensic analysis. And your fingerprints, for the purposes of elimination. And we'll be wanting to talk to you again." There were things Maclennan wanted to know about Sigmund Malkiewicz. But they could wait. His feeling of unease about these four young men was growing stronger by the minute. He wanted to start pushing. And he had a feeling that the one who went to pieces in a crisis might just be the one to cave in.

✧

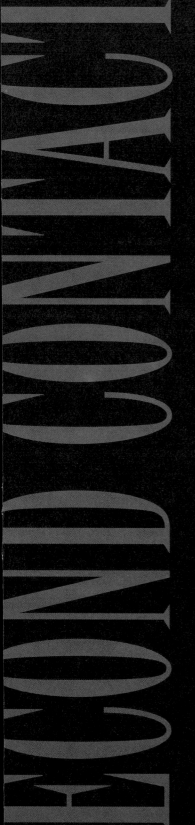

SECOND CONTACT by GARY COUZENS

This collection of sixteen stories, two novelettes and one novella nudges conventional genre boundaries, deftly exploring the fringes of experience to burrow deeply amidst our heartfelt fascinations and fears.

Dissecting the relationships between time and identity, perception and misconception, longing and alienation, Couzens's often cinematic prose evokes realities just below the surface of common experience. For each story here there will be a connection with someone, somewhere.

Second Contact will be available from 1 May 2003, priced £8

Elastic Press, 85 Gertrude Road, Norwich, Norfolk NR3 4SG

Visit www.elasticpress.com for further information

MARION ARNOTT

In 1857, Madeleine Hamilton Smith stood trial at the High Court in Edinburgh. She faced two charges of attempted murder by poisoning, and one of murder. The alleged victim was her lover, Emile L'Angelier. She was found Not Guilty on one charge of attempted murder, and Not Proven on the other two charges. Extracts from her letters given here are authentic.

Marion Arnott is from Paisley, Scotland. Her proudest moments are winning the QWF Philip Good Memorial Prize For Fiction in 1998; winning the CWA/Macallan Short Story Dagger in 2001 (for 'Prussian Snowdrops', *Crimewave 4: Mood Indigo*); being shortlisted for the CWA/Macallan Short Story Dagger in 2002 (for 'Marbles', *Crimewave 6: Breaking Point*); being anthologised in Datlow & Winding's *Year's Best Fantasy and Horror Volume 15*. Proud moments to come include a story collection called *Sleepwalkers* to be published by Elastic Press in August 2003, and an appearance of 'Marbles' in *Best British Mystery Stories of the Year* (ed Maxim Jabukowski, Allison & Busby), November 2003.

Madeleine stepped into the dock. The court was not at all what she expected: it was dim, untidy, and very small, lit only by wedges of dusty sunlight which forced a fuzzy warmth through its tall windows. The roars of the crowds outside – "Hoo-er! Hang the wee hoo-er!" – died down and she was startled by a new sound, a steady drone like the buzzing of wasps in a byke. It was a murmur of excitement from dozens of male throats. She glanced across at the public gallery and saw that gentlemen were lounging with their feet on the brass rails. They were peering at her through opera glasses. And they had kept their hats on in her presence. A warm flush of affront crept up her neck.

The friendly wardress whispered, as if Madeleine were some music hall performer pleased to draw a crowd, that the gentlemen had paid golden guineas to secure a seat in court, and double the amount for a place on the day when her love letters would be read. A high pitched gibber of fear filled Madeleine's head at the mention of her letters. She tried to catch Mr Inglis's eye, needing his granite reassurance, but her advocate was riffling through his papers. She steadied herself with what he had told her: "Evidence of immorality is not evidence of murder, Miss Smith; evidence of the convenience of a death does not prove that it was hastened; and suspicion is no evidence at all." She repeated his words silently, but his mellifluous confidence dried in her mouth and tasted of too much protesting. The crowd had roared 'hang the whore', not 'hang the poisoner'. Immorality could be proved, poisoning not, but would that matter?

It would be better not to think. As the clerk read out three separate charges of wicked and felonious administration of arsenic, she lowered her eyes to her lap, to her small hands gloved in lavender kid, and began to count the stitches in the seams. She counted all through the reading of the charges and the examination of the first witnesses and never looked up, not when the Lord Advocate, the clerk to the court, and the witnesses all in turn mispronounced Emile's name; nor when the pathologist explained that Emile L'Angelier had died of enough arsenic to kill six men; nor when he said that the medium for the poison was likely cocoa; and not even, especially not even, when witnesses described Emile's death throes: his vomitings and purgings, his writhings, his weepings, and his green arsenious bile.

But if Madeleine did not look up, she heard, and her face coloured pink and sweet as an angry rose. She had never heard the like of this evidence in all her life. She grimaced and tugged at the cuff of her glove. They were no true gentlemen who subjected her to such coarseness! And to think that Emile had considered suicide by poisoning a romantic end for a disappointed lover! He was fortunate indeed to have been spared this last disillusion.

Witnesses gave tedious evidence of arsenic mixed with soot, and arsenic mixed with indigo, and which kind it was she'd had in her possession and which kind it was that killed Emile; they produced tables to show that arsenic could not be suspended in cocoa, and charts to show that it could; they opined confidently that Emile's death was convenient to her, and with assurance that it was not. Their certainties brawled and knocked one another out of the witness box. And all the while the opera glasses remained trained on her face.

135

Madeleine's heart lurched. They were looking for signs: gentlemen prided themselves on being judges of dogs, horseflesh and women; they knew what to look for
and if they found her wanting, they would hang her. The opera glasses scanned her
face, seeking out the flicker of an eyelash, the quickening of a pulse. Madeleine's heart
lurched again. The Daniels were come to judgment: my learned friends, the gentlemen of the jury, the gentlemen of the Press, the gentlemen of society who had left
their manners at home with their wives – all were come to sit in judgement. But that
was the way of things – always the gentlemen must be pleased. Quiet rage bloomed
prettily in Madeleine's cheeks.

That night the friendly wardress told Madeleine that she had made a good impression
on the court. She had not been what they expected. Her modest demeanour and shy
blushes had given all present pause for thought, and her purchases of arsenic were
scarce spoken of at all.

Alone at last in her cell in the failing summer twilight, Madeleine studied the
newspaper the wardress had smuggled to her. There was a lurid account of Emile's
death throes and a sketch of him which she disliked on sight: something about his
light waving hair and upturned eyes suggested a martyred saint. She scanned the
densely printed columns: apart from an irritating excess of exclamation marks, the
bulk of the reportage pleased her. It was concerned with her background, her up-
bringing, her education, her stylish new bonnet, her fine grey eyes. Poor Emile, so
vilely mispronounced, so dramatically and excessively dead, had been quite upstaged
– how piqued he would have been had he known!

Editorials agonised over her downfall, demanding to know how it had come to
pass. Madeline stared sightlessly into the gathering dusk. She hardly knew herself
how things had come about. The trouble was that she had changed so much that it
was difficult to remember what she was like at the beginning; that Madeleine was a
stranger to her now, a stiff and distant little figure seen through the wrong end of a
telescope. She had not been what she seemed, that young girl, but then in the end,
neither had Emile.

She took up the newspaper again, and studied the sketch which had been made
of her. Her much admired bonnet was lovingly drawn and shadowed meekly down-
cast eyes. She recognised that posture at least. It had been painfully acquired over
many years. As Mrs Gorton used to say, a young lady's posture must always show her
breeding and education. The younger Madeleine, whom she could not think of as
'I', only 'she' or 'Madeleine', had tried very hard to be what everyone expected . . .

*Madeleine is eighteen and just returned from Mrs Gorton's finishing school, pruned and
shaped into one of her white blooms of innocent womanhood. Papa studies her final report and is not displeased. Her wilfulness, which Mrs Gorton complained of before ("Miss
Smith, no gentlemen will marry a woman of discordant character"), has mellowed to a
decent decorum; she can discourse charmingly about suitable novels and current affairs
("Miss Smith, you were vehement with the curate in conversation last evening; gentlemen
discourse with ladies to be entertained, not to be disputed with"); she can net purses,
paint a little, play the piano prettily, and recite screeds of romantic poetry.*

*Mrs Gorton has only one complaint: Miss Smith's penmanship is impenetrable, sprawl-
ing spikily across the page, right into the margins and beyond ("Miss Smith, how will*

your future beaux ever be able to decipher your billet doux if you cannot control your pen?").

Papa considers. Madeleine flutters helplessly, a sweet and rueful clown, and Mama's fan flaps wildly like a trapped bird; if Papa frowns, Mama will have a fit of the vapours and need the sal volatile *again. But Papa does not frown. "Well, Madeleine, I never intended you to be a clerk. You show every promise of turning out as dear a little woman as your Mama." Mama's fan recovers its equilibrium and Papa gives Madeleine two golden guineas for a new bonnet.*

Later, alone in her bedroom, Madeleine tries on the bonnet and considers her accomplishments. She can flirt discreetly without being in the least forward and has even managed to extract a compliment from that vapid little curate; from her reading of romantic novels, she has discovered that there is nothing a gentleman so admires – no, not even the netting of purses – as a pair of white shoulders rising snowy from the neck of a ballgown; also, by assiduous study of Chamber's Journal, *she has discovered that an application of arsenic in solution is efficacious in whitening the complexion and said shoulders.*

Madeleine poses at the mirror. She is ready for life to begin.

The morning went badly for Madeleine. The Lord Advocate, Mr Moncrieff, appearing for the Crown, established beyond any doubt the fact of a criminal intimacy between Emile L'Angelier and the panel, Madeleine Smith. Madeleine was chilled by the greedy concentration of the court as deceit, furtive slyness, and a depravity beyond the ken of decent folk were all repeatedly proven via the evidence of self-righteous servants and stammering clerks. Her reputation was destroyed utterly. With dull despair she saw her own advocate rise to cross-examine on a painful subject that should have been passed over in decent silence, at least by her own side.

It was some time before she understood what was happening. Mr Inglis had a persuasive voice and a wonderful way with a meaningful pause. Emile's reputation was shredded by the hail of deadly silences which Mr Inglis discharged like grapeshot at the witnesses parading before him.

"Now, sir, this A-meel Long-jelly . . ." Pause for the court to reflect that A-meel Long-jelly was a villainous name and cause for suspicion in itself. "This Long-jelly" – a squint down his nose and a hitch at his gown – "was, you say, full twelve years older than the panel who was fresh from the schoolroom?" Pause. "A wordly man, would you say?" Very long pause. "And he pursued the panel, Miss Smith? He besought you to make an introduction to her? In spite of the differences in age, rank, and education?"

He executed the quick sideways step which Madeleine soon learned was a sign of excited disapproval. You can see how it was, the step seemed to say, you can surely see how it was . . .

Madeleine is eighteen, exotic among the dumpy Bessies and Marys of Glasgow. Her world consists of Sunday to kirk, and weekday visits to aunts who chime the same notes of approval and disapproval as Mrs Gorton. She blooms white and sweet behind her thicket of stern headmistresses and nothing ever happens. She is like to die of suffocation if something doesn't happen soon . . .

"Now, sir, you did not introduce him. Why not? In what way not a respectable person? Come, sir, this is a court of law, not a valedictory service." Pause. "I see. He bragged of his sordid liaisons. A barmaid in Leith? A lady in Dundee who admired his 'pretty little feet'? Sundry females in Paris? A Lady in Fife whose position and inheritance he found appealing? And when he desired to pay his attentions to Miss Smith, he set out to cultivate the acquaintance of people who could perform an introduction?"

Madeleine stared down at her lavender gloves. She and Emile had often laughed together over the superhuman efforts he had made to meet her . . .

A grey February afternoon in Sauchiehall Street. Madeleine shivers and wishes for the interminable Glasgow winter to end, for winter to end and life to begin. And then it does. He looms out of the driving sleet, a smiling blurred shadow. He is elegant and wears his stove pipe at an angle, and is slim pretty, not Scotsman square and sturdy. He is so bold with his eyes that she blushes hotly in the raw air. The introduction is barely proper, the conversation not at all, but she is out of the schoolroom now and despises missishness. And besides, his accent is charming.

That night she lies awake and thinks of M. L'Angelier. She has never known a man so confiding, nor one who has led such an exciting and adventurous life! And when he speaks of it, his skin glows with a spirit which animates his every word and gesture. Madeleine lies awake and whispers his name to her pillow; she tries on his accent with its French precision and beguiling little slurs. "Enchanté, Mees Smeeth," she whispers, "enchanté." She turns restlessly in bed and the darkness is lit by his pale face and burning revolutionary eyes. "In the Révolution of 1848," she whispers, "when I manned the barricades in Paris in the name of Liberté, Égalité, Fraternité; in '48, when I summered with mon ami the baron at his estates in Malmédy . . ."

She mimes and whispers and tries him on. "Malmédy," she whispers, sometimes with precision, sometimes with a slur, "Liberté. Enchanté, Mees Smeeth, enchanté."

She despairs that she will never see him again, that she will live forever behind her thicket and never again catch a whiff of revolutionary cordite.

But she does. When she walks in the Botanic Gardens, he is there behind the hydrangeas; when she visits Mr Ogilvy's bookshop, he emerges smiling from behind the bookstacks . . .

"And he pursued this young girl to the point of obsession, you say? He discovered all her regular haunts and followed her there?"

The bookshop is her favourite trysting place: Emile belongs among the romantic gilt-edged pages of Mr Ogilvy's novels. He stands before her, wrapped in the cloak of his pride, and confesses that he is only a clerk with Huggins & Co, which would matter nothing in France where such things are of no account, but he fears that Glaswegians are flint-hearted and that love means nothing to them, only wealth.

Madeleine is above such small mindedness. She tells him that like Mary, Queen of Scots, she would go to the world's end in her petticoats for love's sake. His eyes moisten. He has found his twin soul, he says, his rebel heart, and they will be together to the world's end and beyond . . .

"Now, sir, let us be clear. He bragged of eating arsenic? Did he say why he indulged in this practice? For his complexion, you say? For the lustrousness of his hair?" Pause to reflect on the oddities of foreigners. A ripple of amused disbelief in court. "And to enhance his . . . what? Speak up, sir." An incredulous pause. "You did say his virility?" A full round turn and two half hitches of the black gown. "I see. His virility." Long and deadly pause. Excited scuttling sideways step. "He was aware surely that arsenic is deadly? Ah, he was. In fact he bragged of it to show his devil-may-care courage. I see. He told the decent young men he worked with about this filthy habit?" Twist of mouth, very like Mama's the evening she had twelve to dinner and found a cockroach in the pastry. "This Long-Jelly, he had the temperament usually associated with gentlemen of continental extraction? He spoke freely of his passions? He threatened suicide when his affairs went not to his satisfaction? Because he liked to impress, you say?" Another incredulous pause. "And it is your recollection that he threatened suicide for the Lady in Fife? And for the panel, Miss Smith's, sake. On many occasions?" The deadliest silence of all.

Emile explains that he is a man who grapples with passions stronger than those of ordinary men. For him, life is only worth living when fired with extremes of feeling. He tells Madeleine often of the boulevards of Paris and the women he knew there, women who lived only for love and thought nothing of dying for it. He himself, he says, has many times been suicidal over disappointments of the heart. He shrugs off her horror with Gallic nonchalance and a swish of his cane which decapitates a clump of daisies under a hedge. "Little Mimi, you are such a child. You know nothing of a man's passion. But in time I will teach you."

She shivers at this talk, hot and cold as if in a fever. But not so much as she does when Papa finds out that she has been seen walking with a gentleman not of his acquaintance. His rage scalds her. He will turn her from his door if she has further connection with that Frenchified little popinjay. Mama takes to her bed with the sal volatile. Madeleine weeps helplessly, her rebel heart broken.

She finishes with Emile, but his bitterness, and the justice of it, wounds her. Oh, but her love is a poor thing compared to his! Night after night she shivers and frets, hot and cold, afraid of Papa and missing Emile, humiliated by her failure to defy Papa, and by her failure to match Emile's revolutionary spirit.

Emile writes that he wishes he were dead and makes her shiver; Papa says he'd rather see her dead and makes her shiver. She must continue in the shadow of the thicket. Oh, God, she shivers, she would rather be dead.

She and Emile are reunited. Love cannot be denied. They cannot be blamed for deceit forced on them by Papa's intransigence. They meet when they can, and when they cannot meet, they write . . .

Every evening, the wardress brought Madeleine the speak of the court. "Oh, the bailiff says none of them like the cut of his lordship's jib one wee bit," she snorted. "Him and his glossy curls and his wee feet and his virility! A queer lot, the French – "

Madeleine forbore to point out that Emile was from the Channel Islands. To the good folk of Edinburgh, the one was as outlandish as the other. And besides, Emile had always been thrilled to be taken for a Frenchman. It was fitting somehow that he should be judged as one.

The day's newspapers were devoted to her case. Madeleine read until the candle guttered, throwing one last shadow up the wall before sputtering out. The dark blue gloaming softened the harshness of her cell while she mulled over what she had read. Much was being made of her practised deceitfulness; and Papa and Mama came in for a good deal of criticism for sending her to England for a newfangled education. Too many novels and nonsense, wrote irate readers from all over Scotland, not enough of household management and a daughter's duty to her father. The more chivalrous pointed to the ladylike humility she had displayed in court as evidence that there was very little wrong with her breeding, but that no system of education on earth could protect an innocent from the machinations of the lascivious French.

There was a good deal about hapless innocence, which comforted Madeleine until she remembered that soon she had to face the public reading of her letters. Mrs Gorton had been quite wrong about her penmanship; no one was having the slightest difficulty in deciphering it, right into the margins of her letters and beyond, where there was nothing at all of helplessness or innocence. Why, oh why, had Mrs Gorton never warned her girls against putting anything in writing . . .

Madeleine veiled herself on letters day and was glad of the concealment: the buzz in court was deafening, and the winking opera glasses dazzled her. The Lord Advocate prosecuted vigorously, fully armed with the dates, times and places of licentious behaviour. He made it clear that murder was the natural consequence of her moral collapse. From the sour faces in the gallery, Madeleine judged that many gentlemen were in accord with him.

Her hand closed around the silver topped bottle of *sal volatile*, sent by Mama who had taken to her bed with an attack of the vapours. As had Papa. It spoke volumes against her that neither parent had come into court. What would the jury make of it? Behind her veil, anger crimsoned her cheeks and she hoped that her parents' vapours might rise and choke them.

The Lord Advocate introduced a selection of her letters into evidence. Madeleine closed her eyes when the clerk to the court, drenched in sunlight and dust motes, rose to his feet, holding her letters at arms' length, and began to read aloud. Slowly the well of the court filled with the musky scent she had doused her writing paper with, and conjured up a new participant in the drama. Emile's naughty Mimi slouched languorously into the dock beside her. Madeleine resisted the urge to draw her skirts aside and endeavoured to look as shocked as everyone else.

The clerk, a little bird-faced man with a high sing-song voice, recited Mimi's musky passions as if chanting the names of strange territories unvisited by civilised persons: "O-my-beloved-why-did-you-not-come-to-me-a-kiss-a-fond-embrace-sweet-pet-Emile-it-was-a-punishment-to-me-to-be-deprived-of-your-loving-me-for-it-is-a-pleasure-no-one-can-deny-that-it-is-but-human-nature-o-my-beloved." The clerk's sinuses were affected by the musk perfume and he sneezed often into the deep silence in court. "ATT-ISH-OO!-I- was-in-my-nightdress-when-you-saw-me-would-to-God-you- ATT-ISH-OO!- had-been-in-the-same-attire."

Papa has her watched and reads all her mail. No matter how often she assures him that she has forgotten a certain person and broken off all contact with him, Papa is ever vigilant. His lack of trust infuriates her, but she will not fail Emile. She writes and writes . . .

The clerk to the court had a special distaste for words like *fondling* and *petting* and spat them out like a boy spitting peas. Madeleine wondered if the words of passion when passion was spent always sounded so foolish. If the Daniels laughed, she would die. But they did not laugh. The explicit words written in heat and musk were punctuated by groans of horror and disgust from the public gallery, and slowly she realised that if they could not laugh at her, then she might really hang.

"Sweet-pet-Emile-I-love-you-truly-fondly-last-night-I-did-burn-with-love-Emile-I-dote-on-you-with-my-heart-and-soul-I-would-be-wishing-you-to-love-me-if-I-were-with-you-now-ATT-ISH-OO!"

She burns for him. Days pass when they cannot meet. Papa keeps her busy and out of mischief. She smiles meekly, but she burns. Every moment spent visiting her aunts, or taking the minister's sermons to heart, is time spent longing to be with Emile, to be his Mimi, to be kissed, embraced, to hear his yearning heart thudding under her cheek. But love finds a way. Emile leaves red roses on her doorstep; she sends him pressed flowers and letters, a snowstorm of letters . . .

The clerk read on. A gentleman leapt to his feet and fled the room, declaring he'd never heard anything like it in his life. Madeleine sniffed delicately at the smelling salts in an appeal to chivalry, but the hubbub in court reached a crescendo: a woman so lost to all notions of decency was entitled to no such appeal. Behind the veil, Madeleine flinched a step nearer the gallows. She struggled for composure, reminding herself that evidence of immorality was not evidence of murder. But the gentlemen were making more of a stramash over her letters than they had over the three wicked and felonious administrations of a noxious substance.

She risked a sideways peep at the gallery and a thought occurred. Could it be true that they had never heard anything like her letters? She pitied them fleetingly; but on reflection, pitied their wives even more.

Mr Inglis introduced his own selection of letters. "May it please the court. An extract from the panel's first letter to Long-Jelly, written within a month of their acquaintance."

"I-am-trying-to-break-myself-of-all-my-very-bad-habits-it-is-you-I-have-to-thank-for-this-which-I-do-from-the-bottom-of-my-heart-I-shall-trust-to-your-telling-me-all-my-little-faults."

Mr Inglis was brisk with witnesses. "Now, sir. He boasted that he would forbid the panel, Miss Smith, to do such and such? To wear such and such? He bragged of his mastery over her?"

"I-shall-love-you-and-obey-you-I-shall-do-all-that-you-want-me-to-I-know-what-awaits-me-if-I-do-what-you-disapprove-of-off-you-go."

This was the acceptable language of love, fragrant with the sweetness of the white flower. The tension in court eased. Mimi the Mistress was nowhere to be seen; Madeleine the Maid, submissive and ladylike, was in every line. Mr Inglis took many excited little sideways steps – you see, the steps seemed to say, you see how her very proper sentiments were twisted by a worthless man to his own vile purposes.

Madeleine understood her defence at last: the worse she behaved, the more Long-Jelly was to blame. Behind her veil, she was brick red with humiliation. She did not care to be reminded of her slavishness, which she found a thousand times more mortifying than her depravity. Her letters were a bitter reminder of that silly girl Madeleine's foolish notions . . .

Emile is masterful and hard to please and Madeleine's faults are many. He warns her that she must improve herself or else be a disappointment to him. He rebukes her for the things she does which cause him unhappiness and constantly seeks an opinion of her behaviour from his genteel spinster friend, Miss Perry. Miss Perry entirely agrees with him that she is not to go to balls or assemblies, no matter what her Papa says, and she is not to be at her flirting, nor is he to wear her fetching pink bonnet; a discreet fawn one is more suitable for a young lady who is spoken for. Madeleine smiles fondly at this. Emile fears that some other gentleman will carry her off. As if Papa would allow any such thing! Or even any flirting!

"I-shall-be-guided-by-you-entirely-I-shall-not-be-thoughtless-and-indifferent-to-you- dear-love-I-shall-be-more affectionate-in-future."

She is to write to him telling him all her private thoughts and all that she does when he is not there to supervise her. He explains patiently that she has only herself to blame if he treats her coldly after she sends him letters which are brief and lacking in affection. Madeleine tries harder. She writes adoringly, effusively, apologetically, for page after page, because he is kinder when she tries to please. He teaches her the joy of making the one she loves happy. And she does love him. He has only to clasp her waist between his two hands for her sure to be sure of that; the swooning heat she feels is proof. If only he were not so hard to please, or if she herself were more adept, like his former loves of the boulevard . . .

"O-dear-love-why-am-I-not-always-what-you-want-me-to-be-but-I-cannot-help-my-carelessness-I-know-your-love-for-me-is-great-when-I-am-good-but-you-are-cool-to-me-when-I-am-bad."

All is not well between them. For months, for a year of months, they snatch at meetings when they can, at one another when they can, in friendly dark corners, in empty rooms when the household sleeps, but their stolen moments leave them irritable and quarrelsome. Emile is disgusted by her refusal to confront Papa with the fact of their secret engagement. Always she must be sorry for her cowardice, for her failures in affection and obedience.

Things are difficult at home too. Papa is distant and suspicious. Always she must be sorry for her past failures in duty and obedience. She quails at the thought of facing him with her engagement and urges Emile to elope with her. She will not mind being poor so long as they are together. But Emile minds: recognition from her family is his right; her marriage portion is her right. And they must consider her reputation.

Their clutching in the dark, once so warm and vivid, is soured. "Let me, Mimi, let me," he gasps at her ear, at her throat, at her bosom, and she is only too willing, but always he pulls back with a despairing reproof. As a man he is subject to his passions, he chides her; as a lady she must never be. Madeleine remembers that Mrs Gorton used to say much the same thing, in much the same admonitory tone, but had never hinted at how difficult it was.

They quarrel endlessly. He threatens that if she does not confront her Papa, he will enlist in the French army, or emigrate to Lima and find work on a coffee plantation. This he will do for her sake; this is how much he loves her.

"Emile-for-pity's-sake-do-not-leave-me-I-will-do-all-that-you-ask-only-do-not-go."

She lies awake at night weeping for fear that he will leave her alone with her ragged nerves and restless burning.

"For-pity's-sake-Emile."

She cannot eat or sleep and suffers from mysterious glooms and spurts of temper. Papa tells her that a certain matter is now forgiven and forgotten and that they are friends again; Mama doses her with her own nerve tonic, but Madeleine cannot stomach it; the doctor prescribes strong wholesome cocoa to soothe girlish megrims. Nothing helps. Desperately, Papa decrees holidays at their country house at Rhu to restore the roses to her pale cheeks.

She weeps at Papa's kindness, which she does not deserve, and at the thought of being separated from Emile, which she cannot bear, and at Emile's anger that she is being taken away from him, because she knows that she will suffer for it. Sometimes Emile follows her to Rhu and they can snatch an hour together; sometimes he does not and spends his time in Glasgow studying the shipping schedules for Lima. She longs for peace of mind . . .

She tells Emile that they must elope; he insists that she must confront Papa. Sometimes he threatens that he will confront Papa himself, or else kill himself for her sake. The thought of either leaves her white, shaken, sleepless and nauseous. Mama makes her drink more cocoa.

She tries to break it off with Emile for the sake of her peace of mind – how she longs for peace of mind – but his throaty endearments lure her to him in the dark. She tells him that she is ill, but he only reproaches her that she has not enquired after his latest cold, caught and suffered in the hideous climate of Glasgow which he only endures for her sake. He is sure that his health would improve in Lima.

"Emile-for-pity's-sake."

Night after night when the household lies sleeping and she flounders in twin pools of despair and yearning, she rises from her bed to write to him. She takes care to write lovingly and with endless concern for his catarrhs and nervous stomach, both aggravated by her lack of true love for him. She writes by moonlight, a blanched flower in the silver beams which wash over her but do not cool her heat. She writes in heat and longing, and by the light of the bright spring moon, she slowly blooms scarlet and wise and understands at last what will bring them peace of mind and happiness.

There comes a May night at Rhu. In the violet twilight, Madeleine flickers like a flame across the lawns, out the back gate and into the arms of Emile. They clutch and hold, but this time she does not let go and they lie all night under the trees.

At dawn in her bedroom with the smell of crushed clover and grass still clinging, she scribbles a letter full of joy and fulfilment. She has the resolution now to face Papa's wrath, she writes, and come what may, they will be together at last.

His reply soon follows. The servant smuggles it to her, and she has to hide it in her long sleeve all day until she has privacy. That night in her bedroom, in the circle of yellow light around her lamp, she reads greedily, and as she reads, she pales and shrinks inside herself.

He got home safely, he writes, although the walk did his cold no good. He was happy with her last night, but . . .

"I-regret-it-very-much-Mimi-why-did-you-give-way-after-all-your-promises-you-had-no-resolution."

"Think-of-the-consequences-if-I-were-never-to-marry-you-Mimi-only-fancy-if-it-were-known-you-would-be-dishonoured-if-Miss-Perry-did-know-it-what-would-you-be-in-her-eyes."

"It-is-your-parents'-fault-if-shame-is-the-result-they-are-to-blame-for-it-all-you-will-have no-one-to-blame-but-yourself."

Oh, but it was a different tune he sang last night. "Let me, Mimi, let me . . ." Her heart turns over at the memory of sighs and groans and cries of pleasure. Aloud, as if he were there, she snaps, "Well, I don't regret it. Never shall!"

She reads again and hears the scandalised delight of respectable spinsters in 'only fancy'; she hears a perfect cacophony of stern headmistresses, disapproving fathers, and prim Church of Scotland ministers. At last he is teaching her something about a man's passions. And she hears the threat not to marry her. She must speak to Papa, he says, or for very shame he will leave the country.

In the yellow lamplight, she shrinks and pales, then flushes with anger. Threats, always threats, always she displeases, always she is to be abandoned. She has fallen from grace, not given it, and Emile has another stick to beat her with. Her mouth twists and she smells a whiff of revolutionary cordite; for a moment she sees him clearly, her shabbily respectable revolutionary, but her own anger frightens her, for there is no going back now that she has given herself to him. What if shame were indeed to be the outcome? They must marry. And soon.

She paces in and out of the circle of light. Emile is overwrought. He has no inner strength. But they can still be happy. She must believe that. But she does not speak to Papa.

The Lord Advocate thoroughly explored Madeleine's illicit connection with the deceased. The criminous intimacy was continued in the gardens at Rhu, in the laundry and drawing room of the panel's home at Number 7, Blythswood Square, in the park behind the rhododendrons at dusk, and – the Lord Advocate was heavily emphatic – at her basement bedroom window where it was her custom to pass Long-Jelly cups of cocoa through the iron stanchions.

The wardress was thoughtful that night. "Well, you're right, lass. They didn't like the letters much. Very surprising from a young lady. But the bailiff says it's clear you were under that puffed up wee Frenchie's influence. How else would you ken how to write all that stuff? Anyway, for all their protests, they're men of the world in that court. They know the ways of a man with a maid." She lifted Madeleine's plates on to a tray, then looked at her with unexpected shrewdness. "And mind, while they're all taken up with fornication, they're not thinking overmuch about arsenic."

Madeline hid a smile. It was just as well, then, that she had never explained that after that one time at Rhu, there was never another criminous connection, not even clandestinely in the laundry.

Emile, shocked by the force of her passion, insists it must be curbed. He has quite forgot that they are revolutionaries. He bleats milk-and-water hymn sheet sentiments at her: her purity; her reputation; her marriage settlement. They return to their old game of pleading and resistance, by which he has some satisfaction and she has none, but which has this to be said for it, that Madeleine does not disgrace herself again. She grows cold to him and discovers the pleasures of making him suffer. She torments him with letters passionately explicit and brings him running to her, his new found virtue in shreds.

"Let me, Mimi, let me."

Earnestly she declares that they must not sully the purity of their love.

"Let me, Mimi, let me. You did before."

She reminds him how conscience stricken he was before.

He sulks and threatens Lima or enlistment. She is silent, but after some consideration, cautions against such rashness; he must realise surely that he is not suited to the rigours of the climate in Lima or the brutishness of military life.

He abandons Lima and enlistment and hints again at suicide. She perfects a half smile in response which goads him to tearful reproaches that she no longer loves him. She smiles again and he looks away. At last they are beginning understand one another. It is an unpleasant experience, but she can't quite finish with him, not yet. She often wonders why.

She has not the slightest intention of speaking to Papa.

The Lord Advocate was in fine form the next morning. "From her letters, gentlemen, it is clear that she promised to marry the deceased in September and refers to him still as 'sweet-pet-Emile-o-my-beloved' while simultaneously she accepts a proposal of marriage from Mr William Minnoch, to whom she writes in more decorous vein:

"My-aim-in-life-dear-William-shall-be-to-study-you-and-please-you."

Madeleine winced. It was just as well that Billy too had taken to his bed for the duration of the trial. What would he have made of all this? He would think her insincere. She knew perfectly well that, as the old song had it, it was best to be off with the old love before you were on with the new, but Emile had refused to be off. She would have liked to be honest, but his intransigence had forced deception on her.

Papa decides that Madeleine is ready for life to begin, and for marriage, which is the same thing. There are new tarlatan gowns and satin lined cloaks and little dancing shoes which are soon worn out; there are routs, assemblies, and balls; there are endless letters to Emile protesting that she only attends these functions at her father's insistence and that she has done nothing to warrant the title of Glasgow's leading belle. As for the gossip about Billy Minnoch and her, it is just that. Gossip.

He does not believe her. His suspicion are dark – he knows full well of what licentiousness she is capable. He warns her that he has a husband's rights, and she the obligations of a wife. That is the law, he says, because they are contracted to one another.

Wearily she agrees and protests her devotion. Wearily she recommends cocoa for his colds, catarrhs and nervous stomach. Wearily she agrees that she has much to learn about being a perfect lady.

Sometimes her patience snaps and she tells him that he can go to Lima or the dark side of the moon for all she cares. Sometimes she means it.

With Papa's approval, and to Mama's delight, handsome Billy Minnoch, rich and charming and the catch of the season, comes courting. He adores Madeleine and finds no fault in her. Papa says she could do worse than Billy Minnoch. She already knows this. She lives in dread of Emile's jealous interrogations and his hectoring sermons, but just when she thinks that she cannot stand one more carping letter, just when she thinks that one more bleating complaint will drive her mad, a look from him, or a touch, or the realisation of his utter misery softens her and she steps weeping into his arms and he is loving and kind. She often wonders why falling out of love has so few of the certainties of falling in. But she knows that a future with Emile is impossible, would be intolerable, and has known it since Rhu.

Life is complicated. She must assure Emile of her undying devotion but that the time is not right to speak to Papa; she must assure Billy of her undying devotion but ask that their engagement be postponed until the spring, her favourite time of year. And before that time comes, she must disentangle herself from Emile.

She picks quarrels, ignores his letters, and has no time to meet him. He suffers it all. The man has no pride. Finally, she writes in the coldest terms that their engagement is ended.

He laughs at her. She has given herself to him and he has her letters to prove it. He has only to show them to her Papa, has only to broadcast her looseness, and what man will marry her then? She is to fulfil her obligations to him or she knows what will happen. She is to be quite clear about that. Madeleine is clear and is devastated.

"Emile-on-my-bended-knee-do-not-denounce-me-it-will-kill-my-mother-I-humble-myself-before-you-I-crave-your-mercy-despise-me-hate-me-but-do-not-make-me-a-public-scandal."

She begs hard enough to please him. Graciously he forgives her. They are reconciled.

That night the wardress was especially kind. The Lord Advocate would sum up next day. Already the timetable of events had been laid before the jury: the proposed spring engagement to Billy Minnoch, Emile's two sudden and desperate illnesses just before it was announced, her last letter to him, inviting him to visit her, his death that very night. The wardress shrugged. "The whole business is the talk of the town. The betting's on Mr Inglis, though. He's a canny lawyer and the bailiff heard him say they've proved nothing, only thrown a lot of mud."

Madeleine sat alone in the gathering gloom, aware that the tide of public sentiment had turned in her favour. The world loved a repentant fallen woman, it seemed. She had letters, dozens of letters, from gentlemen all over the country, offering their forgiveness for her erring ways, which they dwelt on in nauseating and lingering detail, along with their hearts and hearths and gentle guidance for the future. As if she hadn't had enough of men's hearts and guidance to last her a lifetime.

"O-my-beloved-come-to-me."

Her last letter to him. To hear the Lord Advocate, it was a declaration of intent to murder. "She invited him, and he came. The panel insists that he did not keep the appointment and that the arsenic she purchased had nothing to do with his death. She bought it, poured it in a basin, and washed in it. Gentlemen of the jury, do you believe that? He told his friend that more than once he had been taken ill after imbibing cocoa served to him by her. He said that if she were to poison him, he would forgive her. What was it that had aroused his suspicions? Should not we also be suspicious? It has been suggested that he killed himself for her sake. Is it conceivable that a man would attempt such a death, such an agony, three times?

"O-my-beloved-come-to-me."

Mr Inglis was succinct. "There is no proof that the letter refers to the night that he died; there is no proof that they met on any of the occasions when he was taken ill. If it is inconceivable that a man would attempt such an agonising suicide three times, is it remotely conceivable that a man who suspects he is being poisoned would continue to accept cocoa from her hands? Long-jelly was an hysteric: he threatened suicide many times; he told his friend that if he could not have Miss Smith, then no one would, that he would make sure of that; he declared that if she were to poison him, he would forgive her. Long-jelly had the overheated temperament of a parlour-maid. Have we a case of murder to try? Or a suicide? Or a Machiavellian conspiracy to punish Miss Smith for her audacity in rejecting him? Could his death in fact have been an accident? It is known that arsenic eaters often kill themselves by mistake. Any one of these explanations is as likely as any other. Gentlemen, the picture is murky and there is much reasonable doubt. Consider carefully."

It was time for the jury to decide. Madeleine watched the jurymen's thoughts march across their faces. The opera glasses were trained upon her again, magnifying her, as if by enlargement the secrets of her heart would be exposed and the events of that night at the window of her basement bedroom put on show for all to see.

There were two versions to be considered:

"O-my-beloved-come-to-me."

He did not come. She waited. At length she put out her lamp and retired to bed. L'Angelier's movements that night were unaccounted for. He was missing for five hours. Maybe he got his death elsewhere. Maybe he killed himself in despair. Maybe he was careless with his poisonous medicine. Any one was as likely as the other. The picture was murky.

Or the other possibility:

"O-my-beloved-come-to-me."

He came. He tapped at her window. She opened it, standing in her nightdress with the yellow light behind her, her hair flowing darkly over flounces and ruffles of white lawn. And then – the picture was murky. There might have been an impropriety or a murder or both or neither.

Madeleine knew from the wardress that these were the scenarios being considered by the jurymen. All Edinburgh was considering them along with its tea and scones. Madeleine needed no opera glasses to see what happened that night. She thought of it occasionally, at unexpected moments . . .

"O-my-beloved-come-to-me."

He comes, stooping out of the darkness to tap at her window, blinking in the lamplight.
   She smiles a welcome, a well trained bitch brought to heel.
   He is pale. His stomach, he says, has not settled since that last bad bout and his cough is worse. He has strange, frightening tinglings in his fingertips and toes.
   Madeleine is all concern. He must see a doctor. She told him so last time, but he never

listens.

His eyes, dark and watchful, lighten. She would not mind if he saw a doctor? An expert? It would not trouble her? Truly?

The more expert the better, she says smiling. Why on earth would she not want him to consult such a person? The illness continues too long and must be investigated. This is only common sense.

Yes, he says, common sense. He smiles and his pale face glows.

She clasps his hands through the bars at the window. Perhaps he should accept the invitation to visit his friends in the Isle of Wight. The mild air would benefit him. He should go next week. And consult a doctor there.

His eyes darken with suspicion. Why does she want him out of the way next week?

She says she only wants him to be well soon, so that they may marry.

Marry? he says. There are rumours of a marriage. Billy Minnoch's marriage. That it is to be announced soon.

She weeps. These endless suspicions. She has told him over and over that there is only friendship between her and Mr Minnoch. She cannot be held responsible for gossip. Cannot he forgive past misunderstandings?

He forgives, he says, but cannot forget. She understands, doesn't she, that he will never let her marry another, that she will never be rid of him?

She presses his hands between hers. She does not want to be rid of him. Why must he torture her so?

He weeps and says she does not know the meaning of torture. She cannot know what it is like to be him and to be so tortured.

He tortures himself, she says, but soon he will never know another moment's unease on her account.

He raises her hand to his lips. Yes, he says, they will be happy when they are wed.

She says his lips are cold. It is a raw night. He must have something to keep out the chill. She has cocoa warming on her little stove. She brings it to the boil, stirring all the time to make it smooth. He complained of grittiness last time. Drink it down, she says, while it is hot. It is good for a nervous stomach.

He warms his hands around the cup. If he is harsh, he says, it is only because he loves her. In future his reproaches shall be more gently given.

Yes, she says, yes. For her part, she is only sorry that she has been such a trial to him.

He drinks deeply. Does she truly love him?

Yes, yes.

He presses his forehead to the bars and weeps. Sometimes he thinks she only says things for form's sake.

Emile, she protests gently, I have always loved you. Always.

He drains the cup and kisses her between the bars. Love will find a way, he says. He goes home happy.

She wipes her mouth carefully and rinses the cup and the saucepan several times. Oh, that dreary wee man! He should have taken his chances in Lima.

The verdict, when it came, provoked a storm of cheering the length of the Royal Mile. Madeleine was displeased by the wishy-washy Not Provens, and also by Mr Inglis's pointed refusal to shake hands with her. But she shrugged off the insult, which was of no consequence. She was free and ready for life to begin at last.   ⬦

JAMES SALLIS

Jim Sallis's books include nine novels, multiple collections of stories, poems and essays, a biography of Chester Himes, and a translation of Raymond Queneau's *Saint Glinglin*. A new novel, *Cypress Grove*, will be out shortly from No Exit.

Each day we're required to assume the identity of one of the other students. At first, when we knew so little of one another, it was less difficult, but we're well along in the program now and have gained considerable personal knowledge. On the other hand, all those early, generic assignments, impersonating postmen, policemen and the like, have paid off. This has been going on from the first day. We're graded on how well we bring it off:

Preparation. Equal parts Research (on the internet) and Observation (finding those physical, character and speech traits of the target that others in the class will recognize).

Persuasiveness. This one, like much else in life, is mostly attitude. You must charge right in and right along, pursuing your objective and game plan, oblivious of all objections, challenges, detours and roadblocks.

Perseverance. You do not, whatever happens, surrender. Even in the face of certain defeat, cover hopelessly blown, revealed for what you are, you do not give up the pretense.

Yesterday I received the only 10/10/10 of the semester. Called upon first thing in the morning, I stood, walked to the front of the class and began my presentation, continuing same, with scheduled breaks, of course, until almost five in the afternoon. This time I had become not a fellow student but our instructor, Mr Soong. As Mr Soong sat in the back of the classroom smoking cigarette after cigarette and looking ever more nervous, I taught the class he might have taught, sketching out details of a standard shadow-agent operation, citing examples from my own (his own) field work and my (his) personal history.

The secret-agent school is located on a strip mall in the far-southeastern reach of the city, just at the boundary where the city goes down for the third time into suburbs. One end of the mall's held down by a Petsright, the other by an upstart home-supply center. An income-tax service, a cut-rate office-supply store and two food shops, Ted's Fish N Chips, Real-y-Burgers, straggle down the line. Standing apart across a narrow empty lot chockful of go-cups and partial frames of shopping carts like disabled vehicles left behind on battlefields, a shabby cinema plays last year's forgotten films at a dollar a shot to sparse audiences of forgotten people.

"A moment, if you will," Mr Soong announced as, taking my seat near day's end, I passed both torches, classroom and identity, back to him. He held up a finger profoundly nicotine-stained to the first joint and only seriously stained to the next – a characteristic of which I had made full use. By now, mindful of rush hour, students are compulsively checking watches as though they're detonation devices. The next wave of hopefuls, buying their way towards certification as nursing assistants, teems on the sidewalk outside. The storefront classroom's on time-share between various vocational schools. *Stuck in a dead-end job? You're only ninety days away from an*

151

exciting career as _____. *You can make the difference*, etc.

"Violence, I'm afraid, has paid a visit," Mr Soong said, British locution and Indian rhythm chiming together like two dice in a cup. "At or about one o'clock this morning, noticing that lights remained on well after hours, a squad car on routine patrol pulled up in front of the Rialto." Everyone hereabouts called it The Real Toe. "One officer stayed behind to radio in, the other went into the lobby. There he found a young man – the assistant manager as it turned out, an eighteen-year-old who closed each night after seeing the rest of the staff out – lying in front of the popcorn machine, quite dead."

Lying in a pool formed of blood and piss in equal parts, with a small pool of Real Butter Flavoring nearby, lesser lake among the greater – but Mr Soong doesn't say this.

"Both the mall's proprietors and school officials have asked that I urge you all to exercise caution today as you leave. Please do so." That index finger went up again, pointing to the sky like a saint's. "Observe the buddy system." Now a second finger. "Be aware always of your surroundings." And a third. "Walk purposefully." Little finger. "Make eye contact with anyone you encounter." Lady Thumb. "Have your car keys out and ready."

Because it was the first Friday of the month, tuition was due. One by one we filed past Mr Soong's makeshift desk to pay up, settle, render unto Caesar, etc, before filtering out onto the parking lot where a magnificent sunset burgeoned parachute-like above the horizon as the next generation of students prepared to clamber in. Many, as always, paid in cash. Some, surely, are illegal; others, for whatever and various reasons, have or lay claim to no bank accounts.

I sat in my car smoking a last cigarette, radio tuned to the local NPR, as late arrivals rushed from car to classroom in search of the excellent salary and fulfilling career promised them by late-night TV ads, and as day's parachute collapsed into darkness. At Standard Uniform in Twin Cedars Mall a mile or so further along towards the city, they've all purchased green uniform tops, white shoes, shiny scissors, gleaming stethoscopes.

I watched Mr Soong cross cracked pavement to his yellow Honda. Often, I know, once all are gone, Mr Soong returns to the classroom to work.

On the way home I listen to an interview with a writer who's published a book about caged birds taken as safeties into coal mines. "Mute, unsocialized birds are best for the purpose," he said. "Mockingbirds with their vast repertoire proved worthless: they sing and sing up till the very moment they keel over."

The color of the universe, another interviewee, a physicist, insists at length, is beige. He also has written a book which expounds his beliefs. The world is fast filling up with news and interviews, books and belief. Soon there'll be no room for people.

Next morning, Miss Smith pulls into the spot alongside as I'm sitting there with windows rolled down listening to bad country music and finishing up my large coffee and egg-and-bacon sandwich. I stopped off at the Greek's diner as always. We go in and find Mr Soong lying in a pool of sticky red stuff. Soon other students begin arriving; more than one stumbles back outside to throw up.

"Maybe this is our final exam," I say to Miss Smith.

Mr Soong, get up. Light a cigarette, smile your lopsided smile, and grade me. Tell me how I did. ✿

RAY NAYLER

Ray Nayler was born in Quebec and educated in California, where he studied American Literature and Film Noir at the University of California, Santa Cruz. His short stories have been published in a variety of professional magazines.

Ray's first novel *American Graveyards* was also the first Crimewave Special. It was received extremely well by critics and readers alike, so much so that we have reprinted the book – see the ad on the previous page for more details or visit our website at www.ttapress.com.

I had a father for six months.

I met him when I was seven years old. There was a knock on the door of our prefab house, and my mother, who had been in the kitchen throwing cut vegetables into a bubbling pot of Ragu, smiled down at me and said, "Who could that be? Why don't you go and see, baby?"

She knew who it was, of course.

It was June 5, 1976 and my father had just been released from prison for burglary. I knew none of this. My father had taken a Greyhound Bus from Folsom to Albuquerque, New Mexico. He had been on the bus nearly two days. He had spent his time playing Go Fish with a couple of kids about my age, whose mother wanted nothing to do with them. She had a headache.

I knew none of this.

My mother never had a headache.

I threw the door open.

The man was tall and very thin and a bit pale. He had a bunch of daisies in his hand, wrapped in cheap green cellophane and with the price-tag still on them. He looked around a hundred years old to me, but I was seven and anybody over thirteen was over the hill. He had a red baseball cap on, the kind that's sized, not the cheap plastic-backed kind with the adjusting tabs in back. He had a baseball glove in his other hand, which he had stolen from a kid's backpack at the Greyhound station in Phoenix, Arizona, while the kid was in the bathroom taking a leak. He had a big stupid grin screwed to his face, and there was a tooth missing on one side. A bicuspid, knocked out by a prison guard who caught him smoking in the laundry room, instead of folding.

He said, "Hey, buddy. How's it going?"

I turned around and yelled: "It's some guy selling flowers!"

He said, "I guess you don't remember me."

I was confused because he wasn't a Mexican like the other guys who wandered around selling Cheapo Flores in Albuquerque.

"Better let him in, honey. It's hot out there."

My mom must be nuts, I thought. I'm not letting some jerk in our house.

Some Jerk said: "I'm your Dad. But you don't have to call me that, just yet. I guess I'll have to earn that."

My mom came up behind me, wiping her hands clean on her yellow half-apron, and they stared at each other. I don't know how long. I was in my room with the door slammed shut, face-down on my bed. It could have been hours.

It was a big shock for me, seeing my father for the first time. My father who had been 'away' since before I could remember. Just 'away', and somehow I had known never to ask questions. I had seen pictures of him, but pictures are just shapes on paper and this was a man. The glove he gave me helped me get over the shock. You can buy kids off easy.

That evening we played catch in the flat white light of the motion sensor lamp mounted over our front door. He would be still for a moment, and it would go dark. He would move to throw, and the lamp switched on, and there was the ball, already halfway to my mitt, coming out of nowhere. I would catch it most times, or miss it and it would bounce away, out of the light, a dull whitish spot under the half-grown bushes that framed our property. If I caught it he said, "Great catch, buddy!" in a way that made me want to cry and throw myself at him, burrow right into him and stay there loving him, hugging him so he would never go 'away'. And if I missed it he would say, "Don't worry about it," in a voice that made me want to kill myself because didn't he know I was a failure, a scabby little brat with an upcoming F in math that I hadn't told my mother about?

Everything was love and death.

When he stopped moving the light went out with a click and he was gone.

When he moved he was there again. Like a magic trick. I scrambled to catch the ball.

He had no glove but caught the ball bare-handed and didn't even wince. Because he was magic. Because he was my dad already, even though it would take me a month to say it to his face.

Even though I couldn't stand it when he touched my mother.

We lived way out on the West Side of Albuquerque, where it starts petering out into the desert again. We lived a stone's throw from Route 66. There were plenty of lumpy vacant lots to go BMXing in with the other kids, but that was about it. The ice-cream man didn't make it out that way much, but there was a market where you could buy pop-ups and orangesickles. I sped around on my BMX, new that Christmas, jumping off the dirt mounds, spectacularly happy because it was summer, because it was Saturday and because I had a dad. My friend Jimmy said, "Hey, who's that guy sitting out fronta your place?" and I said, "That's my dad, you dumb bastard."

My dad.

Not just Some Jerk.

A man who could catch a baseball bare-handed.

A man who knew how to break glass quietly by taping it, and then pulling it away in a single piece.

A man who had spent five years in prison sharing a cell with Harley Madson. He called himself Harley, but my dad said his real name was Kimberley. His parents had wanted a girl.

My dad said a lot of things.

In prison you end up owing people. My dad owed Harley, for reasons I would never know. For reasons he didn't talk about. So when Harley showed up at our doorstep and needed a place to stay the night, he stayed.

The two weeks before Harley came were the best fourteen days of my life. My new dad was gone all day looking for work. He had been a mechanic, and he had been a janitor, and a pump jockey, and a barback and a dishie and a short order cook. But he had also been a felon, and that was what people saw. Like an angry red scar down the side of his face. Like a missing eye. Felon. Jailbird. Thief. Liar. Dirt.

In the evening we played catch. He fixed the chain on my bike and showed me how to patch a tire. He sat in a lawn chair on the doorstep, and my mother sat in a lawn chair next to him, and between them their hands were linked. They didn't talk much, but sometimes my mother's eyes glittered, and sometimes my father would lean over to her and whisper something, and then they would go inside. I would hit the jumps on my BMX and fly up into the hot red desert air and come down easy. I would fall and not wince. I tried not to think of him touching her. I could never get used to that. Holding hands was okay, but inside they did something else. Something you turned the lights out and locked the door for, and I didn't like it.

It was the price I paid for having a dad.

That was the way I saw it. It was like dues.

My mother had hair the color of postcard sand, and brown-gold eyes. Like whiskey in the bottle, with the sun coming through it. When Harley came my dad got the door, and in the kitchen my mother, who was straining macaroni noodles, closed her whiskey eyes and put her hand to her forehead, like she had a fever. I was standing in the middle of the kitchen saying, "Mommommom." Because my inside clock had gone off and I had to make sure dinner was coming in say the next five minutes or so.

In the front room my dad's voice said: "Honey, is there enough for a fourth?"

A new voice said: "Don't worry about me, David. I don't – "

"Honey?"

My mom opened her eyes again and said, "Of course there is!" in a sweet voice that didn't match the empty, awful look in her eyes. She blinked like someone trying to wake up.

I wanted to go in the other room to see who it was, but somehow I was scared. I didn't like the way my mother was acting, and I didn't like the way my dad's voice sounded. Weak. Like a kid's voice.

"Honey, come on in here and meet Harley Madson. We shared a cell in Folsom."

We sat around the table and ate macaroni and cheese and drank Pepsis. Harley did most of the talking. He was a big man with an even bigger voice, and a tattoo of a carp swimming down his right arm – splashing out at the elbow and darting toward his wrist. My new dad laughed at all of Harley's jokes, which mostly went over my head, being about women or prison, two things in which I was inexperienced. My mother laughed, but her laugh was polite and stiff. Harley kept looking at her in a way that made me want to stab him with my fork. Her cheeks were red.

"Time for bed, champ." My dad winked at me. I didn't want to leave. I felt somehow like I needed to stay. To keep an eye on things. But I had never made my dad angry. I didn't know him angry, and I was afraid (with that instinct of a child) of what I might see.

I lay in the dark and listened to Harley's big laugh, my father's little laugh, and the polite titter of my mother. Harley had been nice to me. He'd winked at me and told my mom how big I was and how strong I looked. If anyone else had done those things, I would have liked them. But I could not like Harley. There was something about him. Something that then I could not put into words, but now I can. Every expression Harley made was a different mask. His face was not his own. His expressions were exact, and the emotions they conveyed went no deeper than the muscles he had trained to take their shape. His eyes watched from behind. Flat blue eyes the color of faded denim. His eyes were murderous, even crinkled at the edges in a smile. Anyone should have seen he meant no one in this wide world any good.

My mother saw it.

My dad, for some reason, could not.

If he could, everything would have been different.

Harley spent the night, but was gone before I got up in the morning. He had a job at a warehouse all set up by some of his other prison buddies, but he hadn't gotten a place in Albuquerque just yet. He found an old Airstream trailer for sale and parked it in the parking lot of the warehouse. He got my dad a job at the warehouse as well. I thought it would make my mother happy, my dad getting a job and becoming a 'citizen' again. "A productive citizen. That's my goal," my dad would say. "I don't want to do anything fancy. Just make enough for bread and take care of you and buddy there."

My mother kept working at the laundry, like always. She said she would quit as soon as they were sure the job at the warehouse would hold. She squinted her whiskey eyes when she talked about 'The Job', as if it were not a real job. Even though he came home tired and sweaty from unloading trucks. It seemed real enough to me.

Sometimes, he didn't come home until late. Sometimes, until after midnight. There was a strangeness to him then. His voice was growly and slurry, and his eyes would coast over me, not really seeing me. He smiled different. And he stank.

I understood that these times he had been out with Harley. That they had 'tied one on'.

On those nights my mother was very quiet. She sat at the table in the kitchen turning the pages of a book or a magazine while the blue light of the television flashed in the living room. I would sit on the kitchen floor shoving my Hotwheels around their orange track and watching her out of the corner of my eye. Had she gotten smaller? Was she shrinking? Sometimes my heart pounded. I was scared without knowing why. I loved her more than I loved myself.

Those nights I did not like my dad. I peeked in on him, slumped in the battered armchair in front of the TV, smiling that new stupid smile, nodding along with the voices on the TV until his head stopped coming up and he was asleep. I wanted to kick him, to punch him.

Other nights it was all right. He bought himself a glove and a bat and we played ball out in the lumpy vacant lot. High pop-flies lost in the evening sky. The chirping of crickets that fell silent when you came too close. His skinny arm lofting the ball and the crack of the bat.

"Great catch, buddy."

"Don't worry about it."

Love and death.

Harley came by sometimes. Those were the worst nights. Sitting around the table and listening to his stories. Listening to my mother try to laugh. And watching him watch her. Was my father getting smaller as well? Were both of my parents shrinking? Harley was huge, his belly sagging over his belt, his carp-arm swimming over the table to shovel more food onto his plate. After dinner they sat in the living room emptying a bottle of Jack.

My mother would walk with me on those nights, down to the liquor store. The evenings were warm. The ground kept the day's heat inside itself. The ground pulsed with heat like skin. You could feel the earth breathe. We went the long way and under the street lamps I stared at her. The filament glow of her sand-colored hair, her crooked front tooth when she smiled down at me.

Sitting on the curb in front of the liquor store, sucking on my creamsickle, I asked her the question. "Is Harley a good man?"

She looked at me like she'd never seen me before. "I don't know . . . I guess he is. What do you think?" She was always asking me that. And she always meant it.

"I think he's a fat dumb lying bastard. And his stories suck."

She put her hand on my head. I loved it when she did that. I knew it meant that I'd done something right.

The bad nights came around more often. The weather started to change. School started, and the high desert winter came, the cold cutting wind sweeping off the mountains, the dirty scum of snow and black ice at the curb. My dad would drop me off at school. In the warming car he wanted to talk. Sometimes I would talk to him. Sometimes – after a bad night – I would just stare out the window. He never got angry at me. Even though I wanted him to. I wanted him to shake me and yell at me and ask me what was wrong with me. Then I would have told him how much I hated Harley. How Harley was eating them up. How they were getting smaller, and I could see it.

He never got angry.

Even when Harley grabbed my mother's butt while she was getting up to refill their drinks. "She's really something, pal. You got lucky."

My dad's laugh was a small thing. A cricket ready to stop the moment something came too close.

I was trying to decide whether to stab Harley with my knife or my fork when my mother looked at me and mouthed the word: "No."

I bunched my fists under the table. Angry. Hurt.

My dad never got angry. He just got smaller.

And then he was gone.

I was up because my mother had been up. Because she had been sitting in the kitchen, not crouched over *Vogue* or over a book as sometimes she was. Not simply sitting as sometimes she did. Sitting with a bottle of Jack, as my father and Harley sometimes did. Sitting and pouring this liquid the color of her eyes from bottle to small glass to mouth. Sitting there and not seeing me crouched on the floor. Playing with my Hotwheels but not playing. Moving the Hotwheels on the floor because if I stopped moving them, if I stopped making engine-noises and pushing the little chunks of metal and plastic across the floor she would think that something was wrong. And absolutely she could not think that anything was wrong with me. Absolutely not. I made myself invisible through movement and play. I acted out the motions of an unconcerned child. On the digital clock over the stove the blue numbers read 1:20. She got up. She staggered, leaned against the wall. Full of Jack, her voice swimming in it. "Going bed now baby you too 'kay."

"Night mom." I would not look at her.

Pushing my cars. Not seeing her hip whack into the door frame. Not hearing her fall in the hallway, or her crying. Push the cars. Push the cars around the orange track and make engine noises. Push them and do not hear. Hear maybe but do not listen. She was going into her room now. She was crawling. Push the cars. Make engine noises. Vroom. Brrrrr. Sobbing and then silence and then a heavy breathing from the bedroom. Asleep now.

Like a zombie I began doing things I had been told never to do. I made myself a bowl of cereal, climbing up on the counter to get at the high cabinets. I took it into the living room, where I switched on the television and stared at it, shoveling Cocoa Puffs into my mouth. I could not begin to tell you what was on the television, besides bright movement that dulled whatever anger and hate were in my mind. Besides voices, like my own moving the cars in the kitchen that made things invisible.

I heard the screen door pulled open, the hand fumbling with the doorknob. I did not move.

The door was flung open with a bang, and the frame filled with a dark shape, a pale and sweating face. Harley. He stumbled into the room. He'd tied one on, I guessed. But where was my dad? I got up and ran into the kitchen. From the drawer next to the sink I got the largest kitchen knife we had.

"Hey, boy! Boy!"

I peeked around the corner.

"Where's your mother?"

"Not here."

Harley's face was pale and wrong. His mask had slipped off. His eyes rolled in the naked flesh. He tried to assemble the mask. Smiled. "She ain't gone, is she boy? She wouldn't leave you here. Pretty woman like that . . . leaveyoualone."

I got the half-empty bottle of Jack and brought it in to him. Slapped it down on the TV tray. "She'll be back. Went to the store. Here. Drink this."

His eyes rolled. He picked the bottle up. Hands shaky. Brought it to his mouth and made half of it go away. "Got to have her . . ."

Have her? I was tight, a little coil of wires. Have her.

"Got to have her drive me."

In the bedroom my mother's breathing was loud, but he didn't hear it. Would he hear it? Go in there? Have her? I would stab him. I would kill him.

"She be back?"

"She just went to the store. Where's my dad?"

Harley shrugged. The sweat poured down his face. He smelled of something awful. Stink. Human waste. Maybe metal in there somewhere. Sweat. "Dumb son-of-a-gun. Should've known better . . ."

He was trying to get up. Couldn't somehow. In the flickering light of the television his face was a round whitish ball, a fat floating ball with eyes painted on it. The television laughed at him. It was funny. This big man who could not stand up.

"She better get back soon."

"Yeah," I said. "Soon."

He picked the bottle up again. His eyes closed and I came at him with the knife. I brought it down and it clanked off the bottle, just then lowered. His eyes widened. He grabbed my wrist. "What's the big idea, kid?"

He squeezed and the knife dropped to the floor.

"I won't let you," I said.

"Wh – what?"

"Have her."

He smiled sloppily. His face ran with whiskey and water. The smell of him made me gag.

"That's funny. Have her. I just . . ."

He had let go of my hand. He was doubled over, now. Breathing hard.

"You let me know when she gets back, kid."

"Where's my dad?"

"Ha. Where's yer mom?" he said into his knees.

He stayed that way. Doubled over. I picked the knife up and sat, Indian style, in the hallway. Watching him. This man who had made my parents small. This man who had come to have my mother. I would not let him! But he did not move. He stayed doubled over a while. Finally he slid out of the chair and lay on the floor, a big curled up lump with a fat belly. I did not see the blood beneath his jacket. I did not know it when he stopped breathing and died there, shot through the gut, bleeding to death in our living room.

I waited for dad to come home. This would make dad angry. This man coming in the middle of night to have mom. I imagined my dad coming through the door. Big again. Hard baseball catching hands. Hard no-wince face.

He would set things right.

Now he would be angry.

My dad was dead.

He'd broken into a rich man's house, up in the Northern foothills. He and Harley. Half drunk, doped up on cocaine. The owner, a retired Albuquerque sheriff, a man who wore cowboy hats and wide turquoise-studded belts, woke up to the sound of the two of them crashing around down there. Descending the stairs calmly, in darkness, with his Colt Peacemaker he saw two shadowy men, carrying his television set out through the door. They were laughing, and one of them was saying, "Shh. Shh. Cut it out."

The man fired two shots.

The first hit my dad in the back of the head, killing him instantly and knocking the sized red baseball cap into the air with a small round hole in its wool front, just above the brim.

The second hit Harley in the back, just to the left of his spine. He ran screaming out of the house. He drove his car swerving through downtown Albuquerque, losing blood, vacating his bowels on the seats. Half a block from our doublewide he drove the car into a ditch. He left a clear trail of blood from the car to our house, where he expired a few hours later, under my watchful eye. Waiting for my mother to come home, so that she could drive him to the hospital.

The warehouse where my dad worked was a front. They shipped stolen property out to points all over the country. Some of it was burgled from houses, but most was stolen from other warehouses and off the backs of trucks. It was a lucrative business, but it was shut down after the police found Harley dead on our indoor-outdoor carpet, and discovered where he and my father worked.

I knew none of this.

I kept expecting dad to come through the door and put an end to my vigil. But it was the cops who came, early in the blue desert morning. I was surprised but it was all right because I liked cops. They were big men who talked loud and who always, always seemed angry. They tousled my hair and told me what a good, brave kid I was. They gave me a small plastic badge to replace my dead dad.

I still have it.   ✿

'American Waitress' is the latest in an ongoing series of 'unsung heroine' stories Chris has been writing, in which ordinary people – servers, housewives, teachers, students – experience extraordinary moments in their lives that help to define them. Chris says: "I've always been typecast as a 'supernatural' writer, wrongly so, because I've only written two novels with supernatural elements, and in one the element was added at the insistence of an editor." His next novel is a Bryant & May murder mystery called *Full Dark House* published by Doubleday in August. This is followed later in the year with *Demonized*, from Serpent's Tail, then another mystery, *Plastic*.

The woman on Table 4 has a laugh like a hen getting sucked into a jet engine. She's been sitting there for hours fooling around with a tuna melt that's gone grey on her. Clearly she has nothing better to do than sit there taking up a whole booth, filling in time between the carwash and the nail bar, yakking with her friends about what one woman said to another, and how the husband is fooling around on both of them. It never ceases to amaze Molly how small the talk can get toward the tail-end of the afternoon, when the orange light is low and fierce behind the restaurant blinds.

She's managed to keep the four till twelve shift at the restaurant so she can work with Sal, who has more years on her and won't work after midnight, because she has a little girl with a twisted spine who won't let anyone else put her to bed. Sal lives in an EconoLodge near Junction 17N which is filled with frat boys throwing parties and looking to get laid, but it's safe enough for the kid, who feels safer where there's noise. Sal is a classic; she washes her hair in bleach and keeps it filled with pins and pencils in case any guy has a mind to run his fingers through it. Molly likes her; no Ps and Qs but no airs and graces either, so they help each other in the two hours that their shifts overlap.

Molly likes her job, and she's good at it. Her mother was a waitress in those chrome-fitted fifties roadside diners that have mostly been demolished now, except in states like Missouri and Florida, where they've been preserved with a kind of airquote-irony she doesn't take to. As a kid, Molly passed her life in diners and family restaurants waiting for her mother to come off duty. She never got bored. She read the books diners left behind, or watched the cook orbiting elliptically between the counter and the grill. Her mother yelled the old diner slang; Adam 'n' Eve on a raft, murphy in the alley, shingles with a shimmy, burn the British, hounds on an island, nobody uses that stuff anymore.

Now her mother is gone, and Molly has been a waitress long enough to type any customer within seconds of him coming through the door. That's how she knows the guy on Table 7 is going to be trouble. True, he doesn't have any of the usual tell-tale signs, he doesn't look angry or drunk or both, but there's something about him she doesn't want to get too close to. For a start he looks like he has too much money to be eating in a place like this; forget that crap about family restaurants being great social levellers, you don't eat here unless you're watching the pennies more than the carbs. He's in a blazer, tie and cotton twill slacks, high-top boots and some kind of fancy silver watch peeking out from his sleeve, and it just doesn't feel right. Still, he's in her section so she has no choice.

Molly's worked everywhere, Eat 'N' Park, Chili's, Hooters, Village Inn, Denny's, Red Lobster, Tony Roma's, Chi Chi's, Houlihan's, Applebee's, Red Onion, Lone Star, IHOPs, TGI Friday's, but she prefers the little family places away from the highway, where the regular trade consists of couples who've been coming there for years, local workers and lonely widowers who won't cook for themselves. Plus, you get people passing through who are just looking for a place to eat where the arrival of their eggs won't interfere with their reading of the newspaper.

In some places the work is seasonal, so it requires her to move across state. Molly doesn't mind; she has no kids to worry about uprooting, so she follows the job. But the mom and pop joints are disappearing as more people eat on the run. The chain takeouts are carefully situated to cater for office crowds. What they serve is less important than where they're based. The chains purchase tactical real estate, and keep throughput high by avoiding the comfortable familiarity of diners. They expand ruthlessly, encroaching on each other's territory so much that Molly has to look harder than ever to find the places she likes to work. Eventually she'd shifted all the way from Arizona to Florida. She likes warm weather and doesn't want to head up-state, but knows she might eventually have to in order to find a place where she can more easily afford to live.

Molly side-glances the loner as she grabs the coffee pot and swings by his table, dropping the menu in front of him. He's staring at her strangely. *Okay, I've got a weird one*, she thinks, unfazed. Some eateries attract nothing but crazies, they're situated too close to the bus station, but this place isn't one of those, even though they make you wear pink nylon uniforms that gather more static than thunderheads. She glances at Sal, with her hair like a ball of unravelled blonde wool, stuck through with pens, and wonders how she does it. Sal has five full plates and a coffee pot in her hands. Like Molly, she's on an eight-hour shift making two dollars seventy an hour plus tips, and she never stops smiling. "Honey, I can outsmile anyone if I have to," she tells Molly, "some days it feels like I have a clothes hanger in my mouth." She can handle eight tables at a time, no problem, more if she has to. There are seventeen tables in Mickey's, so the girls take turns to pick up the overlap. She'll give refills on coffee and water but not soda (although her offer to top 'em up gets noticably slowly after three trips) and she takes no shit from anyone.

Molly stands beside the guy at Table 7 and offers: "Hi, what'll it be?" because he's closed his menu.

"What's the special?" he asks, making eye contact and holding the look too long, too deep. He knows damn well what the special is because it's on the board right over the cook's hatch. He's late twenties but going to seed young, too tanned, watery brown eyes, expensive clothes that fit a little too snug. He looks like he doesn't get laid too often.

"Meatloaf, mashed potatoes, onion gravy." Molly stands with her pen poised.

"You have a really pretty face, you could try smiling like your friend over there," he tells her in a refined, not-from-around-here voice.

"I'll smile when I finish my shift. You want the special?"

"No, I'll have the hash and an egg-white omelette."

"We finish breakfast at midday. I can do you the hash as a side."

He sighs and reopens the menu, taking a while to choose, finally settling for chicken-fried steak. Molly checks out his waistline and thinks maybe he shouldn't be opting for the most calory-laden dish on the planet, but keeps the thought to herself.

"Coffee?"

He nods and she goes to pour when his hand flashes out and grabs her wrist, twisting it hard until she's forced to drop the coffee pot, which bounces on the formica-topped table and cascades scalding liquid into his lap, soaking his crotch and thighs. He doesn't flinch or make a sound. Weirder still, he looks like he wanted this to happen. Then the flicker of a smile vanishes and he explodes, jumping up and batting at his wet pants in mock-horror. "She goddamned scalded me!" he shouts so that everyone turns. "Jeezus!"

"Sal," Molly calls, "some help here."

Sal slides her plates down and shoots over to the table, but so does Larry, the assistant manager, who makes things worse by taking the customer's side without even checking to see what happened.

"I'm burning here, Christ," yells the scalded guy, hopping around, "your waitresses don't even know how to pour coffee, I'm gonna sue you for every fucking penny you've got and put you out of business, man. I have the best lawyers in town, you are *so* history." Sal drops a wad of napkins on the table and throws the scalded guy another wad, saying, "You knocked that out of her hand, mister, I saw you do it you lowlife, you can clear your own damn mess up," and with that all hell breaks loose, with customers taking sides and Larry fighting both of them, standing in front of the scalded guy like a shield. And that's when Molly knows this job is gone, because the customer won't let it go and the management has already decided who's right.

But she can't allow the incident to bug her. You let one mis-step like this throw you off and you're sunk. Money runs so tight that it only takes a small miscalculation to drop you into a whole world of ugly-ass debt, and once you fall down you never get back up. So Molly checks in her uniform and says goodbye to Sal, who ruefully promises to stay in touch. Then she begins circling the wanted ads, and the next place she can find that's hiring is called Winnie's Home Cookin', a dozen blocks further to travel from her apartment, twenty-eight tables split three ways, red plastic banquette seats and no tourists, because they stay uptown where there are no burned-out buildings or mean-faced homeboys sitting on the backs of bus benches.

She chooses the place because of the menus, which at Winnie's are bonded carriage trade leather with linings, not sponge-cushioned PVC, and a sign that the place once saw better times. It's as good a way as any to pick a job when one restaurant is so much like another. A few years back, rafia-covered menus became popular, but customers picked the corners off and one pat of butter would ruin them. The public doesn't realise how much of a server's job is side work, clearing and cleaning and replenishing, and one mushed butter-pat can really throw you off. Molly waits tables in places that have cooks, not chefs, where the portions are big and hot, the salads still sweat ice from cold storage, the pie cream comes in a spray can and every other condiment from dressing to creamer is in a fluted plastic pot. She's given a two-to-ten shift with a half-hour break and an unflattering licorice-red uniform with a nametag she has to get printed herself. The busboy is Indian and speaks better English than her co-workers, Marla and Jeanette, both of whom have allowed their everyday conversation to elide into shorthand order-speak.

The place is really busy tonight, and the table configuration is a bitch to get used to, but she's good at realigning herself to any environment, a homeostatic impulse that serves her well as she moves from job to job across America. Molly knows the secret of staying on top of the work is to be on good terms with the cook, because if he takes against you, your whole shift can go to hell. Unfortunately she got off on the wrong foot with Jomac by accidentally parking in his space. The heavyset cook looks so uncomfortable in his sweat-sheened body that she half expects to see him step out of it like a discarded jumpsuit.

She's keeping busy in a quiet patch, folding cutlery into paper serviettes, thinking about the loss of her last job with some annoyance, when the guy from Table 7 walks right in, bold as a peacock. She recognises him instantly, because you never forget the face that got you fired, but she's careful to act like she's never seen him before, even when he arranges to be seated in her section. Her first thought is: *how the hell did he find me?* The only other person who knows where she's moved is Sal, and she would never tell.

This time he's wearing a blue double-breasted blazer with gold buttons and has blond-frosted hair, a low-rent version of a high roller, like he has money and wants folk to think he's someone special but doesn't have the taste to pull it off. Molly makes sure she keeps the coffee pot well clear of him, and her hand is steady as she pours. He never takes his eyes off her, but she won't be drawn, because if she catches that look he'll know that she recognises him. Her rent is overdue because of the days she lost switching jobs, and she can't afford to screw this one up. She tries to sound casual as she takes his order, which he changes and fools with, trying all the while to connect with her, but she's steel inside, never once letting down her guard.

Placing the order at the hatch, she grabs a glimpse at the table and is shocked to see that he's still staring after her. She wishes Sal was here to back her up. She can't confide in Marla or Jeanette, who share a rented trailer together with Jeanette's boyfriend, so they obviously have no secrets and no time for anyone else's. She'll have to deal with it alone, but forewarned is forearmed, and this time she's not coming anywhere near his reach. When the meal arrives she slips the plate across from the far side of the table, smoothly withdrawing her hand before he can get near her, although he makes no attempt to do so.

She comes back from the table, serves the couple on 12 with lurid emerald slices of Key Lime pie, and is refilling their plastic water glasses when she hears the cry. She instantly knows where it's coming from, and looks over. He's sitting there clutching his mouth with both hands, and there's a thin trickle of blood coming out of the corner between his fingers. She tries to ignore him but knows he is calling to Marla, who's just passing his table. Her world slows down, because it has suddenly been rendered fragile.

She wonders what could be wrong. He couldn't have burned himself on the plate or found a piece of glass in his potatoes – Jomac is so meticulous in his preparation of the food that the servers are constantly hassled by impatient diners. Her mind flashes back over the service she provided – nothing she's done could have caused him injury; she's in the clear. He's yelling like crazy now, and if she pays no attention it'll look like she has something to hide, so she goes over and stands beside Marla, watching the performance.

The restaurant moves in a strange half-time as she watches Marla trying to convince the man to take his hands from his mouth. He tips the crimson-stained palms away and parts his bloody teeth as Marla probes. Molly sets down the water jug and realises, as her gaze travels up her uniform, that she is no longer wearing her name badge. She washed the outfit last night, as she does most nights, and ironed it before she left the room, pinning the badge in place as she walked down to her sideswiped Nissan, but sometime between then and now it has disappeared, and she has a terrible feeling that it is in his mouth.

Sure enough, the pin is hooked into his gum, but Marla's strong fingers pull it free, she just reaches in there without thinking, not worrying about HIV or anything, she used to be a nurse at the city hospital, and he retches and spits onto the tabletop, the little red badge skittering out in front of him. Molly snatches the thing up, wiping blood from the raised letters to reveal her name. The pin has been jammed in his mouth so hard that it's almost bent double. Marla's trying to wipe him down with a wadded cloth but he's still yelling blue murder, and now the temporary manager, an ineffectual, almost ghostly Texan kid who goes by the wholly appropriate name of Sketch, is calling her over with a look of anger on his face that's the first genuine emotion she's seen him show.

It's raining hard, the first time in over a month, and it's falling too fast for her wipers to clear, pelting through the smashed window and soaking her shoulder, so she pulls over beside a phonebox. She no longer has her mobile – that was one of the first expenses to go. She's lucky – Sal is just leaving to start her shift.

"How he could even convince people he'd accidentally eaten it, for God's sake, it's a name-tag, he said it had been deliberately pushed into the mashed potato where he couldn't see it, I mean, what is this guy's fucking problem?" She listens to Sal, who's a mix of common sense and Southern toughness, a woman who once went back on a double shift within hours of an abortion in order to pay the doctor.

"No, I didn't report the car window because what's the point? He obviously recognised the vehicle in the restaurant lot, looked in and saw my badge on the seat or the floor. Well it seems pretty obvious to me that's what happened, 'cause I sure as hell didn't come near enough for him to rip it off me in the restaurant." She listens some more. The rain is steaming off the car hood like mountain mist.

"The same as before. Won't press charges if they let me go, yadda yadda, they couldn't get me out of the door fast enough, everyone's so shit-scared of lawsuits. Marla with blood all over her, unbelievable. God, no, I don't want to track him down, I just want to stay the hell out of his path. I wouldn't even be able to give the police a clear description, he looked kind of different this time. Sure I recognise him, but that's because of his manner, you know how you do in this job, complainers stay with you. But I'm going to change the car, that has to be how he found me. I have to anyway, I can't afford to get the window fixed, although what's gonna be cheaper than this heap of junk I don't know. No, I have no idea what car he drives. No, Sal, it's celebrities who get stalkers, I'm just a waitress, but I'd like to know what the fuck he thinks he's doing." She scans the straight wet street as she listens. The sky is darker than the buildings. "Sure, I'll be in touch just as soon as I get something."

After hanging up she goes into the convenience store on the corner and collects the freesheets. She needs to start looking for hirers right now. She can sell the Nissan and go to Rent-A-Wreck until she's back on her feet, the cash will tide her over between jobs, but doesn't know how she'll ever cover the gap and save for another car.

Back in her room at the motel – she swore she'd never rent like Sal, the margin for financial error is just too slight, but there's no alternative now that she's moving around again – she looks at her face in the bathroom mirror, and knows that some restaurants will rule her out. She was always pretty, but the look is getting hard. She's not as light-hearted about the job as she used to be, and it's starting to show. The management want their 'girls' looking fresh, not troubled. She's always been good at hiding her worries behind a smile, has no problem with being on her feet all day and knows the work better than any of the younger ones, her customers always tell her that. If she'd been an executive she'd have risen through the ranks by now, but when you're a waitress there's nothing to be except another waitress, and the older you get the more management start thinking you'll want to use their health plans.

The tips at Winnie's were solid, she needs another place like that. For a while she toys with the idea of taking a second job, just until she's out of this money-hole. She could do mornings in a mall, grab a couple of hours' sleep and keep her regular afternoon shift, or just work one restaurant and pull a double every three days or so, but first she has to find one job, let alone two, and the ads aren't promising.

The first interview she gets is a disaster, a dingy deep-red ribshack staffed by downtrodden-looking migrants with ESL and a scary supervisor called Ethel who warns her that they don't tolerate slackers. The next, which she passes on the spot, is in a diner set behind the grafitti-blitzed bus station, populated entirely by derelicts surviving on handouts of old coffee. Getting in and out of the building involves walking through shadowed no-go zones to an unlit car park; and with her stalker waiting out there somewhere, it's not worth the risk.

Finally she gets a decent slot at Amanda's, a dessert-heavy joint in an unsafe but thankfully well-lit downtown neighborhood where the kids hang out in chicken-wire basketball courts smoking, dealing and constantly shifting loyalties within their social groups. Amanda's desserts are a source of fascination for Molly. They sit in a tall glass cabinet lit spearmint-neon in the middle of the restaurant, and appear to have been manufactured from entirely alien ingredients. The jello is coloured in eye-watering shades that don't exist in or out of nature, the cream is so white that it looks like plastic paint, and the pumpkin pie appears to be made of orange sofa foam.

But hey, it's a job, and the other girls seem okay, if a little distant. They're scared, she can see that, scared of slowing in case they stop altogether, like wound-down clockwork toys. The bad news is she gets the late shift, which is until 2:00am with another half-hour of clearing away after that, but servers can't be choosers and at least night diners aren't so picky about their food.

The motel where she's staying smells of damp and fast sex. It has a filthy pool, a scared-looking Mexican cleaner and a weird reception clerk who concentrates on comic books as though they were Dickens novels. She gets back from Amanda's too tired to wash out her uniform, but it has to be done the night before or it won't be dry in time. The tips are lower because the desserts are cheaper, which is no surprise considering how they taste. Amanda was the original owner, but the place killed her and now it's working on the rest of the staff, who have the bad skin and downbeat demeanor of drug mules.

In the moments when the work eases off, and she looks out through the plate window at the windy, desolate street, Molly sometimes wonders how it's come to this. She has no real friends to speak of, no one to share private jokes with, no loyal lover who waits up to tell her things will all turn out fine. And on the bad evenings, when rain weighs down the red plastic canopy and the place is deserted, she asks herself how long she can go on pretending that everything is fine, how long it will be before her ready optimism and her hopeful smile crack and die with the weight of getting by.

But you think like that and you're already lost. So she covers the burns on her wrist caused by hoisting the coffee pot and shows the surliest diner that she cares, and works on autopilot until at the end of the week, one rainy Sunday night, she doesn't even notice that he's back, the stalker is back, and has slipped into a booth at the end of her section just before the restaurant's due to close.

The lights are dim over the crimson seats, so when she catches his face it's a shock. He looks terrible, like he hasn't slept for a month. He looks like a serial killer haunted by his deeds. His hair has grown out and he's added a moustache that ages him, and she knows she can't ask Rosemary, the other waitress, to take over because her section is empty and she's slipped into the alley for a cigarette.

Ted, the cook, is nowhere in sight. No one can help her. She drops the menu onto his table and beats it, checking that her name-tag is in place as she goes. But she has to return to take his order, because that's her job, it's what she does. And he says: "Molly, I've been looking for you everywhere. You're the only one who can help me. Please, don't go, I won't do anything bad."

She wants to go but has to stop and ask. "Why did you get me fired?" She's holding the coffee pot high above him, ready to throw it in his face if he moves an inch toward her.

"You're too special to be working in a diner," he tells her, watching her eyes. "Such big blue eyes, like an angel. You're a good woman, Molly. You know how much it hurt me to let you go? The first time I saw you I knew you could save me from myself, stop me from doing harm to others."

"You're crazy, mister," she tells him. "I can't even save myself."

"Molly – " He reaches out a hand.

"You don't use my name, and if you move one more muscle I swear to God I'll pour boiling coffee over you," she warns. "Now you can either eat and leave or just plain leave, there's no way I'm listening to your bullshit." Her hand is shaking, and she's not sure how much longer she can hold the steel pot aloft.

"Apple pie and coffee," he tells her, as normal as any other diner. "I won't make any trouble in here." She goes to the cabinet and cuts the pie, slipping the knife into her apron pocket, but he's as good as his word. He eats as meekly as a punished child, and leaves a twenty dollar bill on the table without asking for the check. He picks up his raincoat and goes so quickly that she has no time to see which direction he's heading.

She's due off duty in five minutes, and there's no more side work to do tonight because they cleared and reset as the restaurant emptied. Outside, it's raining fit to drown rats. There's a stippled yellow pool stretching across the road where the drains are backed up. No cars, no people, like a movie set waiting for its cue. She thinks of asking Ted to walk her to her car, but doesn't want anyone to think there's something wrong. So she offers to close up for the night, and waits as the others pull their jackets over their hair and head out into the downpour. She douses the lights and watches, but there's nothing happening outside. Finally the waiting gets on her nerves, so she digs out the keys and locks the front door behind her. From the canopy to the car park is a couple of hundred yards max, but she needs to plot the route because parts of the broken tarmac are flooded and her canvas trainers will get soaked.

She negotiates an isthmus through the water toward the Rent-A-Wreck Datsun and already has her keys out when she realises he's sitting in the car, and the headlights come on as he pulls around her, shoving open the passenger door and dropping across the seats to pull her in, but she's fast and lashes out at his face. She's not expecting the pad across her mouth, though, and the gasp of surprise she takes draws chloro-form into her lungs. That's the trick, not to put it across the nose like they do in movies, and now it's too late because everything's pressing in on her, and she knows she's losing consciousness. He's going to kill her and leave her body in a ditch, she realises stupidly, and that's not at all what she had planned for herself.

But not before she's pushed her way back out of the car, and although she's dis-oriented by the rain and the bitter smell in her head, she knows she must breathe clean air fast or she'll go down, and he's slowed up by having to stop the car and come around from the other side. And man, either he's slow or she's fast because she's stumbling back at the door of Amanda's before he comes sliding around the corner toward her. If she can shut the door she'll have won, but his strong hand covers the jamb and pushes back, and all it takes is one clean sharp punch in the face to floor her cold.

"Nurses are strong, of course, but they care in an entirely different way, and they empathise way too much."

She hears him before she sees him. Her right eye is sore and feels swollen shut. She has a fat lip, a metal taste in her mouth, a jackhammer headache, but at least she's upright in one of the darkened booths, so she can get her bearings.

"You, though – " he shakes a finger at her as he paces about " – you're a real piece of work. I've watched a lot of waitresses, and you're a classic. A dying breed. Like those Newfoundland women who gut fish all day, nothing touches you. I like that. A true *enfant de malheur.*"

"I don't know what that means," she says thickly. She needs a drink of water, something to stop her tongue sticking to the roof of her mouth.

"It means you've had a tough time, Molly. It shows in your face. It's what makes you strong."

"Just tell me what the deal is here." She can't see him clearly. Why the hell doesn't he stand still for a moment? "What's your name?"

"Duane," he says softly.

"Well, Duane, what is it you want?"

"I know you're alone. I know you're broke. Christ, I've seen where you live and I have *no idea* how you can stand it." He angrily throws out his hands. "What is it that keeps you going? You've nothing, nothing at all. But you don't have to be alone. You don't have to fight so hard. I could help you."

"Do me a favour." She points at the counter behind him. "Flick that switch down."

He looks around and sees the steel coffee pot. "Right, sure," he smiles and shakes his head and the orange light goes on, then turns back to her. "I promise you, Molly, I didn't want to hurt you and never will again. But I had to get you to listen to me. All I want is for you to be happy, and if we can come to a deal that will make me happy too, well hey, everybody wins."

She tries to focus, to measure how far she is from the phone, the door, the kitchen knives. "What did you have in mind, Duane?"

"Okay." He perches on a corner of the orange leatherette seat and slaps his hands on his thighs, pleased with himself. "I come from a pretty wealthy family. We owned half the car lots in this city. When my old man died he left me a shitload of money. I can give you whatever you want. You'll never need to worry about making ends meet again. This country favors the wealthy, Molly. If you haven't got it now, there's no way you're ever gonna get it. But I can take care of you."

"You're not in love with me. I got no real education, I got no money, I wait tables and fetch people coffee for God's sake." She glances at the pot. The orange light has clicked off.

"You're strong, Molly. Nothing fazes you. That's what I need, a really strong woman."

"I need caffeine while I think about this. Could you grab me some?"

He rises, then seems to change his mind. "You fetch it. You said it's what you do."

She wonders how nuts he is to let her go near the boiling coffee pot. Maybe it's a trust thing. Maybe he just likes her to wait on him.

That's when she realises the true nature of his proposition. He loves her strength so much that he wants her to use it against him. He wants her to fling the hot liquid in his face, to stab him, to punish him, to make him cry, to expose his helplessness before her.

He's making her an offer. It's a fucked up world, he's thinking, but there are worse deals going. She could be alone for the rest of her life.

She fills the thick white cups that hold less than they look. With a steady hand she carries them together with the pot to the shadowed table. His eyes never leave hers as she sets the cups down and raises the hot steel container level with his face.

He dares her. "Do it, Molly. Do it, and I'll make sure you never have to work in a hellish place like this again. I'll never hurt you. I'll look after you like a princess. There's crazier men than me out there." He licks his lips. "Come on, baby, show me what you're made of."

Molly considers the idea for a moment, then lowers the coffee pot. She absently touches her swollen mouth before she speaks. "You have a hell of a nerve, presuming this is what I need, just because of what I do."

"Everyone wants to feel needed."

She could throw the boiling coffee in his eyes and run out, but then it will never end. Instead, she sets the pot down quietly and walks to the door. "Let me tell you something. I wait at your table, I take your shit, but you can't get inside me. I'm not running across town from you anymore, Duane. You come after me again, I swear I'll end up going to jail for killing you."

"You stupid bitch," he shouts after her, and she realises he's saying that because torture and death at her hands is what he most desires. She wonders what happened to him as a little boy that placed him in the sexual thrall of strong women. "What have you got here? You'll grow old and die serving shitty food to people who don't give a fuck about you. You've got nothing and you'll get nothing."

"That's right, lover," she smiles to herself beneath the rain-sparkled streetlight, "this," she throws her arms wide, "this is what I do. But you only have to do one thing well to have a reason for getting out of bed every morning. And I'm a damn good waitress. What keeps you alive?"

Later, she'll sit in a bar, have a drink, maybe cry. But right now, as she walks away into the night rain, she's already thinking about the ad she saw for the Chicken Lodge downtown, a rundown family joint, good shifts, minimum wage plus tips.

Four months on, there's a two-line piece in the *Cleveland Plain Dealer* about some rich guy found stabbed to death in a quiet family diner. Police want to interview the woman who served his final meal. ✿

TIM CASSON

Tim Casson lives in Cardiff and works in theatre. He was once (briefly) a trade union rep within the local authority and attended several courses including first aid (the inspiration for 'Squeamish'). He owns a highly erratic mobile paper shredder which looks exactly like a Staffordshire bull-terrier. He is currently working on his first novel.

S eren says it's all about cost. "The Authority can't afford to squander a slice of the budget on losers. They'd only have to go and train someone else. And these courses are expensive. That's why they make sure nobody fails." Seren says this after telling me I have to go on the damn thing. "*Nobody* fails. You turn up," she says, "listen for five days, do a bit of practical, a straightforward exam on the Friday then collect your certificate. Simple."

"Not for me," I say. "There's something about the idea of being around sick people – real or imagined – that unsettles me."

"A person on your salary shouldn't get *unsettled*," she says. "How much did you earn last year?"

"Money's got nothing to do with it. Everyone's different."

"There *was* a woman who didn't get through once."

"Aha, see! People *do* fail."

"No they don't! Everyone passes."

"But you said . . ."

"A cleaning supervisor. Doesn't count as a failure. She turned out to have literacy problems, dyslexia or something like that. Poor love kept it to herself, didn't tell the trainer, so when it came to the written multiple choice questions she just ticked some boxes and hoped for the best. Needless to say . . ."

"I don't like blood."

"Blood? There won't be any blood."

"I'm squeamish."

"I don't believe you. You're behaving like a child. Just what the hell is your problem here?"

"I'm trying to tell you."

The trainer's name is Phil. A fit-looking paramedic. He wears a white shirt, pressed black trousers and a black tie. His shoes are highly polished. He explains briefly what we're going to be doing over the next five days then asks whose Porche is parked outside near the ambulances. I raise my hand, wondering if I'm obstructing an emergency vehicle in a life-threatening situation. What a start that would be! What a prick I'd look like.

Instead Phil makes a quip about being in the wrong business: "There's no money in saving lives!"

My fellow students laugh – a light-hearted moment – though I sense some tacit hostility. The car confirms my outsider status. This lot couldn't afford my hubcaps!

"Okay, we must press on," Phil says clapping his hands. "We've a lot of work to get through."

Seren knows all about these courses. After all, she wrote 'Violence at Work Policy', 'Equal Ops', 'Harassment', 'Recruitment' and 'Selection'; then she devised an accessible and *entertaining* course for each policy which has since benefited thousands of Council staff. She was responsible for bringing my consultancy company in. The Authority wants a workable Stress Management Forum, with the aim of saving £6 million per annum on staff sickness. I'm an expert on stress and the recognised methods of tackling it. I also know they've no chance of saving *three* mil let alone six, but I don't divulge this. My company wouldn't like that. We deal in profit, not honesty.

We're to work together on the project, Seren and I.

Seren's very precise. When she removes my clothes she takes her time. Eyeballs my naked body for ages, way too long, like she's searching for something inappropriate perhaps, something that would best be deleted. She insists on looking down on me in bed, staring like that. Light and bony, I flip her about, strum her ribs, slap her little arse for fun.

"If I did that to you in work," I say, "would I be sacked?"

"Depends on whether it's . . . unwanted . . . inappropriate . . . contact," she gasps, thrusting her sharp pelvis back and forth.

"How is a bloke supposed to know if it's wanted or not?"

She snorts, screws up her face.

"Should he approach by memo in the first instance?"

"Shut *up!*"

There's a small kitchen next door. We make coffee, take it into the main room and chat for a bit, then we brush up on what we did yesterday.

Phil shows us some slides. He explains about backslaps and abdominal thrusts. He says it's not possible for a person to choke to death on a fish bone – too thin and flimsy. A bigger object, such as a marble, could be very nasty for a child if blocking the airway.

Why did you do nasty things to the little girl?

There's a middle-aged woman from Human Resources who holds up the course with improbable anecdotes. Sparing no detail, she tells us about a friend who choked to death on a green olive. This woman seems to have experienced every accident and illness mentioned in the book – sometimes personally but more often through someone she knows.

Little Jennifer?

I can't speak. It's like an adult has their thumb pressed into my Adam's apple.

My mother is there. Answer the doctor, she says. The doctor isn't like a GP. He's the other type of doctor.

I . . .

Why did you do those things to little Jennifer?

The wallpaper is yellow; the lighting soft, mellow, unthreatening.

It was just a game, I manage to say. Maurice went too far.

Maurice?

My mother waves a dismissive hand, laughs nervously. She says, It's his . . . you know . . .

The woman from Human Resources is still speaking. Apparently her friend choked on the olive while on holiday in the Algarve. It also triggered an asthma attack at the same time. The friend turned blue, then white, then the same shade as the olive. The waiters were hopeless, the ambulance took ages negotiating the narrow streets and when it did arrive her friend was dead.

Unfortunately this starts off the young lout from Refuse and Cleansing, who relates horrific, semi-fictional tales of severed arteries and crushed limbs he's seen on cable

TV. I keep my own stories to myself, thank you. Little Jennifer is my business.

"Okay, we must press on," Phil says patiently, having heard it all before.

Later that evening Seren asks: "How was it today?"

She's found something interesting on my back. She's tracing her fingers over the area, examining.

"We did the recovery position," I say, turning round and manoeuvring her onto her side. "Like *this*."

I feel her hot breath on my arm. I touch her short hair, which is a watery orange colour, same as the herbal tea I have to make her. I stare at her freckles, fumble for a pulse in her stringy neck.

"The priorities are," I say, "airway, breathing and circulation – a, b, c. You're not dead *yet*."

Afterwards I make the mistake of querying something from one of her policies. They're laid out on the table, fresh white blocks: the sacred texts. I think *tablets*, I think *Ten Commandments. Thou shalt not . . .*

"It's down to the definition of violence," I say.

"What is?"

I flick through a hefty draft. "For the purpose of this document," I read aloud, "violence is defined as thus: the calling of inappropriate names (especially regarding race, gender, or sexuality), raising one's voice, slapping a surface (such as a desk) in a manner perceived by the victim to be threatening . . ."

"That's correct," confirms Seren. "That is violent behaviour in the workplace."

"Then what's a punch in the face?"

"*What?*"

"You know. What do you call thumping the shit out of someone? Hitting them so hard and so many times they're no longer recognisable. That must be a fucking nuclear strike, right?"

I really wish I hadn't said that. It's much more fun being a closet heretic. This woman could make a lot of trouble for me.

That night I dream about the woman from Human Resources. She doesn't stop talking. She describes breaking bones that make audible cracks before poking through trouser legs, epileptics quivering like jellyfish as they crash-land jumbo jets, heart-attack victims turning ash-grey as they carry on working without knowing they're having an attack and then – *boom* – too late! I beg her to stop but she continues her incessant chattering. It's a relief when Seren's caresses wake me.

I walk into the room and there are dummies all over the floor: limbless torsos, hairless heads. I don't like looking. My heart quickens as I step around them. We make coffee. Then it's period revision. Phil talks for an hour, fails to mention the dummies or what we're going to do with them. I can't concentrate on what he's saying. Nobody else seems too concerned.

"Okay, let's start the practical training," Phil says, smiling to himself.

My turn comes. Everyone watches. I approach my dummy with feigned concern. "Are you okay?" I ask it. I forget to look for danger so Phil stops me. An embarrassing slip.

I shout for help but it doesn't sound convincing. I kneel down, check breathing. "You're poorly," I say.

Me? Jennifer asks.

No, stupid! Your doll. I mean your baby. He's poorly. Is it a he?

She nods.

Then he needs an operation.

Concern shows on Jennifer's pretty features. An op . . .

I'll be back soon, I say, grabbing the baby in its white crocheted shawl.

When I return a few minutes later I lay her baby on the grass and kneel beside it. Jennifer stands next to me, fascinated. Can I be nurse? she asks.

No. You flunked the exam. Anyway you're the mother. You should go in the waiting room but just this once I'll allow you to watch.

Maurice says we must begin.

I take my mother's sharp vegetable knife and cut off one of its rubbery arms. Jennifer gasps.

That's better, I say. Gangrene. We've solved that *problem. Now we need to examine his cancer.*

"You forgot to check the mouth for obstructions," Phil points out. "After you raised the chin. Not very good I'm afraid. You would've failed the exam."

The lout from Refuse and Cleansing says, "Ha, I pity your girlfriend, mate!"

The students laugh. Another light-hearted moment at my expense.

Later that evening Seren asks how it went.

"The trainer insisted I would've failed," I say. "See, it *is* possible to fail this course."

"He's just saying that," she tells me, "to make you try harder next time."

"I don't see the point of me doing this course."

"So you keep saying. It's important you experience what's available to Council staff. It won't take long. Knowing first hand how we do things round here can only be beneficial to the Stress Management Forum."

"You're no different to anyone else," I point out. "I've put together dozens of these things for corporate clients all over the country without having to do their courses."

"There are subtle differences," she says. "You get to meet people from various departments. A diverse mix. Mingle with staff on the lower pay scales. Cleaners, binmen, gravediggers. See what makes them tick. Find out what stresses them out. I think it's important. Anyway, we agreed, remember?"

"*You* agreed."

The lout from Refuse and Cleansing is telling us about his poisoning experience. "We got a call saying there was a dead yeti dumped on the tip," he says. "Honest to God! The bloke that made the call was adamant, said we should ring the *Fortean Times*. But when we got there we saw it was just a big dog, the twisted body of a Great Dane. Been poisoned. Someone gave it dodgy meat. Chucked it over the wall deliberate, like. It must've died in agony. We had such a *laugh!*"

The woman from Human Resources sees this as an opportunity to slip in a dog bite anecdote.

"We must press on," Phil says, holding up his hand.

As usual, I keep my stories to myself.

I'm starting to get the hang of this resuscitation stuff. We're all getting quite proficient. I place my lips over the dummy's open mouth, pinch the soft plastic nose, give two ventilations. I trace my fingers down to the breastbone, look for the spot and with the heel of my hand push down. I wonder if the sound is the same on a real person – *fump, fump, fump.*

Cancer? little Jennifer says.

Yes. Your baby will rot if we don't stab its cancer.

Oh my!

Maurice suggests I make an incision in the chest.

Jennifer is transfixed as a thin line of blood follows the vegetable knife's vertical descent. I press down firmly and blood squirts over my hands.

Jennifer screams. But she doesn't move. She doesn't know whether to run or pick up the butchered baby.

I look at her with a solemn expression, shake my head. I'm afraid he didn't make it, I say. He's passed on.

Some time later I explain to the doctor that it was just ketchup. Maurice told me to unscrew the head, fill the hollow torso with red sauce then replace the head.

My mother confirms this, though she says it was me *and not Maurice. She says she couldn't understand why a brand new ketchup bottle was sitting on the shelf empty. She was furious with me because I ruined a perfectly good T-shirt. The smell!*

My mother used to stroke my cheek and tell me I was beautiful, I had an angel's face, she whispered. Didn't know where my looks came from, she said, not from her. She made a decision at that point to defend me. From that day on there was no turning back for her.

It got harder, like a few years later when she found that thing in my room. She opened the handkerchief. What is . . . this? she said, bursting into tears.

Go to your room and stay there, I told her.

"Okay, what's important here?" Phil is asking.

I open my eyes. My vision is blurred. I feel devoid of energy. The students are standing around me with their hands raised.

"First we remove the danger," the woman from Human Resources says.

"Correct. Good."

"We check for airways, breathing, and circulation," someone else says.

"Correct. And?"

"Lay him down on the floor," the lout from Refuse and Cleansing says. Everyone laughs.

"He's already on the floor!" Phil says. "He's pale and sweaty. What happened to him?"

"He fainted."

"*Right*. So what do we treat him for?"

"Shock?"

"*Correct*. Which means?"

"We raise his feet."

Everyone applauds. What a show!

The woman from Human Recourses lifts my feet and rests them on a box. Congratulations all round.

Later on, when I'm able to stand, Phil claps me on the back. "In all my years of doing this," he says, "I've never had a *real* case among the students where someone actually needed treating. Thanks for that."

"You're welcome," I say.

That evening, when Seren asks how I got on, I tell her that I fainted. I'm not sure she believes me. There's no chance of throwing a sickie now. If I'd kept quiet from the outset and then just sprung it on her I might've got away with it. Too late now.

It's the morning of the exam. Seren wakes me early with her usual demands.

"Who's Maurice," she says afterwards.

"I don't know, why?"

"You said the name in your sleep last night, several times."

After showering and a light breakfast I leave her flat and head for the ambulance station. The traffic's bad. I arrive ten minutes late. They probably think I'm being arrogant. Phil says it's no problem. He tells me to get a coffee. Phil briefs us for half an hour, says we'll go straight into the written test and then at about 11 o'clock there's the practical in front of two trained examiners.

"Whatever you do," he says, "don't be nervous. Relax. They're nice people. They're going to create a scenario, different for each one of you. We'll be done by lunchtime."

The multiple choice questions are pretty straightforward and I only have to make a guess with two. After that we wait in another room for our names to be called. When my turn comes I shake everyone's hand and wish them luck. The lout from Refuse and Cleansing eyes my watch then tries to crush my hand.

I knock on the door. A woman is seated with a clipboard and pen. A man is lying on the floor pretending to be injured. He moans. His trouser leg is rolled up and there is fake blood on his shin. Broken sugar glass and an aluminium stepladder are close by. I do everything by the book, quick and efficient. I answer the woman's questions and she stands up, smiles, says congratulations.

She fails to see the irony. *Me* – a life saver?

I'm feeling quite pleased with myself, even though no one was meant to fail.

"You were right," I say to Seren. "Everyone passed. It wasn't as bad as I thought."

Seren seems preoccupied with something else. She looks at me eventually. "I've decided I want our relationship to be on a professional level only," she says.

"Oh . . ."

"Okay?"

I nod my head slowly.

"Good, then that's out of the way. The first draft's over there," she says, pointing.

"First draft?"

"The Stress Management Policy. Take a copy. Some things of yours are in that bag by the table."

"Is there any reason? I mean, have I done something wrong?"

"I've made my decision."

"Can I stay for tea?"

"I want you to leave now."

"Now?"

"I'll see you Monday morning in the office. Nine sharp."